AGGRESSOR

Also by Nick Cook

Angel, Archangel

AGGRESSOR

NICK COOK

St. Martin's Press   New York

to Ali

ISBN 0-312-07623-1

First edition: February 1993
10 9 8 7 6 5 4 3 2 1

PROLOGUE

THE RUSSIAN VIP and his Syrian host paused on the metal gangway. To the Russian the centrifugal compressor didn't look like much—just angular pieces of metal joined by solid old-style Soviet riveting—but the deafening howl of the gas turbines and the energy that shook the platform told him otherwise.

He mopped the sweat from his brow and looked to his host, then toward the door. The Syrian minister of the interior seemed to take the hint. The militiaman swung the door and gestured the two men outside with a deep, exaggerated bow.

"Congratulations, Minister," the Syrian said, the noise of the turbines behind them. "It is a masterpiece."

Mikhail Koltsov, Russian minister of gas-petrochemical industrialization, forced a smile.

He had hoped it would be cooler outside, but it was like the heart of a foundry. The compressor station lay in a slight depression in the desert. The sun, now at its zenith, reflected off every grain of sand. The temperature was well over forty degrees Celsius. He wanted nothing more than to board the air-conditioned bus for the return journey to the airport.

"My government was only too glad to be of assistance," Koltsov said stiffly.

The truth was that Russia needed dollars; and the Syrian government, flush with the discovery of vast new natural gas reserves, had plenty of them to spend. But the al-Hasakah–Latakia pipeline was a project of which Russian engineers could be justly proud. It had taken five years to build and there was nothing else like it in the world. Koltsov saw the pipeline as a symbol of hope for his country. Just because the Soviet Union was dead and buried, it didn't mean that almost eight decades of technical achievement had to die with it. And it was Russia, not the Ukraine—or any other former Soviet republic— that was the rightful heir to that distinguished reputation. The pipeline, here, was proof of that.

A gleaming steel duct, two meters wide, pumping gas twenty-four hours a day, 365 days a year, from al-Hasakah, a barren heatspot in the furnace of the desert, across 450 kilometers of the al-Jazirah to Latakia, a port on the Mediterranean coast. It surpassed even the technology employed on their Urengoy "supergiant" gas field in western Siberia.

Outside the concrete shell of the pumping station, the whine of the two gas turbines was audible, but only just. The engines, each rated at a staggering 230 kilonewtons, were adaptations of jet engines normally employed on giant Russian transport aircraft. It required two such powerplants to pump the gas along the pipeline to the next booster station, 150 kilometers to the east, where it would receive one last injection of energy for the journey to Latakia.

And for once, Moscow had driven a straight cash deal instead of another of those crazy barter arrangements that characterized Soviet export policy in the years before Gorbachev. This time it was different. Syrian petrodollars, 10,000 million of them, for Russian engineering expertise—the new capitalism at work.

Farewell handshakes were exchanged between Koltsov's eight colleagues and their hosts.

The Syrian turned to him with outstretched arms and Koltsov obliged by kissing him in comradely fashion on both cheeks.

"A safe trip to Moscow, God willing," the Syrian said.

"Thank you."

The Russian looked around gratefully for the bus, spotting it a little way off in the shade of a tin shelter just beyond the perimeter fence. He set off, the Syrian minister at his side. The thirty-strong party, which included a squad of heavily armed troops, shuffled along in his wake. He thought of the Syrian transport aircraft sitting on the tarmac at al-Hasakah, sixty kilometers away. A thirty-minute flight to Damascus and he would be reunited with their Air Russia jet bound for Moscow. His mood lightened. He had had enough of the heat, the dirt and the flies that had plagued his three-day trip. It was time to go home.

The door at the front of the bus opened with a hiss of compressed air. Koltsov stepped inside, relieved to feel the air-conditioning chill the sweat on his brow.

The driver, a kaffiyeh protecting his face from the sun, lolled in his seat with insolent disregard for the VIPs.

Koltsov waved to his host from his seat by the rear window. But the interior minister was preoccupied now with his own departure plans, pushing his minions out of the way to reach his air-conditioned limousine. As the bus pulled away into the desert, the Russian was left staring at the concrete heart and steel arteries of the pumping station.

At first, Koltsov thought he imagined it, that the heat shimmer was playing tricks upon his eyes. The concrete roof of the compressor station seemed to lift by as much as a meter, then settle, intact, upon the walls of the blockhouse amidst a light cloud of dust.

He had time only to brace himself against the headrest of his seat for the massive explosion that followed the detonation deep within the bowels of the blockhouse.

The shock wave radiated outward, engulfing and igniting everything in its path. The pumping station, the perimeter wire, the shelter, the soldiers, the Syrian delegation and the limousines fused with the inferno, each fueling the reaction, each adding to its power.

The pumping station disintegrated with the destructive force of a small nuclear weapon.

Shards of glass flew through the bus as the rear window blew in. Koltsov came up from behind the seat and was knocked backward by a second shock wave. The bus veered sharply in the grip of a pressure roller, but somehow held the road.

As they slowed to a stop, the minister looked into the dazed faces of his colleagues. He saw terrible cuts, but they would live.

Nobody spoke. Eyes were captivated by the flames that leapt into the sky behind them. The sand around the compressor station had been turned to glass.

Koltsov was aware of noise and movement around the wheels of the bus. He leaned over the edge of the shattered window and saw men armed with assault rifles crawling from the luggage bins. Before he could signal the alarm the driver was on his feet, shouting for them to stay in their seats with a force out of tune with his earlier lethargy. It was only when the minister saw the automatic pistol in the driver's hand that he realized why.

One by one, the stowaways stepped on board. Koltsov counted five, not including the driver. They wore combat fatigues topped by T-shirts, and strips of cloth tied across their noses and mouths.

The first of them spoke sharply to the driver, who proceeded to gun the engine and turn the bus off the road, weaving between the boulders and scrub.

The minister's curiosity overcame his fear. Encouraged by the mounting cries of indignation from his colleagues, he fixed his eyes on the one who had barked the commands.

"Who are you?" he demanded.

The terrorist swung the muzzle of his rifle in the direction of the voice and told him—told them all—in a tone that did not betray the slightest hint of emotion. Then he turned back to the driver.

Koltsov held the chair back in front of him for a good minute, eyes wide with shock. When he dared to look at the rest of his party, he noticed that the outrage that had begun to show on their faces before had just been killed stone dead.

■   ■   ■

ULM HAD rerun the scene maybe a dozen times in his mind. Shabanov had kicked the door down and rolled through the opening. He had been right behind, covering the Russian's back. The room was small, only about fifteen by twenty feet, but it was smoky from the stun grenade tossed in by Shabanov a few seconds before.

Shabanov had come up, his automatic sweeping the four corners of the room. Ulm braced himself to hear a string of shots from the Russian's weapon, but he was greeted only by the single word: "Clear." No time to stop and rest—they had to go on to the next room. It was unrelenting. He'd always hated house clearing, because it took so long. Airliner work was different. That was over in seconds. Either way. Them or you.

It was then he saw the figure advancing through the smoke for Shabanov. He pushed the Russian to the floor and fired his Kalashnikov. The figure went down like a target at a carnival shooting gallery.

When the invigilators burst through the door a moment later he knew he'd blown it. They raced to the point where the figure had hit the floor, their Russian babbling made doubly unintelligible by the gas masks they wore. They raised the figure until it locked back in the upright position. When the wind lifted the smoke he saw it was a mother carrying a young child. Had they been real, not cardboard, both would have been dead.

He and Shabanov walked back to the debriefing center, the Russian full of well-meaning comments about the fog of war and the inevitability of civilian casualties. For Colonel Elliot Ulm—head of the U.S. Air Force's elite antiterrorist unit, the Pathfinders—the humiliating fact remained: he had shot the wrong target and the Russians were laughing at him behind his back.

The humidity at the training compound, centered on marshland some 150 kilometers outside Moscow, was insufferable. It was a vast complex sealed from civilian life, filled with hundreds of different stages and backdrops that had been designed by the Russians as likely arenas for low-intensity conflict. There were whole towns here, buses, airliners, airport buildings, even sections of supertankers and cruise liners. And Spetsnaz, Russia's own special antiterror squad, practiced against them all—day in and day out. They were, Ulm had to admit, remarkable troops.

The woods crackled with the sound of near and distant gunfire. Occasionally, he saw Spetsnaz going about their work, but for the most part their operations remained stealthy, unseen. The Russians, after all, didn't want to show him too much. In the New World Order, special operations lay at the heart of a nation's defense.

The Romeo Protocol was designed to overcome this natural reticence. The agreement that had brought Ulm here was established to pool the resources of the United States and the Soviet Union—and now Russia—in the war against terrorism.

But like the CFE treaty limiting their conventional arms, the Romeo Protocol was an agreement that worked better in theory than reality. It was a politician's dream and a soldier's nightmare. For the moment it remained secret, its existence to be unveiled only after the two sides had been into battle together and brought one more terrorist outfit to heel.

Ulm hated the idea of going into action with Russian special forces—so much could go wrong. He tried to put it out of his mind. He was going home that night to prepare for Shabanov's exchange visit, set for two week's time. He would fly back from the Pathfinders' base in New Mexico to Europe, meet Shabanov at some obscure rendezvous and then escort him into the States. It was altogether safer that way—no awkward questions at immigration, that kind of thing. The precise meeting place hadn't been fixed yet, but at least it wasn't going to be Russia. A month on little better than K-rations was quite enough.

They reached the barracks that served as the debriefing center. Shabanov pushed the door open for Ulm and they stepped inside.

In the gloom of the corridor, Shabanov was greeted by a deferential private, who snapped to attention and passed him a note. Shabanov read the message cursorily before stuffing it into a top pocket of his camouflage tunic.

"Excuse me, I must make a call," he said to Ulm. Shabanov's English was perfect. Active colonels in Spetsnaz were expected to have at least one language under their belts. Shabanov had several.

■　　　　■　　　　■

As ULM headed on to the briefing room, Shabanov entered his own office. It was a Spartan affair, with nothing but the bare essentials: shelves crammed with military textbooks, foreign defense magazines and a lone copy of *The Rubáiyát of Omar Khayyám,* a gift from his mother. In the center of the floor was a utilitarian metal desk, its surface adorned with an in-tray and a telephone.

He raised the phone and dialed. The connection established in seconds, but to Shabanov it seemed much longer. Events in Syria the day before were preying heavily on his mind.

"You took your time, Roman Makhmadzhanovich," the general said. "I've been waiting."

"My guest and I were doing a little shooting in the woods, General."

General Aushev grunted. "You don't have to be circumspect,

Roman. This is one line in our wretched country I know to be secure."

Shabanov knew it, too, but he never talked tactics or operations on an open line unless the general invited him to do so first: force of habit in a country with the worst communications network in the world.

Shabanov mopped the sweat off the back of his neck with his T-shirt. "I'm sorry, General, I only just received your message. I've been on urban area training with the American for the past two days."

"Then you won't have heard the news," Aushev said.

Shabanov felt a tightening in the pit of his stomach. "What news?"

"We've found the Sword. Someone has come forward. An old contact from the Middle East."

"Firm intelligence?" Shabanov asked.

"Unquestionably. Tomorrow, I'm sending someone to London who can bring the details home. A time and a meeting have been established already. It's going to cost us, but then we knew it wouldn't be cheap."

"I take it you can trust our . . . courier."

"He is an unprepossessing character, but less conspicuous than you."

"He won't be missed, then."

"No." Aushev paused. "Not particularly."

Shabanov noticed a slight edge to the voice on the other end of the line.

"Two weeks tomorrow, General, I go to America. Colonel Ulm has just confirmed the dates with his people."

"Then we don't have much time, Roman."

"I know, General."

■　　　　■　　　　■

SHABANOV'S MIND was buzzing when he put the phone down.

It was typical Aushev to pull something from the bag at the eleventh hour. But then General Aushev's whole career had been an unconventional combination of luck and daring.

Shabanov had first met him almost two decades earlier, when Aushev was just beginning to fast-track up the GRU, the intelligence wing of the Red Army. Shabanov remembered the day well.

He had been on home leave in Moscow, his nose buried between the breasts of the horny bitch who lived in the apartment next door, doing his best to forget about the frozen hellhole he'd been assigned for two years—Kamchatka, Siberia. The call came to report to the offices of one Colonel Viktor Nikitovich Aushev at the government buildings on Krasnovodsk Street, just behind the Frunze Academy. A highly unusual summons.

Being the good junior captain he was, Shabanov had got his ass there quick. The area around Frunze was known for its ties to military intelligence; and one look at Aushev told him the effort hadn't been a waste.

Although not on the tall side, Aushev, with his cropped hair—steel gray even then—and his piercing blue eyes, was someone you couldn't forget in a hurry.

Standing at attention before Aushev's desk, Shabanov had listened intently as Aushev outlined his offer: an instant transfer from Kamchatka upon agreement to lead the special operations unit that was being formed under Aushev's overall command.

''Why me?'' he'd asked.

''Because you have what we need. Skill, determination, dedication, loyalty . . .''

''You can find men with those qualities anywhere in our armed forces, Comrade Colonel,'' he'd stammered.

Only then did Aushev smile. ''I also need an Arabic speaker. And you, Comrade Captain Shabanov, are fluent in the language.''

Shabanov stared at the Arabic copy of the Rubáiyát on the shelf above his desk and the years bounded forward again. Of course he was fluent. Arabic was almost his mother tongue. Though an Uzbek by birth, Shabanov had been brought up to read and write Arabic. Later, he learned to speak it.

In the eighteen years since that meeting he'd learned a lot about his boss; not least, his stupendous achievements in the Middle East.

Aushev's first foreign assignment had come in 1969, as a military adviser in Iraq. Two years later, and still in his mid-thirties, he'd transferred to Egypt. In the one year he'd spent there before President Sadat expelled him and the thousands of other Soviet 'advisers' from that country, he'd got firmly into his stride, establishing a network of agents, many of whom were still in place today. And given what had happened to his own country in the intervening years, Shabanov reflected, that was no mean achievement at all.

Five years after '72—and a succession of other regional postings—

Aushev, now a colonel general, was recalled to Moscow. He'd been tasked with setting up a special antiterror unit prior to the Moscow Olympics, then three years away. Arab terror was on the increase and the Kremlin wanted nothing to darken what promised to be the most glorious event in Soviet sporting history.

Under Aushev's guidance, Shabanov's special unit established itself quickly and in the utmost secrecy. Within a few short years it had been honed into a supertough fighting force that was ready for any contingency the Olympics had to throw at it.

And then came Afghanistan, altogether an episode in his country's history best forgotten. The same could be said for the Olympics, because the damned Americans went and boycotted the event in protest of the invasion.

Aushev had done all right, though, rising even higher through the GRU to the lofty heights of the Second Chief Directorate, the department in charge of all army special operations activity. For some reason best known to itself, the Politburo had assigned the GRU—military intelligence—responsibility for all Spetsnaz operations.

And there Aushev, now a full general, had remained, watching over the succession of desperate events that had overtaken their country since the late 1980s: withdrawal from Afghanistan, the dissipation of the Warsaw Pact, the loss of the Baltic states, the August coup, the collapse of communism and the economy, the death of the Soviet Union itself, the formation of the Commonwealth—and its rapid dissolution—the food riots and the growing unrest on Russia's southern border.

Somehow, throughout it all, Aushev had clung to power. The liberals had tried to remove him on several occasions, but Aushev was too wily to allow himself to be put out to pasture just yet.

Maybe it was the Romeo Protocol that had kept him there, Shabanov mused. After all, Aushev was just about the only man, other than the Russian president himself, who could pick up the phone and link directly with the United States National Security Council, Washington's supreme crisis body.

Back in Russia, liberals were wary of Aushev principally because of his vast knowledge. Almost thirty years in the army's intelligence service had made him a very powerful man.

In times of crisis—and there was little doubt Russia was facing its worst since the Great Patriotic War—for Shabanov, it was good to know that he, General Aushev, and men like him were all on the same side.

BOOK 1

CHAPTER 1

ALMOST THIRTY-SIX HOURS AFTER AUSHEV BRIEFED SHABANOV, another, quite junior member of the general's staff emerged from the depths of the London underground into the damp summer's evening above Hyde Park tube station.

Boris Sinitsky shunned a slight feeling of dizziness and looked at his watch. His run around the network had taken him an hour. He had not been followed.

His stomach churned as he recalled the air of the trains, heavy with the aroma of expensive soaps, after-shave, women's scent and the soiled clothing of the tramp in the seat beside him. The odors had combined in his head, wreaking havoc with his senses.

He sucked in the cool air of the park and let the nausea subside.

London was a long way from the Second Chief Directorate's headquarters in the tree-lined suburbs behind Moscow's Dinamo soccer stadium.

Sinitsky felt proud to have been entrusted with the general's mission. His task was to obtain the missing piece of a jigsaw puzzle from a man who had cause to volunteer it. General Aushev had not seen fit to brief him on the wider context of the operation, but Sinitsky had little doubt it was something to do with the abduction of the Russian delegation in Syria.

It was almost dark. Away from the throng his sense of isolation was acute. The case he carried hung heavily in his right hand.

A signboard by a newspaper kiosk caught his eye. More unrest back home, this time in one of the former Central Asian republics. The stark words of the headline stiffened his resolve. He walked briskly through the underground walkway that went beneath Hyde Park Corner. Above him he could hear the rumble of traffic as it inched toward Piccadilly and Marble Arch. The lights in the dank, gloomy passageway flickered.

As he crossed Rotten Row, a few pedestrians passed him, their heads bent low against the drizzle that had begun to fall in the gathering darkness. When he reached the long, rectangular pond he turned left and started counting. One, two . . .

At the third bench he stopped and put the case down. He looked left and right, but could see no one. Where was his contact? After two minutes, he pulled a pack of Marlboros from his coat, put one in his mouth and struck a match. The box was damp and the match tore uselessly at the striking paper.

"A lighter is better than matches, I find."

Sinitsky looked up to see a man in a raincoat standing before him. His complexion was dark, swarthy. Cheap, flimsy trousers protruded beneath the hem of the coat, making his appearance seem out of step with the bad weather. The Russian looked around him, but could not establish the direction from which the stranger had come.

The man offered him a light. The tip of the cigarette glowed dimly. Sinitsky shielded it from the drizzle.

"Disposable lighters—cheap, but reliable," Sinitsky said. His English, taught well, was strong and fluent.

The other man looked down at the case. "The money . . ."

Sinitsky could smell garlic on the man's breath and a spicy odor on his clothes. For a moment the bouquet of the claustrophobic subway returned to him.

Sinitsky shook his head. "First, the information."

The colonel from the Popular Front for the Liberation of Palestine, General Command—the PFLP-GC—smiled.

"In the Jebel al-Baiyada, a mountain range in southern Lebanon, there is a peak called Ayn an-Nasr, the Eye of the Eagle; in its shadow is the valley where the Sword and his Angels of Judgment have made their camp.''

''What is the valley called?''

''It does not have a name.''

''How will we know it is the right place?'' Sinitsky asked.

''The camp itself is a deserted *khan al-qafila* . . .'' He paused, searching for the English. ''A caravanserai.''

Sinitsky's brow furrowed in confusion. ''Caravanserai?''

The Arab nodded. ''An ancient building, a resting place.''

''And the meeting?'' Sinitsky had learned the questions back in Moscow. All he had to do was memorize the answers, as per General Aushev's instructions.

''The *shura?* It is to take place in four weeks. On August fifteenth, to be precise. On that day, the Sword will deliver his message. He will have quite an audience: al-Haqim of Black June, Abu Ya'aqub of the Palestine Liberation Front, al-Ghanem of Fatah, those madmen from Hizbollah and our own dear Jibril.''

Sinitsky winced. Some groups were pro-PLO, others, like the colonel's PFLP-GC, against it. Hizbollah was something quite else, but Sinitsky couldn't remember quite what. He memorized the names, but gave up on their affiliations. They concerned the general, not him.

The Arab's face tensed. ''I need Aushev's assurance. He must leave no one alive.''

Sinitsky nodded. The general had told him about this moment. ''He gives it.''

The Arab counted the bundled wads quickly. It was all there.

He hawked some phlegm from the back of his throat and spat it at Sinitsky's feet.

Sinitsky felt the bile rise. He turned on his heels, his mind already dividing the information he had acquired between the essential and the trivial.

Sinitsky walked on past the old lido and the restaurant, turning back only once. His contact had disappeared as stealthily as he had arrived. He prepared himself for a circuitous walk back to the embassy in Kensington Palace Gardens. The rain was falling more heavily now and he cursed. His cigarette had gone out.

At least he didn't have to get back on the metro.

■   ■   ■

THE COLONEL was the deputy leader of the PFLP-GC, second in command to Ahmed Jibril and like Sinitsky a long way from home. In contrast to the Russian, however, he knew London well. He now turned north, walking quickly past the bandstand toward the Bayswater Road. He did not have far to go. The safe house in Westbourne Terrace, just around the corner from Paddington Station, suddenly seemed very inviting. His last night in London would pass quickly; there would be much talk with his compatriots, several bottles of *araq*, a woman, perhaps . . .

He had much to celebrate.

His ticket, booked under a false name to match the alias carefully prepared for his new Moroccan passport, would be waiting for him. Tomorrow he would pass through Athens on the way to Damascus. He was confident his absence would not have been noticed.

He held the case close by his side. Funds for the cause and the knowledge that in a few weeks he would become the dominant leader in the holy war against the Israelis had made him a happy man.

Jibril's having shared the information about the *shura* with him had enabled him to hatch his plan. The Russians were willing accomplices in the achievement of his ambition. General Aushev had long been a man with whom he had been able to do business.

He left the path to take the most direct route across the park toward Albion Gate.

Halfway across the grass, he heard a noise behind him; only slight, but unmistakable. A footstep sinking into the rain-soaked earth. The colonel turned, saw the man twenty yards behind silhouetted against a distant row of street lights. He dropped the case, his hand moving up the lining of his coat, fumbling for the inside pocket where the automatic lay flat against his heart. He saw a light somewhere in the depths of the long, silenced barrel, but his ears never registered the dull sound. The bullet hit him squarely between the eyes and removed the back of his cranium.

■   ■   ■

GENERAL AUSHEV wasn't given to good moods, but as he slipped the twenty-kopek piece into the change machine in the lobby of the metro station at Ploshchad Sverdlova, he felt a certain excitement.

Aushev collected the four five-kopek pieces, tucking one of them into the pocket of his greatcoat. He joined a queue of shuffling Muscovites for the Gorkovsko–Zamoskvoretskaya line. After what seemed an eternity, he reached the automatic barrier, pushed the three remaining pieces into the slot and passed through to the head of the escalator. Within minutes he was boarding an underground train that would take him the four stops from the heart of Moscow to Dinamo station.

On that day he had abandoned his Zil for a less ostentatious mode of transport. It was, in fact, the only way of accomplishing his "accidental" meeting in Moscow with Sinitsky, who had just returned from London.

The rendezvous had gone according to plan. Sinitsky and he had met in the northwest entranceway of the old state department-store, GUM. They had strolled through the evening air, catching the last rays of light as the sun had slid behind the Grand Kremlin Palace, while Sinitsky had reeled off the information he had acquired.

As the train trundled toward Dinamo, Aushev reviewed the news. He had all the information he needed; he'd covered his footprints. There was now only the matter of dealing with Sinitsky before implementing stage two. Aushev was lost still in the details when the carriage doors opened onto the platform at Dinamo.

A minute later and he was on the wide *prospekt*, dodging the rain-filled potholes as he walked back to the offices of the Directorate. It had been decided some years back to locate the GRU nerve-center of special operations—Spetsnaz—planning in this remote area, because it was deemed the last place the CIA might consider looking.

As a result of the Romeo Protocol, the care that had gone into that detail now seemed little more than a joke.

When the general secretary, dear old Mikhail Gorbachev, signed the agreement all those years ago, he might as well have given the Americans Aushev's address and telephone number.

Aushev recalled Gorbachev's very words. "Viktor Nikitovich, you are to be a point of contact between us and the Americans. Under your guidance and with American help, we will eradicate terrorism from world society. The Romeo Protocol is just the beginning of that vision."

He cut through the wide squares and alleyways of the Frunze

Military Academy. A group of laughing officer cadets almost collided with him as he rounded a corner. The sharpness of their salutes gave him deep satisfaction. Though just turned sixty, Aushev was still lean, with none of the fat on his face that distinguished those of his military contemporaries who had sold their birthright for the Yankee dollar. He knew that his appearance, combined with his rank, was still enough to put fear into the heart of any officer his junior. Except one. Colonel Roman Makhmadzhanovich Shabanov was different.

Aushev reached the ordinary-looking office block on Krasnovodsk Street and sprang up the stairs to the second floor. He punched in the combination on the push-button entry system and opened the door. Few of the twenty-five computer console operators looked up from their work.

The general proceeded straight to his office and shut the door behind him. He picked up the phone and dialed a number that had long been etched in his memory. One advantage of working at the Second Chief Directorate was the newly installed secure digital network, which obviated the need to wait for a line on the ailing national telephone grid.

He heard the click as the receiver was lifted.

''Roman Makhmadzhanovich? Get your ass on a flight up here right now. We have things to discuss. The operation starts today.''

■   ■   ■

ON HIS way home that afternoon, Sinitsky never saw who shoved him from behind. In the throng of people lining the platform, the movement went unnoticed by everyone else. He sprawled headlong into the path of the train, his mind too numb to hear the screams of the onlookers, his eyes locked on the wheels that sliced him into three neat parts a second later.

CHAPTER 2

THE JUDDERING HAD BEGUN as a tremor soon after the Tornado slowed to subsonic speed and descended below the clouds on its final dash to the target. Girling thought it would pass. But as the aircraft left the clouds behind and hugged the contours of the ground, the shaking had intensified. Now it was relentless.

The electronic picture swam in and out of focus. Every jolt of turbulence jarred his bones.

Like a powerboat on a rough sea, the Tornado plowed on, its nose carving a swath through invisible pockets of air that flexed the wingtips and bucked the fuselage.

Half of him wanted to tear his gaze from the radar screen, but a voice in the back of his head told him not to break concentration.

He had invoked everyone and everything he had ever held dear in a vain plea for the sickness to leave him, but it persisted, a cold ball in the pit of his stomach.

There was always the bag.

He had glanced at it a minute before. The writing had swum before his eyes: ''Bag, Air Sickness, NATO Stock No 8105–99–130–2180.''

They had given him two in the briefing room. Just in case.

He would hold on. It had to pass.

He saw the object grow in the center of the screen and braced himself. Another hill. A second later and the Tornado pulled up sharply, pushing three Gs on his shoulders, then rolled onto its back. Girling opened his eyes and looked up to see a treetop flash past the canopy at over five-hundred knots.

Girling forced his chin onto his chest. He inched his gaze back to the instrument panel and found the radar picture again. The concentration helped.

They were still upside down. Although his attention was seized by the screen, depriving him of spatial awareness, he could feel the sweat dribbling past his hairline into his helmet.

The pilot burst through over the headset, his voice strangled and distorted from the strike aircraft's fight with gravity.

"Terrain-following-system, State-of-the-art. Hands optional."

Girling swore he heard Rantz laugh. He forced his gaze ahead. Behind the top of the ejection seat, the pilot was waving his arms about the cockpit.

He wanted the strength to record the surreal scene before him. The aircraft upside down, the ground rushing past less than a hundred feet from his head with his pilot suspended from his straps shaking his hands around like a lunatic.

The sickness paralyzed him. Finding the camera was out of the question.

The Tornado rolled back to right side up. Girling unclipped his oxygen mask, remembering to turn the intercom switch on its snout to the OFF position. He did not want Rantz to hear him retch.

Girling sucked in ambient air from the cockpit, not caring that it was thick and rancid with sweat. It was good to get the rubber mask off, good to feel the swish of recycled air from the conditioning system on his face. He couldn't give a fuck for Rantz and his orders about keeping his helmet visor down at all times. A bird strike, right then, the bones, feathers and mashed flesh exploding into the cockpit with the force of a high-velocity projectile, would be the least of his problems.

Throwing up would be easy. It was what Rantz wanted him to do.

He pictured himself descending the ladder from the cockpit holding the full blue-and-white bag, and Rantz smiling. Another puking hack to chalk on the side of the fuselage.

He gritted his teeth and thrust the bag back into the thigh pocket of his flight suit. A small point of honor, perhaps, but he wasn't going to give the asshole the satisfaction.

He took a glove off, pulled a Biro from his top pocket and pushed the point into the open palm of his left hand.

Girling clamped the mask back to his face, locked the catch down over the snout and felt it seal against his sweat-soaked cheeks. He breathed in and waited for the pervading smell of rubber to bring the bile to the back of his throat.

Instead, he felt the sickness ebb, replaced by a dull ache in his hand. He looked down to see the point of the Biro lost in his torn flesh.

Girling pocketed the pen, slid the glove back and concentrated on the pain until the sickness became a memory.

His hand moved up to the intercom switch. "How far to the target?"

"You're supposed to tell me."

"Give me a break," Girling muttered. The words were lost in the relentless battering of the slipstream. He knew that most of his instruments were duplicated in the front cockpit.

"Five minutes, fifteen seconds to the IP," Rantz said. "Switch TF radar to standby."

Girling moved the the dial on the radar console. The Tornado was out of its automatic terrain-following mode now. Another jagged Highland peak loomed beyond the nose of the fighter-bomber. This time Rantz saw a gap and pushed the aircraft toward it.

The gray, scree-strewn slopes of the mountain whistled past the right-hand wingtip. He pressed himself back into his seat and flexed his feet. His straps had been pulled so tight he could barely feel his legs anymore.

The Tornado belted out from behind the mountain and a screech, like a fingernail pulled across a blackboard, filled his headset.

"What's that?"

Rantz's voice came calmly back to him.

"Search radar. Probably from a SAM battery at the target. Sky Shadow should take care of it."

Girling knew from the premission briefing that the Sky Shadow pod beneath the Tornado would be classifying the nature of the threat and jamming it.

The screech wavered for a second, then steadied. The "enemy" was either employing electronic counter-countermeasures—ECCM—or the pod didn't work.

Rantz came through over the electronic howl. "Get a fix on it from the threat-warner."

Girling's mind raced. Threat-warner. He thought back to the simulator at Marham. A whole afternoon spent in the damned thing and he couldn't remember where the threat-warner was. If he was going to participate in Exercise Stalwart Divider sitting in the navigator's seat of one of Her Majesty's twenty-million-pound aircraft, then he was going to have to learn a navigator's duties, Rantz had said.

The screech was piercing his head. The turbulence blowing off the Highland mountain ridges was making the Tornado buck like a stallion. The whole instrument panel was still little more than a blur.

"Come on, he's about to lock us up and you're just pissing about back there." The crackle on the intercom made it difficult to hear. "Try the right-hand side of the panel."

A red box containing threat data was blinking in the top quadrant.

Girling screwed his eyes against the glare on the screen.

"E-band surveillance radar," he said. "Dead ahead."

Rantz's voice crackled in his headphones. "Let's stick an ALARM down his throat and see how he likes it."

Girling racked his brains, trying to remember what the acronym stood for. Air-Launched Anti-Radiation Missile. Designed to knock out enemy radars by homing on a preassigned signal, shooting hypersonically down the line of the offending beam until impacting the antenna, or exploding close enough to put the system out of action. It had received its combat baptism in the Persian Gulf.

Beneath the wings, a facsimile missile, rigged with an ALARM seeker head and processor, squawked its attack signal to the nearest ground tracking station. If the missile could lock on to the simulated enemy radar and register a hit, the radar would be marked out of the game by the examiners on the ground.

Unlike a live firing, there was no plume of flame, no streak across his vision as the missile homed in on its target. All that, he had to imagine.

The screeching stopped. Simultaneously, the red box on the threat-warner winked out.

Six days before, a Tornado from Rantz's squadron had plowed through a Devon village, leaving twenty-seven dead, almost all of them schoolchildren. They never found the pilot, but it was assumed he had had a heart attack. The navigator wasn't testifying either. He'd ejected at the last moment, but as the Tornado was three-quarters inverted at the time, his seat had fired him straight into the ground.

The press had had a field day.

Parliament resounded to the cries of back-benchers, from both sides of the House, demanding an immediate moratorium on low flying. It was a time to put constituency interests before party loyalty. Time, if you were an MP, to get your face on the TV and convince the electorate that you were doing everything to protect its safety.

Demonstrators, activists mostly, had hurled abuse and bricks at the unrelenting walls of the Ministry of Defence, and were probably still doing so.

It made good copy, of course. Kelso, Girling's editor, told him to go out and get some words, find some new angle. The public had been treated to five days of torrid abuse against the RAF from the tabloids. Even some of the weightier nationals had joined the outcry.

As *Dispatches*' science and technology correspondent, Girling went to try to see the story from where the pilot sat. He found it quite a welcome diversion. Nothing much else was making the news. Girling had been tempted to look into reports of a violent gas pipeline explosion in Syria a week before, but it wasn't really his kind of a story. Not any more.

So they had arranged for him to fly back-seat in a Tornado, the principal all-weather, twenty-four hour strike asset of the Royal Air Force. Its primary task, the mission for which it had been designed, was precision delivery of nuclear or conventional ordnance against the Warsaw Pact.

Girling smiled. Warsaw Pact. What was that?

The Royal Air Force, anxious to put across a good case for low flying, had been happy to accede to Girling's request. Kelso's enthusiasm for the story soared when he learned that Girling had been granted exclusive access to Exercise Stalwart Divider, a war game to test Britain's air defenses.

They'd given him a crash course in navigation and weapons-system operation, and finally introduced him to Squadron Leader John Rantz. Rantz was twenty years in the service, combat-tested in the Gulf, and terminally pissed off because he was heading for a desk job in Whitehall in two weeks and had better things to do with his time.

Their Tornado, hurtling toward the target at 560 knots, or the length of three and a half soccer fields a second, was the lead element in Red Force, a strike package composed of British and American fighter-bombers. Their target was a railway bridge, a leftover from the days when steam trains thundered across the great Scottish rivers on their way to and from London, now a rusting relic on the weapons range.

Girling had been on base, waiting for three days to scramble, banned from even so much as placing a phone call to the office, or even his daughter. Exercise rules. No communication with the outside world. No radio, no TV, no tabloids.

Even the manner of his mobilization had been carried out without concession to his civilian status. Just one call from the MoD's PR men to report to Marham at 0900 the next morning. There had been barely time to dispatch Alia to his parents before making the trip to East Anglia.

Rantz's voice came over the intercom.

"Arm the bombs."

Girling leaned over and found the switches. "Bombs armed."

"Switch on the radar."

Girling moved the dial on one click from STANDBY. "Radar on."

"See the IP?"

Girling peered into the radar picture. It took almost two million pounds of taxpayers' money to train a professional to interpret the thing and he was being asked to "read" it after two hours in the simulator.

Initial point, the IP. A strong navigation feature, in this case a factory chimney, from which the pilot could plot a course to the target. Chimney, oh fucking chimney, where were you? Girling's mind fogged over as he thought of football pitches, scores of them, rushing beneath the plane's belly.

"I said, can you see the IP?"

The beam swept the picture, highlighting objects in a dazzling green-

and-black contrast that made his eyes water. He could make out hills, valleys, but nothing that resembled a . . .

"Okay. Got it." A needle of light contrasting against the background clutter, just as the instructor had said. "Straight ahead. About ten miles." He could see the target, too, a little way off, its features clearly defined on the radar screen.

"Take your time," Rantz muttered.

Girling strained past Rantz's ejection seat for a view forward. Out of the corner of his eye he noticed the pilot grab the IP-to-target map and clip it to a knee pocket. The chimney reared out of the haze a fraction to the left of the fighter-bomber's nose, a beacon on its rim flashing high above them. He saw Rantz adjust course a fraction, advancing the throttles as he did so.

The chimney filled the canopy. It seemed, for a moment, as if they would scythe it in two.

"Standby . . ." Rantz yelled. He jerked his hand down as he depressed the button on his stopwatch. The chimney shot past the left wingtip in a blur of mottled browns and reds.

"Viking zero-one?" A new voice in Girling's headphones. The pilot of the airborne laser designator.

"Roger."

"I've got the target, sight's on."

Girling looked past the swept wing for a glimpse of the stand-off designator aircraft, another Tornado equipped with a thermal imager and laser target marker. He could see nothing except rolling greenery, but he knew the second aircraft was close by.

A glint of reflected sunlight in the forward hemisphere made him switch his attention to the front again. The river snaked in the distance from right to left just below the horizon. Spanning it, the majestic arches of the girder bridge were clearly visible.

Girling felt the Tornado jink left, then right as Rantz maneuvered his sight over the target.

"Sight's on, sight's on," he called. A brief pause. "Bombs gone."

The Tornado leapt skyward, relieved of almost four thousand pounds. The two laser-guided bombs, dubbed Paveways, streaked off in the general direction of the bridge. Without laser guidance from the stand-off designator, the Paveways would coast blind, their stubby fins generating enough lift to fly several miles, eventually splashing into the river or the muddy ground beyond. Once the laser was directed at the target, however, the bombs became surgical strike weapons, able to hit any point designated by the laser operator.

"Stand by to lase . . . lase now," Rantz called to the Tornado designator. Even before Rantz finished the command, he was pulling the Tornado into a tight turn to starboard, away from the SAMs and radar-guided artillery.

Girling tried to keep his eyes on the bridge, but it disappeared into the haze behind them.

Two miles away, the seeker heads in the Paveways responded to the laser energy scattering off the third girder of the bridge by snapping the control fins hard over, first left then right, until the bombs locked on course. Only the laser operator, watching the bridge through the high-powered electrooptics in the tip of the designator, would be able to see the results.

Four seconds later, they got the news.

"Two strikes, bridge destroyed. Nice work Viking. See you back at base."

When the Tornado leveled out, Girling was surprised to see they were up to a thousand feet and over water. He looked down at the moving map. They were flying southwest along the Firth of Lorn, just to the south of the island of Mull off the Scottish west coast.

"Pull me up the first way-point for the return leg," Rantz said.

Girling punched in the commands on the buttons by the TV-tab display just as they had shown him on the simulator. The message was relayed to the pilot on his CRT. Rantz pulled the Tornado back on a course that would bring it to the west of Glasgow and thence on a direct line southeast to Marham, now something under half an hour away.

The Tornado decelerated. Girling settled back into his seat, happy in the knowledge that there would be no further need of the sick bag. In the less turbulent air of their cruising altitude, the return journey would be a breeze.

"Just make sure you tell it how it really is," Rantz said, suddenly.

"Enlighten me."

"We fly above a hundred feet on the day and they'll have us. It's as simple as that. Your friends on Fleet Street make out we do this for fun. One cockup out there on the range just now and I would have buried

The static hiss changed in tone. A second later, Girling heard the controller, "Go ahead, Viking zero-one."

Rantz gave a succinct damage report and requested permission to land. The static seemed to build in intensity. They were taking their time.

"Come on, you son of a bitch," Rantz said.

It seemed minutes before the tower came back. "Viking zero-one?"

"Roger."

"You are clear to land from the northeast. Wind speed fifteen knots. Crash crews alerted."

"Thank you, Machrihanish." There was more than a trace of sarcasm in Rantz's voice.

Girling's helmet dug into the back of his skull and the hole in the palm of his hand throbbed.

The Tornado passed over the coastline at two and a half thousand feet. The wings swept forward, ready for landing, and flaps and slats were extended into the slipstream. The straps dug into Girling's chest as the aircraft slowed for the approach. Three green lights appeared on Rantz's instrument panel. Girling heard the wheels lock in place.

The aircraft pulled around in a tight turn between two fifteen-hundred-foot peaks and passed over the peninsula's eastern coastline. They were now over Kilbrannan Sound. Away to their left, Goat Fell, Arran's highest hill, thrust up from the center of the island toward a patch of low cloud scudding in from the southwest.

The runway lights sparkled in the distance.

"Port engine's playing up now," Rantz said, too calmly for Girling's liking. "I think we're only going to have one stab at this."

Girling's grip tightened over the firing handle of his seat.

The Tornado swept over the shoreline. They seemed to be heading for the runway at a phenomenal speed. Behind the airfield a twelve-hundred-foot plateau rose menacingly out of the evening mist. With one unreliable engine there was no chance of the Tornado clearing the rising slopes and going around again for another attempt.

"Brace yourself," Rantz said, his voice strangely detached.

The Tornado cleared the last row of approach lights and banged down hard onto the runway. Girling heard Rantz bring off the power. The Tornado was still doing about 130 knots.

The crash trucks were already moving by the time the Tornado rumbled past their position at the runway's halfway mark. Rantz was standing on the brakes, while Girling could do nothing except watch the far perimeter fence grow through the Tornado's front canopy frame.

It was only when he noticed a fire truck pull alongside the aircraft that he knew they had made it. The Tornado shuddered to a halt, the vibration from the carbon brakes rising up through the airframe.

Orders from Rantz burst into his headset. For a moment, Girling could only think of their deliverance. He had forgotten they were on fire.

"Get the safe-arm pin back into the seat. Quick, come on."

Girling snapped out of his torpor, found the pin on the canopy frame and pulled it from its stowing position. He pushed it down under the seat, desperate to find the hole, his fingers desensitized by the thickness of the gloves. Until he replaced the damned pin his seat was still alive, ready to catapult him into space. At last he managed to click it home.

Rantz was already getting out of his seat when the canopy sprang open and hands pulled at Girling's body. He looked up, dazed, at a crash attendant, his face masked by asbestos-and-foil headgear. One turn of the harness in his lap and he too was out of the cockpit, trailing the umbilical that had plugged him into the aircraft.

From a safe distance, Girling looked back at the Tornado, the rear half of its fuselage covered in fire-fighting foam from the surrounding trucks. It no longer looked the pride of the RAF's strike force.

Rantz shook himself. "Come on, let's go and get some tea."

Girling limped after the pilot, his leg muscles protesting at every step.

"Well, you got your story," Rantz said, dropping back for him.

Girling noticed the strain around the pilot's eyes. "I came to do one story on low flying. My editor doesn't like melodrama—not the sort I write, anyway. We leave that to the tabloids." He paused. "In any case, I reckon I owe you something for getting us down in one piece."

"You're not going to write about this?" Rantz looked from Girling to the Tornado. A bitter, squally wind was blowing across the airfield, whipping the foam off the aircraft and scattering it like tumbleweed across the concrete. Summer seemed to have given Scotland a miss.

"It's not what the magazine's about. Pity, really. Maybe I'll call *The Sun* . . ."

Rantz laughed. "Very funny, Girling."

A detachment of six heavily armed men rounded the corner of a building and headed straight for them.

"Here comes trouble," Rantz muttered.

"Our reception committee?"

"Looks like it."

With the troops still a hundred yards away, Rantz lowered his voice conspiratorially. "Don't tell them you're a journalist, okay? Unless they specifically ask you for ID."

Girling looked at him.

"Otherwise, we'll be here all bloody week. Just leave all the talking to me. They'll assume you're my navigator."

The troops were upon them. Army, Girling noticed, not RAF Regiment as he had expected.

The sergeant saw Rantz's rank and snapped into a salute. "Orders to escort you to the crew room, sir."

"Thank you, Sergeant. Why the firing squad?" He smiled.

"Regulations, sir."

Rantz raised an eyebrow.

"Exercise rules," the sergeant added. "We're on heightened alert."

They turned toward a group of buildings a little way beyond the concrete apron.

"Good to see our defenses working as well on the ground as they do in the air," Rantz said cheerily.

The sergeant said nothing, not quite sure whether Rantz was pulling his leg.

They reached the crew room. Rantz removed his helmet and asked how they might arrange travel back to their own base.

The sergeant pointed to the phone, explaining that it connected to facilities on the other side of the airfield, where his request could be processed. Machrihanish was only a standby RAF base, he said, apologetically. The accommodations were a little Spartan. As he retreated out of the crew room, the sergeant suggested it would not be a good idea to wander outside. Machrihanish was assigned to NATO and the American contingent tended to lock up first and ask questions later. Rantz nodded his thanks. They would wait there until someone came to get them.

"So far so good," Rantz said, when they were alone. He consulted an index by the phone. "Now let's see if we can get out of here."

He dialed a number, jammed the handset to his ear and stared beyond the peeling window frame across the windswept airfield. Thick clouds from the North Atlantic had begun to bring rain with them.

"Bloody awful place," Rantz drummed his fingers on the window-sill waiting for the connection.

Girling realized it was likely to take some time. Good opportunity to take a leak.

Rantz turned from the window. "Don't go wandering off."

Girling grunted.

The pitch-dark of the corridor made the howl of the wind all the more noticeable. Somewhere upstairs a door slammed. Girling found a wall switch and peered through the dim light cast by the low-watt bulb for signs of a bathroom. The signs on the three doors announced that they were offices.

He took the stairs and found himself in a control tower converted into a pilots' recreation room. There was a Ping-Pong table in the middle, a coffee machine by the wall and even the odd magazine scattered around the chairs.

The toilets were off an adjoining passageway. Someone had left one of the frosted-glass windows ajar, causing the cubicle doors to batter against their frames in the wind. Girling shivered and moved toward the urinals. The cumbersome flight gear—G-pants, in particular—made even the most innocuous pee something of a ritual.

Standing there gave him a clear view through the gap in the window. And what he saw made him catch his breath.

He had only ever seen pictures of the 76 before. It was a big aircraft, shorter than a Boeing 747, but about the same diameter, giving it a disproportionately tubby appearance, especially from the rear. It was sometimes confused for the Lockheed C-141, another large airlifter and troop transport, but this was no C-141.

The Ilyushin Il-76, the Russian jet transport known to NATO as "Candid," was inching into a giant hangar on the opposite side of the airfield, the sound of its four engines carrying on the wind. Because of the buildings that surrounded the crew room, it was only possible to obtain a view of the hangar through this one window. Had he been anywhere else, he would have missed it.

He zipped up his flight suit and moved to the window, adjusting the frame so it was fully open. He never noticed the spots of rain on his face.

The Candid was still painted in the colors of Aeroflot, the Soviet state airline. But as the aircraft's engines and systems were shut down, twin guns slid into their stowed position beneath its massive T-tail.

The giant doors began their slow journey across the front of the hangar.

Girling remembered his camera just as the doors had reached the halfway mark. He could see people buzzing around the Candid and stairs being pushed across to the door just aft of the cockpit. And one caught his attention: a stocky man walking back and forth in front of the aircraft with a restless energy, a walkie-talkie alternating between his ear and his mouth. From his nondescript fatigues it was impossible to tell whether the man was Russian or British. He tore at the Velcro lining of his flight suit, set the autofocusing Pentax to full zoom and started shooting.

He managed to get off half a dozen pictures before the doors slammed shut, the boom as they met rumbling across the airfield. Girling shoved the camera back in his suit and retraced his footsteps to the crew room.

As he went downstairs, he could hear Rantz giving someone a hard time on the telephone. When he reached the room at the end of the corridor, Rantz had established that there was a flight out that afternoon. He reserved two seats and hung up.

"That's fixed," he said. "We're on a flight to Northolt. I'll make sure someone forwards your kit from Marham tomorrow."

"Perfect."

Rantz glanced at the wound on Girling's hand.

"What the fuck's that?"

Girling was sheepish. "For a moment, back there, you had me worried."

He thought Rantz was going to laugh, but he didn't.

"You and me both," he said.

CHAPTER 3

THE ELEVATOR DOORS opened and Girling stepped into the newsroom.

"Ah, Tom." Kelso glanced at his watch. "Good of you to join us. Still in one piece, I trust."

Girling threw the briefcase on his desk, nodding to Kelso, who seemed to have avoided any trace of a suntan from his vacation. He sat down and turned on his PC. He looked over his computer screen at the clock and saw Kieran Mallon wince. It was close to eleven-thirty.

Kelso wouldn't want to hear about the rigors of his journey from Machrihanish, how he'd been unable to fall into bed until four that morning. The trip south had been made in an ancient, propeller-driven Devon. The rickety plane's turbulent passage through the night cumulus had sent at least one naval officer scuttling for the head.

From Northolt, Girling had headed straight home. It was a long and expensive taxi journey to his flat.

Kelso wasn't interested in long journeys and late nights. He cared only about the magazine hitting the newsstands every week with the best damned stories his editorial budget would buy. As he was liable to remind the staff, it didn't matter how good the story was if the subeditors didn't receive the words. The week was drawing to a close and there were pages to fill.

"Meeting in five minutes," Kelso said, looking over the top of his glasses. "You're just in time to tell us what pearls you scooped from the mouths of our death-defying RAF friends."

Kelso swiveled on his heels and strode back to his office.

Girling went over to the coffee jug. He looked at the four-day-old stains at the bottom of his mug, thought about washing it out, then poured the coffee anyway.

Mallon turned his chair. "How was World War Three?"

"Don't talk to me about it," Girling said. He took a sip. "Your coffee doesn't get any better."

Mallon smiled. He was ten years younger than Girling and more or less straight out of Queen's University, Belfast, having had one stint on a local paper. "You should try washing the cup now and again."

Girling managed a smile. His whole body ached from lack of sleep. He had never even heard the alarm clock.

"So, who won?" Mallon pressed. "Us or them?"

"The truth is, they're worried there's no one left to fight. The Warsaw Pact's gone, the Iraqis are all in. Who's left?"

"Don't you believe it," Mallon said. "For as long as there have been people on God's Earth, war's been at the top of the hit parade." He grinned. "And we're just the boys to write about it."

"Hell of a way to earn a living."

"Better than working," Mallon said. "Talking of which, what did you pick up?"

In his mind's eye Girling saw the Ilyushin trundling into the hangar.

"Not much. Just some stuff on low flying; a few facts and figures."

Girling pulled his pad from the briefcase and started flicking through the pages for the notes he had made during Exercise Stalwart Divider.

"That's all well and good, but I want the Beirut story," Mallon said. Girling only half-heard. "Beirut?"

"So far, Kelso's gone for all the safe, old hands. Moynahan, Gilpatrick, Stansell . . . I know I could do a better job than Moynahan, for Christ's sake. He spends most of his time in the Press Club."

"What about Beirut?"

Mallon looked at him disbelievingly. "Are you serious?"

"Kieran, I haven't seen a paper or heard the news for three days. News blackouts. World War Three, remember?"

"Sounds more like World War Two."

Across the large, open-plan office, the rest of the editorial staff was filing into the conference room for the news meeting that doubled as Kelso's end-of-week address. Girling and Mallon picked up their coffees and headed in the same direction.

"Well?" Girling prompted, as they walked over. "Beirut?"

"Two days ago, a bunch of lunatics, probably PLO or something, hijacked a Jumbo at Dubai and flew it on to Beirut. They're holding, among several hundred others, a high-ranking group of American diplomats. Poor bastards were part of the Gulf peace initiative, on their way back to Washington to report on the cease-fire."

"What's the latest?"

"All quiet. Negotiators are still trying to make contact."

"And what does Kelso see in it for us?"

Mallon shrugged. "He wants to dig up dirt, find out what's really going on behind the scenes. He's relying on us to put one over the competition. He's really got it in for the Sundays at the moment. Ever since he got back from holiday."

That figured, Girling thought. Kelso fancied himself as the big editor of a national Sunday paper.

"Sounds like the big boys are squeezing his nuts."

After the early summer job lay-offs, the magazine was under pressure to recapture its flagging circulation. Lord Kyle and the board were leaning heavily on Kelso to produce results, or face the consequences.

Girling closed the door behind them. About twenty of the editorial staff were positioned around the table, with Kelso in his customary place at the head. Girling pulled up two chairs, offering one to Mallon.

Kelso was a heavily built Scot in his early fifties, with a gruff face hidden for the most part by a straggly beard. Behind his half-moon, tortoiseshell glasses, he had eyes that were black and bottomless. Shark eyes.

"Right, what have we got?" Kelso asked, turning to the news editor.

Jack Carey reeled off a number of issues that had been put to bed on the magazine's early pages. Most were pretty familiar: the U.S. primaries; Russia's offer to cut a third of its submarine fleet—again;

Pakistan's covert nuclear-weapon tests; a serial killer on the loose in Berlin; more Gulf news; and the gas pipeline explosion in Syria.

Though the magazine predated Kelso's arrival, *Dispatches* was very much Kelso's baby. His curriculum vitae was a litany of famous newspaper names. He was an editor of the old school and held to his principles. As the papers themselves had moved from central London and as old Fleet Street had all but died, Kelso had been approached to mastermind the relaunch of *Dispatches*. In his five years as editor he had built up a strong reputation for hard-hitting news.

Kelso turned his attention to the page plan. "Okay, we've got fifteen pages that still need filling." He turned to Girling. "Tell us about this war game of yours, Tom."

"Exercise Stalwart Divider was the biggest test of Britain's air defenses since the first talk of 'peace dividends.' And against the background of the Devon school disaster, it was controversial. In view of the vast cost and the danger to civilian life, people are asking why we have to stage these things at all now that the Soviet threat has disappeared."

"And your facility—your three days at the base—were exclusive to us?" Carey asked.

"Yes."

"It's certainly topical."

"And expensive," Girling said. "Half the U.S. Air Force was there."

"Official figures?"

"I picked up a USAF press release at the Tornado base. It seemed to contain all the facts."

Carey stared at his page plan for a moment. "I'll buy around five hundred well chosen words on the financial and political cost to the government of military low flying."

Kelso looked at Girling over the top of his glasses. "You flew in one of those jets, so why not give the punters some of your celebrated techno-jargon—tell them how it is from the other side."

Girling thought about Bag, Air Sickness, NATO Stock No 8105-99-130-2180. He was glad to have a chance to put across the pilot's viewpoint. But he would leave out any reference to the in-flight emergency. He owed Rantz something for getting them down in one piece.

Carey scratched his chin. "Seems to me we should split the story in two. We'll box up your firsthand impressions of the exercise on the same page as the main angle. A thousand words tops, all right?"

"And I want to see it by two o'clock," Kelso said. "Anything else we should know about?"

Girling turned to Carey. "There was a Russian military transport aircraft at a base on the west coast of Scotland yesterday. A place called Machrihanish."

"How do you know?" Carey asked.

"I was there. Got pictures, too."

Kelso said: "The Russians are probably starting charter services between Scotland and Murmansk. Who the hell cares, Tom?"

Girling put his notes away. He would follow it up another time.

"I've got other things on my mind," Kelso continued. "Just when everyone thought hijacking had gone out of fashion and it was safe to get back on a fucking plane, these jokers pop up from nowhere and do a number on the American ambassador to Saudi Arabia and his negotiating team. This time, the American public has gone apeshit. My guess is Washington's going to send in the marines, or that antiterrorist outfit of theirs."

"Delta Force," Carey prompted.

Kelso twitched. It didn't do to show him up in company.

"I mean, talk about balls," Kelso continued, his gaze fixed on Girling. "Did you see how they got on board?"

"I haven't had a chance," Girling said.

"Well, read the cuttings file, Tom. It'll take your breath away."

The shark eyes swept the assembled company.

"We need to find out what's happening in Washington," he said. "It's been too quiet for my liking since that 747 touched down in Beirut. We need to steal a march. Show the world we've still got teeth."

"What's the word from the States?" Girling asked. They had to have some news.

Kelso looked to Carey.

"Claudia's done a piece on the knee-jerk reaction over there." Carey picked up the cue. "But it's the usual trawl through her sources in the administration and Congress. So far she hasn't turned up anything we can stick on page one." He paused. "We've also got

Stansell working the story out of Cairo. That should produce some results.''

"If he can get his nose out of a bloody bottle," someone whispered, too low for Kelso to catch. Girling turned to see Moynahan smiling sweetly at him.

Girling stiffened. Coming from Moynahan, the two-faced bastard, that was rich. "What's Stansell's brief?"

"Find out the identity of the hijackers, their motives, see if there's any word of state involvement on the streets. Maybe Libya's up to its old tricks. The usual shit.''

Girling's brow furrowed. "You mean, these guys haven't said who they are yet?"

Carey shook his head.

"What about demands?"

Girling felt himself drawn toward the story. He bit his lip. He was done with that kind of thing. He had promised himself, as much for Alia's sake as his own.

Only Kelso caught his reaction. "Zilch. We're dealing with some hard bastards out there. You might find them interesting." He smiled beguilingly. "As I say, why don't you pull the file from the cuttings library, Tom, and take a look. After you've turned round your copy, of course.''

Girling went back to his desk and flicked through his notes.

He pounded out the details of his trip with Rantz—up to the point where the bombs destroyed the bridge: the nausea, the concentration, the sweat and the fear that accompanied a Tornado crewman as he hurtled supersonically toward the target, his wings level with the tops of the trees.

As science and technology correspondent, Girling had written many such pieces. Today, he pounded out the story mechanically, with little enthusiasm for the words.

"What is it?" Mallon asked.

Girling paused.

"I was thinking of all the useless knowledge that's stored away between these two ears, with maybe a total of three pages a year on which to dump it. Seems like a hell of a waste. I mean, tens of thousands of pounds of taxpayers' money have been spent training me to fly aircraft and helicopters, drive tanks, fire guns—''

"Sounds fun to me," Mallon said.

"Don't get me wrong, it is. But in the end I just get to file the copy if I'm lucky and then kiss all this knowledge good-bye."

"Short of fighting a war, there's not a whole lot you can do with it."

The picture editor arrived with photographs of a Tornado similar to the one in which he had flown with Rantz, and the burnt-out shell of the little Devon village school. The one with the rag-doll body of the child in the ruins that had been splashed across the front pages of so many tabloids the day after the disaster.

Girling sighed. "Kelso?"

The man nodded.

If orders came from the board to take *Dispatches* downmarket, it looked like it would be a short journey.

Girling hit the key to save the file, entered it into the network system and dispatched it electronically to the subeditor's desk, where it would be hacked about before being put into production, finally ending up on an inside news page.

CHAPTER 4

GIRLING PULLED THE cuttings from their file in the library, took them back to his desk and started to read.

The hijackers had boarded a Pakistan International Airlines flight at Karachi bound for Paris. Somewhere over the Arabian Sea they had made their move, storming into the 747's flight deck and killing the copilot; there had been no time for the crew to send a distress signal.

An hour from Dubai International Airport, the hijackers ordered the pilot to make an emergency descent. Dubai tower picked up a Mayday indicating the Jumbo had suffered explosive decompression at thirty-two thousand feet. The tower was informed there were casualties on board.

The pilot requested an immediate descent into the airport and called for ambulances to meet the aircraft as soon as it rolled to a stop.

Once on the ground, the hijackers waited for the medics to board the plane, overpowered them and donned their uniforms. The aircraft was then booby-trapped with explosive devices positioned around the cabin. The terrorists told the passengers and crew that the detonators were primed with infrared sensing fuses and the slightest movement would set them off.

The terrorists—witnesses later described them speaking Arabic—boarded the ambulances and moved across the airfield to the TWA 747, on which the U.S. ambassador to Riyadh and his staff were sipping their champagne in the first- and business-class sections, while their captain waited for takeoff clearance. All flights out of Dubai had been put on hold pending resolution of the emergency on board the PIA flight. The moment the hijackers had sent out their false Mayday over the Arabian Sea, they had established a schedule to which everyone else—including the captain of the TWA Jumbo—played along. These guys were good.

Predictably, the newspapers had been quick to chastise the U.S. government for allowing so many of its diplomatic staff to travel on the same commercial flight. In fact, because of the flurry of diplomatic shuttle missions around the Gulf that week, all U.S. Air Force VIP transport aircraft in the region were already in use.

If U.S. protection policy for its diplomats had received a pasting from the press, the security arrangements on the "airside" of Dubai International, normally an exemplary airport, fared worse.

The terrorists had been able to park their ambulance by the wheels of the TWA Jumbo and were not so much as challenged until they boarded the aircraft. Two air marshals mingling with the passengers had tried to resist, but were shot dead, their bodies thrown onto the tarmac.

The terrorists told the pilot to taxi out for takeoff. The leader of the group made it clear to the tower that any form of obstruction would result in the aircraft being blown up.

The 747 left the coastline of the United Arab Emirates at 0530 and headed northwest up the Persian Gulf. Ten minutes later, the police entered the PIA 747 through the forward wheel well and managed to deactivate the somewhat crude infrared trigger linked to the explosives.

The New York Times established that a Royal Saudi Air Force E-3A AWACS—complete with U.S. crew members—had been scrambled to track the 747's progress up the Gulf. The AWACS vectored F-14s from a carrier near the Strait of Hormuz to intercept the airliner and coerce the hijackers into turning back.

The 747 beat the F-14s to the coast. Low on fuel, the navy planes were forced to turn back to rendezvous with a tanker.

The airliner flew on, passing briefly through Jordanian and Syrian

airspace. Above the wastes of the Syrian Desert the hijackers announced their intention to land at Beirut International. After frantic
dialogue between the copilot and the tower, the 747 touched down in
Lebanon some four hours after it had left Dubai.

Beirut, as ever, was perfect. The airport was in a state of chaos, as
it had been for years. Though held by Amal guerrillas, no one was
really in charge.

In the mayhem within the perimeter fence, no one noticed the group
of commandos stealing across the tarmac until it was too late. Their
strength boosted by reinforcements, the hijackers began to appear
unassailable. For the Joint Chiefs of Staff in Washington the rescue
options were running out.

Since then, the Amal militia groups "guarding" the Jumbo had kept
a respectable distance. Even they seemed to fear an unpredictable
response by the terrorists.

In the three days that the 747 had been there, languishing in a
desolate corner of the airport, there had been no end of rumor
mongering by the tabloids—as well as some of the more respectable
papers—about the likelihood of a storming operation by Navy SEALs
or Delta Force, the U.S. Army's elite antiterrorist unit.

This anticipation was heightened by the arrival of the Sixth Fleet's
carrier battle group off Lebanese waters.

Just as awesome, even to the war-hardened Lebanese, was a
small-scale invasion of Beirut's suburbs by the more intrepid members
of the world's press corps. Even though regular flights in and out of
Beirut were sporadic, there were established routes into the capital for
those who knew them. Sensing safety in numbers, the press was lodged
in an encampment of tents on the edge of the airfield. Through the
miracle of satellite transmission, people were able to catch up on the
hijack drama through snatched glances over cereal bowls, or in the
windows of TV retail stores. From Arkansas to Archangelsk. It was
like Baghdad all over again.

Just about every nation in the region had its forces on alert. The
Middle East, for decades a tinderbox of prejudice and racial hatred, had
become set to explode once again. In the twinkling of an eye, the focus
had moved from the Gulf to the Levant.

Girling stared hard at a newspaper photo of the 747, prominent against a background of desert scrub and the Mediterranean beyond. A hijacker's masked face was visible at one of the windows.

"Who in hell are you?" he heard himself whisper.

In three days, no one had managed to make contact with the hijackers. Grainy pictures of shadowy faces, masks twisted by the distorting effects of the aircraft windows, were splashed across some of the newspapers. The tabloids ran headlines like "the face of terror," or "the mask of death" above them.

The terrorists had made no demands and had not issued the customary declaration of their identity or political aims. That alone set this incident apart.

Against his better judgment, Girling found himself taking notes.

Yesterday's evening papers had carried the news of the biggest breakthrough. The terrorists, quite unannounced, had released all Arab nationals. These people were the first to give eyewitness accounts of conditions inside the aircraft.

Every hostage had a story of terror to tell, but it was the plight of Ambassador Franklin which touched Girling most. Separated from the rest of the hostages, he had borne his torture with courage and dignity. Girling, well hardened to stories of suffering, could not hide his revulsion at the accounts of the ambassador trussed to his seat. Artists' impressions in some of the papers depicted the wire running across his neck that led to the grenade taped to the back of the chair.

In that morning's press, no one was any closer to establishing the identity of the terrorists, although most "observers" and "experts" called upon by the media believed an Iranian-backed Shi 'ite group to be responsible. Knowing something of Washington's own confusion, Girling knew that the pundits were shooting in the dark.

He tilted his chair and stared at the ceiling. So what were the options for ending the incident? A negotiated settlement seemed unlikely— even attempts to deliver food and water to the aircraft had met with stony silence.

After the Arab exodus, there were still almost a hundred mouths to feed. Pretty soon, people would start dying of thirst.

Where were the demands for the release of political prisoners from Israeli jails, or fellow "freedom fighters" from the cells of the West's prisons?

The failure to negotiate was a worry to everyone. If these guys were Hizbollah, then they had every good reason to be concerned.

On October 23, 1983, Hizbollah, the sprawling Iranian-backed terror organization, had issued no warnings, no demands to the French and American peacekeeping forces in Beirut. But by the end of that day 241 American marines, 58 French paratroopers and two more martyrs of Islam were dead.

The truck which struck the U.S. Marines' complex contained six tons of explosives. The detonation was the single largest nonnuclear blast since the Second World War.

Organizations with links to the Palestine Liberation Organization operated with a shade more method in their madness—but not much.

Girling closed the file and walked it back to the library. Others— people like Stansell in Cairo, for instance—could handle the story. He was best out of it.

By the time Girling was back at his desk, most of the staff had gone home. He raised his eyes to the TV, which remained on throughout the day in the corner of the newsroom, pumping out the usual diet of CNN news bulletins.

A Jumbo jet was sitting in the glare of media and arc lights at an airport some two thousand miles away.

"You got time for a drink?" Mallon asked, getting to his feet. "I'm heading down to the Punch."

The Punch was the office watering hole a few blocks away.

Girling looked at his watch. "Not tonight. Got to get back home." He'd promised he'd speak to Alia that evening and already it wasn't far from being her bedtime. She'd been with her grandparents for the best part of a week and he missed her terribly.

Mallon pulled on a jacket. "I'll see you tomorrow then."

Girling gave him a half wave. "Good night, Kieran."

There was no one left in the newsroom, except for the night editor, Joe Cornelius, an old hand from the days when the Street hummed with the presses of newspapers most people had never heard of. Cornelius sat in a stupor at his desk, his eyes raised to the TV.

The box, perched on a shelf in the corner of the room, pulsed out its mute images, the volume turned too low for Girling to hear. In another corner, one of the wire machines jerked into life. Cornelius rose to inspect the message, glanced at it cursorily and moved back to his seat.

On the TV, the talk-show host grinned into the camera, then turned back to his guest. Girling reached out and shut down his PC.

It was only when he was on his feet that he noticed the package from the photo labs in his in-tray. He had not spotted it amongst the cuttings, press releases and scrawled notes that lay strewn across his desk.

He pulled the six glossy enlargements from their folder and began to leaf through them.

He smiled to himself. His efforts to capture the Il-76 Candid at Machrihanish were somewhat haphazard. One of the pictures was wide of the hangar, but showed the hills and the stormy sky behind to advantage.

Of the rest, one was reasonable enough to print. The guy with the walkie-talkie was screwing his eyes against the bright hangar lights behind the great white fuselage of the transport aircraft, his arm raised. The object of the man's attention was hidden by the partially open cabin door.

Girling reached for his coat, then hesitated. He might still catch someone at the Ministry of Defence.

He dialed the number of the press office and waited. If any of them were working this late, it would be a miracle, but it was worth trying just to establish the MoD's line on the Candid's presence at Machrihanish.

The phone was answered on its first ring. Girling recognized Peter Jarrett's voice on the other end of the line. "What are you still doing there, Pete? This was supposed to be a long shot."

"Who's that?" The voice sounded tired and irritated.

"Tom Girling, *Dispatches*."

"Tom, sorry, didn't recognize you for a moment. Contrary to what you lot think, some of us do actually put in some hours here." Jarrett paused. "Well, if you must know, the wife's coming up to town. We're going to catch a show in the West End tonight. What can I do for you?"

Girling pulled a notepad out from his top drawer and scribbled on a page to ensure his pen was working. "It's about something I saw during Exercise Stalwart Divider. You know your boys arranged an exclusive facility for us to cover the story from the backseat of a Tornado . . .''

"Oh yes," Jarrett said. "I remember."

"Well, we had to divert to RAF Machrihanish with a technical problem."

"Did you now," Jarrett said. Girling could almost hear the alarm bells ringing in the press office at Whitehall. "I suppose we're going to see this splashed over your lead page this week."

"The Tornado is not the reason I'm ringing."

"Go on," Jarrett said warily.

"While I was on the ground at Machrihanish I saw a Russian transport aircraft—an Il-76 Candid. Do you know the thing I mean? A big four-engined bugger."

"Yes, I know the type. It looks a bit like a British Aerospace 146. I bet that was what you saw. The Queen's flight has 146s, you know."

"Come on, Pete, you know me better than that. This was a Candid. I've got pictures."

"There's bound to be a very good reason for this, Tom. I doubt very much whether there's a story in it for you."

"I'll be the judge of that," Girling said. He hated to be fed that line by press officers.

"The Russians come into the U.K. on a regular basis these days," Jarrett continued, getting into his stride. "It's all to do with verification. CFE treaty and all that. We allow them to check our equipment levels, make sure they adhere to treaty rules and they let us see theirs." Jarrett chuckled. "It's bloody daft if you ask me, but you'd better not quote me on that."

"I'd appreciate it if you'd check all the same," Girling said.

His eyes started to roam around the room. The talk-show host was staring straight at him, laughing. "Perhaps this is a question for another department. I could try another desk tomorrow if you prefer."

Jarrett coughed. "No, that won't be necessary. I'll ask the right people, but I think I know what the answer will be. As I said—"

"Verification," Girling cut in. "Yes, I know."

"Precisely, Tom. When do you close for press?"

"Tomorrow night."

Suddenly, Girling's attention was riveted to the TV screen. The picture had changed from the talk show to a shaky view of bright lights against an inky backdrop. Girling caught a glimpse of an aircraft on the ground. It took him a second to realize it was the Jumbo.

"Tom, are you still there?"

"I'm sorry, I've got to go," Girling said firmly. "Something's going down in Beirut."

He hung up and sprinted across the newsroom, turning the volume up as soon as he reached the set. Cornelius's expression of irritation changed the moment he saw the reason for the intrusion.

The TV picture was still veering about the screen. There was the sharp crack of gunfire, followed by a burst of excited voices. The BBC's Middle East correspondent, James Cramer, whom Girling knew well from the old days in Cairo, was doing his best to describe what was happening. But it sounded as if his view of events wasn't any better than theirs. The cameraman focused shakily on the cockpit of the airliner. Girling could just make out a shadow on the flight deck.

". . . There were several shots, we heard them quite distinctly, one of the bullets ricocheted off the building behind me. I can see a hijacker in the cockpit. He's pointing a machine gun out of the window . . ." There was another crack and the picture went haywire again. "That was extremely close. The gunmen appear to be firing indiscriminately around the airport."

The voice cracked. "Someone has been hit. I can see one of the newsmen to my right on the ground . . . his colleagues are dragging him across the tarmac to cover." There was a brief shot of a body being carted along the ground. Then more firing. The screen was filled with a blurred picture of sandbags five inches from the camera lens. The correspondent's rapid breathing pounded over the TV's loud-speaker.

Despite his absorption in the drama, Girling could sense Kelso moving across the floor from his office to join him and Cornelius.

The Jumbo lurched into view again, its great white body illuminated by the glare of the arc lights. The intensity of the lights left ghostly traces across the video picture with each oscillation of the camera.

The picture steadied as the cameraman appeared to find a niche from which it was safe to film.

The door immediately aft of the cockpit sprang open. A man in a light-colored suit appeared, hesitated a fraction too long and jumped. The figure lay motionless for a moment on the tarmac before commencing a painful crawl toward the scant cover offered by the nosewheel.

A second figure appeared at the doorway. Girling took in the mask, the sleeveless T-shirt and the Kalashnikov pointed purposefully at the ground. There was a ripple of light from the muzzle, the passenger writhed for a moment, then lay still. Before the cameraman pulled back the shot, Girling saw a suit dotted with weeping black holes.

Cramer, off-camera, swore, then asked the cameraman if he got the shot. Somehow, he managed not to make it sound offensive.

"Christ, why doesn't someone help these bastards?" Cornelius pleaded. "Why doesn't the local militia move in? Where's fucking Delta Force?"

Girling was too horrified to answer, but somewhere at the back of his mind the questions registered one by one.

For Beirut's Amal militiamen, weaned on the law of the Kalashnikov, this was one battle they would want to sit out. This wasn't their fight. As for Delta, or whoever the Americans had out there, they probably couldn't get near the beach, let alone the aircraft. This massacre had taken everyone by surprise.

A violent explosion tore the picture in half. The entire tail section of the Jumbo fell to the ground.

"This is terrible," Cramer said, his voice breaking under the strain. "The whole of the rear of the aircraft is in flames. I can see people jumping to the ground, their clothes on fire . . . now there's movement at the front, by the cockpit . . ." The camera adjusted to capture the nose of the Jumbo. Girling moved closer to the screen. A group of people was sliding down an escape chute. At first he thought they were just passengers, but then he noticed some of them carried guns.

About twenty of them gathered around the front of the plane before wheeling away from the burning airliner, away from the glare of the arc and camera lights. Girling was reminded of a flock of sheep worried by dogs.

Cramer's voice broke over the speaker. "I can see Franklin, the ambassador. He's in the middle of that group by the front of the plane."

Three shadows passed across the front of the lens, one of them distinguishable as Cramer, the other two carrying camera and sound equipment. There was a brief interruption as the transmission switched to the new camera.

Girling dropped his eyes to the floor. "Cramer, you always were a stupid arsehole," he whispered.

Kelso looked at him questioningly.

"He's going after them," Girling said. "James Cramer wants to be a bloody hero."

The picture jumped from the potholed concrete of the taxiway to the sand dunes of the beach beyond. Behind the newsmen there was a huge explosion from the airfield as another set of fuel tanks exploded inside the Jumbo. The fireball that rose into the sky illuminated the waves, a hundred yards distant, as surely as a star shell from a flare pistol.

It was clear the terrorists had no idea they were being followed. From the shaky picture, Girling built up an image of Cramer and his camera crew bobbing in and out of the dunes after their quarry. After several minutes, the camera motion stopped and the picture settled. A little way off, it was just possible to see the terrorists and their captives squatting in a hollow between the dunes.

In the background, Girling heard the distant screams of burning passengers and the crackle of flames.

Cramer's voice came over the speaker as a hoarse whisper. "They're signaling to someone or something out there. Wait. I can see a boat."

They all felt the tension in his voice.

A forty-foot fishing smack bobbed on the waves, just beyond the gentle breakers, its deck windows reflecting the flames from the airport.

The terrorists herded their captives down to the water's edge. Flanked on all sides by the masked men, the prisoners formed a single file and headed gingerly toward the boat.

"Can't they do something?" Cornelius croaked.

"With these pictures the Americans should be able to pick them up," Girling said. He sounded dispassionate, but it was the last emotion he felt.

Cornelius's eyes never left the screen. "But it'll be black as pitch out to sea."

"Not to a radar or FLIR operator, it won't."

Girling hadn't finished the sentence when the picture died and the screen went blank.

"Oh, Jesus," Cornelius said.

Cramer and his crew had just bought the farm.

CHAPTER 5

BARELY ONE HOUR after the flames had been extinguished at Beirut International, the U.S. government's counterterrorism committee, TERCOM, convened in the situation room on the third floor of a discreet government building on Connecticut Avenue, Washington, D.C.

Joel Jacobson got to his feet. If his four colleagues across the table were waiting impatiently for his situation report, they did not show it. There was not much Jacobson could tell them that they did not know already or that they had not seen via the live TV coverage from Beirut.

Except for the Russian development. But Jacobson wanted to hold that back a while.

The dim overhead lighting accentuated Jacobson's pallid complexion and pockmarked cheeks. At forty-five years old, Jacobson was the youngest member of TERCOM. It was a job he relished because it gave him unlimited access to everything the USA had ever gleaned about the Middle East. *Everything.* But it still wasn't enough.

Take the al-Hasakah gas pipeline explosion two and a half weeks ago in Syria. Through their satellites they had see the conflagration, but it was information on the ground they lacked. Jacobson often wondered what had really happened to Russian minister Koltsov.

The region was a place that consumed him utterly, for the simple reason that it was a teasing conundrum. He had made its study his whole professional life.

He had spent the last two hours staring into a terminal linked to the National Security Agency's Magnum SIGINT/COMINT satellite, which was scouring for the merest whiff of the terrorists who had absconded from the beach at Beirut. Thanks to the British Secret Intelligence Service, which had passed on an interesting set of visual clues contained in some BBC news film, the NSA knew what kind of radio equipment the boat carried. It was a useful pointer that enabled the NSA to narrow its search of the airwaves, but so far it had picked up nothing. Had there been any information, it would have been passed on to the navy, which was conducting a more upfront search for the boat in the eastern Med.

Jacobson's monologue began with a status report on known casualties at Beirut. More than a hundred U.S. citizens were feared dead. The terrorists had achieved their breakout from the airliner by planting bombs throughout the cabin and detonating them, either by remote control, through preset timing mechanisms, or infrared triggers.

The effect had been devastating. In the ensuing confusion, the terrorists had rounded up Ambassador Franklin and his staff and shepherded them away from the airliner to the beach. It had been confirmed that there were up to sixteen terrorists on the 747 at the time of the breakout. They were calculated to be superfit and highly trained. And now they had ten U.S. hostages to play with.

Jacobson looked up for a reaction, but his audience remained impassive.

He moved on to the more sensitive issue of why the United States had been surprised by the breakout.

Although there had been a Delta Force detachment waiting offshore in one of the ships of the navy task force, it had not been moved into position. As he spoke, someone was roasting for that mistake, but Jacobson conceded—for the politicians, at least—it had been a tough choice. If U.S. forces had been caught on the ground without Lebanese government approval, there would have been hell to pay, since Lebanon's allies, the Iranians, were making noises about belligerent U.S. behavior again. No one wanted to bring about a new Middle East conflict so soon after the last one.

TERCOM's recommendations had always been clear-cut: dispatch half a wing of F-15Es to the United Kingdom and send Delta Force into Beirut. The rescue completed, the F-15Es would have gone on a little retaliatory raid to teach the terrorists' sponsor a lesson—Israeli style. It would have been quick, clinical and a clear signal that the United States would not tolerate terrorist acts.

But it wasn't to be. The doves in the National Security Council had blocked any such move on the grounds it was highly provocative. And now, to make matters worse, they still knew nothing about the terrorists. It was not the first time he had felt so utterly at a loss. The trouble with their intelligence machine was it was so damned . . . patchy. They had made the Libyan connection in 1986, but it had been close. This one was shaping up to be a bitch.

He continued reading aloud. Terrorists and captives were met by boat, a local fishing smack, and removed from the beach. Within minutes they had sailed into the night.

"Which brings me to current events," Jacobson said. "We're still looking for that boat. The navy does not believe it can get very far. And as soon as it is located, there is a detachment of SEALs on standby to go in and rescue our people."

There were a few curt nods. TERCOM was managing to maintain an even keel. Its present mood was in keeping with its tough reputation in the White House.

Following a presidential decree, the top-secret committee was set up in August 1990 to coordinate the counterterrorism activities of U.S. Special Operations Command, USSOCOM, and Washington's diverse intelligence agencies.

From the start there were difficulties. One of the main ones was the antipathy between TERCOM and certain members of the National Security Council, the president's inner circle of political advisers, who saw TERCOM as a threat to their collective status as crisis manager.

However, within informed military circles, TERCOM's creation was hailed as a turning point, the seal on American military resolve to fight the new enemy.

In a crisis situation, the president and the NSC injected political reality into TERCOM's decision process. Once the necessary political approval had been given, TERCOM passed its directives to USSOCOM, which had at its disposal almost forty thousand active-duty and reserve troops. These troops were ready, twenty-four hours a day, to wage low-intensity warfare against America's unconventional enemies.

Jacobson glanced at each of the four faces opposite him.

TERCOM was chaired by Ryan Newhouse, former congressman and founder of the Corbeau Corporation, a Washington-based think tank. In the beginning, Newhouse had nursed the organization along with a few meager DoD contracts, but by the early eighties he had sculpted it into a monolith.

As for the three other members, whether by coincidence or design, they had been drawn from the rich vein of professional Cold Warriors who would otherwise have been forced into early retirement by the fall of the Berlin Wall: a general who had been forty years with the U.S. Army Rangers, a former head of the National Security Agency's East German section, and a former director at the Defense Intelligence Agency.

Jacobson himself had been a senior analyst in Middle Eastern affairs with the Central Intelligence Agency. Disillusioned with the way things had been drifting in his department at Langley, he had been only too glad to step on board at TERCOM after Newhouse had explained its mandate.

It amused Jacobson that TERCOM had been left to administer the Romeo Protocol. This secret agreement, signed between the presidents of the United States and the Soviet Union in Moscow in July 1991, allowed for the cooperation of U.S. and Soviet special forces in times of mutual crisis. Like the arms treaties, the Romeo Protocol survived Gorbachev's abdication. It was now just the Russians and them. Combating terrorism, insurgency, regional warfare and violence engendered by narcotics trafficking was predicted as the chief military priority of the 1990s, so TERCOM linked the Soviets' elite Spetsnaz antiterror force with a USAF outfit that specialized in antiterror operations—though it was one of the United States' most singularly lackluster special operations units. Jacobson couldn't remember its name, but it was led by a man who had disgraced himself during a penetration mission into Panama in December 1989.

The Russians, TERCOM believed, wouldn't notice the difference. But they would learn nothing of military significance during the exchange visits that had been set up. USSOCOM was happy, because its special ops techniques remained secret. And a select few politicians

He got up, avoided the shards of glass that mined the floor, and
[wa]ndered back to bed.

[T]he pains were getting worse. As if two competing forces were
[wre]stling for supremacy. He could not account for that because over
[th]e years the painful intensity of the dreams had not diminished at all.
[H]e accepted it as part of his life. Dreams and work; the only things he
[ha]d besides his little girl.

slept better at night knowing that relations between the nuclear
superpowers had thawed a little more as a result of their secretive
efforts.

The thought coincided neatly with the last item on his sitrep.

"I should say, gentlemen, that we have received an offer of
assistance from the Russians through the channels established by the
Romeo Protocol. According to General Aushev, they have specific
intelligence on the identity of these terrorists should we agree to accept
his offer of help."

The chairman leaned forward into a pool of light cast by the recessed
bulb above the table.

"How has the White House reacted to this offer?" Newhouse asked.

"With some gratitude," Jacobson admitted. "The NSC wants our
formal response urgently."

"I think we already know the answer."

Jacobson preempted him. "That any dealings with Moscow would
be premature while our own sea-search is under way."

Newhouse nodded. "Premature, yes."

There were gestures of assent from the others.

"What if the sea-search proves . . . unfruitful, sir?" Jacobson
asked.

"Impossible," said the former Ranger general. "There's enough
radar painting the eastern Med to bring it to a boil."

Jacobson coughed. "I would remind you, General, there has been no
sign of anything that fits the description of that boat so far."

Newhouse sat back and brought his hands together. "See that the
Russians are informed of our gratitude, Joel. But tell them there will be
no need for any cooperation this time."

Jacobson closed his clip file. "Yes, sir."

■   ■   ■

GIRLING AWOKE suddenly, his mind filled with images of terrible
violence. He switched on the bedside light, noticed the time—past four
o'clock—and threw back the bedclothes.

A black-and-white movie was playing on the TV. He killed the
picture as he walked past to the kitchen.

The glare from the kitchen track lighting accentuated his curious
existence: remains of a late-night takeout and dregs of an unfinished

whiskey sat on the table beside Alia's cup, the one emblazoned with the picture of the cartoon pony.

He grabbed a bottle of mineral water from the fridge and swigged deeply. When he closed the door he noticed his daughter's red rubber boots in their niche between the fridge and the wall. He thought he'd remembered to pack her off with everything, but the suddenness of the call from RAF Marham had claimed some casualties after all. Neither Alia nor her grandmother had mentioned their absence during his last phone call, which meant Alia was being spoiled. She hated walks. Whenever they did go out together in the park, Girling usually relented and lifted her to his shoulders. Somehow she knew how to manage him. Not having a mother around had given her a resourcefulness beyond her four years.

Although the flat wasn't big, it seemed to rattle without his daughter there.

At nights, after he had put her to bed, he felt the tempo of her breathing around him, no matter whether he was cooking, working to music in the sitting room, or talking business on the telephone.

To say evenings gave him a feeling of rapt pleasure was an understatement. They brought out protective instincts in him which were lionlike in their intensity. He supposed that the absence of a woman in the house had contributed to the depth of feeling. He was father and mother to the little girl now, which explained the cocoon he had wrapped around her.

Evenings with Alia were precious. They imbued him with a sense of calm that he found nowhere else in his life.

As for their daily routine, it seemed to teeter constantly on the edge of disaster. He dropped her off at school on his way to work and relied on a neighbor to collect her, give her tea and look after her until he returned from the office. Then there was a quiet period—comparatively speaking—when he would read to her for an hour, or talk. Sometimes Alia would ask questions about her mother, questions he always answered truthfully. She never pressed him on the subject, seeming to sense his vulnerability.

Soon after his return to England, Girling placed photographs of his wife on the shelves, chests and tables of the apartment. He felt a need to be surrounded by them. Then, one day, he gathered them into a box and consigned them all save one to a dark corner of the cupboard

beneath the stairs. He put the lone photograph in A could be near her mother. For Girling, the pain wa needed.

Whenever he could, Girling would work from time with his daughter. When foreign assignments were only too willing to come to the rescue and Stalwart Divider trip was typical of the time he woul home on any one occasion.

Girling's parents lived in a small village outside (since his father retired from the diplomatic serv before.

He had called them shortly after his return fro discussed arrangements for collecting Alia with promised to drive over the next evening, the preci arrival dependent on the usual last-minute complicat panied press night. He anticipated he would be there His mother was delighted. Visits from him were so ra be grumbles about promptness from his father. Son changed. His father was the last person to understand reason his only son rarely came visiting.

Outside Girling's second-story apartment, London sle thousand miles away, the ashes of a five-hundred-seat still be smoldering. And within the hospitals of Haifa doctors would be working through the night to save liv

Girling had fallen asleep to the pictures of American ters shuttling survivors to hospitals in Israel, thoughts of James Cramer's fate in his head. But his dreams wei images of a killing on a dirt road in a provincial tow sweeping, majestic river and the barren wastes of an endle accepted the dream, because it was part of the price of hi dream was a vent, through which the feelings he denied hi were allowed to escape.

The pain hit him in the stomach and he doubled ove falling from his hand and smashing on the tiled floor. His down instinctively, hugging a point below his midriff, feeling was focused.

Girling held himself until the knife in his gut was pulled t the agony dissipated.

CHAPTER 6

GIRLING HEARD THE NEWS on the radio: the *Washington Post*'s exclusive about U.S. plans, now aborted, of course, to send F-15Es based in the United Kingdom on a retaliatory raid. It made the second slot, just below the lead item detailing the disappearance of the hijackers and their captives.

The jets were to have flown the moment the identity of the hijackers and their sponsor nation were established by Delta Force, the hostage-rescue unit on standby in U.S. Navy ships off the Lebanese coast. Only Delta never got its shot at the big time; the hijackers' unexpected and violent getaway had seen to that.

The implication of this story was worrying: it appeared that nobody had the slightest idea where these terrorists had sprung from.

As he walked to the station, Girling could feel still a dull throb in the pit of his stomach. The pain was a reminder that he had flown too close to the flame. Prudence suggested it was time to lay off the ball-grabbing exclusives.

Still, the thrill of his old work—once his stock in trade—drew him like a bottle pulls a drunk. It would be so easy to indulge himself.

Technical journalism kept him on the right side of the tracks, but it was no compensation for the adrenaline that accompanied the reporting of world news.

When he entered the building, the workstations lay idle, a sign there was another news meeting in progress.

Girling went straight to the conference room to find Kelso, who was sitting at the head of the table, calling the meeting to order. He took a seat at the back of the room.

"What happened to you?" Kelso asked.

Girling shrugged. He knew he looked terrible. It would wear off.

Kelso didn't look so good himself. He looked tired, and when he was tired he was testy. He began shuffling a sheaf of papers, until the rustle of pages was the only sound in the room. When he had everyone's attention, Kelso got to his feet.

"We've all seen the news. Last night you lost a colleague. I know some of you have worked with Cramer." He paused. "So here's some good news. Whatever the speculation last night, Cramer's alive."

Kelso could do that sometimes. He had a way of breaking news to people who were paid to gather it, day in and day out. It was one of the things that had kept him in the business through the years.

"I was called to an editors' meeting at the Ministry of Defence this morning," Kelso continued. "Among other things, they told us he's safe."

"But his pictures went off the air," Mallon said. "We thought—"

"I know what you thought. That's what all of us were meant to think. The fact is, Cramer's pictures had become useful."

"So someone pulled the plug," Girling said. "That's pretty extreme."

"The government is asking for the media's cooperation. They've asked us to hand over any information that might be relevant or useful before publication. That was the gist of the meeting this morning."

"Washington must be leaning on its allies pretty hard," someone said.

"Are we going to play ball?" Carey asked.

He had a point. Requests for media cooperation were not binding.

"That depends," Kelso replied, resuming his seat. "We've still got a bloody magazine to get onto the streets by tomorrow morning. And there's no obvious lead. What did we get through last night?'' His gaze fell on Carey.

The news editor looked at his clipboard. He had a list of stories that had been ''dropped'' into the electronic mailbox by their stringers and correspondents around the world during the night.

''Gilpatrick's filed her political sketch, plus a short piece on last night's press conference at the White House.''

Kelso, like most of his staff, had seen the president speak on the late news. ''Did she manage to get anything beyond all that shock, horror and outrage?''

''She checked her sources on the identity of the terrorists, on who might be behind them, and on possible military retaliation. No comment. If they know, they're not saying.''

''Jesus, how much are we paying that girl?'' Kelso demanded under his breath.

''Come on, Bob,'' Carey said. ''This is a tough one.''

''It seems that the CIA, or whoever checks these things, has no more idea who carried out this attack than we do,'' Moynahan, their diplomatic editor, said. ''That's a fair assumption, isn't it?''

Girling saw the tic pull at Kelso's right cheek. Moynahan, his words as ponderous as his gait, irritated Kelso. Girling knew that the editor had been seeking an excuse to sack him for months. No one would be sorry to see Moynahan go. He spent more time at the Press Club than he did in the office, which made his gibe about Stansell all the more odious.

''I don't want fucking assumptions,'' Kelso said. ''I want facts.''

''But the hijackers and hostages have disappeared into thin air. You heard the news, didn't you?''

''Doesn't mean to say no one knows where they've gone,'' Kelso said. ''Maybe that's what the CIA wants us—and the terrorists—to believe.''

Moynahan slumped back into his chair. He looked exhausted, his lackluster eyes in reddened sockets.

''Bob's right,'' Carey said. ''We can't make any assumptions, especially with a story of this complexity. We shouldn't simply assume that Washington is groping in the dark.''

Kelso cut him off. There was a wild look in his eyes. ''Listen, all of you. We're going all the way on this one. I want us to break the identity of these bastards. Find out who these terrorists are, and who's behind them. It's got to be our very own story. Our exclusive.''

Girling thought there was more to this outburst than pure indignation. He heard the rustle of money behind Kelso's words. All he could see was Kelso standing before Lord Kyle and attempting to justify the magazine's profile against the latest circulation and advertising figures.

"Time's running out, Bob,'' Carey said. "We've got ten hours, maybe twelve tops, if we're to put that story in this week's edition. It doesn't look too promising.''

There was a look of desperation on Kelso's face. "What's Stansell filed? He's closer to it than any of us. He's got to know something.''

Carey produced the clipboard again and rummaged through the reports until he found the page with the Cairo dateline. "He's sent in a piece setting out the background to Islamic terrorism—''

Kelso brought his palm down on the table. "Background, background. That's all I'm hearing. Hasn't anyone got any news, for Christ's sake?''

Carey grabbed his coffee before it swilled over the edge of his cup. "Stansell's still working the news angle. Along with a few other people.'' The news editor looked sidelong at Moynahan for a sign that he had managed to turn up something during the night. The old hand shook his head.

Carey grimaced. "I think it's worth pointing out what we could be dealing with out there, how these terrorist groups cooperate, their aims, beliefs and so on. Stansell has done that. I think people will want to know.''

Carey had a knack for keeping a cool head when things got bad. And, just as important, he knew how to play Kelso's temper.

Kelso's anger subsided. "Give us the short version.''

Carey pulled Stansell's copy from the clipboard. "There are two principal threats, the Palestine Liberation Organization and Hizbollah.'' His eyes ran down the page. "Each is an umbrella organization, overseeing dozens of groupings—small armies in some cases—all of them as committed to the cause today as they ever were, whatever their more moderate leaders say.''

"The cause?'' Mallon asked.

"Clear in the case of the PLO—the annihilation of Israel and destablization of the Mideast peace process. Less so with Hizbollah, but essentially the establishment of a pan-Islamic Shi'ite state.

"Behind the two umbrella groupings are a number of sponsor nations, the most prominent being Libya, Syria and Iraq for the PLO, and Iran for Hizbollah."

"I thought the PLO and Hizbollah hated each other," Kelso said.

Carey smiled. "They do and they don't. It's a kind of love-hate relationship. On the surface, they spend more time fighting each other than they do their own traditional enemies, but at an unofficial level there is communication. It's bizarre, but then Islamic terrorism is a world of contradictions, like Alice and the looking glass. Once you're through, it becomes a web, a whole network that sprawls right across the Middle East—and beyond. Stansell points that out somewhere and no one knows better than he does," he added, putting the copy down.

"All right," Kelso said, "pass it over to the subs desk." He turned to the senior subeditor. "Box it up on the spread. And dig out a picture of the bombing of the marines' complex in '83. That should show people what we're dealing with out there. Now all we need is some news."

Kelso paused a moment, letting his gaze brush each of them. "What happened after the terrorists slipped away from the beach? Somebody's got to know. Somebody we have access to."

Girling felt a nest of insects stir in his stomach.

Kelso swung round to face him. "Well?"

Girling managed to keep the strain from his voice. "Tech-Int would know."

"What?" Kelso's forehead creased.

"Technical Intelligence. The MoD's technical analysts—the people who do nothing but assess the bad guys' hardware. I deal with them all the time."

Girling stared into a wall of uniform incomprehension. "How do you think I get all that information on Russian military equipment? From the Russians themselves?"

Kelso frowned. Girling realized he might as well have been talking Chinese.

"Remember that defense exhibition in Baghdad all those years ago? I gave Tech-Int a set of photographs—around five hundred prints in all—the day after Saddam Hussein invaded Kuwait. Tanks, aircraft, missiles—the Iraqis had put everything on display except their nuclear, biological and chemical weapons. And I was the only Western journalist to show up with a decent camera. Tech-Int confessed that their military attaché in Baghdad had been on holiday at the time. They were delighted. We've been best buddies ever since.''

"What's that got to do with our friends in Beirut?'' Kelso asked.

Girling took a deep breath. "A pound to a penny Tech-Int has sucked Cramer's film dry for evidence that could point the finger at the terrorists. I know the way they work. They would have passed that information to MI5, who would have sent it on to the Pentagon. That being so, they would have received feedback from Washington, too.''

"Can you get to them?''

"We would need to talk about that.''

Kelso pushed back his chair and got to his feet. His eyes remained on Girling. "Okay. This meeting is adjourned for everyone except you.''

The two of them strolled back toward Girling's desk. Like some heavy piece of mechanical engineering, the newsroom began to swing into action around them. Carey was shouting for copy over clattering keyboards and the trilling of phones. It was press day.

They stopped in front of Girling's desk. Kelso hitched up a trouser leg and sat down on the one corner free of papers. Girling stood facing him.

"I need you on this story, Tom.''

"I don't mind talking to Tech-Int.''

Kelso shook his head slowly. He took off his glasses and rubbed his eyes. "I mean for the whole shooting match. You know the Middle East, what we're dealing with out there. And I haven't got any reporters working this one.''

"What about Kieran Mallon?''

"I mean real reporters. Mallon's too young. Lacks experience.''

"You could do worse than give him a break. I've never seen a kid so hungry for the story.''

Kelso watched Mallon walk back from the coffee station to his desk. He had already made up his mind. "Another time, maybe. I want you to take charge of this one.''

"I'm not sure I can.''

"I'm prepared to take the risk. Listen, Tom. I've stuck my neck out for you. I've let you pursue your *Boy's Own* stories." He smiled to himself. "I confess that most of your stuff goes straight over my head, but then I'm a little old-fashioned. For Christ's sake, you're too damned good to end up on the scrap heap."

"Funny as it may seem, Bob, I enjoy what I do. Besides, it makes me feel better."

"Don't think I haven't seen that look in your eyes. You want this story."

"Maybe. But then I'd like a cigarette, too. Doesn't mean I'm going to start smoking again."

"That's no answer."

Girling gave his editor a reproachful smile. "Yeah, I know." He felt the insects stir again. "Look, Bob, if it's just this once . . . ."

Kelso slapped his thighs and got to his feet. From deep within the shark eyes a light shined. "Good man."

"Is that all you can say?"

"You'll be all right, Tom. Trust me."

■   ■   ■

GIRLING ORDERED two pints—a bitter for himself and a stout for Mallon—and carried them over to the table where the reporter was waiting. He glanced at the wall clock on the way. He had another hour before he was due at the top floor of the large ministry building on Northumberland Avenue, where Technical Intelligence was located.

There was a keen look in Mallon's eye. He was still young enough to thrive off office intrigue; and the business with Kelso during and after the news meeting had more than aroused his curiosity.

"You angry you didn't get Beirut?" Girling asked.

Mallon shrugged. "Not really. It happens."

Girling smiled. Mallon, the philosopher, strangely at odds with the character who routinely terrorized the MoD into giving him answers.

"Anyway, I see Kelso's put you onto the story," the Irishman said.

"A temporary arrangement, I can assure you."

"So how come you get to do it? You're supposed to be the science and technology correspondent."

"I used to cover the Middle East beat. In Kelso's book, that's important. I still think any reporter with a nose for a decent story could do the job."

"I heard what you said about me, you know."

For a moment Girling thought Mallon was accusing him. His brow furrowed.

"The recommendation you made to Kelso," Mallon prompted. "About me doing the hijack story. Thanks for trying."

Girling shifted uncomfortably. "That's a hell of a pair of ears you've got."

Mallon laughed. "Maybe I'll insure them one of these days."

"So what else did they pick up?"

Mallon traced a finger idly across the head of his Guinness, then stuck it in his mouth. "More than a tinge of desperation in our great editor's voice."

"Thanks for the vote of confidence."

"Come on, Tom. You know I didn't mean it like that."

"Relax. I was kidding."

"You could tell me why Kelso's so keen for you to take charge of this job, though."

"I know the Middle East. And I used to be a reporter. It's that simple."

"The work you did for the *Times,* right? I heard about that. What happened?"

"There's not a whole lot to say," Girling said.

"Why does everyone talk in riddles when they're around you? Now you're doing it yourself."

"I'm not sure I follow you."

"When Kelso asks you to talk to these Defence Ministry whiz kids, you turn round and say, 'We'd need to talk about that.' As if you were striking some sort of deal with him. What's there to talk about, for Christ's sake? If I were to try and negotiate with Kelso over a story, he'd throw me into the street."

"That's just because you're not yet part of the furniture."

Mallon's blue eyes bore into him. "I ask a few people later what the big mystery is about you and they just shrug, or clam up on me. And then I come back to my desk to find Kelso kissing your arse because he wants you to take charge of the whole story. You, the technology correspondent."

Outside, it was raining heavily. The traffic moved slowly down Fleet Street toward Ludgate Circus and St. Paul's Cathedral.

Girling looked at his watch.

"Well?" Mallon's eyes shone like a child's before a bedtime story.

"You don't give up, do you," Girling said.

The Irishman shook his head. "Persistence. It's what I'm paid for, remember?"

Girling took a cigarette from the pack Mallon had left on the table and rolled it between his fingers. He was just about to place it in his mouth when he thought better of it and stuffed it back into the box.

"All right, so you know that I used to work for the *Times*. I was their Middle East correspondent. People said I was on my way, and I believed them."

Girling watched the traffic crawl through the rain. He picked out a harmless-looking man, roughly his age, sitting on the top deck of a bus, and tried to lose himself in imaginary details of that ordinary life.

"Tell me what happened," Mallon said.

Girling spoke, but his voice had changed. "I suppose I could have done something about it. They told me afterward that she was beyond help, but to this day I keep thinking . . ."

"Done something?"

"About the slaughter. No other word for it, really. Murder doesn't describe what they did to her."

Mallon lost all interest in his beer. "Murder? Who was murdered?"

"Her name was Mona. Mona Hamdi. You wouldn't have heard of her. She was a young Egyptian photographer. Did some free-lance work for us. For the *Times*, I mean. She would have been very good." He smiled distantly. "She was already pretty good."

Girling gulped at his drink, but the alcohol wasn't working. His stomach felt as if it were on fire. "Kelso thinks that this hijacking is going to send me off the rails again, but he's in a tight spot. You were right about him being desperate."

"You said murder."

"I did? Must be the drink."

"Stop pissing me about, Tom. What happened to Mona? And what has she got to do with you?"

"What is this?" Girling said. "A one-on-one?"

"I'm sorry."

Girling never heard Mallon's apology. He was halfway to the equator, on a dirt road in a provincial town in Upper Egypt. "Mona was killed by fundamentalists. She was dragged from my car, before my eyes. Slaughtered . . .''

He turned to the window.

"They stoned her to death. Rained the rocks down until her head cracked open and the blood was all over the road, while I just watched.''

"Why, for God's sake?'' Mallon touched Girling gently on the arm.

"There must have been dozens of them, whipped into a frenzy. She hadn't done anything, except take a few pictures. Bastards held me, while their leader laughed in my face, his hands red with blood from the rocks. . . . I'll never forget that face. It was twisted with loathing. For me, for her, everything we stood for. I don't want to forget that. I won't forget that.''

■   ■   ■

MALLON KNOCKED on Kelso's door and walked in, even though the editor was in the middle of dictating a letter to his secretary.

"Yes?'' There was a look of irritation on Kelso's face.

"I'm sorry, but I'd like to talk to you privately,'' Mallon said. "It shouldn't take a moment.''

"Is anything wrong?''

"Yes, I think there is.''

Kelso's secretary was still waiting expectantly for her next line of dictation. Without uttering a word, Kelso gestured her to the door. "I'll buzz you when I'm through.''

When they were alone, Kelso shuffled the sheaf of papers on his desk and popped them into a drawer. "Well?''

Mallon suddenly felt awkward. He searched for a way to convey his concern without directly criticizing Kelso's approach.

"It's about Girling,'' he said. "He's just told me what happened in Egypt. About the riot.'' He paused, but Kelso wasn't giving him any help. "I had no idea,'' he stammered.

"Nasty business,'' Kelso said. "Incredible how he manages to keep it to himself.''

"I never knew what he was carrying around with him, Bob. But it runs deep, very deep, and this business over the hijacking . . . it's not doing him any good. He said something about going off the rails, just like last time. What did he mean by that?''

Kelso scratched at the skin beneath his beard. It made a curious, rasping sound in the silence that hung between them. "He blamed himself for what happened. In a nutshell, he cracked up. Hospital case."

"A breakdown?"

"Something like that."

"What were these riots?"

"They hardly made the news over here. An outbreak of student rioting—serious stuff, mind you. Burning, looting, killing, the lot—and all started by the Muslim Brotherhood, the Egyptian secret religious society. All roads and communications in the south were down, so Girling and Mona set off upriver in a bid to deliver an exclusive to the *Times*. They felt they could get through where every other reporter and photographer had failed.

"They reached Asyut, the center of the troubles, and it was like a bad day in Beirut. Girling tried to persuade Mona to remain outside the town, but she wouldn't have any of it. They were driving through the streets, when a mob sprang up from nowhere, spotted them and pulled Mona from the car. Local reports said it took ten minutes for the stones to kill her."

"What happened to Tom?"

"They started on him next, but the cavalry arrived in the nick of time. An Egyptian Army patrol reached him before they could finish him off."

"Finish him off?"

"He was half-dead," Kelso explained. "And they never did catch Mona's killers. As far as I know, they're still at large today."

"But what made them do it?"

"Who knows? An Egyptian girl, a Muslim, caught with an unbeliever. Perhaps that's reason enough to people like that. Anyway, the point is, Girling blamed himself for what happened. Only time he ever talked to me about it, he told me he wished he'd died with her. Funny thing is, if it hadn't been for Stansell, he probably would have been granted his wish."

"Our Stansell?"

Kelso nodded. "Stansell turned up at the hospital a few days later. He was doing a feature on fundamentalism and the return of the Brotherhood. He wanted to get Girling's own story. You should find the back issues and read it for yourself. It's vintage Stansell—a graphic, vivid account of a grubby Middle East dustup that most of us never even knew was going on. Anyway, Girling wasn't eating, or accepting medication, so the Gippos just left him to die. Stansell had Girling shipped over to his apartment and simply refused to allow him to give in. Don't ask me how he did it. I've known Stansell a long time, but he's never told me the full story. You haven't met Stansell, have you?''

Mallon shook his head.

''He's a funny old sod. He must be sixty by now. One of the old school. You know the type—he's married to the job. Was married for real once, but it didn't last long. Likes a drink—a bit too much, as it happens. It's been showing in his copy, or lack of it, for some time. Still, in his day, he was a bloody fine foreign correspondent. Loves the solitary life. He could spend weeks incommunicado and then—*wham*—up he popped with some amazing exclusive. Loves the Middle East, too. Covered everything from the Six-Day War to the Soviet invasion of Afghanistan. Always on the spot. I used to rank him one of the best in the world.''

''What happened to Tom?'' Mallon asked.

''The *Times* replaced him, of course, because he refused to file anything, or was incapable of filing anything—I don't know which. He didn't touch a keyboard for months, not until Stansell coaxed him back to it. But by then he was through with hard news. He went back to his roots—technical journalism. He'd started out that way, writing for some popular science magazine, oh, years ago. But he was an ambitious bastard in those days and chucked it in to become a reporter, eventually working his way up to the *Times*. He did well there. So much so that they sent him to Egypt. The rest, as they say, is history.''

''So why the hell did you put him onto this story? It was just a matter of time before he flipped his lid.''

Kelso bristled. ''He's got to snap out of it sooner or later.''

''Oh, really? You don't need him because this magazine's in a bit of a tight spot, I suppose.''

''Careful, Mallon.''

''I'm sorry,'' Mallon said, then regretted it. He'd meant every word.

''Girling's got to leave this psychosis behind,'' Kelso said. ''He's too good to spend the rest of his working life writing about machinery."

"Don't you think he should be free to work out his own destiny, in his own time?"

"Bah." Kelso searched the cracks in the ceiling for an answer. "If man had always remained on safe, solid ground, if he'd never taken risks, we'd still be staring at the moon and wondering if it's made of cheese. Girling has to confront this. When I was looking for someone on the science and technology desk, it was Stansell who persuaded me that Girling was good enough for the job. I've never regretted it. He has a knack for turning high-tech jargon into good reading. But it's time to move on."

"Well, you've managed to shed light on one mystery, anyway," Mallon said.

"What's that?"

"Why Girling talks about Stansell sometimes like he's his old man."

"Girling would die for Stansell," Kelso said. "He's never forgotten that he saved his life."

He picked up his phone and asked the secretary to come through and finish taking his letter. "Girling's a distant kind of bloke. Half his problem is that he doesn't want anyone to know he has a problem. But you're as close to him as anyone in this building, Kieran," he added, turning back to Mallon. "Keep an eye on him, will you? I think this will all pass, but if I'm wrong . . . I wouldn't want him or his little girl on my conscience." He stood up, came round the desk and clapped a paternal arm around the Irishman's shoulders. "If he looks like he's going over the edge again, I'll take him off the case, that's a promise."

"I never even knew Girling was married, let alone a father," Mallon said, getting to his feet.

Kelso stared at Mallon.

"I thought Tom must have told you. Mona Hamdi was his wife."

■   ■   ■

IT WAS late afternoon when Girling returned to the newsroom.

Mallon was on the phone. Carey had asked him to turn his hand to covering the spate of antiwar demonstrations that had sprung up in London and other European capitals on account of the U.S. military buildup in the eastern Mediterranean. At that moment, Mallon was trying to interview an opposition MP well known for his controversial views on Middle Eastern affairs. The parliamentarian was running out of steam, but Mallon willed him to keep talking, for the handset had become a convenient shield from Girling. He was worried that on reflection, Girling would be furious about the grilling—and his revelations—at the Punch.

Girling's shadow fell across Mallon's desk just as he was replacing the receiver.

"Want a coffee?"

Mallon looked up and blinked. Girling was waving two empty cups in front of him.

"No thanks," the Irishman managed.

Girling shrugged, then moved to the coffee station and filled his cup. "Can't say I blame you," he said, sniffing the steam that belched from the mouth of the carafe.

Girling stirred his coffee with an absent, tranquil look on his face. It was as if the incident at the pub had never happened.

He walked back to his desk and began rifling through the pile of papers teetering on the top basket of his in-tray.

"Any messages?"

"Stansell called a couple of times."

"What did he want?"

"Didn't say. He's not very talkative, is he?"

"He takes some getting to know," Girling said. "Does he want me to call him?"

"He said he'd call back."

Girling nodded.

"I take it you have been at the Ministry of Defence most of the afternoon," Mallon said.

Girling sat down and swiveled the chair to face Mallon. "Uh-huh."

"So how were the back-room boys?"

"Tech-Int? You have to bring something to the table, otherwise they don't play ball." He tapped his jacket pocket. "So I borrowed the tape of the interview with the Russian defense minister—the one we're running in the magazine next month. Tech-Int was particularly interested in the part about the offensive capabilities of their new aircraft carrier, the *Kuznetsov*."

"It was hardly your interview to give."

"In a few minutes the cassette will be back where I found it. Moynahan will never know."

"Well, put like that . . ."

Girling produced his notepad. "Anyway, it didn't take long for the conversation to shift to last night's events in the Lebanon. I was right. Details of the BBC's film of terrorists and hostages getting off the beach—the stuff that we, the public, never got to see—are now in the Pentagon." He paused to sip his coffee. "Not that it's going to be of much use to the U.S. Navy."

Mallon leaned forward. "What do you mean?"

"To put it simply, our violent friends have disappeared off the face of the Earth. Or from the surface of the sea, strictly speaking. Which is pretty bloody astounding, seeing as the navy had P-3s, E-2s, A-6s, S-2s—basically, a lot of metal in the sky—looking for that fishing boat."

"Are you sure about this?"

Girling smiled ruefully. "The intelligence community is awash with it. I'm afraid the secret won't last the night." He gestured to the TV. "It'll probably be on the evening news. Certainly in tomorrow's papers. Kelso's going to have to start looking somewhere else for his exclusive."

"There go our jobs," Mallon said.

"No kidding," Girling said, rolling the coffee cup between his palms.

Mallon's expression darkened. "Do you think Lord Kyle will shut us down?"

Girling shrugged. "I heard a rumor there's a meeting tomorrow and all the big guns will be there. It explains why Kelso's been busting his balls to put such a hot edition to bed this week. It might end up being the difference between a desk and the dole queue."

"And I was just beginning to enjoy journalism," Mallon said.

"Chin up," Girling said, mimicking their editor. "We'll be all right."

Mallon returned the smile. "It's certainly good to see you back to your old self."

"Me? I'm fine. Always have been."

"I meant . . . well, about what happened at the pub."

Girling waved a hand dismissively. "I get a little morose sometimes. Don't take any notice."

"I know she was your wife, Tom. Kelso told me. I'm really sorry. I shouldn't have pried like that. I had no right."

The phone trilled by Girling's elbow.

The receptionist's voice came on the line. "It's Mark Stansell for you," she said. There was a click and he was through.

Mark Stansell? Girling smiled. No one ever referred to him by his Christian name. She must be new.

The line was crackly. In Egypt, Girling had become used to the vagaries of their telephone system. Now he shouted to make himself heard.

"I hear you've been drafted into Kelso's army," Stansell said. "Welcome back."

"Thanks," Girling replied. "It's only a temporary arrangement, although I'm still not sure I'm doing the right thing."

"You'll be fine, Tom Boy. Just make sure you fly low and slow. Don't rush things."

"Sure," Girling replied. "Tell that to the guys who made an even bigger mess of Beirut last night. How are you doing on the ID front, Stansell?"

Stansell said something, but he missed it in a sudden burst of static.

"Say again."

"I said I think I've cracked it," Stansell said, as the noise subsided.

"Cracked what?"

"Who they are. Our terrorists." Stansell paused, leaving Girling just enough time to worry about the difference he heard in the voice on the other end of the line.

"Do you have a name?"

"Yes."

"Well, for Christ's sake let's have it."

"Are you alone? I mean, is there anyone nearby?"

Girling looked up. Mallon was chatting to the attractive girl on the subediting team who had stopped by his desk on her way out. There was no one else around them.

"I'm alone. Stansell, what is this?"

"Well, it's a bit awkward, really. You see, I'm not sure I can use the information as it stands."

Girling swallowed. "In case you hadn't heard, this is working up into a pretty big news story over here."

"There are one or two things that don't quite add up. I have to check them out."

"Stansell, it's press day. You said you'd cracked the identity of these monsters. Let's use it."

"I said I *thought* I'd cracked it."

"Who's the source?" Girling asked.

"That's the thing. He's been solid in the past. Every one of his stories have checked out. But this time . . . You see, I'm sure I've come across this outfit before. Not here, though, somewhere else. Trouble is, I can't bloody well remember where."

"Just give me the name, Stansell. If you're worried about validity, maybe I can second-source it."

There was another interminable pause.

"Dust off your Arabic dictionary," Stansell said at last. "But first, you must promise me something, Tom Boy."

"Sure."

"Whatever you do, don't use this until I give you the all clear. Even if you're able to second-source it with your contacts. And for God's sake don't give it to Kelso until I say it's okay. Have you got that?"

"Yes. I understand. But why?"

"I can't go into that. I'm already late—I'm meeting someone across town who could confirm what I'm about to tell you."

"Come on, Stansell. The suspense is killing me."

"Malaak al-Hissab," Stansell said.

"What?" Girling's pen hovered over his notepad.

"What happened to your Arabic? The Angels of Judgment. That's what they're called. They're a hard-line, fundamentalist outfit operating from a base deep within southern Lebanon—at least, that's what my source says. And they're led by some character who calls himself al-Saif—the Sword. They're supposed to be independent of all other religious and political groups which, according to my man, explains why we've never heard of them before."

"Except you think you have," Girling said, resting his pen.

"Maybe. The Sword's a common enough pseudonym among militant fundamentalists. But that's not the name I'm reaching for. It's those damned Angels of Judgment that bother me . . ."

"Right now, everyone's shooting in the dark, including the Americans. I just heard that the U.S. Navy has lost the boat the terrorists used to escape from the beach."

"Bloody hell. Has that broken yet?"

"No, but it will. That's why it's important we lead with this. It's one big break for us, Stansell, and we could use it right now."

"I know."

"You don't sound very sure," Girling said.

"If we use this information and I'm wrong, it could be extremely dangerous."

"Dangerous?"

"Tempers are high, Tom. One word out of place by us, the media, and this whole region could blow again. It's an awesome responsibility we carry sometimes." He paused. "Not everyone sees it that way."

"Kelso?"

"I gather he's got a lot on his mind. Maybe his judgment isn't quite what it should be right now. That's why it's important you don't do anything until I've checked this thing out. I trust you, Tom. I'd trust you with my life, you know that."

"Hey, relax. You have my word, okay?"

Girling could hear Stansell's hard breathing over the atmospheric hiss.

"Look, I want to tell you how glad I am Kelso's tempted you back."

"Under some duress," Girling said.

"You have talents, Tom. Don't waste them. I'm not saying anything Mona wouldn't have told you herself."

"Thanks, but I don't need the lecture, Stansell. How long do you think it will take to confirm that these characters are behind the hijacking?"

"Maybe a couple of hours. Depends how many sources I have to plug on this one. If the first one fails, there's one other . . ."

His voiced trailed away again in the ether.

"Remember what I said, Tom. No confirmation, no story. Look after yourself, boy. I've got to go." And with that, he hung up.

Girling replaced the receiver. Stansell, impossible to ruffle, had the jitters. It came to him that this was like the moment he had discovered as a child that his father wasn't invincible, but frail and human, just like everybody else. He looked at his watch. It was close to five o'clock. "Shit."

Mallon stopped flirting with the subeditor and turned to him. "What's up."

"Lots to do and not much time to do it in. I'm expected at my parents' place outside Oxford this evening. And I haven't even briefed Kelso yet."

Girling set off for Kelso's office. He knocked on the door and walked in.

Kelso listened first with excitement, then disappointment to the tale of the hijackers' disappearance and the imminence of the news's appearance in other media outlets. Girling promised to type up what he knew before leaving for Oxford. Some other poor sod could have his evening wrecked working it into shape for the edition.

Girling took a step to the door, then stopped and turned.

"Look, Bob, you ought to be aware, too, that Stansell has a significant lead on the terrorists' identity," Girling said. "He just called in."

"What do you mean, 'significant lead'?" Kelso asked.

Girling took his editor through the conversation slowly, leaving out the name of the terrorist organization and making it clear that Stansell's caveat—holding off until his say-so was received—was sacrosanct.

Kelso nodded slowly. "He's cutting it mighty fine. I'd like to use it, but I can delay the printers only so long."

"I know. But Stansell said wait."

"What is he trying to prove?" Kelso said angrily.

"Maybe he wants to make sure it's right. We do still do that, don't we?"

"Don't break my balls, Tom. I've had a hell of a day."

"When do Lord Kyle and the board decide our futures?"

Kelso rubbed his eyes. "Tomorrow. Shit, I wish I was a hack again sometimes."

Girling took two paces toward him. "Look, the only reason I told you about this is because you, as editor, should know."

"Stansell didn't want you to tell me at all, right?"

"Everyone knows the pressure you're under, Bob."

"So, it's got to the point where even Stansell doesn't trust me anymore."

"He's just protecting his investment. If he can get confirmation this could be a hell of a story."

"Mm. And he told you the name of this outfit?"

"Yes."

"Are you going to tell me?"

"I can't. I'm sorry, Bob, but I promised."

"And what if Stansell staggers out of a bar and falls under a bus?"

"Oh, come off it."

"You know what I'm talking about, Tom."

"He's still the best."

"He's getting . . . erratic."

"There's always my notes," Girling said.

Kelso stopped kneading his eyes. When he looked up, they were bloodshot and watering. "Maybe I'll give the old bastard a call in a couple of hours; chivvy him along a bit. Or that new girl, the Egyptian. Maybe she can tell me when Stansell's going to file."

"Sharifa?"

"Old friend of yours, isn't she?"

"Kind of." He paused. "She was Mona's best friend since school."

Girling looked at his watch. "I'm late for my parents and I've still got some work to do. Will you excuse me?"

"Sure. See you tomorrow."

Girling went back to his desk and typed up what he had gleaned from Tech-Int about the missing hostages and the U.S. Navy's abortive search for them. Then he left the office, took the tube home, picked up his Alfa-Romeo and was soon heading down the highway toward Oxford, his mind free of work, the Angels of Judgment, Kelso and Stansell.

He was seeing his daughter again.

■   ■   ■

JACOBSON WAITED for the first ring of the phone, his eyes still glued to the third of five TV monitor screens set into the wall opposite him.

He was in TERCOM's mini–situation room, a boxlike affair with no windows, making it impossible to tell—but for a digital twenty-four-hour clock—whether it was day or night. He was surrounded by every conceivable device man had ever invented for communicating covertly or otherwise with the outside world. Among the SATCOM transmitter-receivers, the VLF submarine communications equipment and the teletypewriter decoding machines were five ordinary TV sets, each tuned to a different station.

His gaze was fixed on the one which belted out news coverage in a relentless stream of bulletins.

Cable News Network had just reported that the U.S. Navy had lost all contact with the terrorist boat that had slipped away from the shores south of Beirut almost twenty-four hours earlier. The reporter wasn't revealing how he had come by the information, but Jacobson guessed it had been leaked by someone in the Pentagon who was unimpressed with naval aviation's reconnaissance efforts. That suggested the culprit to be someone senior in the air force. Each rival service never lost a trick in pointing out the others' deficiencies.

The media were having a ball.

As he looked on, the picture switched to the Pentagon's chief spokesman, fidgeting nervously beside his podium in the DoD's media room. When Jacobson looked at the other sets, he saw that the other stations were also covering the event. The spokesman straightened his suit and walked to the microphone.

At that moment the phone rang.

"Are you watching this?" Newhouse asked. "I've just had the national security adviser on the horn. The president wants to know why he had to learn about this from the media. For Christ's sake, Joel, finding this fishing boat was meant to be easy."

"The navy was overconfident, it seems."

"Then what's happened? Has the boat sunk? Is Franklin dead?"

Anything was a possibility, Jacobson admitted. Nothing was as it seemed in the Middle East. His exhaustive studies of the area, its history and its culture had provided him with that much, gratis.

"But the Russians believe he's alive," Jacobson said.

"They've communicated again?"

"Aushev called a few minutes ago. Same message. They have specific intelligence on the whereabouts of Franklin and the rest of our people."

"Well, where the hell are they?"

"That's all the Russians are saying, sir. They're pressing us to respond."

Newhouse fell silent for a few moments. "Has the NSC contacted you about this yet?"

"Not yet."

"Then it seems we're in time. We've got to pull ourselves out of this shit."

"Sir?"

"Contact Aushev on the Romeo channel and tell him we accept his offer. We await his further instructions."

Jacobson smiled. Here we go again, he thought.

"Do it quickly," Newhouse said. "We'll worry about the consequences later."

CHAPTER 7

Shabanov flexed his upper arms in a vain bid to restore their failing circulation. With both his hands clamped to the top of his head for something over two hours—although not having access to his watch it was impossible to be precise about elapsed time—he had long lost the ability to feel any sensation in his muscles, which was probably a blessing. The pain was focused in his shoulder joints instead. He began to imagine that the limbs had been wrenched from their sockets, but chastised himself as soon as he became conscious of these wild and irresponsible thoughts; it was best not to drift, even if this was just an exercise.

"Move again and I'll shoot, you Russian son of a whore," the woman screamed in Arabic. Her accent was unfamiliar, but he understood enough to stop the movement.

Shabanov raised his eyes to hers. The .45 was pointing straight at the center of his forehead. He held her gaze and noticed the deep brown eyes flash angrily again. She was startlingly attractive. Her long black hair had tumbled over her face, but she made no effort to sweep it aside. Beneath those soft dark strands, the silky complexion, full lips and perfect straight nose were strangely at odds with the bitch's demeanor.

"You haven't got the guts to use that thing," he said, the edges of his mouth breaking into a smile. "It is just a toy in your hands." He spoke a different dialect from hers, but it was good Arabic nonetheless.

He saw the confusion sweeping her face. She brushed the hair away from her eyes, cocked the gun and rammed the barrel up against his jawbone.

"Keep your mouth shut," she screamed, "or I'll blow it off."

She adjusted her stance. Out of the corner of his eye, Shabanov could see her wiggling her hips as she settled into the new position against the bulkhead of the airliner. He was captivated by the shape of her body. He could picture every inch of it beneath the rough texture of her combat fatigues.

Rarely had Shabanov felt so alive. They had told him at training school that the feeling was not uncommon during moments of acute danger. But they had not prepared him for this. He felt he could do anything, he was better than all of them. And he would take the bitch afterward for his pleasure.

About three seat-rows behind him one of his fellow hostages, a woman, groaned. Her husband asked the man known as Mahmoud for water again. He was greeted with the light sound of the Kalashnikov's safety catch slipping off.

"No water till the aircraft is refueled," Mahmoud shouted in English.

Shabanov thought there were four of them, but he couldn't be sure. There was Mahmoud, the girl Layla, a lanky, gun-toting youth at the back of the aircraft and another man with a grenade on the flight deck. There was always a chance that there were others, but because he had not been able to turn around since the beginning of the ordeal, it was impossible to tell.

Layla pulled the .45 away from his face and leaned back. Although the blinds were still pulled down over the windows, Shabanov could see the last rays of sunlight slipping behind the horizon beyond the cockpit windshield. It was probably three hours since the terrorists had made their move. Something had to break soon.

He heard a brief commotion on the flight deck, then saw the man with the grenade beckon Mahmoud up to the front of the airliner.

The tower on the line again.

"Fuel, I want fuel," Mahmoud screamed, pressing a communications set to his head. "If we do not receive it within the next five minutes, another hostage will be killed."

Shabanov had not seen the execution. He had heard the man's screams and the sharp crack of the Kalashnikov on single shot; that had been enough. From the way Layla was looking at him, he reckoned he was up next.

Mahmoud walked down the gangway toward his position, roughly in the center of the airliner. The manual said to avoid eye contact with these people. You had to believe you were invisible to avoid being singled out for special attention. Shabanov met Mahmoud's gaze and held it. Fuck the book.

Mahmoud looked at Layla, then nodded to Shabanov. She grabbed him by the collar and pulled him out of his seat. Shabanov twisted and wrested her grip from him. For a moment she seemed captivated by his appearance. He was wearing the full uniform of a Guards airborne assault colonel in the Russian Army. There were three rows of medal ribbons on his chest. He was tall and lean-faced, with cropped black hair that accentuated the lines of his skull. A small scar on the bridge of his nose marked the spot where an Afghan tribesman had slashed him during hand-to-hand fighting in the hills above Jalalabad. Shabanov knew that his greatest strength in a hostage situation where there were women among his captors lay in his looks. They could gain him vital seconds in any confrontation. He gave her a half smile and let her catch a fleeting glimpse into the depths of his blue eyes. She seemed to draw back a little, until a low growl from Mahmoud stopped her in her tracks.

She thrust the gun up against his temple. "Move," she hissed, "to the front of the plane."

Shabanov was about to take a step forward when the lights in the roof went out. He knew what was happening. The next moment he was on the floor, his hands clamped over his ears, his eyes screwed shut. A split second later the two doors over the wings, about four rows forward from him, blew into the airliner. Even though his eyes were shut, he saw the intensity of the flashes through his eyelids.

Shabanov looked up to see a figure clad in black, clutching a machine gun–flashlight combination, his outline faintly illuminated by the atmospheric reflection of the flashlight beam.

"Everybody stay down, stay down," the figure shouted, voice muffled by the gas mask.

Layla was still standing in the aisle. Shabanov saw a look, like that of a frightened animal caught in a car's headlights, etched on her face. The Heckler and Koch jumped twice in the hands of the assault commando and she fell to the ground, a deep red stain over her T-shirt.

Behind the lead commando, a second figure fired two shots into the prostrate body of Mahmoud, who had been knocked off his feet by one of the doors.

The first commando probed the smoke with the beam of his flashlight and fired twice again. That took care of the stick insect behind him.

There was another explosion at the front of the aircraft, the flash and blast catching Shabanov unawares. When his vision and hearing returned, the man with the grenade lay sprawled on the floor by the forward toilet. The commando who shot him kicked the grenade from his hand out into the dawn air through the still smoking doorway.

The man behind him tried to move. His wife began screaming.

"Keep down," a remote voice shouted.

The black figures roamed up and down the aisle, the light from their torches stitching across the seats and the startled faces of the passengers.

"Everybody make their way to the escape chutes," a muffled voice said. It was calm, but authoritative.

Shabanov got to his feet and helped the woman in the row behind to hers. He ushered her to the nearest exit, picked her up and threw her on to the chute, which had already fully deployed from the fuselage to the ground. Then he jumped himself.

He ran across the tarmac to the minibus, which had not moved from its position at the outset of the incident, and rapped on the door. There was a brief pause, some muffled sounds from within, then it slid back on its rails.

Shabanov found himself staring into the face of a USAF officer.

"How long?" the Russian asked him.

Colonel Elliot Ulm, commander of the USAF's 1725th Combat Control Detachment, better known as the Pathfinders, looked again at the stopwatch. "One minute, thirty-five seconds, from the moment the doors blew to your knock."

"Congratulations, Colonel," Shabanov said. "That's quick."

Ulm jumped down onto the tarmac. "Thanks." He looked over to the airliner, an old Boeing 727 the unit had managed to scrounge off one of the airlines for next to nothing. It was in the airlines' interest for the Pathfinders to get it right. One day soon it would be for real. The Gulf war had shown what terrorism, or even the threat of it, could do to revenue.

The last of the eighty-two passengers was coming down the rear exit chute. This time, they had lost only one. "Only one" wasn't good enough, but it was doubtful whether there was any way they could have avoided it.

Still, Ulm thought, they were getting better. Not as good as the Russians in all-round terms, maybe, but they were improving.

Ulm turned to face Shabanov. "Did you survive your ordeal, Colonel?"

"More than that. I enjoyed it," the Russian said.

"Hardly a term I would have used."

Ulm couldn't make the guy out, even after his two weeks in Russia and the couple of days Shabanov had passed so far in New Mexico. Shabanov was engaging, beguiling almost, but still one of the hardest bastards he had ever come across in almost twenty years of the special operations business. Maybe he'd get that officer from psy-ops to have a look inside the Russian's head.

Ulm took the evening air deep into his lungs. A light wind had sprung up with the setting sun, scattering the tumbleweed across the New Mexico desert and over the crumbling concrete of the runway. The 727 was flanked a little way off by the disintegrating carcasses of combat aircraft. The sun found a single piece of shiny metal on an old F-106 and sent a beam into Ulm's face. The special forces colonel let the light dance in his eyes for a moment. The pinprick of warmth on his skin felt good, but it could not compensate for his malaise.

An old boneyard, a scrap-metal dump—the epitome of his worth in the eyes of the Pentagon. The Red Rio Range, part of the White Sands Reservation in New Mexico, was a weapons training area for A-10 ground-attack aircraft. The dilapidated combat aircraft on the disused runway gave them something to aim at. Ulm's unit, based at nearby

Kirtland Air Force Base, shared the Red Rio training ground with rusting relics of the Vietnam era.

He wondered if Shabanov had any idea to what extent the Romeo Protocol was a sham.

A black-suited figure loomed out of the gathering darkness. Master Sergeant Nolan Jones pulled the mask and balaclava from his head. Jones was from The Everglades, scalp and gristle above the neck line, muscle from collar to feet.

"All passengers present and accounted for, Colonel. Four terrorists dead. Aircraft safe from explosives." He smiled at his commander, exposing a row of chipped, stubby teeth. "We took the mother down, sir."

Ulm congratulated him. "See you at the debrief in a half hour, Spades."

Shabanov watched Jones amble back to the team's minibus, which had drawn up under the wing of the 727. "Spades?" he said.

Ulm had almost forgotten about his guest.

"During his selection test, Jones listed ax-throwing as a special skill. They encourage individual talents in the special forces, so they put him to the test. During his trial they discovered he could slice a melon into two equal halves with a trench spade at twenty yards. We look for people like that in the Pathfinders."

"I see," Shabanov said. "There is a master sergeant, a Starshina, in my unit, Starshina Bitov, that I would like him to meet. They would be quite a team."

Beyond Ulm's shoulder, Layla appeared at the doorway of the aircraft. The wet stain on her T-shirt accentuated the shape of a perfect left breast.

Ulm caught the direction of Shabanov's stare. "Normally we would put a couple of shots straight between the eyes," he said. "These training sessions are meant to sacrifice nothing for realism, only those dye-filled capsules we use can blind if they hit you in the eyes. So in training we go for the heart."

Shabanov followed Layla's progress across the weeds and the concrete. "And where do you find your terrorists?"

"Layla's an air force captain," Ulm said. "Second-generation American. Her grandparents were Lebanese. The others are all brought in from various branches of the armed forces. They'll go back to their units tonight."

As she strolled past, Layla gave Shabanov a smoldering look. Then she smiled warmly. He flexed his fingers behind his back and returned her grin. Another time, perhaps.

"In the old Soviet Union we had many ethnic minorities. I myself am descended from the tribesmen of Uzbekistan in Central Asia. With so many republics, it was hardly surprising that our recruits came from different cultures and backgrounds. But I had no idea the makeup of the American services was so . . . diverse."

"Uzbeks. They've been involved in all that unrest down south, haven't they? I was reading an article in *Time* about—

Shabanov cut him off. "There are many people in Central Asia. Turkomans, Khirghiz, Tajiks, Azerbaijanis, Uygurzt . . . There are bound to be tensions, Colonel," Shabanov said stiffly.

"The march of Islam," Ulm said. "It seems unstoppable."

"And nationalism, Colonel. This is the price Moscow has had to pay for giving us our democratic rights. It is not easy for us seeing our country torn apart."

Ulm thought he might have touched a raw nerve. "That was insensitive of me. As an Uzbek, you're probably a Muslim, too, I'll bet."

Shabanov remained impassive. "I *was* an Uzbek. But now I am a Russian—second generation, like your Layla, Colonel. My family has been living in Russia for almost fifty years."

Ulm searched for a way out of the minefield. "Look, let's drop the formalities," he said, extending his hand. "It's Elliot."

Shabanov shook it. "Roman Makhmadzhanovich," he said.

Ulm flinched.

"Roman is enough," the Russian said. "Makhmadzhan was my father's name. Makhmadzhanovich means son of Mohammed. The last trace of my ancestry."

They started back toward the airliner. "I wanted to extend the same courtesy when you were with us," Shabanov began. "But you saw how it was there. There were many people looking over my shoulder. This protocol is too adventurous for some of my countrymen."

Russia's Higher Airborne Command School was still vivid in Ulm's mind. Nor had he shed the ignominy of shooting the wrong target at the

nearby training ground. Shabanov had shown no danger of shooting
women or children during his two days so far at Kirtland. From the
minibus, Ulm had even seen Shabanov shepherd an elderly woman to
the aircraft's escape chute.

Shabanov gazed at the 727 fuselage. "Our Spetsialnoye
Naznacheniye—our Spetsnaz special-purpose forces—could not have
done this." He pointed at the blackened doors of the aircraft.

Ulm suddenly pictured the life-sized cutout of woman and child.
Was Shabanov just saying that to make him feel better? The Russian
was as much a diplomat as he was a soldier.

There was a shout from the minibus, Ulm's mobile communications
wagon. The 1725th's intelligence officer, Captain Charlie Doyle, was
beckoning them from the open door. Ulm sprinted over, followed
closely by Shabanov.

"It's USSOCOM, sir. General McDonald's about to come on the
line. Wants to talk to you personally."

Ulm hid his surprise and took the receiver. General James L.
McDonald was commander in chief of the U.S. Special Operations
Command. Serious shit.

He gave Doyle a signal to distract Shabanov, get him away from the
phone. He was still wondering what the general wanted with him, when
the man himself came through via the satellite communications link.

Two minutes later Ulm replaced the phone on the hook.

Doyle left Shabanov, who was watching the sun set over the New
Mexico scrub. He found his boss in a state of visible excitement.

"From that look on your face, I'd say something pretty big must be
going down."

"You could just be right, Charlie. I've got to get my ass up to
Washington as if my life depended on it. A C-21's coming into
Kirtland in an hour and I'm on it."

"A Learjet?" Doyle could not contain his surprise. "The 1725th
must be going up in the world. What happened to that shitbox Beech
they used to send? Someone must want to talk bad. So things are
getting busy around here at last." He jabbed a finger at Shabanov.
"What do I do with him while you're gone?"

"That's the weirdest thing," Ulm said. "The general told me he's
coming along for the ride. He gets dropped at the Russian embassy and
I go on to . . ."

"Where?"

"I don't know. I guess I'm just going to have to find out when I get there."

■   ■   ■

THE WIND was up and it was raining heavily when Girling swung his Alfa-Romeo into the drive of Rigden Court. The gravel scrunched under the tires. It was a sound he associated with a world in which he had never felt particularly at ease.

His parents' house loomed tall in the moving beams of the headlights. He could not understand why his father should want to have retired to a place of such mammoth pretension. His mother, he knew, would have been happy with a small cottage somewhere in Dorset. But his father's decree was absolute and his mother accepted it meekly.

Girling turned off the ignition and listened to the rain drumming on the roof. He pulled up his collar and ran across the last few yards of open ground to the front door. Once inside, the flagstones in the hall rang out with the sound of his footsteps.

He rounded the corner to find his father fixing himself a gin from the large liquor cabinet beneath the stairs. He looked up and said hello as if Girling had just come in from a walk around the garden.

"Your mother's putting the child to bed. Help yourself, won't you."

His father walked back into the drawing room, leaving Girling to hang his jacket by the other raincoats in the hall.

His mother stopped reading to Alia when she heard Girling's footsteps at the top of the stairs. She appeared outside the door and greeted him with a fleeting kiss. He had never been so struck by his mother's fragility. Her skin looked almost translucent.

"She's sleepy," his mother said, "but insisted on staying awake. I'll leave you to chat to her."

It was a large room for a small child, but his mother had done her best to make it warm and cozy. Alia's face peeked out from the sheets. Her eyelids flickered and she smiled drowsily when she saw him.

He bent down and kissed her on the forehead.

"When am I going home?" she asked.

He brushed a lock of hair from her eyes. "Soon, sweetheart."

"What's the matter, Daddy?"

"Nothing. Everything's fine," he said.

"Then why can't I come home now?"

"Because . . ." His fingers scurried up the blanket like a spider and tickled her under the chin. She giggled, but he could tell it was simply to please him.

"Don't you like it here?"

"Oh, yes," she replied. "Except for all the walks. Grandpa loves walks. Why doesn't he use a car like everybody else?"

They both laughed.

They talked a little about what she had been doing since she arrived. She enjoyed feeding carrots and apples to the horses at the end of the garden and she had made friends with some of the children who lived in the village. As she spoke, her eyelids would droop, then snap open in her determination to keep him there for as long as possible.

Finally she turned onto her side, her face away from him, and he watched over her until he thought she was asleep.

He turned off the light, kissed her on the top of the head and tiptoed to the door.

"Please get better, Daddy."

The words, barely audible, made him stop before he reached the door. He turned to answer, but the tempo of her breathing told him she had been talking in her sleep.

His parents were seated at the dinner table when he came downstairs.

As they ate, the chink of cutlery was only interrupted occasionally by conversation. It was a familiar pattern. His mother would inquire awkwardly about the women in his life; his father would make observations about the sorry state of the world. The two would be quite separate. It was at such times that he wondered how they had stayed together.

"I'd like you to look after Alia a little longer," Girling announced suddenly.

"I thought you were taking her back with you tomorrow morning," his father said.

"Things have changed, Pa. It's difficult right now. I'm heavily involved in this hijacking business."

"You're back on current affairs?" his father exclaimed. "Why that's the best news I've heard in years, Tom. I never could understand

why you buried yourself in all that science and technology nonsense. I always said it was kid's stuff.''

His mother took a sip of water. She looked as if she were going to faint. "I hope you won't be going back out there, dear. We were horrified to see what happened to all those poor people on the television the other night."

"I'm not going anywhere," he said. "I'm only doing this because my editor needs some extra help right now." Girling turned to his father. "Then I'll be going back to the kid's stuff."

His father put down his knife and fork and stared at him angrily from across the table. "You should be making your way back up the ladder. It's time you were on a proper newspaper again."

"I've told you before, Pa. I'm quite happy doing what I'm doing. For the moment."

"Happy? You wrote damned well when you were on the *Times.* You got right under the skin of the Middle East. Everybody said so. We were so proud of you."

His mother tried to change the subject. "Why can't you take Alia home with you, Tom? You know we love having her here, but she's been missing you terribly."

"I think she's safer here with you right now."

"You're not in any kind of trouble, are you?" she asked.

He smiled. "No, Ma."

She wasn't convinced. "It's Mona, isn't it?"

Girling said nothing. He looked straight ahead at one of the family portraits on the wall. "You have to forget, Tom," she whispered. There were tears in her eyes.

"I can't," he said simply.

"Of course you can," his father said. "It's all in the mind."

"I'm only too well aware of that, Pa."

"Then discipline yourself, laddie."

Girling felt his skin prickle. He looked his father straight in the eye. "I can't forgive them for what they did, Pa. Could you?"

His father shook his head. "It's a savage part of the world. Always was, always will be. It was a risk you took when you decided to live there."

Girling knew that this was as close as his father came to asking why his only son had not married an English rose.

"You've got to forge a new life for yourself," his father said. "If only for the girl's sake."

He saw his mother nodding hopefully.

Girling made his excuses shortly after dinner. He pretended that he was needed in the office early the following morning. It was better that he made the journey back to London that night.

Before he left he crept up to Alia's room. He replaced some blankets that had fallen off the bed, making sure that he did not wake her when he tucked them in.

■   ■   ■

HIS WATCH showed a little after midnight.

As soon as he picked up the drone of the AC-130 gunship, his signal, he roused his men into action. The platoon stole across the edge of the airport, each of the sixteen men seeking the target he had been assigned.

The colonel picked out the personal transport plane of the country's self-styled "Maximum Leader" from the others. He clipped the selectable strike beacon, the SSB—a small device hardly bigger than his car stereo—to the wing of the VIP jet, switched it on and stole back to the edge of the concrete.

The AC-130 was close now. The colonel knew the coordinates from the SSB were being fed into the targeting computer, the guns primed. He did a head count. His Pathfinders were all there. Time to be leaving.

His deputy nudged him and pointed. Across the airfield there was movement. He raised the imager to his face and saw a column of troops moving across the concrete.

"PDF," his deputy whispered—Panamanian Defense Forces—and smiled, his white teeth stark against the night.

The column was almost upon the cluster of private aircraft primed with their SSBs. Above them, the drone of the AC-130 Specter rose to a crescendo.

The colonel felt his blood run cold. They couldn't be PDF; they were moving too stealthily. He knew then that he was watching a U.S. Army Ranger detachment in the wrong place at the wrong time.

He opened his mouth to shout the warning a second before the first aircraft blew up.

The 105-millimeter shells rained down from the AC-130, patrolling unseen in a tight circle two thousand feet above them. The colonel ran across the grass and grabbed the radio operator. He pointed to the carnage, then to the sky, shouting his order above the din of explosions. The operator tried to raise the crew of the Specter, but without success.

The colonel ran towards a soldier, stump bleeding from an amputated leg, and dragged him across the concrete to cover. Above the boy's screaming, the detonations, and the pom-pom beat of the Specter's 40-millimeter gun, he heard his name repeated over and over again, as if someone was working a bullhorn . . .

"Colonel Ulm, sir . . . Colonel."

Ulm's eyes snapped open. They looked straight into the face of the pretty female copilot who had come back from the flight deck of the C-21. He saw, too, the shock on her face. The same look on the face of his wife whenever she woke him from the dream.

Ulm was drenched in sweat. His face was gray, drawn; and he was shaking.

The captain managed to control her voice. "Colonel, we'll be touching down at National in ten minutes. You ought to prepare yourself for the landing."

He grunted his thanks and watched her move past him to Shabanov.

Ulm looked out the window and saw the Washington monument pierce the horizon.

Even though it was the Rangers who had been in the wrong place that night, it was he who'd been blamed—not them—because the Pathfinders had been using the wrong radio frequency, making it impossible to call off the Specter. After the court-martial, his punishment had been an unspecified period of exile for him and the rest of the 1725th Combat Control Detachment, his Pathfinders, at Kirtland Air Force Base, New Mexico—just about as far as you could ever get from the nerve center. But in those days, before the Gulf war, when people came to accept it as part of the battle, death by friendly fire was an ugly embarrassment.

Was this their way of saying sorry, or that enough was enough? Were they giving him another chance? Was his advice sought over recent developments in the Middle East? After the dream, his mind was too fuzzy around the edges to provide any answers.

The copilot slipped back to the flight deck, giving him a strange look as she passed his seat.

Whatever the truth of the matter, there were those who said the Pathfinders had had their chance and blown it.

Confirmation of his worth—or lack of it—had come on the day USSOCOM told him he had been selected to enter into a secret bilateral exchange program with Spetsnaz. He was warned against showing the Russians too much. The Romeo Protocol, USSOCOM pointed out, was hatched by politicians who did not understand the ways of the military. In other words, he'd been given an assignment that was hollow almost to the point of being a sham.

As the Learjet swept into National Airport, Ulm cast a glance back to Shabanov. The Russian's eyes darted eagerly over the sights of the capital. No longer in uniform, Shabanov passed for any other U.S. serviceman heading into D.C. on legitimate business.

Two bumps through the airframe signaled they were down.

■   ■   ■

ULM ALMOST asked the driver if there had been some mistake. After dropping Shabanov at the Russian embassy, he had expected the car to swing south for the Pentagon. But instead, they had kept going deeper into the tree-lined suburbs of Washington's northwest district, eventually stopping outside a mundane office building a short distance from the National Zoo.

The driver walked around and opened Ulm's door. Ulm was led across the sidewalk to the building. The entrance hall was cool, its floors and walls lined with dark polished stone tiles. A middle-aged woman, sitting behind a desk against the far wall, looked up as soon as his footsteps rang out across the atrium. Ulm kept walking. It was only when he reached the desk that he realized his escort had gone. He turned to see the limousine pulling into the early-morning traffic beyond the double plate-glass doors.

Ulm had expected a military facility, but there was not a shred of evidence that a single cent of the DoD's budget had gone near this place. The woman looked at him expectantly. He gave his name.

She smiled again, filled out a form and handed him a pass, which he clipped to his jacket. Then she lifted the telephone and announced his arrival as if he had been expected for a week. She pointed to the elevator and told him he would be met on the fourth floor. As he turned, Ulm glanced up at the board behind the desk listing the companies in the building. For the fourth floor, there was just one entry: Comco Software, Inc.

The elevator did not stop at any of the intervening levels. When the doors parted, Ulm was met by a sallow-faced, studious-looking man in his mid-forties.

"Colonel Ulm? Welcome to TERCOM. I'm Jacobson." He offered a delicate hand, which Ulm shook suspiciously. "You probably have a thousand and one questions, but if you'll be patient a while longer, I promise that you will get your answers. If you'd like to follow me, Colonel."

Ulm stepped into the corridor and was struck immediately by the absence of natural light. There was an unpleasant, artificial odor and a hum of air-conditioning about the place, too, which exacerbated his growing feeling of isolation.

Jacobson led him into a dim room with a large oak table in its midst. He was offered a seat and accepted a cup of coffee. Jacobson had one already. There were two windows set in the wood-paneled walls, but the blinds were down, allowing no early-morning light to creep into the room.

Jacobson took a seat opposite Ulm. The ex-CIA man clasped his Styrofoam cup between both hands.

"It will probably help you to think of me—and this place—as your direct link to every asset this country possesses for the neutralization of the terrorist threat," Jacobson said. "By comparison, your General McDonald at USSOCOM is limited in the resources at his disposal. Believe me, Colonel, that there is absolutely nothing I cannot call upon in the pursuit of that goal. You see, we—that is my colleagues and I—have a mandate from the highest possible authority. General McDonald has therefore temporarily assigned you to us."

"That's very impressive, Mr. Jacobson," Ulm said dryly. "But maybe you could start by telling me what I'm doing here."

"Simple, Colonel. We want you to go after the people who carried out Beirut. We want you to find Ambassador Franklin and bring him and his staff home—alive. And we want the people who perpetrated this deed punished. Is that a mission you feel you are prepared for, or able to undertake, Colonel?"

Ulm battled not to let his feelings show. "The 1725th is ready for anything," he said. "But—" Ulm looked at Jacobson again and was reminded of one of the Pentagon prosecuting attorneys at his court-martial. A jumped-up little bureaucrat with a big opinion of himself who was real good at talking and full of ideas about the way things should be done, but pig-ignorant of the realities. Ulm thought he'd like to see Jacobson handling a PDF sniper with a night-vision scope on a pitch-black night or trying to defuse an Iraqi chemical mine with the fur flying around him. Jacobsons used people as stepping stones through shit to further their ambition.

"Yes, Colonel?"

"Why us? Why not Delta or the SEALs? From what I've seen of this case, it's more their style."

Jacobson chuckled. "But there is no provision under the Romeo Protocol for Delta or the SEALs to work with the Russians. You see, you'll be going in with Spetsnaz on this mission."

Ulm felt his blood run cold. "You're pulling my chain."

"No, I'm not, Colonel. This will be a joint U.S.-Russian operation."

"But everybody knows the Romeo Protocol is a sham," Ulm said. "God knows, I've been playing my part, but it was always intimated that we would not have to go into action with them. At least, that's the way SOCOM explained it."

"With respect, SOCOM has no idea how deep the shit is around us," Jacobson said. His expression had changed. He looked like death.

"What do you mean?"

"In simple terms, the Russians have access to information that is denied to us at this time. They are willing to share it, but the price of admission is a joint operation."

"It won't work," Ulm said adamantly.

"You said you were ready for anything."

"On our own, yes. But the only contact between Spetsnaz and the Pathfinders has been at commander level. As it happens, Colonel Roman Shabanov is with us at the moment."

"We know," Jacobson said, before pausing to take a sip of his coffee. "Have you been watching the news lately, Colonel?"

"Of course."

"Then you will have seen the items about the disappearance of that boat."

"Sure, but that's public-consumption shit, right?"

"Wrong. That, I'm sorry to say, is how it is."

It took a few moments for the impact of Jacobson's statement to sink in. "Jesus, Jacobson, what kind of outfit are you running here?"

"I don't like it any better than you," Jacobson said. His voice never wavered from a dull, impassive monotone. "But for the past two decades my colleagues at Langley relied heavily, far too heavily, on sophisticated surveillance methods in the Middle East. Sure, we have space-based radar, infrared satellites, plus every conceivable ELINT and COMINT platform above the eastern Med and the Gulf sucking intelligence out of the rawest data you can imagine. Between ourselves and the NSA, we can position a communications- or signals-intelligence ship off, say, the coast of Libya and listen to Qadhafi talking into a mobile phone from his toilet."

Ulm sat back in his chair. He felt numb. He let Jacobson's words wash over him.

"I would not have known how to begin looking, however, for a bunch of two-bit terrorists roaming around southern Lebanon."

"Why not?"

"Because we've lost the ability to do the one thing we used to do well—HUMINT. Human intelligence, Colonel. Having a guy on the ground who does nothing but good old-fashioned cloak-and-dagger work."

"When peace broke out between East and West, the budget resources allocated to the CIA, DIA and NSA were pared back to record lows. We were trying to reestablish a new network in the Middle East when the finances were pulled from under our feet. Then the Gulf crisis came along. The dollars started flowing back again, but it takes years to get people back in place and we're not there yet."

Ulm recalled the collapse of their network in Iran, Lebanon and Syria following the kidnapping of the CIA's Beirut station chief, William Buckley, in 1984. Within a few months, every single operative had been wiped out.

"And in the meantime," Jacobson said, "the Israelis had stopped helping us because we'd been leaning on Jerusalem too hard over nuclear proliferation."

"What about the Brits?"

"MI6? You know what the Brits are like. They're good at asking, but they sure as hell don't like sharing it. Basically, though you won't get anyone to admit it, we're blind from the eastern Mediterranean to the Asian subcontinent.''

"Which leaves the Russians,'' Ulm said.

The rattle of the air-conditioning system seemed to fill the room.

"Precisely, Colonel. I should add that we are under some pressure here to make this thing work. Politically speaking, that is.''

Ulm got the hint. It was obvious from its elaborate front that TERCOM received its funding from the administration's ''black'' accounting jar, the source from which most classified programs obtained their money. As a result, TERCOM was at its master's beck and call.

"All right, suppose we can make it work,'' Ulm said. ''When would I be briefed about the target?''

"That is being arranged, Colonel.'' Jacobson looked at his watch. "We have a preliminary briefing scheduled in an hour's time. Until then, why don't I show you around?''

The tour took something less than an hour in the end. Ulm saw everything from the front company that had been created to protect TERCOM from prying eyes—a fully funded and functional computer software house—to the dark workings of the organization's communications room. Throughout the tour he was conscious of Jacobson's mounting agitation. The agent punctuated his talk with frequent references to his wristwatch.

The phone buzzed in the midst of a demonstration of TERCOM's VLF communications suite. Jacobson picked the receiver up and listened intently for a few seconds. He left Ulm alone for less than five minutes, returning to announce that their briefer had arrived.

Ulm followed him along the corridor, conditioning his mind already to expect a whole lot of things about what lay ahead—things he wasn't going to enjoy hearing.

It was this discipline that undoubtedly saved him from an exclamation of surprise when he reentered the conference room, for on the other side of the table, it was Colonel Roman Shabanov who rose to greet him.

■   ■   ■

"You two, of course, know each other,'' Jacobson said, a smile thinning his lips. He closed the door behind them with a soft click.

As Shabanov rose from his chair, Ulm couldn't begin to think what the Russian—scarcely a four-star general—was doing with information of the caliber required by TERCOM for a joint operation. Had he been in possession of the salient facts all along, or had he merely collected the information from the embassy as messenger boy for the Kremlin?

Either way, the Russian had been a sleeper, waiting for orders. It was a timely reminder that Spetsnaz was indivisible from the GRU— military intelligence. And however Westernized Shabanov seemed, Spetsnaz had drawn its recruits from such hard-core Communist organizations as the Komsomol until the death of the Party in 1991. Altogether too recently for Ulm's liking.

Jacobson gestured for Shabanov to take his chair again. With Ulm to his left, he took his seat opposite the Russian.

"The floor's yours, Colonel," he said. "Make history."

Shabanov remained unmoved. He raised his eyes from the table and stared straight at Ulm. "I have known about the organization which carried out the hijacking for some time. Let me tell you it has not been easy, Elliot."

Ulm held the Russian's stare. "We all have our orders." Privately, however, he could not shake off an irrational sense of betrayal.

"General Aushev has empowered me to deliver the identity of the terrorists as proof that the Romeo Protocol can succeed. Our motives are not altruistic. The general wishes me to be honest with you. For us, cooperation in the counterterror field has a very practical purpose. Terrorism inside Russia is on the increase. In the past three months, thirteen internal flights have been hijacked. Yet a few years previously, Russians did not know the meaning of the word. You and your allies have had time to formulate your counterinsurgency doctrine and practices. As I said to you yesterday, Elliot, Spetsnaz can do many things, but we are still learning. There is much you can teach us."

"And vise versa," Ulm said. He thought of mother and child, three neat holes drilling each head.

"Doubtless, you heard about one of our top military advisers in the Yemen, General Churmurov, killed by a terrorist car bomb in Sanaa, last February. In the following month, an Air Russia Ilyushin Il-96 blew up at cruising altitude on a routine flight between Moscow and Tashkent. There were no survivors."

"I remember the day," Jacobson said.

"We found ourselves in a war, Mr. Jacobson, and we didn't even know who had declared it upon us. There has been so much unrest in my country over the last few years it was difficult to isolate these two acts as the work of one group. Except in one respect. In both these instances, no one claimed responsibility. That struck us as strange."

Ulm looked at Jacobson as Shabanov continued.

"By early summer, when our scientists were able to match the explosive used in the airliner to the bomb in the general's car, the civil intelligence service—formerly the KGB—knew, without doubt, that they were looking for one organization. In their minds, all other pockets of unrest became of secondary importance, for they realized they were dealing with a new terror outfit; one with the ability to operate both inside and outside Russia, but whose focus was turned on the destruction—or at the very least, the destabilization—of our apparatus. But who were they? The civil intelligence service was without any leads. And so it was that they handed over the entire investigation to the GRU."

"Jesus," Jacobson said. "I bet you were surprised."

"I was not personally involved at this point, but certainly, General Aushev was taken aback. There is little affection between the GRU and the old KGB."

Jacobson removed his glasses and began cleaning them with his tie. "I'll say," he muttered.

"As soon as the Second Chief Directorate assumed responsibility for the investigation, General Aushev sent word out through our embassies that this matter had become a priority. All GRU operatives were made aware of its criticality, its vital importance. Old contacts with guerrilla organizations, such as those in Lebanon, Libya and Syria, were renewed. We made it clear that we were looking for any information leading to this organization; and that we were prepared to pay."

Ulm noticed the way Shabanov had glossed neatly over the matter of Russian, formerly Soviet, "contacts" in the Middle East. Before the New World Order, the Kremlin had financed organizations like the PLO in the fight against the West. He cracked his knuckles under the table, the sharp pain reminding him that this was real.

"For several months there was silence," Shabanov continued. "Then almost three weeks ago, al-Hasakah blew up in our faces."

"That was them?" Jacobson gasped. "We thought al-Hasakah was an accident."

"Wait a minute," Ulm said. "Would you mind telling me what the hell you're talking about."

Jacobson turned to him. He seemed elated. No matter that their Middle East intelligence network had let them down again. The sands of the Middle East had shifted to reveal a tantalizing new truth.

"A Russian-built gas-pumping station at al-Hasakah in the Syrian Desert blew up during an inauguration ceremony. The explosion killed the Syrian minister of the interior, dozens of other attendees and, crucially, it wiped out a Russian delegation led by Mikhail Koltsov." He turned back to Shabanov. "Your minister for gas-petrochemical industrialization, I believe."

"Correct in all but one detail, Mr. Jacobson. Koltsov and his associates did not die. That information was released to spare our ally, Syria, any extra embarrassment over its appalling lapse in security. No, our delegation was captured in its entirety. And by the same organization that perpetrated this latest outrage at Beirut. We have firm proof that both Koltsov and your ambassador, Franklin, are being held at the same location."

"How can you possibly know that?" Jacobson demanded.

"Because the day after al-Hasakah our intelligence network in the Middle East bore fruit. Someone in Lebanon had information and was prepared to part with it—for a price. A meeting was requested in London and one of the general's men was sent there for the exchange—"

Jacobson cut Shabanov dead. "So it was you guys who killed the PFLP-GC's second-in-command in Hyde Park. I had his boss, Jibril, down as the instigator of that one; or at the very least, a rival Palestinian group."

"General Aushev is a brilliant man," Shabanov said simply.

Jacobson was still shaking his head in ill-disguised admiration. "Go on, Colonel."

"Before he was . . . removed, al-Azeem told us who these bastards were. There was a buzz of anticipation throughout the Second Chief Directorate. Spetsnaz was put on alert. We were to be sent in to destroy this organization and rescue Koltsov and his delegation. Preparations were being made. We would have done it, too."

"But they wrong-footed you when they took our ambassador," Ulm said.

Shabanov turned to him. "The very day our friends decided to declare war on the United States as well as Russia."

"So who are these people?" Ulm asked.

"They call themselves the Angels of Judgment," Shabanov said. "They're a staunch, ultra-fundamentalist Islamic organization led by a man who operates under the nom de guerre al-Saif. Or in English, the Sword. Their base is located in a secluded valley in southern Lebanon. And that is where he is holding our hostages." He stressed the word "our."

"I've never heard of them," Jacobson said.

"Believe me, Mr. Jacobson, the information surprised your counterparts in Moscow also. Yet it is beyond doubt."

"In south Lebanon?" Ulm said. "But everyone saw that boat head out into the Mediterranean."

"Yet your navy never found it." Shabanov glanced from Ulm to Jacobson and back again, waiting for a denial, but he got none. "That is because the terrorists transferred the hostages into small rubber craft, scuttled the fishing boat and put ashore farther down the coast. As we speak, they are established within the boundaries of the Sword's camp."

"How come you're so certain about all this?" Ulm asked.

"Once you know where to look, the rest is relatively easy," Shabanov said. "General Aushev has all facts at his disposal. I was able to receive a full rundown on the situation while I was inside our embassy just now."

"Then you must know who is behind these . . . Angels of Judgment," Jacobson said. "From their modus operandi, from the advanced state of their technical know-how, it seems obvious to me that the sponsor nation must be—"

Shabanov moved to silence him. "Nobody, Mr. Jacobson. The Angels of Judgment would appear to be a new dimension in terror. They are entirely self-sufficient. Of course, it is no secret that we used to finance such organizations—just as you, Mr. Jacobson, supplied the mujahideen with the Stingers—but that is all behind us now. Without superpower support, many of these terrorist organizations have simply ceased to exist. But not the Angels of Judgment. They have established themselves in a secluded location that is difficult to spot from the air, that is heavily fortified against attack, and which supplies all their needs . . . housing, agriculture, schooling, training. The Sword has thought of everything. What worries the GRU—and will doubtless be of concern to you, Mr. Jacobson, being a Mid-East specialist yourself—is that there is a fascinating precedent for the Sword and his Angels of Judgment.''

Jacobson nodded slowly as his mind chewed over the clues. ''But to find it you would have to go back many centuries, Colonel.''

''To the end of the eleventh century, to be exact,'' Shabanov said. ''When Hassan Sabbah established himself in an impregnable fortress called the Eagle's Nest in the mountains of Persia. Having built his self-sufficient community, Hassan trained his terrorists in the art of political assassination, indulging them with excess as incentive and reward. Wine, women and especially drugs, hashish, were given to his warriors.''

''The Hashisheen,'' Jacobson said. ''The Assassins. Scourge of the ruling Seljuks and later the Crusaders who invaded from Europe. Hassan was the world's first Islamic terrorist. And he, too, declared war on the East and the West. The parallels are, as you say, fascinating.''

But Ulm's thoughts had drifted beyond the history lesson to an aspect of Shabanov's briefing that he found almost as disturbing.

''Roman, I notice you have not mentioned the precise location of this camp,'' he said, choosing his words carefully. ''When would we obtain that information?''

''In good time,'' Shabanov said.

''The price of membership?''

''I don't follow, Elliot.''

''We don't get to know the location until . . . the day of the mission itself, maybe?''

Shabanov's blue eyes blinked innocently. ''Let me put it this way, Elliot. General Aushev thought that your premature possession of such knowledge might endanger the spirit of cooperation between us.''

''You mean he's worried we'd go off and do this thing on our own.''

''Is that true?'' Jacobson asked the Russian. ''The Romeo Protocol is meant to be an expression of trust between our two countries. The very highest expression, in fact.''

"Really, Mr. Jacobson?" Shabanov inquired. "Imagine our surprise, then, when we found that Spetsnaz, Russia's elite, was to work with a unit that had disgraced itself in Panama. A unit that is now exiled in the wastes of the New Mexico desert. Is that your highest expression of trust, Mr. Jacobson?"

"Now wait a minute—"

Ulm raised his hand. "Forget it, Jacobson. Why pretend?" He turned to Shabanov. "What are you saying, exactly?"

The Russian smiled. "Whatever your worth in the eyes of the Pentagon, Elliot, I have complete faith in you and your Pathfinders. I want you to know that."

The declaration made Ulm feel no less uneasy. He felt disoriented, unsure as to which of these two men was his best ally.

"All right, Roman. Let's talk tactics. You and me. Alone." Ulm turned to Jacobson. "Give me a day and I'll let you know if this thing's workable or not. After that, it's in your hands."

■　　　　　■　　　　　■

THE WAITRESS with the Texan drawl and endless legs came over to the table to take their order. Ulm asked for another beer, while Shabanov stuck to bourbon. Ulm noticed the girl's lingering looks over Shabanov's athletic body. Even out of uniform, the Russian was a striking man.

Ulm, at something under five feet and nine inches, with a twice-broken nose, short, thinning hair and the body of a prizefighter past his prime, couldn't exactly say the same about himself, but he never begrudged his somewhat brutish looks. His womanizing days had been over for a long time. He admired the waitress's ass, delicately hidden as it was by the tassels of her miniskirt, as she disappeared off to the bar. Marriage had been good to Elliot Ulm, but it hadn't stopped him from looking.

The low-lit bar of the small, seedy hotel across the street from TERCOM stood in stark contrast to the helicopter gunships, assault rifles, stun grenades and other hallmarks of low-intensity conflict that the two of them discussed all afternoon in the cold isolation of the briefing room.

By the end of the day, both he and Shabanov had a good idea of the sort of resources they would need.

The piped Muzak delivered its rendition of a song Ulm recalled from his college days. It was the third time it had come around that evening. The only other drinkers in the room got up to leave as if in protest. Apart from the waitress, he and Shabanov were the last occupants of the room. It was fast approaching one in the morning.

During the afternoon, Shabanov had drawn sketches of the terrorist camp, marking its location at the end of a steep-sided valley, the dimensions of the compound and the layout of the buildings and its defenses. The Russian had announced his intention to build a facsimile of the terrorist encampment close to their training base, so that Spetsnaz and the Pathfinders could practice their assault until perfect. It seemed a good idea. Ulm wished he could say the same for TERCOM's overall strategy. There was something inherently wrong about doing business with the Bear.

"The war's over, Elliot."

Ulm wondered if mind-reading figured amongst the Russian's many talents. "For some people."

The Russian waved his glass theatrically. "Where do you stand?"

"I'm paid to obey orders. Some are good, others suck. But they're there to be carried out. It'll take time for us to adjust."

Shabanov leaned forward conspiratorially. "That's why our task is so important. A joint mission in a field as sensitive as special operations is truly historic. And a rescue operation, more so. Everyone talks about the New World Order, but there will be no law, no order in that world without policemen. Don't you see, Elliot? This mission, once it is announced, will show the world that Russia and the United States will have earned the right to be the guardians of the new law."

"As long as people like your General Vorobyov exist, you can stick that in a book of dreams." Just a few days before, Major General Vorobyov had given an interview that more or less advocated a return to the cold war. It had fed the fears of alarmists in most U.S. newspapers.

"Ah, but Vorobyov is a reactionary."

"Who believes your president's disarmament policy is a joke. That's a dangerous kind of reaction."

"Vorobyov and men like him have retired. We are the new generation." Shabanov shrugged. "Of course, when I was a younger man I shared some of their sentiments. But you have to see things in perspective. We believed NATO was our bitter enemy. We were conditioned to think that way. As a soldier I have always obeyed my orders without question, as you would expect. When I was recruited into our special forces it was a different time, like a dark age for us. What you saw at the training camp bears little resemblance to the army I entered almost twenty years ago.''

Shabanov took another sip of bourbon, rolling the alcohol on his tongue. ''I remember the day my training school commandant accused me of stealing another recruit's food. In front of the whole school he told me to stick my fingers down my throat and empty my stomach onto the frozen earth of the parade ground. We were treated worse than dogs, our hearts filled with malice, ready to discharge it against the enemies of communism. A lot has changed . . .''

''What made you change?''

''Afghanistan.''

Ulm noticed a slight slurring of the word. ''Why?''

''Nine years of . . . special reconnaissance, that's why.'' He took another pull from the glass. ''At least, that's what we called it. Hill fighting, close-quarter work, scouting, forward air control, designating guerrilla targets for our jet bombers . . . all in a day's work.''

Shabanov stared into his glass. ''Some of the men went insane and there were suicides.'' He snorted. ''Not during the war, you understand. When we got back. Those fucking peaceniks. To them, special reconnaissance was rape, murder, burning, looting . . .'' He emphasized each one by thumping his fist on the table. ''For a while, the radical papers were full of it. I think we Afghantsi deserved better, but glasnost consigned us to the rubbish heap. Only Bitov, my senior sergeant and I, remain from my platoon of '79.'' He drained his glass. ''Glasnost has a lot to answer for.''

''Maybe General Vorobyov hasn't retired after all,'' Ulm whispered.

''Huh?''

''Nothing.'' Ulm felt like someone had just walked over his grave.

The waitress approached with the check. Shabanov made no move to pick up the tab, but that didn't bother the American. It had been made clear to him by USSOCOM that the Russian was their guest in all matters.

He looked up to find Shabanov standing over the waitress, a good head taller than she was, in spite of her legs. She held his gaze, as if he had her in a kind of spell. Ulm blamed the surrealism of the scene on the number of beers he had drunk, but something in her eyes made him look again, lower this time. Shabanov had pulled her skirt around her midriff and was moving his hand up the inside of her thighs toward her paper-thin panties. It was at that moment that Ulm realized that what he had read as complicity in her eyes was in fact a look of horror and revulsion. Then, like an animal breaking the lock of a car headlight beam, she brought her hand up and slapped him hard on the face.

The waitress ran crying from the room and Shabanov tilted his head at Ulm, laughter rocking his body. Ulm pulled the Russian from the hotel into the rain. He hailed a taxi, ordering the driver first to the Russian embassy, where he deposited Shabanov, then to TERCOM, where Ulm would spend the night.

CHAPTER 8

"GOOD MORNING. Here are the BBC news headlines at seven o'clock. . . ."

Girling pulled the pillow over his head to block out the newscaster's voice. He could have used a week's extra sleep.

". . . There has been a vital breakthrough in the hunt for the terrorists who carried out the Beirut massacre two nights ago and the simultaneous kidnapping of the U.S. ambassador to Saudi Arabia and nine of his staff. . . ."

The words barely registered. It was publication day. There were another seven days before the next edition of *Dispatches* hit the streets. Today he could have slept, but he had forgotten to reset the clock radio and it was too far away to turn off.

At the back of his mind, however, a voice told him to listen. He was no longer merely Tom Girling, Science and Technology Correspondent. Beirut was his story now.

". . . According to a report in *Dispatches,* the authoritative weekly current-affairs magazine, the attack was the work of an extreme Islamic terrorist organization called the Angels of Judgment. . . ."

Girling lifted the pillow off his head. That was their story. Stansell had called back with confirmation. He was pleased. Pleased for Stansell; and pleased for Kelso. Their editor had found his exclusive at the eleventh hour and then some.

And now the Angels of Judgment were making the lead spot on the national news. No doubt, it was enjoying similar billing with other media outlets. The wire agencies would have picked it up; Reuters, the Associated Press, Agence France-Presse . . . all flashing the news around the world. And *Dispatches*' name was up there, too, in lights.

Girling smiled. Kelso, the survivor, had his big stick for the meeting. Lord Kyle could not possibly shut them down now, could he?

''We have this report from Douglas Kennedy. . . .''

Girling listened as the principal facts of the story he had written down the night before from the nuggets Stansell had provided were churned out by the radio reporter. That the BBC had credited *Dispatches* so generously did not surprise him. The magazine had a very competent publicity machine that was ready to disseminate its best stories to the mass media in return for a hefty acknowledgment.

The line trotted out in the report was that the Angels of Judgment seemed to be a new breed of terror organization. Independent of larger groups like the PLO and Hizbollah, they were resourceful, dedicated and furnished with the necessary funds to carry through a complex operation like Beirut. Worst of all, no one knew where they had come from.

It was then that Kelso himself came over the airwaves. His voice conveyed a sense of gravitas that befitted the story. Even if *Dispatches* was able only to cite ''diplomatic sources in Cairo'' as its primary informant, Kelso's deep and somber tone gave it an unquestionable authority. The interview had been recorded over the telephone, probably late the previous night. Girling could hear the self-satisfaction in his editor's voice. Kelso was enjoying himself.

''. . . our exclusive report highlights a number of interesting points,'' Kelso said pompously. ''The ability of a hitherto unknown group of terrorists to strike with seeming impunity at innocent civilians, despite recent assurances by Western governments, is particularly alarming. Secondly, so-called experts in other sections of the media have been laboring under the misapprehension that a substantial Middle Eastern power such as Iran or Libya was behind this incident.

Our report has shown this not to be the case. The Angels of Judgment are very much on their own. . . .''

"Would you care to comment on yesterday's reports that the terrorists and their captives have given U.S. forces the slip?'' the reporter asked Kelso. "We gather you have independent corroboration.''

It sounded spontaneous, but Girling knew that the questions would have been rehearsed. Kelso had been furnished with all the answers he needed following the visit to Tech-Int.

"Absolutely,'' Kelso said. "Sources within our own Ministry of Defence, which is collaborating closely with the Americans, have confirmed that the boat in which they escaped has completely disappeared.''

"Despite the massive sea-search?'' the reporter probed.

"I'm afraid the Angels of Judgment have been one step ahead of Western intelligence all the way. It's a political embarrassment, not to mention a tragedy.''

"A tragedy, indeed,'' the BBC's studio anchorman said at the conclusion of the bulletin. "Robert Kelso, editor of *Dispatches,* ending that report there by Douglas Kennedy.''

Girling climbed out of bed and walked to the kitchen. Outside, it was still dark. Inside, the flat was bloody cold. He had no sooner filled the kettle than the phone rang.

"Tom?''

Sally Gordon-Jones of Channel Four News was quick off the mark. He saw her from time to time in the circus of press conferences, interviews and briefings that went with the job. Although a general reporter, she quite often covered science- and defense-related subjects.

Girling carried the phone over to the kitchen counter and tipped a spoonful of instant-coffee powder into a cup.

"I just heard *Dispatches*' piece about the hijackers on the radio,'' she said. "Was that for real?''

"Kelso's going to look pretty stupid if it's not.'' He paused. "I'm joking, of course, Sally. Yes, it's for real.''

"Humor at this hour,'' she said in mock admiration. "Who filed the piece?''

The kettle wheezed dismally. Girling willed it to boil so he could take his coffee back to bed. "Stansell,'' he said. "Out of Cairo.''

"The great Stansell. It has impeccable credentials, then."

"Sally, I'm freezing my nuts off. Please get to the point."

"Well, we wanted Kelso in the studio to record a piece for tonight's news. But apparently he's not available."

Naturally enough, Girling thought. Today was Kelso's big day with the board.

"We were wondering if you'd mind substituting as the talking head, Tom."

"Why me?"

"Kelso's office said you helped put the story together."

He thought about it. "What do you want to talk about?"

"We're getting a Middle East expert in to talk about the rise of independent terrorist groups like the Angels of Judgment. What we really need is someone to explain how they were able to disappear into thin air. Technicalities being your forte, naturally I thought of you."

"Sally, like a good many people right now, I haven't got a clue."

"You must have some idea how they evaded all those U.S. Navy radar planes. Speculate a little."

"Okay. It's your money."

"Thanks, Tom. By the way, are you always this grouchy in the morning?"

"Only when I'm standing half-naked in a cold kitchen unable to make my first cup of coffee because some strange woman is asking me to appear on TV."

She laughed, then apologized. "I'll make it up to you one of these days."

"Don't tempt me."

"Promises, promises, Tom."

They agreed on a time and she hung up. Moments later, the kettle boiled. Girling wandered down the corridor, coffee in hand, and ran himself a bath.

As soon as the temperature was bearable, he lay back in the water and closed his eyes.

There had been a time when he thought he liked Sally a lot. They had a few dinners together, but the one time she had returned with him to his apartment, the air between them thick with lust, she discovered Alia, sleeping blissfully under the watchful eyes of a baby-sitter, and fell promptly in love with his daughter instead. Sally's maternal feelings destroyed any prospect of sex. He was not prepared for a relationship which smacked of commitment. Girling found himself making excuses about the busy day ahead and Sally left. They had managed to remain friends since.

Thoughts of work reminded him to call in. Kelso's secretary could tell her boss that he would be out for the morning; not that Kelso, his mind on loftier matters, would be that bothered.

He clambered out of the bath, dried himself and padded back to the kitchen.

Kelso's secretary sounded as if she, too, had not had her requisite intake of caffeine. She perked up a little when she realized that he would be appearing on TV that night, and she asked what it was in connection with. He explained how the laurels belonged to Stansell, not him.

"What time did his call come in last night?" he asked.

"There was no call," she said, puzzlement in her voice. "Were you expecting one?"

"Bob agreed not to run the story until he heard from Stansell. It was a condition."

"Oh, I wouldn't know anything about that," she said defensively.

"Maybe Stansell reached Bob at home," Girling said, trying to rationalize what he had heard on the radio. Or maybe there was another explanation altogether. He brought his hand up to his head. "Holy shit, no . . ."

His notes.

"I beg your pardon," she said indignantly.

Girling never heard the voice on the other end of the phone. He had left his fucking notes in the office. Surely to God Kelso wouldn't have . . .

He managed to keep his voice steady. "Has Kelso gone to his meeting yet?"

"Yes," she replied. And it would be in progress all day.

Girling tried to dismiss the notion while he dressed, but it clung to him like a bad odor.

Finally, he picked up the phone and dialed their office in Cairo. Egypt was three hours ahead, so Stansell should have read news of his story over the wire by now or maybe heard it on the BBC World

Service. Girling tried to convince himself that had Stansell been in any way troubled he would have called.

It wasn't Stansell, but Sharifa who answered. Sharifa Fateem, Mona's best friend, now Stansell's editorial assistant. Stansell had hired her a few months before because he needed help and had come to know Sharifa after Mona's death. It suited both parties well. Sharifa had wanted for a long time to break into writing, and Stansell justified the appointment to Kelso because he needed someone he could trust and rely upon. And there weren't that many people in Cairo you could say that about.

They chatted for a while, then Girling told her about his concerns.

She hadn't seen Stansell since the previous afternoon. He rarely checked in before lunch, but just to reassure him, she promised to phone him back at the office the moment he did or if she had any news.

■   ■   ■

"We've isolated the leak and it has been dealt with," Shabanov said. "The mission remains uncompromised, of that I assure you."

Jacobson tried to take it in his stride, but Ulm could see he was shocked. Shabanov had commenced the briefing by announcing that the Russian military attaché in Cairo had been caught supplying classified information about the Angels of Judgment to a British journalist. The story, naturally enough, had made the BBC's breakfast bulletins and had spread like wildfire through the U.S. media.

"I thought this information was with only a very small section of your intelligence community," Ulm said. He tried to keep the animosity from his voice. The memory of Shabanov's treatment of the waitress lingered.

"That is true, Elliot. But this man was one of those who had worked closely with General Aushev. Cairo, Damascus and Tripoli were key coordination centers in our search for the Angels of Judgment."

"So why'd this asshole go shooting his mouth off?" Ulm demanded.

"He was drunk, Elliot. A reception at our embassy . . ."

Ulm nodded, his gaze never leaving Shabanov. He'd seen with his own eyes how the GRU liked to drink.

"But I reiterate," Shabanov said, "it cannot happen again. This man has been flown back to Moscow, where he will be punished."

Ulm and Jacobson said nothing.

"In some ways, this leak has played into our hands," Shabanov continued. "Thanks to the media, the terrorists, along with the rest of the world, believe that they have managed to escape without trace. Only a handful of people outside these walls know the true facts. Surprise remains on our side, for the Angels of Judgment will believe that we have no idea where their hiding place is."

"Let's hope you're right," Jacobson said.

"And that it stays that way," Ulm added. "Which publication broke the news?"

"*Dispatches,*" Jacobson said. "They've been sniffing around this story from the beginning."

"The last place we need another security leak right now is in Cairo," Ulm said to Jacobson. "Shabanov and I have decided that we're going to need Wadi Qena. Will TERCOM be able to fix access to Qena, Jacobson?"

Jacobson's pencil scratched across the paper again. "Access will not be a problem. But why Qena?"

Ulm pulled a large map of the Middle East from his attaché case and pinned it to the wall facing the table. "This plan will be familiar to anyone who worked on Rice Bowl. I don't make any apologies for that, because Rice Bowl was based on sound mission-planning. It just got screwed up in the execution. We've learned a lot since 1980. This time, we're going to make the dice roll for us."

His finger hovered over the Eastern Desert of Egypt for a moment, before landing on a point just north of a large bend in the river Nile, some three hundred miles south of Cairo. Wadi Qena had been the final staging post for Eagle Claw, the operational phase of Rice Bowl, itself the planning portion of the abortive rescue of the American hostages in Tehran.

"We spend around a week in training at Qena before we press the button." Ulm slid his finger slowly northward, until it reached the border of southern Lebanon. "And by that I mean we fly a combat rescue team into the Sword's valley, knock out the Angels of Judgment and bring back our hostages."

He would have liked it a whole lot better if the Pathfinders had been allowed to do it on their own. But that was impossible.

Ulm told Jacobson about Shabanov's plan of building a replica of the terrorist camp in the desert outside Qena to maximize the realism of their training. The mountains of the Eastern Desert were, apparently, similar to the terrain around the target. Mission security would not be jeopardized, because the area around Wadi Qena was deserted but for a handful of bedouins.

With approval, Ulm explained, he and his handpicked team of Pathfinders would leave as soon as possible to reactivate Wadi Qena, which had been abandoned by the Egyptians for almost a decade. The team's equipment, including its helicopters, would arrive by C-5 Galaxy transport a day later.

"Meanwhile, Shabanov returns to his unit in Russia and collects the assets he needs. He arrives at Qena by Antonov transport around the same time we get there. From then on, we train; and train hard. There's a lot of work to be done to get the Pathfinders and Spetsnaz to fight as a cohesive unit."

Ulm outlined the method of getting the Russians' giant An-124 transports into Egypt under cover of night without arousing curiosity. The Russian aircraft would be fitted with USAF transponders and "squawk" on the same identification code as the C-5s, thereby fooling Egyptian radar operators into believing they were C-5s inbound from Europe. Keeping Cairo in the dark about Russian participation was important for security reasons. There were to be no more leaks.

Each side was to bring its own equipment, Ulm explained. Part of the training process would be given over to determining whose hardware would be best for the job. Both he and Shabanov had unshakable faith in their own military machinery. It would be the men—and the harsh desert conditions—that would be the ultimate arbiters.

On the day of the mission—the precise timing would depend on the prevailing set conditions over the next two weeks—Shabanov would guide the helicopter force to the terrorist camp. In-flight refueling would be required depending on which helicopters were used. The Pathfinders aimed to bring their Sikorsky MH-53J Pave Low IIIs; the Russians their new extended-range version of the Mil Hind, the Mi-24J.

"My chief concern is that the Pathfinders won't know the target until the very last minute," Ulm said. "I would appreciate it if you would work on General Aushev to release that information. It would certainly help in our mission planning if we were given more target data.''

''I'll see what I can do,'' Jacobson said. ''Although I'm none too hopeful.'' He turned to Shabanov. ''Is there any influence you can exert in this matter back in Moscow, Colonel?''

Shabanov shrugged, a slight gesture. ''These were not my orders,'' he said. ''In my opinion, there should be complete openness between us, but for some people, the buildup of trust takes time.''

They discussed the plan in greater depth until Jacobson seemed satisfied with the information he had. Then he picked up the phone and requested a car to take him to the White House. The National Security Council wanted this thing done quickly.

''I suggest you make your preparations,'' Jacobson said, getting to his feet. ''I believe the NSC's approval will be merely a formality. There will be a full set of instructions for you in the jet that's waiting to take you back to Kirtland.'' He paused. ''Godspeed, gentlemen.''

Given the godless presence of Shabanov, Ulm couldn't help thinking that Jacobson was pissing in the wind.

■　　　　■　　　　■

GIRLING'S DESK phone was ringing its bells off when he stepped out of the elevator and into the office. There was no one around to answer it. The emptiness puzzled him. It was too early in the week for news conferences. Maybe it had something to do with Kelso's board meeting. The thought of another round of lay-offs gnawed at him as he lifted the receiver.

''Girling,'' he said sharply. He began rifling through his desk. The pad was still there, but . . .

''It's Peter Jarrett here, Ministry of Defence.''

For a moment Girling had difficulty making the adjustment. What did the Ministry want? To give him a bollocking for the low-level flying story, no doubt. He knew there were several things in the piece the MoD wouldn't like.

''You lodged a question with us earlier in the week,'' Jarrett said.

Girling racked his brain, then remembered the Il-76 Candid at Machrihanish.

''Well, I've got an answer for you, but I don't think you're going to like it.'' He paused. ''That Il-76 was on a routine mission. It was picking up humanitarian aid. Food relief.''

''Oh, come on, Pete, that's crap and you know—''

Girling was watching Mallon walking toward him. He had just left the conference room, alone. His face was ashen.

Girling dropped the phone onto its cradle just as Mallon was upon him. He got to his feet. ''It's not about our jobs is it?''

''No. Sit down, Tom.''

Girling suddenly knew what was coming.

He saw the anxiety in Mallon's eyes.

''I'm not going to do anything stupid, Kieran.'' The calm in his voice surprised even him. ''It's about Stansell, isn't it?''

Mallon nodded and the words tumbled out.

''Jack Carey got a call from Sharifa, and we just had it confirmed by the Foreign Office. The Egyptian police found the front door of his apartment hanging off its hinges. There was no sign of Stansell inside, just a handwritten note. In Arabic.''

''What did it say?''

''That he's gone. Snatched in reprisal for our story.''

''Who by, for Christ's sake?''

''The Angels of Judgment.''

Girling swallowed hard. ''I don't believe it. Kelso . . . What the hell did he think he was doing?'' His hand fumbled for the chair back. ''Was there any indication he'd been hurt?''

''I don't know. The details are still very sketchy.'' He paused. ''The Egyptian police believe this may be a local incident. Some Cairo-based outfit—fundamentalist sympathizers, maybe—getting on the bandwagon. They're very confident of finding him alive. You've got to have hope.''

''I'm not big on hope, Kieran,'' Girling said.

''The embassy said the Egyptians are taking it seriously enough,'' Mallon said, trying to sound upbeat. ''They've put their best men onto it. No ordinary outfit, either. Our embassy spoke very highly of them.''

''Oh, Jesus. The *mukhabarat,* the Egyptian internal security police. They're the outfit who investigated Mona's death. They more or less told me I'd imagined what happened to us in Asyut. A promise from them means about as much as a promise from Kelso.''

Mallon searched Girling's face. ''What do you mean?''

Girling told him. "Kelso wanted his exclusive that badly. Jesus, he and Stansell go way back, yet he just sold him down the river."

"Steady, Tom."

Girling waved him aside. "Our illustrious editor was so wrapped up in his precious magazine that he was prepared to betray a friend and colleague just like that. What the fuck have I done?"

"For Christ's sake, Tom, this is not your fault."

Girling shook his head. "I should have watched Kelso. I should have known better than to leave him alone with a story like that."

"Do you think this was why Stansell asked you to hold back? Did he know the Angels of Judgment would come to get him?"

"Whether he's been taken by the Angels of Judgment or local nutters, he's dead either way. The only group in Cairo with the will to strike at someone like Stansell is the Muslim Brotherhood."

"But why?"

"They're fundamentalists, Kieran. Hard-liners. They killed Mona just like that. To outfits like the Brotherhood the Angels of Judgment are heroes. Perhaps this Sword managed to get a signal to them. Who knows what links bind these organizations together? Or maybe they snatched him on their own initiative. Stansell stood out like a beacon after our story ran. He was an easy target."

Girling turned the pages of the pad until he found the jottings he'd made just the day before. Stansell, the Angels of Judgment, the Sword . . . and now the Muslim Brotherhood. Egypt.

He had to go back, not just for Stansell. He had to go back for Alia. For Mona. He had to go back for himself.

He headed for the elevator.

"Where are you going?" Mallon shouted after him.

The elevator arrived and Girling stepped inside. "To a board meeting," he said, just before the doors closed.

He never bothered to knock on the door that led to the office managed by Lord Kyle's secretary. The personal assistant to the proprietor stammered as Girling breezed past her.

"Excuse me, you can't go in there. There's a planning session in progress. You'll have to wait, Mr. . . . ?"

But Girling swept on.

He threw open the door, pausing for only a moment to absorb the scene before his eyes. Lord Kyle, owner of the world's second-largest publishing empire, gaped at the intruder who stood framed in the doorway. On either side of the proprietor's seat at the large conference table, two other main board directors, whom Girling recognized but whose names he'd forgotten, looked on in amazement. The senior publishing executives ranged along the nearest side of the table twisted in their sumptuous chairs to look at the intruder. Behind him, Girling was aware of the fussing secretary, who was trying to get past to blurt her apologies.

Girling surveyed the faces. Then he found the one that had brought him there.

As he strode toward Kelso, whose face seemed to redden with every pace that he took, Girling was aware of the cacophony breaking out around him. Lord Kyle demanded an explanation, while the secretary bleated for her master's absolution.

With the din at its height, Girling leaned over and whispered in Kelso's ear. "I'm going to make a short announcement here, after which you are going to follow me very quietly from this room so we can talk. Just the two of us."

"This is outrageous, Tom. That's Lord Kyle over there."

"Bob, I'm sure the noble lord will be fascinated to hear me brand you a murderer in front of all his friends here. It's a statement I am fully prepared to justify, unless you decide to come with me."

"I haven't the first idea what you're talking about," Kelso blustered.

"You will."

Girling turned to the assembled company. "Gentlemen, our scoop has caused such a stir that I'm afraid Mr. Kelso is required downstairs. A small administrative matter."

He leaned over and whispered again. "Now step outside."

Girling saw the resignation on Kelso's face. He struggled to his feet, mumbling apologies to the board. They left the room before any of the dignitaries could object. Girling held Kelso firmly by the arm and frog-marched him along the corridor and into the toilets reserved for the board.

Kelso could contain his rage no longer. "I'll have your hide for this. I have never been so humiliated in my entire life. What was all that crap back there? You barged in there like you owned the place—"

"Stansell's been kidnapped."

"What?"

"He's been kidnapped, because you decided to have your exclusive, whatever the cost. He's been taken by our old friends the Angels of Judgment, or someone operating in their name."

"I don't believe you."

"It's true. And you as good as pointed the finger."

"Look, there must have been some misunderstanding—"

"Bullshit! I know about the notepad. You knew full well what you were doing." Girling jabbed a finger in the direction of the boardroom.

"What am I going to tell them? They've just voted *Dispatches* another five million."

"Here's how you're going to start spending it. You're going to send me to Cairo. Make me Middle East bureau chief in Stansell's absence."

"You must be mad. Egypt was the reason you gave up reporting."

"I'm not going there to report for you." Girling looked at him levelly. "I'm going there to find Stansell."

"You? What can you do that the police can't?"

"You just don't understand, do you? You're so busy currying favor with your friends down the corridor that you've lost touch with the real world. The reality is that the Angels of Judgment have killed over a hundred people inside a week. And to compound an already dismal situation, the outfit that has been tasked with finding Stansell is just about the most corrupt and incompetent collection of policemen that walks this planet. Why do you think they've asked for news of Stansell's kidnapping to be suppressed? Because it helps his case?" He shook his head. "It's because they know they haven't a hope in hell of finding him. By keeping the lid on news of his abduction, they minimize the exposure of their incompetent efforts. I know, because as you correctly pointed out the other day, I am close to this story— maybe too close. I've been through it before."

■　　　■　　　■

THE SINGLE-FILE column of hostages stumbled along the dusty track.

Ambassador Franklin kept his hand clasped firmly to the shoulder of the man at the head of the column. He had given up trying to loosen the blindfold that had been tied too tightly around his head. The last time he had brought a hand up to his face, the sharp crack of a rifle butt reminded him of the rules that had been imposed upon them. The most rigidly enforced was the one about the blindfold.

When they first began to march, the heat had been intolerable, but now that they were higher up, the air had cooled considerably and, despite their fatigue, the journey had become easier. He had an impression they were passing through a deep ravine. Occasionally, he could hear the noise of scree scattered from under their feet echoing off steep-sided rock walls on either side of them.

Now the ravine was opening. Sunlight streamed onto his face, and he could smell lush vegetation around him.

When the terrorists called them to a halt, he thought at first it was just another rest. But then he heard the door pulled back, its hinges jarring noisily, and he knew that they had arrived at their final destination.

The hand in the small of his back sent him sprawling onto the musty earthen floor. His head hit the far wall, but was saved from bruising by the blindfold. The cloth dislodged, Franklin opened his eyes. Bright sunlight flooded through the diminishing gap as the door was pushed shut behind him.

A moment before it closed, Franklin caught a glimpse of his jailer. The sight of the man, the detail of his clothes clearly visible in the bright sun, made the ambassador catch his breath.

Alone, and in the darkness of his primitive cell, he knew there would be no demands, no ransoms paid.

BOOK 2

CHAPTER 1

IT WASN'T UNTIL three days later that Girling saw Egypt again. There had been much to do prior to his departure. Awaking from a light sleep when the flaps and wheels were lowered, he cupped his hands over the window and peered outside. The Egyptair A300 was descending through the night over the barren desert just west of Cairo. He could see sporadic pinpoints of light, where islands of civilization dotted the desert like fireflies.

As the Nile Valley swept below the belly of the aircraft, Girling settled back into his seat for the landing.

Five minutes later, the wheels greased the tarmac at Cairo International Airport, sending a shudder through the aircraft. Behind him a group of Egyptians cheered.

He descended the airstairs and shivered. Thanks to the six-hour delay, the aircraft had landed during the small window of time when the chill of the night had sucked the last warmth from the land. He looked to the eastern horizon, but the sun was a half hour away yet.

The journey through customs and immigration was the usual maze of triplicate forms and rubber stamps; the massed ranks of officialdom were to be breached only slowly. Now that he had arrived, he felt every delay as counting against Stansell's life. He looked at his watch a third time in five minutes. An immigration officer watched him with suspicion.

Reunited with his bags, he headed out of the terminal, through Cairenes crammed around the exits searching for friends and relations. He looked briefly for Sharifa, but she wasn't there. They had arranged to meet at *Dispatches'* offices if his plane arrived late.

He dropped his cases to the pavement. The sun had started to climb over the Eastern Desert accompanied by the odors of humanity that had been suppressed by the dew of the night. A swirl of choking dust blew in his face, bringing with it the distant cry of a muezzin calling the faithful to prayer.

As Egypt stirred it offered sights, sounds and smells that he remembered so well.

A Mercedes, sporting the familiar black-and-white paint scheme of Cairo cabs, pulled alongside. The driver leaned across the passenger seat and waved him in.

Girling told him where he wanted to go. *Dispatches'* offices were located on the fifth floor of a tall building overlooking the Corniche, the long road that ran almost the length of the Nile's east bank in Cairo.

The driver turned to compliment him on his Arabic and the Mercedes swerved across the carriageway. The closer they drew to the city center the greater the bustle and the noise as ten million people went about the day's business. Ahead, the twin minarets of the Mohammed Ali Mosque, a soaring nineteenth-century edifice built atop Saladin's medieval citadel, swung into view. Girling glanced to his left and saw smaller, less elegant minarets, scattered like rocky outcrops in a plain of whitewashed graves and crumbling mausoleums: the City of the Dead stretched away from the highway until its edges merged with the long shadows of the Muqattam Hills.

As the car sped on by, he watched a little boy, one leg amputated at the knee, hobble from the doorway of a requisitioned mausoleum and disappear down one of the myriad alleys that crisscrossed this sprawling subcity.

Once located beyond the walls of the capital, the City of the Dead was now one of its largest suburbs. The million people living here were from the lowest walks of life; mostly peasants who had teemed into the city to find work, but who quickly ended up picking through the rubbish dumps in search of food.

The City of the Dead attracted every kind of criminal. From the lowest thief to powerful, mafia-style gang leaders. A virtual no-go area for the regular police—the '*askary*—the City of the Dead was a hotbed of Islamic fundamentalism. If Stansell was anywhere in Egypt, there was a better than even chance he was down there, Girling thought, perhaps a few hundred yards from his speeding Mercedes. It was a notion that both exhilarated and depressed him.

Twenty minutes later, he paid the driver and stood with his bags on the curb opposite *Dispatches*' building. He crossed the road, avoiding the wildly converging traffic on the Corniche to reach the sanctuary of the building. In the comparative cool and silence of the lobby he glanced at his watch. It was six-thirty. He decided to go upstairs and wait.

He rode the elevator to the fifth floor and found the door to the office ajar. He swung it gently and peered inside. Never a tidy place, the room looked like it had been turned upside down. Files littered the floor, back issues of the magazine were scattered across tables and desks. There were endless boxes filled with papers and several filing cabinets with their drawers hanging open. Then he noticed the policeman in the corner, his white summer-issue fatigues sullied by dust and soot. He was sitting on a tea chest that was brimming with documents. He looked like he had spent the night chain-smoking his way through a pack of cigarettes, judging from the butts littering the floor by his feet.

Girling coughed and the corporal roused himself self-consciously, anxious to prove he had been doing anything but sleeping. He fingered his 1940s-vintage rifle anxiously, until Girling explained who he was. Girling took a seat in the opposite corner and for the next forty minutes, they watched each other uneasily, neither saying a word.

Presently, Girling heard footsteps in the corridor. He smiled in anticipation of seeing Sharifa again. He wondered as he rose to his feet, how kind the last three years had been to her.

Girling turned to find himself confronting a short man in his early fifties, his face built around small features. A wispy mustache, hairs glistening with droplets of sweat, sprouted from his upper lip. The suit, expensive by Egyptian standards, was ill-fitting, the buttons straining against an extensive belly.

The militiaman was on his feet, hand locked in salute. The fat man waved him to a post by the door.

"You are Mr. Tom Girling, the unfortunate Stansell's replacement." It was presented as a statement of fact, not a question. He took a step forward, hand outstretched. "Captain Lutfi al-Qadi of State Security." Al-Qadi lisped each *s,* leaving Girling with a fleeting impression of something reptilian. The *mukhabarat* was welcoming him back.

Al-Qadi left a thin film of sweat on Girling's palm.

"You are not well, Mr. Girling?"

"It was a long flight, Captain."

"You must be tired."

"You try to get used to it in my business."

"And mine also." Al-Qadi gestured to the mess around him. "Not the best greeting, I'm afraid, Mr. Girling. Our forensic people, you understand."

"Actually, I'm impressed, Captain."

"The *mukhabarat* does not take its work lightly, Mr. Girling. We are making progress."

"Oh?"

"We have recently recovered his contact book, the one filled with names and telephone numbers," al-Qadi said. "I believe it will answer many of our questions."

Girling had hoped that the book had been salvaged by Sharifa instead. It would have been an admirable start to his own efforts. Doubtless, Stansell's contact book would give the *mukhabarat* a sober insight into a first-rate journalist's penetration of the establishment, both in Egypt and neighboring countries.

"I am afraid your Stansell did not believe in personal security," al-Qadi said, shuffling to the large desk in the corner of the office. "In his apartment, he has a piece much like this, only oak, good quality." He rubbed the surface to prove the point. "We found his typewriter, with paper in it, just here. There were signs of a struggle—a broken lamp, an overturned chair." He pointed to the corresponding positions of each item.

"Had he typed anything?" Girling asked.

"On the paper? No."

"Did he leave behind any notes, reporter's notes?"

"I remind you there is a news blackout, Mr. Girling."

"Stansell is my friend, Captain. I think I have a right to know."

Al-Qadi removed a silk handkerchief and mopped his brow. "There was the note from his abductors, but that was all. Both his apartment and this office have been thoroughly searched, I can assure you."

"Could I see it?"

"What?"

"The note."

"This is police business, Mr. Girling."

"We have the same interest at heart, don't we, Captain?"

"Naturally." Al-Qadi's eyes narrowed to slits. "But in Egypt some things are impossible. Do your job, Mr. Girling, and I'll do mine."

"This is my job," Girling said levelly. "How do you know they didn't kill him on the spot?"

"Because we found traces of chloroform on the desk."

"But why would the Angels of Judgment go to the trouble? Out here, miles from home?" He paused. "Do you think the Brotherhood may be up to its old tricks?"

Al-Qadi pulled a pack of Nefertitis from his pocket. "A most convenient theory, Mr. Girling."

Girling watched him take out a cigarette and roll it between his fingers.

"It would be stupid for either of us to pretend," al-Qadi said. He lit the cigarette and sucked hard. The smoke streamed from his nostrils. "About what happened to your wife."

Girling managed to keep his feelings in check. He held the investigator's stare. "As you say, Captain." Even though the *mukhabarat* did not operate with Western-style efficiency, it kept files. "But it doesn't alter the fact that the Brotherhood may be helping the Angels of Judgment."

"Please leave the theorizing to us, Mr. Girling." Al-Qadi took a step toward him. "You would do well to remember that the *mukhabarat* has this investigation in hand. And that the Brotherhood is a spent force here in Egypt."

Girling buried an urge to tell al-Qadi that a *mukhabarat* officer had uttered those same words by his hospital bed three years before, barely two weeks after he had watched his wife being stoned to death by Brotherhood activists. For a moment, the rage swirled within him, but he fought against it. He could not afford to antagonize the *mukhabarat*.

He was saved by a sharp knock at the door.

Girling turned and there was Sharifa, a scarf covering her hair, her eyes hidden behind dark glasses. A slight puffiness about her face told him she had been crying.

"Oh, Tom, I'm so glad you're here."

They held each other for a moment. She took a step back. "You haven't changed."

"Nor you."

They stood there awkwardly for a moment, neither knowing what to say after so long.

"How's little Alia?" she asked, at last.

"She's fine. I've left her with my parents, until . . ." He stopped. "This is over."

Sharifa looked across to the investigator. "I see introductions are unnecessary," she said.

Al-Qadi ground the stub of his cigarette into the floor. He made to leave.

"I hope you have a pleasant stay in Egypt, Mr. Girling. If anything occurs to you that could help our investigation, do not hesitate to call me. Miss Fateem has my number." He clapped his hands and the militiaman took up his position inside the room again. "The guard will see to it that you are protected."

Al-Qadi's eyes rested on the satin-smooth skin of Sharifa's legs for a moment, then he turned and walked from the room.

Girling waited till he heard the elevator doors close. "I need a couple of hours in here," he whispered to her. "I have to check this place out, unsupervised."

She followed his gaze to the militiaman, who was engrossed in the pages of a magazine that had fallen from one of the boxes. Sharifa glanced toward Girling's luggage and asked: "Do you have a carton of cigarettes?"

He shook his head. "I quit." He pulled a bottle of Johnnie Walker from his duty-free bag. "But this stuff always used to be better than currency around here."

Girling handed over the bottle and watched as the transaction was made. Sharifa cooed soothingly at the guard's protestations. There was nothing to fear. She had things, private things, to discuss with her colleague from London. Captain al-Qadi would understand. The militiaman looked at her quizzically for a moment, then headed for the door, seemingly satisfied, his prize tucked inside his tunic.

Girling gestured after him. "Where's he going?"

"To guard the main entrance for a while. You probably have a little over an hour before he gets nervous and comes back. Providing, of course, Captain al-Qadi doesn't beat him to it."

"Unpleasant little runt, isn't he?" Girling said.

"Be careful around al-Qadi, Tom. He's not your average *mukhabarat* field officer."

Girling started with the filing cabinet nearest the door. He picked through the folders meticulously, occasionally removing a carnet and leafing through its pages like a bank cashier counting out money.

"Shouldn't you be getting some rest?" Sharifa said. "You've been up all night."

Girling said nothing, but moved to the next cabinet, pulling each drawer out on its runners in turn and passing his hands over its underside.

Nothing.

"There's a coffee shop around the corner," she ventured. "I bet you could use some real Arab coffee after that flight."

"Sounds good," he said distractedly. He never heard her leave.

Girling moved to the cardboard boxes used by Stansell as surrogate filing cabinets. As he stripped away the layers, he found newspaper cuttings, some in English, others in Arabic, bound with pieces of string or elastic. The *mukhabarat,* he knew, would have looked on the boxes as junk. There had been no attempt to categorize the contents beyond their natural chronology. Yet Stansell knew where to find everything. He had that sort of mind.

With a growing sense of unease Girling moved down the layers until he reached the period when he was last in Egypt. There was a long article clipped from the *Economist* on Libya's return to the Arab fold, headed with a picture of Qadhafi shaking hands with Mubarak on the tarmac at the Cairo airport. Girling remembered the Libyan leader's visit. Qadhafi arrived the day he took his first steps in Stansell's apartment. That placed it around three and a half years ago. Stansell had gone to the airport to watch the plane come in and Girling had decided to use the solitude to practice walking. After two months in bed, it had been more difficult than he'd ever imagined. There were a few more pages of contemporary parliamentary reports. He flicked past them and there was Mona.

The sight of her made him start. It was an enlargement of an official photo from her passport, or ID documents. The picture made her look stern, but then all booth-type snapshots the newspapers borrowed in the aftermath of tragedy appeared to do that. Beneath the picture, set halfway down the third page of the *Egyptian Gazette,* Egypt's English-language daily, the caption read: ''Mona Hamdi, photographer for the London *Times,* killed in Asyut crowd stampede.''

Girling had no desire to reread the official account of her death. He replaced the things in the box and moved to the shelf beside Stansell's desk. It was lined with back issues from Stansell's career, bound religiously into fading volumes. For one so apparently disorganized, Girling thought, it was a curious discipline. Beyond the seven years' worth of *Dispatches,* there were other volumes, all present, all complete. Except one.

Girling's finger stopped at the point where the July–December 1979 *Dispatches* binder should have been. He started to look for it, somehow anxious that this diligent record should be restored to its proper complement, but gave up when Sharifa returned with two copper jugs brimming with piping hot coffee, its strong, spicy aroma instantly filling the room.

''Have you found anything?'' she asked as she poured his coffee into a cup.

''Not yet.'' He took the coffee. ''Thanks.''

''Tom, the police have been through this place already.''

''Their toothcomb,'' Girling said, ''isn't quite the same as mine.''

''They still managed to find his contact book.''

Girling began picking through the contents of a box. ''I know. Al-Qadi lost little time in telling me. Where was it, did they tell you?''

She shook her head. ''Most of what I know about the case comes from snatches of conversations I've picked up around the police.''

''Did you hear any mention of his notebook? Al-Qadi was evasive, or maybe he misunderstood when I asked, but Stansell must have made notes. I know if I were Stansell and I were onto something as big as he was, I would have hidden them somewhere.''

''I have heard nothing,'' she said.

"Then maybe they're still around." He fanned through the pages of a book as he spoke. "By the way, you wouldn't know where a volume of Stansell's *Dispatches* wandered off to, would you?"

She shrugged. "No. Is it important?"

"Probably not." He carried on searching the box.

"Do you think you can find him?" she asked suddenly.

He paused and looked up at her. The dark glasses and scarf made her look like she were in official mourning.

"I've got to."

"Tom, this is Cairo, not Kensington."

Girling tossed the book back into a box. "The *mukhabarat* are just going through the motions. You know that as well as I do. Stansell needs someone else on his case. Well, I'm here now." He looked up at the shelves, the piles of magazines, the newspaper cuttings and all Stansell's other work props. "But I need to get to know him again."

Girling sat at the desk. He removed the top drawer and began picking his way through the detritus that Stansell kept next to him. It was the sort of junk that filled the drawers of his own desk: letters awaiting replies, others lying unopened in limbo between the trash can and the filing cabinet; a bottle of typewriter correcting fluid; a pack of Stansell's business cards held together by a plastic band. Paper clips, endless paper clips.

"I don't suppose he started keeping a desk diary?" he asked.

"No," she said softly. "You know him better than that."

"And his pocket diary was on him when he was taken?"

"I guess so. He always kept it on him. The police certainly don't have it."

"How do you know that?"

"What?"

"That the police don't have his diary."

For a moment she seemed confused. "Did I say that?"

"Yes."

She shrugged. "A hunch. Is it really important, Tom?" she retorted testily.

"Everything could be important. Stansell's somewhere out there and he doesn't have much time. What about tapes? The ones he put his interviews on?"

"The *mukhabarat* took them away."

Girling pulled out another drawer, then stopped. "Tell me what happened the day he went missing."

She had arrived at Stansell's apartment to find the door knocked off its hinges, the note from the terrorists anchored to the desk by an ashtray. She told him how al-Qadi and his team arrived, several hours later, followed by the *mukhabarat*'s forensic people.

Every now and then, Girling questioned her on details; but for Sharifa, recalling the minutiae wasn't always easy. Much of the day in question she had been in shock. When he was satisfied he had all she knew, Girling asked her to cast her mind back six days to the moment the terrorists blew the plane.

"That evening Jack Carey ordered him to drop everything and go for the terrorists at Beirut. He spoke to me, because Stansell was out."

"Where was he?"

"Midday he went to a reception at the Russian embassy, but I don't know what time he left. He didn't always like to tell me where he was going. That said, I—"

"Yes?"

"Finding him wasn't usually very difficult."

He sensed her reluctance. "Go on."

"One day it would be the Metropolitan Club, another it would be the piano bar in the Hilton. Or maybe, the English Pub out at Heliopolis."

"That doesn't come as any great surprise," Girling said. "That was how he liked to do business."

"This wasn't business, Tom. It wasn't just the odd lunch."

Girling had a fleeting image of Moynahan, ruddy-faced and red-eyed, sneering at him during the news meeting. "So Stansell drinks," he said. "He's always been a drinker. That's Stansell." He smiled. "Stansell always liked a drink, Sharifa."

She nodded. "He wasn't happy when you left."

"It's not as if I haven't spoken to him in three years," he said defensively.

Sharifa moved over to the window and looked out over Cairo's skyline. "Couldn't we talk about this later?"

"I want you to tell me now," he said. "What didn't he want me to know?"

She tossed her thick, black hair over her shoulders. "He kept the copy coming in, but he found it more and more difficult. He's not young—"

"You make him sound like a lonely old man," he said. "A drunk, tired, lonely old man."

Sharifa looked away.

Girling managed to keep his voice even. He forced himself back to Stansell's itinerary. "But that day, the day Jack Carey called, you didn't know where he was?"

"No."

Girling sat back in the chair. Suddenly, he felt exhausted. He could have slept right there, but he got to his feet and checked the floorboards. None of them seemed loose. He looked beneath the two tables, but there was nothing taped to their undersides.

"So when did you next see him?" he asked.

"Not until the following day. I arrived at the office early and found Stansell already here. He hardly spoke. He just sat at the desk—right there—staring at the piece of paper with Carey's message on it. Then he got out a map and started writing on it. I don't know what."

Girling stopped pacing. Sharifa had removed her sunglasses. She seemed transfixed by the desk.

"When you were a kid, did you ever put a butterfly that was sapped of strength onto a little bit of sugar?" she asked. "Did you see how it would flex its wings, how the life would come back to it?"

He hadn't, but he understood.

"He threw himself into this story like he was a cub reporter again," she continued. "I knew he was onto something, but he wouldn't tell me about it. He rarely discussed big stories with me. The day . . . that day, he returned here late in the afternoon excited about something. His eyes shone, he was short of breath. He called London and held a whispered conversation with someone, Kelso maybe, or Jack Carey."

"It was me," Girling said. "Looking back on it, I think he might have been saying good-bye."

"He knew who they were, didn't he?"

"He said he did." He didn't bother to tell her about Kelso's duplicity, or his own shame. She would already have got the details off somebody in London.

"That was the last time I saw him," she said.

It was some time before Girling spoke. "Did he talk to you about his contacts, at all?"

She shook her head. "You know what he was like about the people he dealt with."

"The most important thing in Stansell's life was that little black book," Girling said. "I wonder if al-Qadi realizes what he's got."

■   ■   ■

HALF AN hour later, Sharifa dropped Girling at the apartment in Hassan Assem Street, across the river in Zamalek.

"Call me, day or night," she said.

Girling had decided that he would stay at Stansell's for as long as it took. He wanted to immerse himself again in Stansell's shadowy life.

A lone militiaman appeared from the shadows of the lobby. The elevator was out of order, forcing him to hump his bags up four flights of stairs. The hasty repairs to the apartment door were readily apparent—nails hammered through the wood to secure the lock, and a shiny new hinge.

Girling used the key Sharifa had given him and let the door swing open. He stepped just inside and looked slowly around him.

It was as he remembered it, a large, airy affair, filled with functional furniture. Its plainness contrasted with the beautiful collection of watercolors and prints that Stansell had garnered from all corners of the Middle East. To Girling's left was the sitting room. Beyond that, the balcony overlooking the front of the block and the back street below. Before him was the dining room that Stansell used as an office, and to his right, the long corridor, off which were three bedrooms, kitchen and bathroom.

Stansell's desk rested against the opposite wall. Its surface was still covered with forensic powder. The *mukhabarat*'s investigators were long gone, but the powder was everywhere.

Girling lingered in front of the photo frames documenting Stansell's career. There were old pictures of Stansell with Sadat, Qadhafi, Shamir and Arafat, plus some he hadn't seen before, including one of the two of them lifting their Stella bottles at the bar of the Metropolitan, old Mansour, the waiter, looking on benignly. Girling picked it up and blew the forensic dust from the frame. Stansell's eyes appeared strikingly blue in the light of the camera flash. The crow's-feet that creased their edges gave him a scholarly look. He had a full beard graying at the chin. For his age, he was a good-looking man. Girling knew that Stansell, half a head taller than Girling's six foot as they stood beside the bar, would not have succumbed without a hell of a fight the night the Angels came for him, however much drink he'd had inside him.

The picture had been taken the day his job offer came through from *Dispatches.* Mona had been dead six, maybe seven months. Much of the intervening period had been a blur. But the offer had been a big step toward his recovery. And like so much of his gradual recuperation, it had been brought about by Stansell. A week later, Girling had passed by his parents-in-law in Medinat-al-Sahafeen, picked up his baby daughter and boarded the plane for the United Kingdom, a new career and a new life. That had been the theory, anyhow.

Girling replaced the photo, knowing that, sooner rather than later, he would have to see Mona's parents. It was not a meeting he relished having. For as long as he and Mona had been married, they had never accepted him. And in the three years he had been back in England he had not communicated, except to send them a picture of their granddaughter each Christmas.

Girling started with the bathroom. He checked the tiles, inside the toilet tank and behind the panels lining the bath, but found nothing. Next he moved into the kitchen. He flicked on the light and heard the scuttle of cockroaches pelting for the shadows. Like all kitchens in Egypt, Stansell's was dark, functional and devoid of comforts; a place for storing and preparing food, nothing more. He inspected the fridge and the freezer, opening cartons and packets for anything that was not supposed to be there.

When the heat became intolerable, Girling moved to the window and heaved it open. A fire escape led down to the ground. The building was like a bad tooth, scrubbed clean on the outside, but decaying in parts that the eye could not normally see. There was rubbish everywhere and its smell rose to meet him. He shut the window and suffered the heat.

It was late afternoon by the time he finished searching the bedrooms and moved on to the dining room. The desk seemed the most obvious place to start, but it was also where the police had spent the most time, judging from the dust. Girling turned instead to the shelves on the opposite wall where Stansell kept his books. There were hundreds of them. Each would have to be searched. He only wished he knew what he was looking for.

He spotted the missing volume of *Dispatches* leaning against a collection of books on the lower shelf. He picked it up and thumbed through it. Tucked away at the back was a Cairo street map. Girling opened it up and laid it on the dining room table. It was marked in two places, both in the same black ink. A nearby street called Ibn Zanki had been underlined and the number 22 written beside it. Girling made a note of the address in his notebook. And a large black arrow had been etched from Ibn Zanki across town toward the City of the Dead.

Girling refolded the map and put it back inside the binder. Was this what Sharifa had seen him scribbling on in the office?

It took until dusk to go through the other books. And all for nothing. His head throbbed and print swam before his eyes.

It was tempting just to ignore the desk, or come back to it the following day. Sleep beckoned, but Girling shook himself awake. He turned on the swing-arm lamp and inclined it so that it shone directly into the well of the desk. Straight ahead were drawers and pigeonholes. He peered inside the latter. There were electricity and phone bills, a receipt from an electrical shop at the bottom of the street, an empty cigarette packet—the *mukhabarat* had probably helped themselves— and a photograph. Girling held the picture under the lamp. The colors had faded so much that for a moment he thought it was black-and-white. Stansell was on the left of the picture, beardless, slim and handsome, cigarette dangling raffishly from his mouth. A woman, blond hair stiff with hairspray, stood beside him. His ex-wife? Maybe.

He removed each of the four drawers in turn, emptied them and examined the contents.

One item, a letter, made him stop abruptly when he saw the name of the addressee. He pulled the letter from the envelope. Stansell's spidery writing sprawled across five pages. He read the first page and a few lines into the next, then refolded it and put it back, not quite sure what to make of it all, except that he felt grubby and intrusive. There were things in this room that he was never meant to know about. He was glad he had almost finished.

Before returning all the other things, he rapped his knuckles over the desk, satisfying himself that there was no hollow space.

Girling collapsed, exhausted, into one of the armchairs. The police had everything. For all his caution, Stansell had as good as given the tools of his profession to al-Qadi on a plate. As he stared at the photo of Stansell, relaxed and smiling at the bar of the Metropolitan Club, Girling was overcome by a mixture of disillusionment and depression.

CHAPTER 2

SCHLITZ WAS THE INFORMATION OFFICER at the U.S. Embassy. He had an office on the second floor that rivaled Stansell's for chaos. A steady breeze from the air-conditioning unit ruffled the papers on his desk. Rather than clear them away, Schlitz anchored them with ashtrays, a photo frame, some books, an assortment of pens, anything solid that came to hand.

The man chain-smoked worse than an Egyptian, which accounted for the gravelly resonance behind his deep, slow, Southern drawl. Schlitz offered beer, but Girling stuck to coffee. It was not yet nine o'clock.

"Sure you won't change your mind?" Schlitz asked, pointing to the small fridge behind his desk.

Girling held up a hand. "No, thanks. Really." He was sitting directly across the desk from the American.

Schlitz chuckled. "And you say you're a colleague of Stansell's?"

"I'm still acclimatizing," Girling said lamely.

Schlitz patted his considerable belly. "Just so long as the pharaoh ain't gotten his revenge on you yet."

Girling smiled. "I have a tough constitution."

Schlitz studied Girling's business card again. "In this place, you need one! Says here you're the technology correspondent. Is there some kind of exhibition going on in town that I missed?"

Girling shook his head. "I'm minding the Middle East bureau desk for a while."

"You've taken over from Stansell?"

"Only temporarily. The whole thing happened pretty fast."

"So, what happened to Stansell? The old bastard kept this pretty quiet."

Girling leaned forward till his face was in the slipstream of the air conditioner. "Can I rely on your discretion, Mike?"

"That's usually my line." Schlitz stopped smiling when he saw Girling's expression. "Sure, course you can."

"Stansell's been sent home."

"Why?"

Girling leaned back again. Schlitz was the gossipy kind. The fact that he summoned Girling so quickly to his office—when all Girling ever expected was to be allowed to leave his business card at the main desk—suggested the guy had precious little else to do except peddle chitchat with journalists. That was fine by him.

"We ran a story last week about the terrorists who carried out the Beirut massacre—"

"The Angels of Judgment," Schlitz said. "Hell of a story."

"Yes it was."

"Well?" Schlitz asked, lighting up another Marlboro.

"Threats were made. Terrorist threats. Against Stansell. My bosses thought it safer if he were to lie low for a while." Girling looked straight at Schlitz. "So, he's in England until some of the heat dies down. Only trouble is, the old bastard's gone and given me a king-sized problem."

Schlitz took a deep drag and laughed, snorting the smoke out though his nostrils. "Like they're gonna blow your ass away instead, right? Nice friends you keep there, Tom."

Girling laughed, too. "Terrorists are the least of my problems."

"Oh?"

"My editor's going to have my balls unless I maintain steam on this one. His attitude is, *Dispatches* led with it and now we've got to stay ahead of the pack. And Stansell's gone and dumped me in the shit.''

''Tough break,'' Schlitz said. ''So how can I help you?''

''Is there any chance I can meet with some of your military people? The defense attaché, for example. Anyone who could give me some background on the hunt for the terrorists and the hostages.''

Schlitz shook his head slowly. ''No can do, Tom. Maybe in London they've got folks who give intel briefs, but I'm not authorized to do that kind of shit. Besides, I doubt if the DA would want to know.''

''Come on, Mike. *Dispatches* broke this story, for Christ's sake.''

''I'm sorry, but . . .'' He paused. ''I'll give you this for free. Off the record, though, or it'll be me who has your balls.'' Schlitz studied Girling's face for a moment. ''This Beirut business has got everyone jumping around here. Throughout the embassy the teleprinters are chattering like some sort of dawn chorus. I've been in this business a long time—twenty five years, anyway—but I ain't seen faces around me this long since . . . well, since Teheran.''

''So, no progress then?'' Girling said. ''Franklin is still lost?''

''Don't go putting words in my mouth, now.''

''I wasn't.''

Schlitz's eyes narrowed, then his face broke into a smile. ''Never trust a guy you ain't drunk with, that's my motto,'' he said, reaching down behind him. He passed over a dripping can of cold Budweiser.

Girling pulled the ring and brought the can up to his lips.

''I tell you what I'll do,'' Schlitz said. ''How about I get you and the DA over to my place? Shirtsleeve stuff, nothing formal. Do you play volleyball? We play most weekends. The DA does a mean game and his wife's not bad either, if you get what I mean. You married, Tom?''

''I was,'' Girling said.

''Here's the deal, then. If you and the DA get along okay . . . well, what you do after that is your business.''

''I look forward to the invitation. What's his name, by the way, the defense attaché?''

''Lieutenant Colonel Cyrus McBain, United States Air Force.''

Girling got to his feet. ''Thanks for the beer.'' He'd taken just one sip.

They shook hands and Girling turned for the door. His hand was on the handle when Schlitz asked: "Stansell ain't in any kind of trouble, is he, Tom?"

Girling froze for a second. He turned to face the American. "Like I said—"

Schlitz waved him down. "I know what you said. Only I was talking to a guy from Reuters. You ever read any of John Silverman's stuff? He's good." Girling had more than read Silverman's stories, he had kept in touch with Silverman in the years since he had left.

"Seems he got paid a visit by the police—the serious squad, not those jokers from the '*askary*,'" Schlitz continued. "You know who I mean by the *mukhabarat?* Internal security. Some of them are real bad-asses."

"I know the *mukhabarat*," Girling said. "Maybe I should have told you earlier. I used to work here. A few years back."

Schlitz apparently didn't hear him. "The police were asking who Stansell hangs around with, who his contacts are. The third degree. This pal of mine was pretty upset, I don't mind telling you. Journalists around here don't like the *mukhabarat* much. None of us do."

Girling's grip tightened on the door handle. "When did this happen?"

"This morning. I put the phone down on the guy just before you walked in."

Girling stepped out of Schlitz's office. So the *mukhabarat* were leaning on Stansell's pals for details of his contacts. Yet, everything they needed to know should have been under their noses, in Stansell's little black book, the one that was supposedly in al-Qadi's hands.

All of which could mean only one thing. The *mukhabarat* were bluffing. They didn't have it; never had. Al-Qadi had been trying to save face.

As Girling checked out of the embassy into the rising heat, he couldn't help but feel a little elated.

This time he knew just where to start looking again.

■   ■   ■

SHARIFA HEARD a slight sound behind her. The gooseflesh rippled the skin from the base of her slender neck to the hairline above her forehead. She turned and al-Qadi was there, leaning against the filing cabinet. She guessed he must have been there for quite some time, just watching her.

"I have come to talk to you about Girling," he said. "Where is he?"

She said nothing. Defiance leapt at him from her eyes.

Al-Qadi moved toward her. His trousers were damp where his left thigh had rested against the cabinet. Sharifa swiveled to face him, clamping her fingers to the underside of the chair as she did so. She gripped it tightly to stop her shaking.

"I asked you a question," he said, perching on the edge of her desk. He spoke to her in Arabic. In his own language, he lisped just the same.

"I don't know where he is," she whispered.

"It's not quite that simple, is it, *ya* Sharifa?" The investigator drew a pencil from the ornamental wooden box in front of her. He pressed the lead point a little way into his thumb and smiled. It was quite sharp.

Still she said nothing.

"You seemed pleased to see him," al-Qadi probed.

"Tom Girling and I are old friends."

He cocked an eyebrow.

"I was at the university with his wife," she said.

"Of course . . . the girl who died in Asyut."

"Mona was killed."

"If you say so."

"We were best friends."

"And now you are *his* friend."

"We were friends then and we're friends now. We'll always be friends."

"And do you want to pleasure yourself with this '*agnabi,* too, *ya* Sharifa?"

"You bastard!" she whispered.

"Careful . . ." al-Qadi pointed the pencil at her face.

She bit her lip. Tears of frustration and anger welled up behind her eyes.

"I suppose you're going to tell me Stansell was different from the others."

"I loved him," she whispered. For a moment, it was as if al-Qadi was not in the room. As if she heard the echo of her own voice. "I still do."

"How touching." Al-Qadi's eyes traced a path from her neck to the shapely outline of her breasts.

"I want you to swear now that you had nothing to do with his abduction," she said.

"I don't have to swear anything to you, *ya* Sharifa. But let me say this. What purpose would it serve me?"

"If you have lied, I will kill you."

Al-Qadi sighed heavily. "Where was I? Ah, yes. Girling. His whereabouts today are not important." He smiled at her with his tiny eyes. "Because you are going to tell me his every movement."

She gasped. "I'd sooner die."

"I wouldn't say that too lightly if I were you."

Al-Qadi moved quickly, grabbed a handful of hair and pulled her head back sharply until she thought her neck would break. He pressed the tip of the pencil to her cheek. She yelped with the pain.

"I could drive this right through your face," he said. "Such a beautiful face."

She gasped. "No, please."

"Then keep your eyes and ears open. You let me know when you see or hear anything, understand? Or else—" she felt his spittle hit her face.

Al-Qadi released his grip and Sharifa fell back into the chair. She saw the erection straining against the tight linen of his trousers. Al-Qadi looked between her and his watch. Then he gave a cluck of irritation and moved awkwardly for the door.

■   ■   ■

As HE rode the elevator to the ground floor, al-Qadi gave his belt a final tug and adjusted his underwear with his other hand. He wanted her badly. Sharifa Fateem was everything. She was high-class—her father was a rich industrialist—she was smart, she had been well educated, she was beautiful, most assuredly so, and she was a whore. It was the latter point, knowledge that was his alone, that teased him so much.

But today he had other matters to attend to.

The elevator doors opened and al-Qadi stepped through the lobby and into the scorching sunshine.

He was worried that he had underestimated Girling. Maybe he had placed too much faith in the man's records. Yesterday, he had not seen a broken man, a man unable to grip reality after the violent death of his wife. Yesterday, he had not seen the husk of a man described in the records. Until today, al-Qadi had neglected to consider one very important fact. It was Stansell who had brought Girling back from the dead. Now that Girling was at large somewhere in his city, al-Qadi regretted not having put a tail on him from the moment he arrived. As of now, however, Girling would be watched night and day.

He clicked his fingers and the Mercedes with the blackened windows pulled alongside. He ordered his driver to take him back to headquarters in Shubra.

∎   ∎   ∎

GIRLING STOOD before the bar of the Metropolitan Club. The crooked blades of a fan rotated noisily above his head. He surveyed the room slowly. Both the decaying armchairs were occupied; one by a man wearing a shabby suit who was immersed in the pages of *al-Ahram*, Egypt's highbrow daily paper, the other by a portly gentleman whose snores filled the air. Sunlight streamed through a gap in the blinds. The room was filled with a musty smell that reminded Girling of old books. Stansell liked the Metropolitan because it was halfway between a decrepit London club and an opium den.

Girling sat at the bar and hit the bell. The snoring stopped and the newspaper crackled. The man in the suit went back to his reading. The snorer slumbered on.

Girling heard the shuffle of slippers across flagstones. The bead curtains parted behind the bar to admit the concierge. His eyes narrowed momentarily as he tried to remember where he had seen this 'agnabi before. But Girling knew there was only one member of the Metropolitan's staff with that sort of memory for faces.

"You would like a room?"

"No, thank you," Girling said. It was then he noticed that the sherry keg that should have been on the shelf behind the bar was gone.

"A drink, perhaps?" the man asked, following his gaze. "We have beer, cold beer in the—"

"No," Girling said. "Thank you." Mansour was no longer there.

The thought had never occurred to him. Mansour, as old as the Muqattam Hills and just as proud, was the Metropolitan Club. "I was looking for Mansour," he said.

"Mansour?" the concierge asked incredulously. "The old man?"

"Yes."

"Mansour has not worked here for over two years." The eyes narrowed in suspicion. "Why do you seek him, *'agnabi*?"

Girling ducked the question. "It's important that I find him."

"How important?"

Girling slipped a five-pound note across the wood surface of the bar.

The concierge looked down and pulled thoughtfully at the edges of his mustache. "Not that important, then."

Girling reached into his pocket and doubled the amount. "It's very important."

The concierge's fingers went to his mustache again. He began to shake his head slowly from side to side.

"I am a friend of Stansell's," Girling said, anxious to put an end to this game.

The concierge's eyes widened. "Stansell? Why did you not say so before?"

Girling looked down and the money was gone.

The concierge pulled a bottle of *araq* from the shelf behind him. He filled a glass and slid it across the bar. "For a friend of Stansell's."

Girling hesitated. To refuse a gift or favor was tantamount to spitting in the man's face. He tipped the burning-hot liquor down his throat. To his relief, the bottle was replaced on the shelf.

"When you see Stansell, tell him his friends at the Metropolitan Club miss him. He has not visited us in a long time."

Girling had the feeling the concierge missed Stansell's money more than the man. "How long?"

"A month, maybe more."

Which meant more like six months, Girling thought. "You were trying to remember where Mansour had gone," he prompted.

"Ah yes, Mansour."

"Did he have family?"

"No, no family. Mansour was alone. That is why he worked. But his eyes, his legs . . . no good. He had to go."

"Where?" Girling pressed.

"Maybe in Khan al-Khalili. Maybe."

The Khan was a huge, fifty-acre tourist market over in al-Gamaliya, part of the old quarter. Girling knew he could spend a year in there and never even catch a glimpse of Mansour.

"How do you mean, maybe?"

"Someone said he saw him working at Kareem's coffeehouse on the Street of the Judges. But that was nearly a year ago."

Girling's heart sank. Old Mansour was probably dead by now. He got to his feet.

"Where are you going?" the concierge asked.

"To the Street of the Judges." It had to be worth a shot still.

"But it is Friday, my friend. Kareem's is closed until sundown." He bowed his head twice to demonstrate the prayer ritual. "On Fridays, until sunset, the Street of the Judges is a holy place."

Girling swore under his breath. "By the way, that old sherry keg that used to be behind the bar . . ." He pointed to a place between the bottles. "What happened to it?"

For a moment, the concierge was confused. Girling described the sherry keg, with a brand name he couldn't remember written on the side. Mansour had always treated it as his proudest possession.

"Ah, that," the concierge said. "We threw it away. I have seen better trash on sale outside the Cairo Museum. This is a hotel, not a third-rate tourist bazaar."

■　　　■　　　■

THE NOISE of the two Antonov An-124s of Voyenno-Transportnaya Aviatsiya—Military Transport Aviation—rumbled in the heavens as their pilots throttled back to line up on the mobile instrument-landing system deployed by the Pathfinders.

The moment they heard the turbofans, Ulm, Doyle and Jones were out of the hardened aircraft shelter, the HAS, and into the dusk air, straining for a glimpse of them.

It was Jones who first spotted the lead ship as it passed across the ebbing sun, pulling around in a wide bank to line up on Qena's main runway.

The Pathfinders watched in silence as the aircraft, with their capacity to carry even more than America's own giant Galaxies, slipped from the skies as effortlessly as eagles. Even without radar or the luxury of voice communication, the Russians had picked Qena out of the desert like it was JFK.

"Some sight, huh?" Doyle said. The Pathfinders' intelligence officer scratched his head. "Never thought I'd live to see it."

The three of them watched the first An-124 cannonball pass their position, brakes smoking, engines in full reverse as the crew struggled to slow its enormous rolling mass.

Jones followed the progress of the second aircraft down the runway. "Us and Ivan—it still don't feel right."

"At least we're out of New Mexico," the intelligence officer said.

"Well, pardon my French, sir, but this ain't exactly fucking Disneyland."

Ulm wandered away from them, down to the taxiway. The lead Antonov, still a hundred and fifty yards away, dwarfed him.

"What's eating the boss?" Jones asked.

"What do you think?" Doyle said. "Working with Ivan scares the shit out of him, too."

The first An-124 slewed around to face the HAS that had been designated as the Soviets' storage area. The aircraft braked sharply, shivering with the vibration. Thirty feet above the surface of the tarmac a door opened and a telescopic ladder deployed to the ground. Shabanov was silhouetted briefly in the doorframe. He had swapped his clean, pressed uniform for combat fatigues. Poking above the camouflage overshirt was the prized blue-and-white T-shirt of Spetznaz.

Shabanov pounded down the steps and came to attention before the American.

"It begins, Elliot."

"Sure." Ulm found himself shouting over the Antonov's idling turbofans. "How was the flight?"

"A textbook deception. The identification transponders worked flawlessly."

Behind Shabanov, the visor nose of the An-124 was lifting slowly over the cockpit. Under the glare of floodlights in the Antonov's roof, the cavernous interior was bathed in brightness. Already, soldiers strained against the first Mi-24J. The Antonov's ramp had no sooner hit the ground than the helicopter gunship was rolled onto the tarmac.

An officer barked orders and the Mi-24J was wheeled into the hangar, followed shortly by another. There were two more Mils in the second Antonov. The rest of the floor space in both aircraft was taken up with the building materials Shabanov required for his dummy camp in the desert.

Ulm jabbed a finger in the direction of the helicopter. "So that's the Mi-24J. Don't look so special to me." In fact, it looked much like any other recent edition of the Hind, the helicopter the Soviets made infamous during the Afghan war.

"Outwardly the same," Shabanov said. "But inside, a new animal."

"Yeah?"

Ulm had asked Doyle to make inquiries on the Mi-24J before they left Kirtland, but nobody at the Pentagon knew anything about it. It was that new.

"It marries the rotors, engines, dynamics, fire-control system and avionics of the new Mi-38 tankbuster with the Mi-24 airframe. The result, a fifty percent improvement in performance. The Mil design bureau is very proud of it. They believe it will perform well."

"It has to earn the right to fly into Lebanon," Ulm said.

"True." Shabanov looked around him. "Where are the Sikorskys?"

"In the hangars, fueled up and ready to go. Man, I'd forgotten how much helos hate sand. This kind of sand, anyway."

"Give me an hour to stow the equipment," Shabanov said. "Then we hold a briefing for all the men."

■   ■   ■

THERE WERE children dressed in rags playing noisily on the steps when Girling arrived at the apartment block in Medinat-al-Sahafeen, a poor district on the edge of the city.

As soon as they spotted him, the children swarmed around his legs, tugging at the hem of his jacket and the cloth of his trousers. Though there were only six of them, they made the noise of a school playground, hands outstretched for his money.

Girling dug into his pockets and distributed his change amongst them. They ran off into the dust squealing with pleasure.

He knocked on the apartment door. Above him, evening light

streamed through a hole in the roof. There was a shuffle from within and the door opened.

Girling's mother-in-law was dressed in a *helaliya,* a somber all-over garment popular amongst Egyptian countrywomen. Her kohl-lined eyes widened slightly, the only outward show of surprise she allowed herself. In the few times Girling had met her, she had never once addressed a word to him. Custom forbade communication with strangers, and especially an *'agnabi,* in the remote village of her birth. Though her husband was from a simple family himself, neither tradition nor religion had ever placed any such constraints upon his behavior. He had never been afraid to speak his mind.

Girling took a step inside and his mother-in-law retreated behind a door off the living room. He heard her whispers and the gruff response they elicited. There was a metallic creak of bedsprings. It seemed he had interrupted Mohammed Hamdi's late-afternoon sleep.

Girling walked into the sitting room. It contained one or two heavy, ornate pieces of furniture, Egyptian copies of French late-nineteenth-century designs. There was lace everywhere—over the tables, the chair backs, and in front of the windows. There was a portrait of Mona on a small table beside him. It made him feel as if he were in a funeral parlor.

In the short time they had lived together in Egypt, Mona had brought him here just once. Her father never made any bones about his dislike for him. And for his part, Girling had never made any special effort to turn his view around. Out of deference to the two men she loved, Mona considered it best they should keep apart.

After her death, it was only natural that her parents should look after Alia. It was natural, too, that they should form a strong attachment to their granddaughter in the long months of his recuperation. Stansell warned him that they might choose to take the law into their own hands. And so it was that, as soon as he was able, he came to pay his respects and thank them for looking after his baby daughter. He knew from the furtive looks they gave him that Stansell was right, that they were planning to keep her. A week later, on his way to the airport, he arrived without warning. He told them he was taking little Alia home, to England. It had been an undignified, painful occasion. He could still remember the look of rage on Mohammed Hamdi's face and the sound of his wife's wailing behind the closed door of her bedroom as he carried his daughter to the waiting taxi. Because Mona had loved her father deeply, Girling was sad that he had had to act so drastically. But he felt that he had had no choice.

Girling replaced the picture of his wife a moment before he heard the scrape of the old man's slippers on the bare floor behind him.

Three years before, Mohammed Hamdi had been a big man, with a barrel chest, great, strong arms and the largest pair of hands Girling had ever seen. Now, one look revealed the extent to which the cancer had him in its grip.

From behind their thick, pebble glasses, two piercing brown eyes held Girling in a reproachful stare. The look of Mona in those eyes suddenly made Girling's heart go out to the man.

"You know there is only one reason in the world that stops me from throwing you out of this house, don't you?"

"I understand your feelings, Mohammed Hamdi."

"Is the little one with you?"

"No. She is in England."

The light that had shone momentarily in his eyes went out. "I see."

Girling reached for his wallet. He removed a photograph he had taken just a few weeks before and handed it to the old man. "Keep it," he said, awkwardly.

Mohammed Hamdi studied the picture for a little while. "For a moment, I thought . . ."

"I know. But Alia's in England. She's with my parents. She's happy. She has a good school and friends, many friends. You would be proud of her."

Mohammed Hamdi held a thin arm toward the door.

"We have only one thing in common now, and since she is not here . . ." His voice, though weak, was steady. "It would be better, I think, if you left."

"I'm asking for a moment of your time, Mohammed Hamdi."

"Whatever brings you here, it must be the Devil's own reason."

"It is. I'm here because of what happened to Mona."

Mohammed Hamdi lowered himself shakily into one of the lace-covered armchairs. With his face as somber as a judge's, he gestured for Girling to sit in the chair opposite. His hand went instinctively for the cigarette box on the table beside him.

"Explain yourself."

Girling hesitated. "I know you can never look upon me as a friend, but I need your help, Mohammed Hamdi."

His father-in-law had just inhaled a deep lungful of smoke. For a moment, Girling thought he would choke. His eyes watered, but he managed to exhale without spluttering. "My help?"

It took Girling five minutes to explain the circumstances surrounding Stansell's abduction.

"What does this have to do with Mona? What does this have to do with me?" Mohammed Hamdi asked.

"You can help me find him."

"I've been retired two years now. And besides, even if I wanted to help you . . ." He held his two hands, fingers pointing inward, to show the extent of his body's collapse.

"I know," Girling said. "I'm sorry."

Mohammed Hamdi had been a beat policeman for more than twenty years when promotion took him into the criminal investigation branch of the '*askary,* the regular police. For all his dogged thoroughness, he had found his efforts constantly confounded by his rivals in the *mukhabarat,* the hard bastards from internal security. Girling knew, because Mona had told him. She was fiercely proud of her father. A peasant by birth, he had worked hard, in the face of considerable prejudice, to save the money to send Mona abroad. All along, her mother, an intensely religious woman, had objected vehemently to his plans. But Mohammed Hamdi, a true meritocrat, knew the value of a foreign education. And, though his religion demanded otherwise, his desire for his daughter to have the best start in life overcame fears for her soul and the objections of his wife. Mona maintained her mother had never forgiven him.

"I fail to see that this Stansell has anything to do with my daughter," Mohammed Hamdi said.

"When the Brotherhood killed Mona, I turned and ran away, Mohammed Hamdi. I'm not proud of that." He searched the old man's eyes for understanding, but found none. "This time, I'm not running. This time, I have to face the Brotherhood. But first I have to find them. And I don't know where to begin looking." Girling took a deep breath. "These Angels of Judgment could not have operated in Egypt without help. They would have needed a safe house, transport, papers . . . Do you understand what I'm saying? The only people who could have helped them are the Brotherhood.''

His father-in-law seemed flustered. "The *mukhabarat* handled all internal security matters. In the *'askary,* I was responsible for running down petty criminals, car thieves, drug peddlers, burglars, pick-pockets—"

"You know these men, Mohammed Hamdi. I know you do.''

Mohammed Hamdi coughed and shook his head.

"The people who assisted the Angels of Judgment here in Cairo are the same people who killed your daughter. Mona. My wife. I'm talking about the animals who beat the brains out of her on a dirt road beside the Nile three years ago.''

Mohammed Hamdi's hand crashed down on the arm of the chair. "All right, damn you,'' he croaked. "But it doesn't alter the fact that they were outside my jurisdiction, my official business.''

"Official business, yes.'' Girling paused. "But how did you fill the early days of your retirement, Mohammed Hamdi? Before this illness? Did you do nothing but stay behind these doors nursing your grief? If I know you, Mohammed Hamdi, you would have been out there, looking for the killers of your daughter.''

The ex-inspector's head hung limply on his chest. "Yes, I tried,'' he whispered.

Girling barely caught the words. "Then what happened?''

Mohammed Hamdi's hand crept to the cigarette box again. It took him an age to get one into his mouth, longer to make the lighter work.

"I journeyed to Asyut, to the very spot she died. The ground was still stained dark with her blood. I spoke to people, I followed leads. You don't forget how to do your job, you know. I was a detective for twenty-five years . . .''

"And what did you find there?''

"A trail.''

"To where?''

The ex-policeman raised his eyes. They were almost lost in the shadows of their sockets. "Everywhere.'' Mohammed Hamdi held his hands out wide. "It's all around us. It's in the streets, the markets, the garbage dumps . . . everywhere.''

"What is?''

"The hatred that killed her.'' He coughed again and his once-strong frame seemed as if it would implode. "Hatred murdered Mona," he said.

"You found them, didn't you, Mohammed Hamdi? You found Mona's killers."

"No."

"But you know them?"

"Yes."

Girling sat on the edge of his chair. "What are their names?"

"Knowing a name will not help you." Mohammed Hamdi's voice had begun to sound slow, drugged.

"Tell me, Mohammed Hamdi. I need to know it."

"It is not his real name."

"Are you talking about the ringleader?"

"Yes, the ringleader." The voice became still more indistinct.

Girling slipped onto his knees and took Mohammed Hamdi's emaciated hands in his. "You've got to tell me," he said softly.

"Abu Tarek, his name is Abu Tarek. That is how they know him in the Brotherhood."

"And where would I find Abu Tarek?"

"With the greatest of difficulty. Abu Tarek enjoys the protection of God."

A lump formed in Girling's throat. "He's dead?"

Mohammed Hamdi shook his head.

"Then . . . ?"

"Tom . . ."

Girling had never heard him say his name before.

"I loved my daughter far more than my own life. And yet, I think of the power that protects this man when I lie awake in the pit of the black night and I am scared beyond all reason."

"I, too, am scared, Mohammed Hamdi. But I've stopped running. And this time, with your help, I may be able to save a life."

Behind the old man's chair, the shadows moved. Girling glanced up to find his mother-in-law standing over them. He knew his time was short. He switched back to the old man. "Just give me an address. Please. I must act quickly."

"You want to know who killed our daughter?" It was Mona's mother who had spoken. Mohammed withdrew his hands from Girling's clasp.

Girling stared at her. Her face was hidden behind the veil, but her eyes held him like a sniper's open sight.

"Yes, tell me," he said.

"You killed her. You killed our daughter as though you yourself had hurled those rocks." Her veil bobbed lightly as she spoke. "You murdered our daughter the very day that you married her."

Girling glanced from her to her husband, but his head hung heavily on his chest.

"Leave us alone," she said. "You are not welcome here. Get out and don't ever come back."

Girling got up and walked out without saying another word.

It was dark when he left the apartment, and all the children had gone.

■   ■   ■

"ATTENTION," SHABANOV commanded.

Within the cavernous structure of the large, long-abandoned HAS, his voice carried effortlessly. There was a sharp noise, like parachute silk snapping in the wind, as the Pathfinders and Spetsnaz troops obeyed his command.

Shabanov and Ulm stood side-by-side on a hastily erected podium made out of crates disgorged from the C-5 Galaxies. The Pathfinders' own transports had come and gone the day before.

"Pathfinders," Shabanov said. "Do not let your feelings stand before the success of our mission. The fact that it is I and not Colonel Ulm who addresses you is an accident of fate, sealed by the politicians of our two countries. It is not important who leads the operation. American or Russian, his nationality does not matter. If we are successful, we will all share the credit. Try to understand the significance of this moment. Study your colleagues from Spetsnaz and you will see men no different from yourselves.

"We have around a week to prepare for the Angels of Judgment. There will be moments when you question my authority. So, let me give you an insight into the GRU's intelligence. The Angels of Judgment have training, they have sophisticated weapons and they have a fanatical devotion to their leader—not to mention their religion—that we cannot comprehend. The Soviet Army was guilty of complacency when we went into Afghanistan. But we Afghantsi learned our lesson—didn't we Bitov?'' Shabanov turned to a sergeant in the front row.

Starshina Ruslan Bitov, a great ox of a man, raised his left hand. Ulm saw that only two fingers remained. Bitov grinned. ''But they buried the bastard with half my hand up his ass, Colonel.''

''Bitov was fortunate,'' Shabanov said. ''The Angels of Judgment will show us no mercy when we go looking for our captive comrades. In one week, we will have to be drilled to perfection. The focus of your attention during this period will be a mock-up of Judgment's camp, to be constructed by my engineers in the desert. It will take time to find a valley that mirrors the one in which Judgment has made its base; and it will take time to erect the camp itself. In the meantime, we drill. We drill until we have got it right.''

Shabanov drove his fist into the open palm of his hand. ''One, we fly in to the Sword's camp. Two . . .'' the fist rammed home again '' . . . we locate and secure the hostages. Three, we annihilate the terrorists.''

Shabanov's knuckles whitened.

''Because my men have been hand-picked, among other things, for their linguistic ability, English will be adopted as standard.'' Shabanov turned to address his own men. ''Any deviation from this rule will entail punishment.''

There was a sudden roar from outside as the first of the two An-124s thundered down the runway and lifted into the night sky. Shabanov paused until both aircraft had departed, the sound of their engines receding into the night as they set their course for their operating base in Central Asia.

''In summary, by the end of our training you will be neither American nor Russian,'' Shabanov said. ''You will learn to work together, to think together, to trust each other. Such cooperation only comes with practice.

''So, I want you assembled here tomorrow at midnight. You will be organized into pairs—one Russian for every American—and flown by helicopter to separate locations in the desert, one hundred and twenty kilometers from here. It is a classic evade and escape exercise—E and E, as you Pathfinders call it. Each team will make its way back, undetected, within forty hours of the drop-off. Those late back will be made to do the exercise again. Perhaps, too, they will forfeit their place on the mission. I have no room for men who are not fit.''

Ulm studied his men. It was rough, but they could take it. They had endured worse.

''And to make it more interesting,'' Shabanov said, ''our helicopters will fly combat patrols into the desert to find you. Anyone located will be made to repeat the exercise. And they, too, may find themselves dropped from the mission.''

The Russian took a step backward. ''I suggest you rest now. It will certainly be the last you get for two days.''

■   ■   ■

THE TAXI, an Egyptian-made Fiat that had seen better days, clattered noisily along the 26th of July Street.

Girling took in the skyline and plotted the differences over the past three years. The number of luxury hotels had almost doubled; so too, had the lean-tos and corrugated-iron shanties.

The driver pulled up outside the Khan. After the somber observances of the holy day, the market was alive with festivity.

Girling paid the fare, crossed the road and took stock. The Khan stretched away in front of him, a sprawling mass of stalls and shops built up around the tiny streets—some no broader than a man's shoulders—that were the capillaries of the ancient bazaar. The arteries that fed them were five main thoroughfares, one of which was the Street of Judges. Girling consulted the map he had found in Stansell's apartment. By his reckoning, Kareem's coffeehouse lay a few hundred yards distant and straight ahead. As the crow flies. He knew that nothing would be quite that simple at ground level.

That he saw no other foreigners did not surprise him. Although a popular tourist attraction by day, the Khan was not the safest place in town for an *'agnabi* to be walking alone after dark.

Girling pulled up the collar of his jacket and plunged into the market. Most of the shop shutters were drawn. He navigated by the pools of light thrown by hurricane lamps and the occasional string of low-watt bulbs across the entranceways to the coffeehouses. In the dark, there was little to distinguish him as an *'agnabi.* He kept going, twisting and weaving along the tiny streets, mixing with the people as he went. Eventually the alley opened up into a main street. The openness of his surroundings, the blazing lights and the hordes of people suddenly made him feel quite naked. The shops, stalls and coffeehouses lay interspersed amid the mosques and the ancient mausoleums shown on the map. He had arrived at the Street of the Judges. He looked left and right, scouring the billboards for a sight of Kareem's. People had begun to stop and stare. It was with immense relief that he spotted the coffeehouse fifty yards from him on the opposite side of the street.

He brushed past the tables on the pavement, past the old men smoking their hookahs and into the bright, track-light-illuminated interior. No sooner had he reached the back of the shop than the chatter stopped. Girling found himself the object of uniform curiosity. The only waiter, a middle-aged man with brown teeth and a lazy eye, stopped what he was doing and turned around.

"We closed," he said. "Too late." He tapped his wrist where a watch should have been.

"I'm looking for Mansour," Girling said.

Lazy-Eye frowned and shook his head quickly from side to side, as Egyptians do when they are confused, or claim to be.

"Old Mansour," Girling said. "I was told he worked here."

"No Mansour here," Lazy-Eye said.

"I was told—"

"No. You leave now."

Girling hesitated. In the mirror on the wall in front of him he saw three customers get to their feet. Each was too well built for his liking. They began weaving a passage through the tables toward him.

Girling held his hands up. "Okay, I'm going," he said to the waiter. "*Aruh,*" he reiterated in Arabic, gesturing toward the door.

It was as his eyes swept past the mirror again that he saw the keg. It was low down in the reflection, nestling on a shelf under the work surface in front of him.

Girling switched his gaze back to the three bearing down on him. They were almost there.

There was a doorway set in the rear wall, a curtain across it. Girling brushed past the waiter and pushed the curtain aside. The little room was dark except for the glow of a charcoal fire. A man was picking out embers and placing them on small tobacco-filled clays. Some of the clays had been attached to hookahs, ready for delivery to waiting customers outside.

The figure did not seem to hear him enter. Girling heard the swish of the curtain behind him. He took a step forward and touched him lightly on the shoulder.

Old Mansour turned just as Girling's arms were wrenched back in a full nelson. He tried to shake himself loose, but they had him held fast.

Old Mansour stepped away from the fire and Girling felt the intensity of its heat.

As the light shone full on Girling's face, Mansour's eyes widened in recognition.

Behind him, voices rasped as his assailants questioned Mansour. The old man answered them patiently. The next thing Girling knew he was free and Mansour and he were alone.

Girling looked old Mansour up and down. He was a little more bowed in the frame, a little sallower of cheek. But it was Mansour, fit, alive.

"Forgive me, *ya* Mansour," Girling said in Arabic. "I never meant to embarrass you . . ."

Old Mansour replied in English. "It is I who should ask for forgiveness, Mr. Tom. They thought perhaps I owed you money. I am sorry. They were only trying to protect me."

"It is good that you have friends to look after you, Mansour."

"Yes, they are kind to me here."

"Mansour, I am looking for Stansell."

"I know."

Girling took a step closer to him. Mansour had blue eyes that were rare for an Egyptian and a white, bushy mustache. "Tell me how you know that, Mansour."

"Do you remember Uthman, the doctor from Duqqi?" Mansour said.

Girling confessed that he didn't.

"He used to drink at the Metropolitan Club, back in the old days," Mansour said. "Now he comes here for his water pipe. The rose water here is the best, they say, the pipes here the smoothest in Cairo. It was Uthman who told me about Stansell. These are terrible days, Mr. Tom."

Girling felt his pulse quicken. "How did Uthman know about Stansell? The police have tried to keep it a secret."

Old Mansour shrugged. "He works part-time at *mukhabarat* head-quarters in Shubra, working on the bodies—"

"Autopsies," Girling prompted.

"Yes. While there one night earlier this week, he heard about the kidnapping. It came as a great shock when Uthman told me. I liked Stansell very much, you know that, Mr. Tom."

"Yes, I know."

"But now you are here. And you have come for him, I think. This gives me great hope."

Girling didn't answer directly. "I am hoping you may be able to help, Mansour."

"Me? Of course, anything."

"Stansell's contact book," Girling said. "In emergencies, did he continue to leave it in your keeping after you left the Metropolitan Club?"

Old Mansour's watery eyes glazed for a moment. "The little book of names and telephone numbers?"

Girling knew the old man knew exactly what he meant. "Yes."

"Maybe he did, Mr. Tom."

"Do you have it now?"

"I . . . it was a sacred arrangement, Mr. Tom."

"It was the police he wanted you to hide it from, Mansour, not me."

Girling reached out and pressed a ten-pound note into Mansour's hand.

Mansour examined the money for a moment before looking up into Girling's eyes. "You know me better than this, Mr. Tom."

Old Mansour's expression darkened. He walked past Girling and headed out through the curtained doorway.

"Shit," Girling said to himself. The tenner was as much as Mansour made in a month. Yet money did not buy everything in this city. Some people were above bribery. He cursed himself.

He was about to follow after Mansour when the curtain parted again. Mansour was silhouetted against the lights at the front of the shop. He held the mock sherry keg in his hands.

"After the Metropolitan Club . . . dismissed me, they threw this out, too," the old man said.

"The book, Mansour . . ."

"If you ask for it, Mr. Tom, then it must be important."

Mansour twisted a catch at the base of the cask, opened it and pulled out a small pocket-sized volume, its covers held together by an elastic band. He handled it with reverence, as though it were the Koran, his fingers avoiding the dog-eared corners. The book looked as if it would crumble at the slightest touch. He passed it to Girling. As he did so, Girling noticed the edge of the ten-pound note poking above Old Mansour's vest pocket.

"In any case, it will be better in your hands," the old man said. "It will not be the *mukhabarat* that finds him. Uthman says they have put Captain al-Qadi on his case."

"Do you know him?" Girling asked.

"Not me, thank God. But Uthman says he has a certain reputation."

Girling opened the book carefully. Stansell lived a disorganized existence in most respects, but in his professional life he maintained a rigorous discipline. Against each surname was a first name or an initial, a job title, a date—presumably the day of their first meeting—an address and a telephone number. From a brief glance Girling estimated there were hundreds of entries. Maybe finding the contact book wasn't the great coup he had cracked it up to be.

"When did Stansell give you this, Mansour?"

"Five nights ago, Mr. Tom."

The night he was taken, Girling thought. "Did Stansell say where he had come from, or where he was going?"

"He was in a great hurry. We hardly talked. He used to come here to smoke a little. But not that night. He handed me the book, just like he used to do at the Metropolitan sometimes, and told me he would be back for it when it was safe."

"How did he look, Mansour?"

"That night? Like you had never gone away, Mr. Tom." Old Mansour paused. "With Stansell everything used to be laughter, you remember? But many things changed after you left Cairo. When you find Stansell, will you stay?"

"I don't know, Mansour." Girling opened and closed the book as he spoke. "Where did he go when you stopped working at the Metropolitan Club? They said this morning that they hadn't seen him there for a long time. I know he used to meet people at the club on business. Did he tell you where he used to go instead?''

''I only know of Andrea's.''

''Where is Andrea's?''

''Out by the Pyramids. When Stansell was here last—not counting the other night—he asked me why our beer was not cold like the Stellas at Andrea's. He had been at Andrea's that morning. He came here afterward to smoke. For the digestion, you understand.''

''I see,'' Girling said. Andrea's. Maybe it was something worth checking.

Girling glanced down at the open pages of the book. There, halfway down was a name, a date and two telephone numbers. The name was Lazan. But it was the address which had caught his eye. Number 22 Ibn Zanki Street was the address that had been circled and underlined on the map he had found inside the stray volume of *Dispatches* in Stansell's apartment.

''By the way,'' Girling said. ''I never asked you how you got the keg back.''

Mansour's eyes twinkled. ''Stansell found it in the rubbish outside the Metropolitan Club. It was he who returned it to me. Please find him, Mr. Tom. It is not the same around here with him gone.''

■   ■   ■

As SOON as he arrived back at the apartment, Girling went to the phone. Referring to Stansell's little black book, he dialed the second of the two numbers, the one listed for Lazan's place of work. At that time of night, past eleven-thirty, he didn't expect anyone to answer, but there might just be . . .

There was a click as the call connected.

. . . an answering machine.

The woman's voice, very smooth, almost robotic, talked to him in a language he did not understand, before switching to English.

''. . . You have reached the Israeli embassy. There is no one here currently to . . .''

Girling gently replaced the receiver.

''Gotcha!'' he said.

CHAPTER 3

Sᴇʀɢᴇᴀɴᴛ Jᴏɴᴇꜱ ᴡᴏʀᴋᴇᴅ his tongue between his teeth. It had ceased to feel like a tongue; it was more like the crust of a dried-out swamp bed back home. He and Bitov had been jogging for just over four hours. One-tenth of the time allowed to them. And already halfway. Except for the water situation, it wasn't so bad.

Shabanov's last little surprise before they boarded the helicopters had been to restrict each E and E pair to just one water bottle. One fucking bottle between two men. To compensate for this, each team was supplied with a map that supposedly marked all the wells in that section of the Eastern Desert. Some swap.

In the darkness, they had missed the first well. Bitov wanted to turn back for it, but Jones persuaded the Russian otherwise. Now he was beginning to regret it.

He was thirsty as hell, but he tried to convince himself he'd been thirstier. Their situation could have been worse, he told himself. The bottle was still half full and the sun wouldn't be up for another half hour or so; and the next well wasn't so far off now, probably around twenty-five kilometers.

On paper, sixty kilometers was good progress. But in a few hours the heat would descend on them and they would have no choice but to hole up for the rest of the day. In this sort of terrain and with daytime temperatures rising to 130 degrees Fahrenheit, marching by night was the only option.

The terrain here was flat. They had managed to skirt around the mountains so far, but the map indicated that toward the end of the journey there was a solid ridge between them and the air base. And there was no way around it. They would have to go over the top. Halfway in one-tenth of the time wasn't beginning to sound so good after all.

Jones kept one eye on Bitov's outline, a little to his left and in front. He was impressed by the Russian's stamina, but then Bitov was no ordinary man. Six-foot-five and built like an armored personnel carrier, he was ugliest son of a bitch Jones had ever seen. He was damned if he was going to let the Ivan get the better of him.

Suddenly Bitov stopped.

They dropped onto their haunches. Jones scanned the skyline for movement, but could see nothing.

The Russian turned his head to the wind. Whatever was bothering him, it was off toward the west.

"There!" Bitov said softly.

Jones heard only his heart pounding against his ribs.

"Two of them, I think," Bitov said.

Now Jones heard the deep *wok-wok* of the blades. He peered against the night, but they were too far way, at least five miles off.

"What are they?"

Bitov shrugged. "Too far for identification."

There were Mils and Sikorskys out looking for them that night. Jones's mind worked against the fatigue. The difference was critical.

"It's okay, they are far from here," Bitov said. He started to march again. "Let's go."

Jones stayed down. He heard the helos' change of direction. Those turboshafts were distinctive now. They were headed straight for their position at 195 miles per hour. He picked himself off the ground, drove his feet through the sand and launched himself at Bitov. He hit the Russian at waist height, his 225 pounds knocking the *starshina* to the ground.

Bitov reacted instinctively. He swung his arm around and grasped Jones's face between thumb and finger, the claw of his left hand.

"Don't fight me and don't stand, whatever you do," Jones snarled. "Just start digging. We've got about a minute and a half before those helicopters are on us."

Bitov wasted vital seconds as he contemplated Jones's distorted face in the vicelike frame of his fingers. Then he released his grip.

Jones's fingers tore into the sand. He linked both hands and moved pounds at a time, in great scoops. It took Bitov vital extra seconds before he began to copy the American, the fingers of his good hand partially aided by the mutilated stump of the other.

"They will never see us, Jones."

"Wrong," Jones panted. "Those are our MH-53Js, and unlike your birds, they carry FLIR—forward-looking infrared. Worse, they just picked us up."

"From eight kilometers? Impossible."

"We stand out like two virgins in a whorehouse against this cold desert floor," Jones said.

Bitov stopped digging long enough to hear the surge in sound.

"Dig! you big son of a bitch!" Jones shouted. "I don't want to end up a passenger on this operation."

As Bitov tore into the sand again, he ripped a nail clean off a finger on his good hand. He ignored the pain. He knew now what Jones was trying to do.

Jones pushed the *starshina* into the hole.

"Hold your breath and trust me," the American said, throwing his bush hat over Bitov's face. He heaped the sand on top of the Russian's body, praying that the grains, cooled by the bitter-chill temperature of the night, were enough to fool the Sikorsky's heat sensor.

Jones saw two shadows moving against the stars. From the sound of their engines, the helos were now less than two miles away, easily within identification range. They seemed impossibly close already, when he hurled himself into his hole and shoveled the sand over himself. Jones took a last, deep lungful of air and pressed back into his makeshift grave. He heaped sand over his face and the grains poured into his ears and up his nose. He fought an overpowering urge to break free from his claustrophobic tomb and plunged his arm into the cool sand beside him. As he lay in his barrow, Jones felt every minute rock particle vibrate against his skin as the sound from the rotors beat the ground.

Jones's lungs were at bursting point when at last he felt the change in tempo as the MH-53s began their climb-out. He no longer cared which way the FLIR turrets were pointing when he punched out of his grave.

Bitov followed a moment later coughing up dust.

The sound of the Jollies receded to the west. Jones guessed that the FLIR operator would be doing some fast talking, trying to convince his crewmates that he really had picked up two human signatures on his FLIR display. The others would be berating him for confusing a couple of desert foxes for soldiers. There would be a few jokes. Some asshole would wisecrack something about it being easy, mistaking animals for special forces.

"How did you know?" Bitov asked.

"You learn that kind of thing in the Pathfinders," Jones said.

They took a drink and resumed their trek across the desert, settling back into the monotony of the march. For Jones, the action would have provided a welcome distraction, but for the shortage of water. He shook the bottle. The unexpected expenditure of energy had pushed up their water needs. He had had no choice but to sanction half rations. The supply was dangerously low now.

He went back to a detailed examination of the new sores in his mouth and tired to forget about their predicament.

The cool waters of the well that lay somewhere on the edge of the sand sea were not merely inviting now. They would soon be the difference between life and death.

■   ■   ■

GIRLING KNEW the Israeli embassy would be little short of a fortress. Israeli embassies always were.

Being the Sabbath, few had entered and left. The fact that it happened to be the Jewish day of rest helped his case, because there were fewer people to watch. He was sure Lazan was in there somewhere. It was just a matter of time before he or she left the building.

Even though he had parked the car in the shade of a large tree, the interior was sweltering. He took another sip of hot Coke and put the can back on the dashboard.

Using the binoculars to try to peek past the blinds into the windows was a periodic distraction, but it told him next to nothing. A sniper would have been similarly frustrated. The Israelis thought of everything. Here, they would be doubly stringent. The Israeli embassy in Cairo was an island in a sea of potential hostility.

Girling had done stakeouts during his period at the *Times*. Then, it had been okay to distract himself with music, or to let his gaze drift when a girl walked by, or simply to daydream.

Under the circumstances, boredom was a luxury which he tried to deny himself. His reveries always ended the same way: Stansell shackled and chained to the wall, in the dark, his cell little bigger than a cupboard. Sometimes a figure with Abu Tarek's face—eyes wild and black as night—would bring food, or water. And sometimes he would bring a stick, or a steel bar, or a soldering iron attached to a car battery.

He shook his head and the image disappeared. He was left staring at the entrance to the embassy again.

Number 22 Ibn Zanki Street, the place listed as Lazan's home address, had been an apartment block. Girling had studied every person who left the building between six-thirty and nine o'clock. Sitting in the lobby of a hotel opposite, he counted fifteen potential Lazans leaving for work.

Next he picked up a car from a rental firm in one of the major hotels. He went for a BMW, partly because Kelso was paying for it, but also because it was the only car on offer that had decent speed.

The embassy door was opening. It was a curious air-lock—two parallel reinforced glass doors bordered by steel frames. Girling raised the binoculars and adjusted the focus. He tweaked the focus another notch and the picture went crystal sharp.

A woman left the building and strolled, hips swinging, toward the main, outer gate. He scanned her face. She was dark, pretty and a little over forty, but he had never seen her before in his life, least of all on Ibn Zanki Street that morning.

The woman waved cheerily to the guard at the gate. She stopped and talked for a few moments, idle chatter by the look of it, before he let her pass. She walked up the line of parked cars on the opposite side of the street until she was parallel with his BMW.

Girling tucked Stansell's binoculars under the street map on the passenger seat and removed the can of Coke from the dashboard. He bent over the map and let his brow furrow, as if he was lost. When he looked up, she was getting into the back of a taxi. As the driver sped off she did not give him so much as a glance.

His gaze drifted once more to the entrance.

Of the people who had departed Lazan's apartment block that morning, three had been black-skinned—unusual for Israeli nationals, although not impossible—and seven had all the hallmarks of Egyptian businessmen. Girling left nothing to chance. He ruled no one in or out. He made copious notes on each person, even though he knew he could always fall back on a talent that had assisted him at varying times throughout his life: he had an outstanding memory for faces.

That left five likely Lazan candidates. One was a stern-looking woman in her late thirties wearing shoulder pads under a dark suit that was definitely out of sync with the weather. The second was a little too European-looking, but Girling included him on his list of probables. The third walked with a limp, was tall, frail almost, and wore a colorful vest over an expensive shirt with links in the cuffs. Israelis, even civilians, usually dressed down: somber trousers, topped by a short-sleeve shirt. This guy was almost trying to draw attention to himself; and in this neck of the woods—bandit country for anyone from Tel Aviv—that wasn't too bright. The fourth and fifth were his two prime targets. One was tall, wiry, with olive skin, dark hair; about forty years old. The other was somewhat older, short, balding and fit, judging by the way he darted across the road to his parked car. Looked like a military man, definitely the right profile for the defense attaché.

If he'd had time on his side, Girling would have followed them on successive days until the right one led him to the embassy. But he didn't have time. The only other solution was to watch the apartment and the embassy in turn and wait until he got a match.

Girling wasn't sure what he would do if and when he identified Lazan. There was no guarantee that Lazan had any of the answers. But one thought gave him hope. The Israelis were the best watchdogs in the world when it came to their Arab neighbors. They had to be for their own survival. And Stansell had obtained his information from a source of the highest caliber. No one other than a spook backed by a hell of an intelligence organization could have given Stansell the information which set in motion the events leading to his abduction.

In the absence of any further help from his father-in-law, Lazan seemed like the next best place to start.

Across the street, a vendor was wheeling a cart full of cold drinks and shouting his wares at he went. A single block of ice protruded from the midst of the trolley. Girling opened the door and crossed the street, reaching into this pocket for some change as he did so.

Fifty yards away, a car rocked slightly, although Girling, his back turned to it, never noticed the movement. Nor did he hear the squeak of its suspension as the driver shifted in his seat and adjusted his camera's zoom lens.

■   ■   ■

THE WELL was on the edge of the sand sea, its location marked only by a few piled stones. Behind it, the mountains of the Eastern Desert rose in jagged disarray toward the sky.

Jones and Bitov watched from a safe distance; their vantage point a rocky spur jutting into the sand. Both were in bad shape and neither made any bones about his predicament.

Two bedouins, nomads of the desert, each carrying a Kalashnikov assault rifle, sat on the boulders by the well's edge. A third bedouin, also armed, was standing on the rim, dipping the shadoof in and out of the water. Having filled the jug at the end of the long pole, he transferred it to their goatskins. There were four goatskins in all. One for each of them. The fourth bedouin slept beside the camel in the shade of a rock overhang.

The shadoof operator was too busy telling his animated story to notice or care about the water slopping carelessly out of the earthenware jug. The sound of splashing drifted to Jones and Bitov on the hot breeze, drowned periodically by snatches of guttural laughter.

Although they were two hundred yards from the well, Jones could see the sunlight glinting off the droplets. He looked at his watch. They had thirty-five kilometers and a mountain range to negotiate and twenty-four hours in which to do it. Without water, they weren't going to get fifty feet up the rock face on the other side of the wall. Without water, they were going to die.

Their progress had been pitifully slow. While the sun climbed toward its zenith, their water dwindled to nothing. For the last eight kilometers, they had been running on empty. Whatever the map said, Jones was beginning to think the second well had gone the same way as the first when, hugging the mountain ridge for the little shade it offered, they saw it. It was Bitov who spotted the distant circle of stones in the sand that marked the circumference of the well; Jones who saw the nomads chatting in the shade of the overhang twenty yards beyond.

For the past two hours they had waited in vain for the nomads to move. Two hours in which they had done nothing but watch helplessly as the bedouins brewed tea and talked.

''I say we go down there and fuckin' ask them,'' Jones stammered. His tongue felt like it was an alien part of his body, like it had no business being in his mouth. ''I can't keep this up much longer.'' He rolled onto his back and felt the relentless beat of the afternoon sun on his face.

''Impossible, Jones.''

They had been through this conversation already.

''The colonel's orders were clear,'' Bitov added. ''Avoid all contact with the local population.''

''Come on,'' Jones said. ''Tell me how the comrade colonel's ever going to fuckin' know?''

''And anyway, the bedouins kill for their water,'' Bitov said. ''They would not hesitate to kill us. They are armed. We have nothing to defend ourselves but our bare hands.''

''We could still jump them.''

''In your condition, Yankee?''

Jones noticed the blisters on the Russian's face for the first time. Bitov was so pig-ugly, with his split lip and flat nose, that superficial blemishes blended with his features. You had to look hard to see the sores.

''You ain't in much better shape yourself,'' Jones said, rolling back onto his stomach. ''Besides, what the fuck would you have us do?''

Bitov lifted his eyes to the midafternoon sun. ''Stop talking, Jones. Be patient. They will move before long. And then we drink.''

''So how come you're so fuckin' philosophical?''

''Spetsnaz has taught me much.''

''Stop shitting me, Bitov. Were you in Afghanistan?''

"Yes. What of it?"

"Was it as bad as they say it was?"

"It was an experience."

"You didn't answer my question."

"The question was . . . political."

Jones snorted. "Political? What happened to glasnost?"

"It is not a word often heard in Spetsnaz."

"Well, it certainly seems to have given the comrade colonel a wide berth."

"He has much on his mind, Jones. Do not judge him too harshly."

"If he ain't careful, a higher authority's gonna be judging him sooner than he'd like. And it ain't necessarily gonna be the Angels of Judgment that'll put him in the dock."

"Is that a threat?"

"The Pathfinders don't take too kindly to this sort of treatment. Let's leave it at that."

"This is discipline, Jones, nothing more, nothing less. Maybe if the Pathfinders had been more disciplined—"

Bitov stopped short of completing the sentence.

Jones narrowed his eyes. "Don't let me keep you from saying what's on your mind, Bitov."

"We know what happened to the Pathfinders in Panama. Perhaps you should question your own colonel's conduct before criticizing that of mine."

Before Jones's anger could spill over, there was a sudden movement far to their right. The three bedouin had risen from the well and were walking to their camels.

Jones could almost smell the cool, clear water. "Thank God."

"Save your breath."

One of the bedouins pulled a rug from his camel saddle, spread it on the sand and lay down in the scant shade. The two others followed suit. The fourth, the one who had been sleeping, struggled to his feet, stretched and walked to a point between the camels and the well to begin his turn as guard. Even the taciturn Bitov allowed himself a curse.

"Fuck it, I'm going down there," Jones said, stirring himself.

"No."

"Look, if I approach from the desert, he'll never see me. He's staring out over the cliffs, for God's sake."

"You will never make it, Yankee."

"Don't you ever ease up? If we don't get water, we die."

"I stand a better chance than you."

In the end, Jones stuck two clenched fists in front of him and asked Bitov to choose between them. Bitov picked thin air and Jones kept the pebble.

Five minutes later, the American found himself squirming across the sand, the water bottle in his left hand. He kept his eye on the little he could see of the guard. The bedouin was sitting on a cluster of rocks about twenty yards beyond the watering hole, half his body hidden by the stone lip of the well.

Under the sun's blistering heat, Jones's sweat soaked his skin, his shirt and trousers. A thin layer of sand now stuck to his body, giving him a little natural camouflage to help him blend with his surroundings. When he reached the well, he lay there catching his breath for a moment. Then, summoning his strength, he raised his eyes level with the stones.

The guard's back was almost foursquare to him, but his head was turned fractionally, so that Jones could make out the harsh aquiline profile of his face. The other three were fast asleep, the noise of their slumbering audible even above the deep breathing of the camels.

The tip of the shadoof seemed to tower above him, impossibly high. He could tell the jug was partially full, because water was dripping through the porous clay and splashing in the well.

Jones made his move. Silently, he clambered onto the sides of the well and stretched up for the jug, his eyes never deviating from the back of the bedouin. His hand slid over moisture-soaked sides of the jug. He let it rest there for a second. The feel of it was pure magic.

Jones started to pull the shadoof toward him, praying that it would not creak in protest, As soon as the jug was level with his face, he dipped the bottle beneath the water. It burbled slightly as it filled, but nothing like loud enough for the bedouins or even the camels to hear.

Jones placed the full bottle gently by his feet. He was in the act of lowering himself to the ground when a slight breeze blew in from the sand sea behind him. Even as the thought formed in Jones's mind as a radiating pulse of fear, one of the camels jerked as if it had been stung by a scorpion and let out an enormous belch.

Jones froze. He had forgotten one cardinal rule of stealth. He had approached from upwind.

The guard started to laugh. He was pointing at his companion, who was sitting bolt upright, startled by the sound and movement of his beast. The look on his face turned to horror as his eyes met Jones's. The bedouin stuttered a warning, but the guard was too busy laughing. Jones could see the rifle of the startled one poking from the holster in the camel saddle. It would take the bedouin several seconds to reach it, several more to ready it.

Jones ran. He hurled himself first at the guard, grabbing him round the neck and bringing his head down on a rock jutting through the sand. The American pulled himself to his feet, fighting the dizziness. He ran for the second bedouin, just as he was pulling back the bolt of the Kalashnikov. Jones hit him in the stomach in a flying tackle and heard the breath expelled from his lungs. In the split-second advantage allowed to him, he chose between the two other stirring bodies and kicked the man closest to a rifle, catching him squarely under the jaw. He swung round to face the fourth to find a Kalashnikov leveled at his chest.

Jones saw the bedouin's finger tighten on the trigger. There was no question but that the guy was going to do it. Jones braced himself, and swore that he would see Shabanov in hell.

A barely perceptible movement behind the nomad prompted Jones to break his stare. The reflex saved his life, for instead of firing, the bedouin turned to find Bitov rising from the sand like a striking cobra. The Russian, cloaked from head to foot in dust, brought his foot up into the bedouin's groin in a whirl of movement and choking sand. The nomad fell to his knees, dropping his assault rifle. Bitov snatched it before it even hit the ground.

It was the last thing Jones saw. The guard, whom he had only stunned, struggled to his feet and, before Bitov could shout a warning, smashed his rifle stock over the back of the American's head.

■　　　■　　　■

GIRLING TWISTED the ignition key and the BMW purred into life. It was no longer possible to see the entrance to the embassy. He had hoped for some illumination from the street lamps. But either they didn't work, or somebody somewhere had forgotten to pull the switch. He had heard a story once that as fast as municipal workers erected street lamps here, thieves followed and stripped out the cables. Everything had a price on Cairo's black market. Everything.

A lone light glowed dimly above the guard's sentry box, but it was not enough to illuminate the faces of the few people who had left the building in the last ten minutes.

Girling took a last look through the binoculars. Bugs and moths swarmed around the solitary bulb. Beyond, all was black but for a few lights shining on the second floor. Maybe Lazan was working late. Then again, maybe Lazan didn't work at the embassy anymore. Maybe Lazan was in Tel Aviv. Or maybe he was dead.

Too many maybes.

He inched the BMW out of the parking slot. He hoped he could find Andrea's restaurant in the blacked-out countryside near the Pyramids.

■   ■   ■

BITOV COULD go no farther. Not because his courage or strength had deserted him—he derived a certain energy from the fact that he, a Russian soldier, was carrying one of the pride of America's special forces on his back. Bitov knew there was no shame in calling a halt. With the sudden change in gradient and the worsening light, further progress wasn't a question of stamina, tenacity or spirit. It was simply an impossibility.

The Russian let Jones's dead weight slip gently to the ground. He positioned the unconscious form so that it was upright on the rocky ledge, back against the rocks, face turned to the sun as it slipped behind the mountains on the far side of the sand sea.

Bitov sat beside Jones and turned his eyes to the west. All day the sun had been their enemy. Now he was sorry to see it go. He took a sip of water, then tipped some into Jones's mouth. Most of it dribbled onto the Pathfinder's T-shirt, but some found its way down his throat. Jones coughed twice, convulsively, then fell silent. Bitov leaned over and listened to Jones's breathing and checked the wound at the back of his head. There was little change in his condition. Helped by the makeshift bandage that he had fashioned from the robe of one of the bedouins, the gash in Jones's scalp had stopped bleeding, but not before the

American had lost a good deal of blood. His pulse was coming back up, but he was still a sick man.

The ledge was a six-foot-wide notch in the side of the rock face. Its position, around one-third of the way up the escarpment, seemed to coincide with a change in the gradient. The first four hundred meters had been steep, but Bitov, summoning deep reserves of strength, had managed to scale it in a little under two hours with Jones on his back.

Bitov twisted on the ledge until he stared at the near-vertical incline above him. The rest of the way would have been testing enough for the fittest of men in broad daylight. But because night was closing in on them, he would be going nowhere until Jones regained consciousness.

The Russian closed his eyes and felt himself lapsing into a light sleep. He gave little thought to the action that had transpired by the well. What were four more dead after the horrors of the Panjshir, Herat and Jalalabad? To Bitov, soldiery since that winter in 1979 had consisted of little else but killing.

CHAPTER 4

J ONES BLINKED SEVERAL TIMES and brought his hand up to the back of his head. His hair was caked thick with blood in varying stages of congealment.

Stretching away before him was a landscape of nightmarish beauty. A three-quarter moon bathed the rocks in an electric blue-black light and cast shadows of endless depth. The dunes of the sand sea stretched endlessly, far below.

Jones spent long minutes trying to fathom why he was on a ledge, a thousand feet up a mountain, propped against the rock like a dummy, with Bitov beside him, sleeping like a baby. He recalled snatches of his attempt to steal the water from the well, but for the most part, his mind was a blank. He tried to get to his feet, but overcome by nausea and pain, tipped forward, striking his head as he fell.

He dreamed he had pitched headlong into the bedouin well and that Bitov was in there with him, holding him down. He came round to find the Russian bringing water to his parched lips.

"Go on," Bitov urged. "We have plenty." He pointed to two full goatskins farther along the ledge.

"You carried me?"

"Quiet, Jones."

"What happened to the bedouins?"

After Bitov had told him, Jones said nothing. He pulled himself into a sitting position and stared out over the monochrome landscape.

"They caught you stealing their water," Bitov said. "They would have killed you."

Jones grimaced. "It feels like he already did." He raised the water bottle to his lips. Jones wanted badly to hate this Russian, his natural enemy for eighteen years of soldiery, his whole career. Yet the enemy had a human face. And it had saved his life.

Jones lay back against the rocks, trying to ignore the pain in his head. Somehow, he drifted into sleep. When he awoke he was overcome by a feeling of panic. He sat bolt upright. "How much longer?" he stammered.

Bitov remained unruffled. "About twelve hours, with just under thirty-five kilometers to go. Distance is not the problem, Jones. Across the sand, I could carry you for a hundred kilometers, farther even." The Russian pointed to the rock face above them. "That is the problem."

Jones lifted his head slowly. The granite cliff towered above them, its pinnacle lost against a black belt of sky. Just raising his eyes had caused the nausea to return.

"Stay conscious, Yankee, and let me do the rest."

"What do you mean?"

"I can help you."

"It's almost vertical, Bitov. You'll kill us both."

Bitov grabbed Jones by the belt and pulled him to his feet. "Jones, you talk too much. Now you climb."

Jones slipped the toe of his boot into a notch in the rock and pulled himself a few feet up the cliff face. He turned to find Bitov beside him, watching over him like some grotesque mother hen.

"Why?" Jones asked.

Bitov smiled, his one good front tooth glowing bright in the moonlight. "Why? Because I want you to be there when we go into Lebanon, Jones. When we go Angel hunting, I want to know who is best."

For the next two hours, Jones slipped in and out of consciousness.

All the while, Bitov pushed him and pulled him, forcing his fingers into handholds and encouraging his feet into niches in the rock. Sometimes Bitov shouted, sometimes he whispered: whatever it took to drag Jones back from the brink and up to the lip of the precipice.

Jones pressed his face against the rock. It was cool from the night. As he hugged the granite, he caught a glimpse of the sheer drop below him. He no longer knew what was real and what was imagined. His vision swam in and out of focus and the nausea moved like a viscous liquid from the tips of his fingers to the pit of his stomach. It was at that point that he felt the rock beneath his feet crumbling to nothing.

Just as Jones slipped, Bitov grabbed him. He anchored himself to the rock face with a bearlike grip on a granite buttress, steadying the American long enough for him to hook his arm around another pinnacle of rock. Bitov inched himself up the buttress, dragging Jones after him. A ledge, barely wide enough to support both of them, appeared to their right and Bitov maneuvered toward it. As soon as they reached it, they collapsed, shoulder to shoulder, panting for breath. Their bodies shimmered and their chests heaved. They looked like two fish washed onto the rocks.

"Was Afghanistan ever like this?" Jones asked.

Bitov's head and arm dangled over the precipice. His voice was almost lost to the abyss. "I died a hundred times in Afghanistan, Jones."

"Tell me about it," Jones gasped. "Talking helps."

Bitov transported Jones's mind to a mountain fortress called Karagar, where on a single day many years before, he witnessed the comprehensive destruction of his company. While one group of commandos, a Spetsnaz unit attached to troops of the Soviet Army's 105th Division, had stormed the Darulaman Palace of President Hafizullah Amin in Kabul, an elite unit under Captain Shabanov, in which he, Bitov, had been a lowly *yefreytor,* a corporal, undertook an altogether more formidable mission. They had been ordered to take Karagar—and one very special occupant—at all costs.

By the time the battle was over, Shabanov and he were the only Russians left alive. What Bitov omitted to say was that they never found the man who had provided the reason for the mission in the first place. He had disappeared into thin air, just like all the other times.

"It was mountainous country, much like this," Bitov said, his voice hard to hear, half-swallowed by the chasm below. "Except for the snow and ice. It was so cold it froze your breath solid, so cold your bones felt brittle enough to snap. It was Christmas, so they told me. But what did Opnaz care about Christmas?"

"What the fuck's Opnaz? I thought you were a Spetsnaz unit."

Bitov heaved himself around till he face the American. "What are you mumbling about, Jones?"

"I thought—"

"Your mind is playing tricks, Jones."

Jones rubbed the back of his head. Talking with Bitov had made him feel better, helped him focus his mind, or so he thought. Now he wasn't so sure.

"Come," Bitov said. "We talk while we climb."

Summoning the last of his strength, Jones began to haul himself up the last leg of the cliff.

"We were a Spetsnaz unit," Bitov continued, "much like the one here, at Wadi Qena. Only the faces were different." Bitov began edging along another narrow ridge. He held Jones tightly by the sleeve, gently but forcefully urging him to follow.

Jones kept his eyes on the back of Bitov's head. He did not look down. "What happened to them?"

"All gone."

"And you blame yourself?"

"Many of them looked to me."

It took them an hour to complete the climb. During that time, Bitov captivated Jones with a tale of courage, the like of which the American had never heard before. The ferocity of the Afghan tribesmen was described in a vivid, awesome way that Jones would hardly have believed possible from one as ponderous as Bitov. Then again, their very circumstances helped to color in any gaps in the Russian's narrative. Jones heard how the Soviets fought hand to hand with the tribesmen on ledges overlooking drops of a thousand feet or more. During the course of their journey back from the summit, Bitov's entire platoon fell into the abyss one by one, many of them still locked in hand-to-hand combat with the enemy as they tumbled to their deaths.

As Jones pulled himself over the lip of the rock face and looked down at the gentle gradient that would take them into Wadi Qena, Bitov offered him his hand one last time. Jones hesitated. His head hurt, but the dizziness had gone. He didn't need Bitov's support anymore, but he took the hand all the same.

■   ■   ■

THERE WAS no hint of a breeze to dissipate the smoke from the great open fire in the center of the restaurant. It hung in thin layers a few feet above the ground, mingling with the smell from the spiced meats, chickens and small, wild birds roasting on the spits above the grill.

Girling watched a wisp of smoke wind its way lazily past one of the palm tree trunks supporting the thatched roof. Andrea's seemed a favorite place for Egyptian families and foreigners alike. And on that evening, they had gathered en masse. Girling sat at the bar.

Beyond the tables, the still waters of one of the Nile's many tributaries reflected the gaudy lights strung across the rear of the restaurant. A child's laughter pealed across the open room. Somewhere in the distance, a water buffalo lowed mournfully. Girling took another sip of beer. It was cold enough to sting his throat, cold enough to turn the taste of the warm Coke into a distant memory.

When the barman asked him if he'd like another Stella, Girling nodded and reached for his wallet. He produced a passport-sized picture of Stansell and placed it on the counter next to the money for the beer.

"Do you know this man?" Girling asked.

The barman looked between him and the photograph. He was middle-aged, with graying hair and large, understanding eyes. Girling thought he saw a flash of recognition pass across them before the photograph was slid back across the counter, accompanied by a shake of the head.

"Are you sure?" Girling pressed.

"I've never seen him before."

"What about the other staff?"

"They have not seen him, nor do they know him."

"How do you know that?"

"I know everything that happens here."

Girling looked at him across the top of his glass. "Mind if I ask them myself?"

"I don't want any trouble here."

"There won't be any trouble. I just—"

"If you ask questions you will have to leave." The large, doleful eyes briefly registered menace.

Girling held the stare until the barman moved away. He replaced the photograph in his wallet and swore lightly under his breath.

Girling heard footsteps, then the creak of the barstool as somebody came in and sat down behind him. "Why does his reaction surprise you, Tom Girling? Can't you see he is afraid?"

Girling turned, his mind trying to work on the voice even as he faced the man who had addressed him.

The black, silver-topped cane tapped the leg of his stool. "Don't you recognize me?"

"I know who you are," Girling said. "I'm more than a little surprised, though, that you should know me."

Lazan was perhaps five years older than him, but the scars of war had added another ten to his looks.

"Stansell told me much about you," the Israeli said.

"Yes, but—"

"And my secretary filled in the gaps."

Girling floundered for a moment. "The woman outside the embassy?"

Lazan shrugged. "As I said, I know a lot about you."

"And you? Who are you, Lazan?"

"You don't know? I thought . . ." Lazan smiled. "A lowly military attaché. I hope you weren't expecting more." He held his hand out. "And it's Zvi, Tom Girling. Colonel Zvi Lazan. Is there anything else you would like to know?"

In Ibn Zanki Street, Girling had seen a flamboyant man. But the cane and the clothes had distracted him. Close up, Girling saw that Lazan had suffered terrible injuries at some point in his life. The lumps of skin tissue on his face and the peppered holes in his cheeks and neck allowed only the barest glimpse of the good-looking man that he had once been.

Girling tried to keep his voice even, free of surprise. "Why is he afraid to talk to me, the waiter?"

"Because you are being watched by the *mukhabarat.* Did you know that?"

Girling twisted instinctively.

"Oh no, you won't see them," Lazan said. "They're outside. In the blue Fiat. Quite obvious when you know what you're looking for.'' He gestured to the barman. ''He has a good idea that it's you they're interested in. Egyptians are very resourceful people, very intuitive.''

After the inactivity of the day Girling realized he had become careless. ''Aren't you taking a risk sitting here, talking to me?''

Lazan reached for a sunflower seed, cracked the shell with his thumbnail and popped the fleshy kernel into his mouth. ''You know how the *mukhabarat* works, Tom Girling. Its problem has always been a lack of imagination. The two bozos in the car have been told to follow you and that is precisely what they have done. When you leave here, they will diligently pursue you to your home, or wherever you decide to spend the night. And then, when they are relieved of their watch, they will go to their beds and sleep like babies, safe in the knowledge they have carried out their orders.'' He smiled softly. ''But if only they had come in here; how much more al-Qadi would have learned.''

Lazan clicked his fingers and asked for a beer before turning back to Girling. ''Don't worry, my driver will warn me if they make the slightest move.''

''You know al-Qadi, then,'' Girling said. ''Aren't you afraid of him?''

''It would be stupid not to fear such a man. Though hardly a genius, he is most . . . unpredictable.''

''Should I fear you, Lazan?''

The Israeli laughed. ''Your colleague Stansell did not fear me. Why don't you ask him?''

''You know as well as I that that's quite impossible.''

''Oh?'' Lazan lifted his glass and drank.

''You may be the last person who saw him alive,'' Girling said.

''Alive? This is all very dramatic, Tom Girling. First following me, then—''

Girling brought his bottle of Stella down hard on the counter. ''Don't play games with me, Lazan. Sure, I've been looking for you, but it was you who found me, not the other way round. Now why should that be?''

The Israeli lowered his glass. His small brown eyes watched Girling intently. ''Stop talking in riddles, Tom Girling. Get to the point.''

''The point is Stansell's been kidnapped and you know it. You met

Stansell last week at his request. It was the evening after the terrorist attack at Beirut, the day after they disappeared off the face of the Earth taking Franklin and his peace team with them. Do you remember now?''

Lazan said nothing.

''You'd supplied information to Stansell before,'' Girling continued. ''It was natural, therefore, that he should turn to you for help. Our editor had set him an almost impossible task, but what a prize would await him and *Dispatches* should he succeed. He'd been told to unmask the hijackers' identity, a job made none too simple by the fact the government of the United States itself had no idea who was responsible.

''But Stansell turns to you, because he knows that if anyone can give him a steer on Arab terrorism, it's the boys from Tel Aviv. Stansell goes to see you at home and—because you and he are old pals—you help him out. You give him the Angels of Judgment on a plate. You were the primary source. But Stansell is a professional. He has to second-source this information. So he goes across town to see someone who can verify what you've told him. *Dispatches* goes and publishes the story and less than twenty-four hours later, while Cairo sleeps, the Angels of Judgment—or people who call themselves the Angels of Judgment—snatch him from his apartment. I know very little about you, Lazan, but I believe Stansell considered you a friend. I, too, am his friend. And I need to know what you told him that night.''

Lazan cracked a seed between his front teeth and spat the shell on the ground. ''Did you work all this out for yourself?''

''A colleague of mine saw Stansell mark a street map shortly before he left to see you. That map is in my possession now. It marks your house very clearly.''

''Quite the detective, aren't you, Tom Girling?''

''I want to save Stansell's life, Lazan.''

''Like so many journalists, I'm afraid you manage to tell only part of the truth.''

''This is no matter for professional pride, Lazan. I'm happy to admit I'm wrong if it means saving Stansell.''

''And you think you are the one who will find him, is that it?''

''He hasn't got anyone else,'' Girling said simply.

Lazan pulled a slim, ornate case from his vest. He offered a cigarette to Girling, who declined, before lighting one up himself. "Go home, Tom Girling. If these Angels of Judgment have him, then Stansell is past help."

"If?" Girling asked. "You said 'if' the Angels of Judgment have him?"

"There are many groups here who would gladly act in their name."

"That's certainly a theory I'm working on," Girling said.

Lazan nodded, the light of the fire dancing on the right side of his face. "Overnight, the Angels of Judgment have become like prophets to every disaffected, hard-line Islamic group in the Middle East. Only a very special band of Muslim brothers could hold a superpower to ransom, after all. The Angels of Judgment have instilled a new generation of Arabs with inspiration."

"So that's why you decided to show yourself." Girling met the Israeli's eyes. "You've no more idea who they are than the rest of us. The Angels of Judgment scare the living shit out of you, don't they?"

"You don't mince words, do you, Tom Girling?"

Girling studied the battered face for a moment. "Then if you weren't Stansell's primary source, who was?"

Lazan remained impassive. "I'd put my money on the Russians."

"The Russians?" Girling remembered the reception at their embassy. "Why them?"

"Because they expelled one of their diplomats the day after the hijacking. We know the guy was a GRU officer. Military intelligence. Maybe he'd been telling tales out of school."

"That's a bit of a long shot, isn't it?"

"Maybe. Stansell also had good links with the fundamentalist community here. His primary source might well have been inside the Brotherhood. As you know, the Brotherhood here is well connected internationally. There is more than likely an open channel of communication between these Angels of Judgment and the Muslim Brotherhood in Cairo; just as there is with those Iranian-backed fiends, the Hizbollah. They're united by militant Islamic fundamentalism—and next to impossible to penetrate. And like all secret societies they have their ways of talking to each other, ways that outsiders like you and I will never learn. You'd do well to remember that, Tom Girling."

Girling looked Lazan in the eye. "Tell me what happened the night Stansell came to see you."

Lazan pulled hard on his cigarette. "As you now have guessed, he already had the terrorists' name when he came to see me that night. He was after confirmation, but how could I confirm a name I had never even heard of? When he mentioned these Angels of Judgment, I actually laughed. I told him that we would definitely have heard of a group with those kinds of resources."

"But you hadn't."

"Personally, no."

"What does that mean?"

"Tel Aviv is conducting a high-level inquiry right now into the revelations published by your magazine. If the Angels of Judgment exist, as Stansell said they did, then we will find them, be sure of that."

"Is there any chance you could let me in on their findings?"

Lazan let out a choked, gravelly laugh. "Are you mad?"

Girling held up his hand up. "There is a connection between Beirut and Stansell's disappearance. I'm prepared to share whatever I turn up, if you'll do the same for me. I'm not talking about high-level secrets, just a steer in the right direction."

Lazan leaned forward till his face was a bare few inches away. "Then let me give you a steer, right now, Tom Girling. Get on a plane, leave Cairo, leave the Middle East and don't come back. You are pitting yourself against a monster, a many-headed beast. The Angels of Judgment and the Brotherhood are just a part of it. The monster is militant fundamentalism—the force that binds these groups together, from Europe to Central Africa; from the Atlantic Ocean to the Chinese border. And to this monster you will become an irritant—if you haven't already become so—something for it to annihilate without so much as a second thought. It will show you no more mercy than it has done to Stansell. You cannot reason with it, for it knows none. It kills because it is conditioned to kill. It spares life only when it wants something in return . . ."

"Maybe they wanted something from Stansell. Maybe, they want to keep him alive."

"There is only the very merest chance."

"As long as there is that chance, I will continue to search for him."

"Then you should prepare yourself for death also, Tom Girling."

"I almost died once at the hands of these people, Lazan. They killed my wife. They can't do any worse to me now."

Lazan took a deep breath. ''Stansell told me about you and Asyut. Believe me, I am sorry for what happened. But look at me, Tom Girling. In 1982, I got shot down over the Bekáa Valley after a Syrian MiG driver put a heat-seeking missile up the jetpipe of my F-4. It was a bad ejection, you know. The cockpit coaming removed most of my right knee on the way out and I'd broken three vertebrae, although I didn't know that at the time. When I came to, they had me tied to a bed frame in a blackened room, in the basement of some house in a village, God knows where. I could hear my navigator close by, crying. I think he was in a next-door room, or maybe it was upstairs, I don't know. He was a young kid of twenty-one, a good kid, a brave kid, with seven Syrian MiGs and Sukhois to his credit. I thought he was crying for his mother, or that like me, he was scared out of his wits. We had every right to be scared. You see, we had fallen into the hands of the Hizbollah . . .

''When they eventually threw him into my cell, there was just enough light to see him. He was slumped unconscious in the corner of the room, his head hanging on his chest. I called to him, but he didn't answer. I knew he wasn't dead, because he was still whimpering. Somehow, I managed to untie myself and crawl over. I touched him on the shoulder and he fell forward, his head in my lap. There was a lot of blood, mostly on his face. From the ejection, I thought. I tore a sleeve off my shirt and tried to wipe his cheek, but—''

He paused to take one last drag of the cigarette. ''But it just came away in my hand. The whole right side of his face. They'd used acid on him. A whole bottle of acid. Drip, drip, drip, until there was almost nothing left. He died in my arms a few hours later, but it felt like days. Like you, Tom Girling, I was so angry that I forgot my pain. I wanted them to come for me. I wanted to kill them with my bare hands. But that night, when they did come, I saw the thick rubber gloves on their hands, and I saw the smoke-brown bottle one of them carried, and I wasn't brave, I wasn't the lion I convinced myself I had become. I wept like a baby and I screamed when they tied me again to that bed frame. And I carried on screaming many hours after they had finished. Drip, drip—''

''Jesus Christ, Lazan, that's enough,'' Girling blurted. He kept his eyes on the floor, unable now to turn them to the Israeli. The face of the young navigator had become Mona's face.

Lazan tapped Girling gently on the leg with his cane. "I was lucky. I had a combat rescue team come for me in a CH-53. You, on the other hand, are quite alone. Are you sure you are ready to face the beast, Tom Girling? For it is here, you can count on that. Though you cannot see it, it is everywhere. All you have to do is provoke it . . ."

■　　　　　■　　　　　■

GIRLING DECIDED to pour himself a whiskey before he turned in. He sat in one of the big armchairs and willed the alcohol to work on the tautness that had made his muscles and sinews ache and his head hurt. He tried to tell himself that the symptoms were a product of the day's exertions, but it was an unconvincing argument. His mind drifted time and again to Lazan's words. They had raked up such feelings of bitterness in him that his mind teemed with images from the past. He could feel his white side, his positive side, struggling against the black, but try as he might, his thoughts always ended on that stretch of dusty road. He could feel his arms pinioned behind his back. He felt the panic and despair, too, as the life slipped from her with every new blow to her body; and there was nothing he could do about it. Finally, he saw the wild face of the man who gave the orders swing around, his eyes latching onto him. Like a bird of prey, seeing its quarry scurrying for shelter, and knowing there is no escape for it. In the darkness of his apartment, Girling saw that face with a disturbing new clarity. For today, somebody had given it a name.

He snapped on the light. He fumbled for the bound volume of *Dispatches* beside him and began skimming over its pages, trying to distract himself. His fingers flipped the pages mechanically and week after week of that distant year passed before his eyes.

And then his fingers stopped. Girling stared down at the open pages. At first, he didn't know what it was that had made him halt here, then he understood. A page had been ripped from the volume, leaving jagged stubs protruding from the spine of the binder. He pried back the other pages to see if any words were discernible on the remaining scraps of paper, but he could make out no more than a few letters. Girling was reaching for his pen to jot down the number of the missing page and the issue date, when he heard the noise outside the door. His ears pricked at the sound. One of his neighbors returning after a late dinner? But a minute later there was a faint shuffling sound in the corridor. Girling put the whiskey and the binder on the floor by his feet. He stood up and found the hairs lifting on his forearms, the skin at the back of his neck prickling against his collar. He moved quietly to the door.

He stopped and listened. Over the sound of his own breathing and the blood rushing in his ears, he heard clearly the light movement of feet on the other side. For the first time in his life, Girling wished he had a gun. He looked around for something to take to the enemy, knowing as he did so that he had nothing to protect himself, just as Stansell had had nothing . . .

The rap on the door sounded like a burst of machine-gun fire. Long after Girling had recoiled from the jamb, he stood there trying to fight the pervasive numbness that gripped him. He considered shouting for help, but realized that they could have the door down in a moment and history would repeat itself.

And then he heard his name. He reached for the latch and drew it back, his heart hammering so hard against his chest he felt light-headed.

The voice reached him a fraction before the dim light of the distant lamp illuminated the face of the man that spoke.

"So now you, too, have found fear, Tom." It was said without mockery.

Mohammed Hamdi stepped forward a little way, until the glow of the lampshade reflected off the thick glass of his spectacles. "I would have stopped you on your way in just now, but I did not want the *mukhabarat* to see us together. Did you know there are two of them watching you?"

Girling nodded. He ushered his father-in-law inside and shut the door.

"If the *mukhabarat* had seen me speak to you, they would arrive at my door wanting to know why," Mohammed Hamdi continued. "*Um* Mona has suffered enough without the attentions of the *mukhabarat*."

From the way he used this term of respect for his wife, it was as if *um* Mona—the Mother of Mona—had never been given any other name. While Girling caught his breath, the ex-policeman reached for his cigarettes.

"There is a place near here. I meet with some of my old colleagues from work. It does me good to talk, to relive the old days. She's not a bad woman, you understand. But she does not see with the clarity with which I see things now. I do not have much time." He paused. "I cannot stay long, and I do not want to stay long. You and I have never seen eye-to-eye and I doubt if things would have changed had my daughter lived. You are an *'agnabi*. Our ways are different. But until today, I never took you for a man of integrity. I saw the look in your eyes when you told me what you had come here to do. I saw the hatred, and just now I saw fear, too. I never confronted those who took Mona from our midst, for I thought to have done so would have been to question my faith, my very reason for existence. I could not do it, because they act in the name of the God in whom I believe. But I know now how wrong I have been. These people need to be hunted down, all of them."

"Just tell me where I must go to find Abu Tarek," Girling whispered. "That's why you're here, isn't it?"

"If you found him, would you avenge Mona, or would you use him to find your friend?"

"Both, Mohammed Hamdi."

"You cannot have it both ways, Tom Girling." The ex-policeman rested against the wall. Girling offered him a seat, but he refused. "Yes, Abu Tarek killed Mona, but even if you were lucky enough to find him in this vast city, it would not do you any good. You told me you wanted to find this man Stansell and that the only way you knew how was to penetrate the Brotherhood. Abu Tarek is a small fish, a common criminal who obeys orders. He will not know who holds Stansell, but his protector might."

"What protector?"

"They call him the Guide."

"The name makes him sound important, yet I have never heard of him."

"He is one of the most powerful men in Egypt, yet scarcely anyone knows of him," Mohammed Hamdi wheezed.

"I don't understand."

"To understand, you have to go back to Asyut, on the day Mona died. Are you strong enough to do that?"

Girling felt his skin prickle. He had returned there every day since. "Yes," he said.

Mohammed Hamdi stubbed out his cigarette and promptly lit

another. "Asyut is a big city. Its university has many students, the vast majority of them from poor families in Upper Egypt, where I was born. It has long been a trouble spot, a breeding ground for fundamentalism. What happened there three years ago was more than just a riot. It was an uprising, a revolution, an attempt to overthrow the government of this country. And the Guide was the spark who made it happen. He began a campaign against the government through his mullahs, the local priests. Every day they preached to the students about the government's corruption, how it had given itself to the West. The tension rose, until one day, there was an incident with the police, and the town exploded in violence. You and Mona arrived there when the trouble was at its height. Remember, the Guide's mullahs had called for the death of the faithless, the eradication of all profanity; and so it was that his followers turned their hatred on you. Abu Tarek was one of the Guide's right-hand men, like a military adviser, if you can believe such a thing. He was the instrument of Mona's death, her murderer. But in many ways, the Guide is more guilty of her death."

Girling's eyes widened. "What happened to him, this Guide?"

"The troops who moved into the city, and rescued you, managed to capture him. He was brought here to Cairo in the strictest secrecy. But they did not dare try him for Asyut, for his punishment certainly would have been the death penalty. And the last thing the authorities wanted was a martyr and another uprising. So they pretended Asyut never happened and the Guide was sent into exile."

"It was a bad day for Egypt when the *'askary* lost you as a detective, Mohammed Hamdi."

"Thank you."

"But if the Guide's living abroad, how could he know about Stansell? Stansell is somewhere in this city still, I'm convinced of it."

Mohammed Hamdi gave a smile of satisfaction. "Whoever said anything about foreign exile, Tom Girling? This was the government's—or should I say the *mukhabarat*'s—masterstroke. In exchange for the Guide's complicity, his promise to behave, they have let him live out his days here in Cairo. He is a prisoner, certainly, but it is a golden cage that holds him. The Brotherhood knows where he is and the *mukhabarat* knows the Guide is in regular touch with them. But as long as there is no trouble, the Guide stays out of prison. He is, in effect, their puppet, but in a sense, they are his puppets, too. For, it is his word—or rather, his henchmen—who keep order in the streets.''

''Where do they hold this Guide?''

''In the al-Mu'ayyad Mosque. To get there you must go down al-Mu'izz Street, almost to the point where the old quarter meets the City of the Dead.''

''The City of the Dead?''

''Yes, it is close. Is that significant?''

''Maybe, maybe not. How do I get into this mosque?''

''Anyone can get in. There are two guards on the door to ensure the Guide does not leave, but there is little danger of that. He does not want to leave. He has the government by the neck just where he is.''

''How will I know him?'' Girling asked.

''He holds prayers every day. In the morning. At nine o'clock. To the people, he is a great and skillful orator. Yet only a handful know of his true power.''

Mohammed Hamdi turned for the door, then stopped. ''I should warn you that if you go to this man, it would be most unwise to tell him who you are, or the secret you harbor. I cannot say I like you, Tom Girling, but—''

''Say it, Mohammed Hamdi.''

''Little Alia is a beautiful child. Stay alive long enough to kiss her good-bye for me.''

CHAPTER 5

THE SIKORSKY THUNDERED through the wadi at over 160 miles per hour, barely thirty feet above the ground, a fearsome fusion of sight and sound; an enormous, squat insect with seven thousand pounds of shaft horsepower propelling it through the air.

The pilot's gaze did not flicker from the TV display's green-and-black FLIR image just above his knees. At this height, glancing up from the screen was an invitation to fly the helicopter into the ground or the valley walls.

Outside, it was as close to absolute darkness as the desert allowed. Major Bart Bookerman's lifeline was the FLIR camera in the nose of the helicopter. He had vocal assistance from his crew, whose night-vision goggles, NVGs—mini-binoculars hinged down over the helmet—picked up on any ambient light, magnifying it thousands of times to turn night into day. Apart from the copilot, Karanski, all of the crew wore NVGs. While the FLIR acted as Bookerman's eyes ahead, his scanners and their NVGs were his peripheral vision. If he started drifting a little too close to the wadi cliffs, they were there to direct him back on course.

Bookerman loved the MH-53J. Although a big helicopter, it flew like a scout bird. The men liked it, too, because it could get them in and out of bandit country fast and because its three miniguns packed enough punch to help them out of trouble. Thanks to its extensive armor protection, there were very few things that could bring down an MH-53J. A shoulder-launched heat-seeking missile was one of them; a fast, air-to-air-armed helicopter was another. Bookerman had been taught every tactic for throwing off fighter helicopters, and his ESM-ECM suite was more than capable of jamming or spoofing surface-to-air missiles.

So much for the theory.

In the end, their survival boiled down to his ability as a pilot. Right now, he felt sharp, alive. Without the boss peering over his shoulder, his confidence soared. Ulm had assigned himself to Bookerman's ship for the duration, but in his absence, it was just him and his regular crew: Master Sergeant Alejandro Salva, minigunner and scanner; Staff Sergeant Byron Sweet, second gunner/scanner; and their regular flight engineer, Master Sergeant John Leiffer. Depending on where he was needed most, Leiffer hopped from his jump seat between the pilot and copilot to the ramp at the back of the helicopter, where he stuck his head into the slipstream, scouting for obstructions forward and, on a real mission, trouble behind.

Bookerman banked the MH-53J around a rock stack and hauled back on the cyclic to align the helo with the narrow wadi ahead.

"GPS has gone again," Karanski said matter-of-factly.

"No shit," Bookerman said. They'd been having problems with the Global Positioning System. Every time he banked the Pave Low past 45 degrees in one of these sheer-sided wadis, the GPS receiver on top of the fuselage lost its fix on the satellite that beamed them their coordinates.

"Inertial nav has got it covered," Karanski said, his eyes on the multifunction display in the center of the instrument panel. Whenever the GPS winked out, the inertial navigation system cut in to keep the mission computer updated on their position. The nav system, some said, was the very heart of the MH-53J Pave Low III. Unless you could plot your way into the target area with pinpoint precision, there wasn't a whole lot of point in taking off.

Bookerman kept his eyes on the FLIR screen. It took a lot of practice—hundreds of hours of hugging the New Mexico desert and being strapped in the mission simulator—to interpret the green and black contrasts of the FLIR. Even now he didn't find it easy. There was always the temptation to look up out of the window. Whatever happened, though, he had to control that urge. He watched another rock stack form in the center of the TV screen. Were he to look for it with his bare eyes through the clear-glass windshield, he would find only a wall of blackness, an infinite void. He wouldn't catch a glimpse of the stack, even as they plowed into it at close to two hundred miles per hour.

Of course, if the Pentagon had invested in cockpit lighting that was NVG-compatible, then he could be wearing goggles like the rest of the crew. Were he to wear them, however, the instrument lights on the panel in front of him would fry his eyes as the NVGs turned each innocuous dial into a searchlight. Bookerman's MH-53J was to have had the new lighting installed months ago, but because of the budget cutbacks the program had stalled. And, of course, because of Panama, the Pathfinders weren't too high on the Pentagon's priority funding list.

The rock stack shot out of the picture. Bookerman felt its presence somewhere off to his right, but he didn't look up.

"That was pretty fucking close," Sweet said over the intercom.

"Don't fucking swear so much," Karanski said. "How close?"

"About five feet from our fucking tips," Sweet said.

Karanski turned to Bookerman. "Did you get that?"

Bookerman didn't answer.

"I said, did you get that, Bart?"

"I got it."

"Are you all right?"

Bookerman's jaw pounded on the wad of gum between his teeth. "Yeah, I'm fine."

"Sure?"

"I'm not overloaded, if that's what you're driving at." Sometimes a pilot got so much information thrown at him that his brain could shut out life-or-death information. Bookerman had heard of pilots in the Gulf war who were so wrapped up in their mission that they never even heard the warning shouts of their comrades. A data recorder recovered from a shot-down F-15E in southern Iraq showed that the Weapon

Systems Operator had been merrily flying the old precision-guided bomb down the cross hairs on his TV screen, his mind set on destroying that mobile Scud launcher, while his escort was screaming at him to punch out chaff and flares and take evasive action. The first the F-15E crew knew about it was when the SA-16 flew straight up the right-hand tail pipe. Thanks and good night.

He adjusted his course fractionally, lining the helicopter up as best he could on the valley's center line.

Until this mission came along, Bookerman was beginning to think that professional life had passed him by.

He'd joined the Pathfinders in 1986 after a distinguished, if short, career with the Military Airlift Command, flying AC-130 gunships. After transitioning to helos on the UH-1, he gradually moved up to the MH-53J Pave Low III, graduating on CH-3Es and CH-53As along the way. Bookerman had just finished learning everything there was to know about low-level penetration missions at night and in bad weather when Panama came along.

On that fateful night, he'd inserted Ulm and the rest of the hit team into the jungle without a hitch. As much as he wanted to blame Ulm for what happened at Los Torrijos, he realized that it could have happened to anybody. But the Pentagon wanted a scapegoat and they'd all been tarred with the same brush. *C'est la guerre,* Bookerman mused. While other USAF Pave Low units were rushed to the Gulf to ready for war, he had had to sit it out in New Mexico, champing at the bit whenever he heard of a coalition aircraft downed behind enemy lines. Rescuing pilots was just one of the many missions for which the Pathfinders had trained him.

The ultimate humiliation came on the night that Ulm told him, his voice quavering with emotion, that the Pathfinders had been picked to wet-nurse Soviet officers on an exchange program formulated as part of the politicians' vision of a New World Order.

Bookerman was no great fan of the Russians.

He pulled the helicopter out of the valley and the desert opened up before them.

"How'd we do?" he asked Karanski.

The copilot peered at the digital readout on the multifunction display. "Thirty-seven seconds out, Bart."

"Shit!" Shabanov would have his guts for any timing discrepancy beyond the half-minute mark. He pulled up to a hundred feet and bled off some speed.

"What are we going to do?" Karanski asked.

"What's our fuel like?"

"Twenty-two hundred gallons."

"Then we do it again."

There were muttered protests from the three scanners. They had been in the air for four hours, most of the time at low level. It was unrelenting work. No one could afford a lapse in concentration. A blink of the eye at the wrong moment and they were all dead.

Bookerman pushed the stick forward and the helicopter plunged back toward the desert floor. Life at thirty feet. What a bitch.

"Time to first way-point?" Bookerman asked.

"Two minutes, twenty-three seconds. You should have it on screen any second. I've got it on radar."

Bookerman screwed up his eyes against the black-and-green TV picture. There, right on the periphery of the stabilized FLIR camera's range, was their entry point into the mountain range. The two peaks, known locally as Satan's Horns, were distinct in the way their summits arched toward each other. They would show up like neon signs on Karanski's terrain-following/terrain-avoidance radar screen.

"We've got company," Leiffer said suddenly from the ramp.

"What kind of company?" Karanski asked.

"Another helo. About half a mile back. On our six and a little ways out left. He's tailing us at about five hundred feet."

Karanski turned to Bookerman. The skipper's face was drenched with sweat.

"Are you getting any of this?" Karanski asked.

Bookerman kept his eyes glued to the FLIR. He chewed his gum rhythmically. "Uh-huh."

"Any ID on our friend?" Karanski asked Leiffer.

No answer.

"Who is that guy back there, John?" Karanski repeated.

"Can't tell, sir. There's a lot of shit from our downwash. I can't get a clear view. I can see navigation lights reflecting off his rotors, though. It's a helo, not fixed-wing."

"I can't see shit either," Sweet said. He was positioned on the wrong side of the helicopter.

"I see him," Salva said. "Man, he's right behind us."

"Come on, Salva. What the fuck is it?"

"It looks like a Hind."

"Do the Egyptians have any Mi-24s?" Sweet asked.

"No," Karanski said. He looked across to the skipper again. Bookerman was flying the MH-53J like he was on autopilot. "It looks like we've got an Ivan out back who wants to play games. Do you want to call this thing off?"

Bookerman's face glowed in the reflection from the FLIR screen. "No. How long to the way-point?" The valley between the two peaks was a black hole in the center of the picture.

"About twenty seconds."

"Okay, let's take him with us."

"Are you sure that's a good idea?"

"No Ivan's going to push me around the sky."

"He's diving," Salva said, excitement in his voice. "He's right down on the deck now. Same height as us. Is this guy crazy or something?"

"This has got to be Shabanov's idea of an initiative test," Bookerman said through clenched teeth. "Okay, hotshot, eat this."

The MH-53J roared between the two peaks into the wadi.

Karanski logged the way-point. "Mark."

Bookerman rolled the helicopter into a bend and felt the Gs come on. Two times gravity, he calculated, from the way his eyes bulged in their sockets. The very edge of the Sikorsky's structural tolerances. "Where is he now?"

"He's still hanging in there—real close, too," Leiffer said.

Bookerman threw the MH-53J into another sharp bend and heard Leiffer's curse over his headphones as the engineer-scanner was hurled against the wall of the helicopter.

"Check your harnesses, all of you," Karanski said.

Leiffer picked himself off the floor and buckled his harness to the cabin wall. He crawled back to the half-open loading ramp, his eyes straining against the dust cloud behind them.

"He's fifty feet behind," Leiffer said.

The nose of the Mi-24J, its blister canopy bulging like an insect eye, edged forward.

Bookerman swore and advanced the power setting. The new Hind was good. He pushed the Sikorsky lower, until it was ten feet off the deck. "How's that?"

Leiffer wriggled farther into the slipstream. "He's somewhere in the dust storm thrown up by our rotors. He's got to pull up now. No one can fly in that stuff."

Suddenly, there was a warning shout from Sweet. "There are freaking camels up ahead."

Only then did Bookerman catch them on the FLIR, the camels' bodies showing up as two giant heatspots in the center of the picture. "Where the fuck did they come from?" He pulled back on the stick, his mind filled with the FLIR's negative image of a bedouin rousing from sleep, the fear in his features detailed on the edge of the TV screen.

The Sikorsky was up to two hundred feet before Bookerman even knew it. He pushed the stick forward and felt his stomach lurch toward his throat. Two hundred feet on the day and the shoulder-launched SAMs would have him. He had to get down on the deck again, fast.

"We're approaching the target area," Karanski said. He was counting off the miles on the multifunction display in his head.

From his prone position on the ramp, Leiffer watched, a mixture of fascination and horror on his face, as the nose of the Hind edged out of the maelstrom boiling up behind them.

He yelled a warning and Bookerman sucked yet more power from the engines. The vibration jarred his teeth, the very marrow of his bones, making even the act of thinking laborious. The ground was flashing past so close he felt he could reach out and touch it.

"My God," Leiffer said, his eyes locked onto the nose of the Russian gunship. He could see the pilot hunched over his controls in the upper cockpit and the gunner immediately below.

"What the fuck's happening back there?" Karanski shouted.

Leiffer shook himself. "He's still out there." He paused. "I think he's trying to get past us."

Up ahead the wadi began to widen. Karanski counted down their estimated arrival from the time-on-target function on the Doppler.

Bookerman tightened his grip on the cyclic and felt the sweat ooze between his gloved fingers.

"Thirty seconds to target," Karanski said.

"He's going past us now," Leiffer said. "I'm losing him."

"I've got him," Sweet said, as the Hind slid alongside his position. "Easy as you go, skipper, this guy's in the fucking haircut business. His rotor's about three feet from ours."

The Hind started to pull past them.

Karanski: "Twenty seconds to target."

Knowing he had been beaten, Bookerman chopped power and pulled up out of the wadi. "Fuck the SAMs, this guy's trying to get us all killed."

The Hind filled Bookerman's FLIR picture. Beside him, Karanski cranked up the magnification on his FLIR scope so that he had a clear view into the Mil's cockpit. He expected fully to see the Russian gunner looking over his shoulder and giving them the bird. What he saw instead was pandemonium. The pilot, in the raised rear seat, was crouched over his instruments, hands darting left and right as he threw switches and checked dials. When the gunner did turn, he was craning for a view of his pilot. Karanski saw that his eyes were wide with fear. The blaze of warning lights across the instrument panel told him why. Suddenly, the Hind pulled up like a rearing cobra, its nose pointing toward the stars. Bookerman didn't even have time to exclaim. He thought momentarily that the Hind was trying to follow him up into the sky, although later he realized that no helicopter pilot would have tried such a maneuver.

Traveling at close to two hundred miles per hour, the Hind had almost nine times the forces of gravity driven through its airframe. Its five blades sheered off at the hub as one, sending the helicopter into a ballistic arc that was cut short by a rock stack jutting out of the desert floor. For some reason, it did not explode, despite the cascade of sparks that lit up the night sky. The impact broke the fuselage in two, the tail boom burying itself in the desert floor of the wadi amid a cloud of dust, the cockpit and cabin flying on another hundred feet before being crushed against the unrelenting face of the wadi's sides.

Inside the Sikorsky, nobody spoke for a long time. Bookerman had seen enough to know that there were no survivors. He pulled the Sikorsky into a turn that would take it back over the crash site.

Karanski's burst transmission to Wadi Qena was succinct. They had a helicopter down in the desert.

■   ■   ■

GIRLING WALKED briskly along the street known as al-Mu'izz, a lone focus among the traders and the faithful. He was the only foreigner in the street, the sole *'agnabi*.

It was a little before nine. In the distance, he could just hear the muezzin calling from his platform high above the al-Mu'ayyad Mosque. The street traders had already hit their stride. Girling tucked his head down and tried to mingle with the droves of men heading for the prayer meeting, but it was impossible to escape the attention of the shopkeepers for long. They dangled wares of leather, cotton, silver and gold before his eyes. Despite their persuasiveness, he steadfastly but politely refused them.

As he pressed farther into the heart of the old quarter, he began to sense a new mood. The traders looked at him with deepening suspicion. It was as if they knew he had not come to their street to buy. For all his attempts to appear like an innocent tourist—guidebook in his hand and camera around his neck—Girling knew he was fooling nobody. As more and more shopkeepers retreated into the shade of their stalls, their overtures rejected, he imagined he heard the rasp of their curses behind him.

When he thought about Lazan's warning and what Mona's father had told him, he tingled with the realization that the street could swallow him in a moment and no one on the outside would be the wiser except, perhaps, Sharifa. He had phoned her at her apartment first thing that morning to tell her he was heading for the al-Mu'ayyad Mosque. He called her from a shop around the corner from Stansell's, thereby avoiding any tap the *mukhabarat* had put on his phone. When he explained about the Guide, she begged him not to go. But he had made up his mind the previous night and nothing was going to deter him, not even the *mukhabarat*. He had slipped from the apartment via the fire escape, neatly avoiding his two shadows out front.

From the moment he arrived, Girling had known that time was running out, as if Stansell were being kept in a sealed box with a finite supply of air. If the Guide was as powerful as his father-in-law claimed, one word, should he choose to give it, would be enough to secure Stansell's release.

Girling raised his eyes to his surroundings. Al-Mu'izz was caught

like a trapped nerve between the affluent bustle of the Khan, a few
hundred yards away, and the grinding poverty of the City of the Dead,
a stone's throw to the south. The necropolis sprawled somewhere
beyond Bab Zuweila, the southern gates of Cairo's medieval wall. The
al-Mu'ayyad Mosque, the Guide's open prison, nestled in the shade of
the gates. On hot days like this, al-Mu'izz festered like an open sore.

Years before, when Mona had brought him here, showing pride in
the craftsmanship paraded in these shops, it had seemed a different
place. But that was before the Gulf war and before he had even heard
of the Brotherhood.

Upon its founding in the late 1920s, the Brotherhood's twin aims
had been the eviction of the ruling British elite and the establishment
of a fundamental Islamic state. It took the Brotherhood just two
decades to realize the first goal, and although a comparatively quiet
period followed, it never lost sight of the second. A vivid reminder of
its presence hit the world between the eyes when a breakaway group,
the Partisans of Allah, assassinated Egyptian president Anwar al-Sadat
in 1981. Sadat had been trying to woo the Brotherhood into main-
stream politics, recognizing that it was gaining strength daily, that it
was wresting the country from him inch by inch. But the Brotherhood
could not negotiate with a man who had sold the Arab birthright for
peace with Israel, the Brotherhood's sworn enemy. And so one day it
rose up and killed him.

Girling rounded a bend in the street and saw the two minarets of the
mosque. The sunlight soared between them, refracted by the dust and
the flies that swirled in the air.

As the faithful tramped through the doors of the mosque, Girling
scouted for guards. He soon spotted them, two policemen squatting
beside a small gas burner in the shadows at the top of the steps.

Girling adjusted his camera, making sure it hung obviously by his
side, and slid into the midst of a group of prayer-goers as they marched
up the marble steps. At the top, a column of warm light hit him in the
face. He squinted past the turbaned heads of the people in front of him
and caught a glimpse of trees and ornate ponds in the open courtyard.
The people were already sitting on the floor, ranged in lines before the
miqra, the pulpit where the Guide would make his speech. Girling was
inside and looking for a place to sit out the service, when a hand
grabbed him by the shoulder and spun him round.

The policeman shook a finger in his face. "Entry *mamnoo'a,*" he said in hybrid English-Arabic.

Girling's brow furrowed in confusion.

"Forbidden," the other guard explained.

Girling produced the guidebook and began to thumb through its pages. "This is the al-Mu'ayyad Mosque?" he asked, his eyes wide-eyed in innocence. He pointed to a page for emphasis.

"No speak English," the first policeman said. He pointed down the steps. "Go."

Girling laughed disarmingly. One of them smiled back. "I just want a few pictures," he said, lifting his camera.

The first policeman shook his head. "For-bid-den during prayers."

"I see," Girling said, pretending to understand only then. "Okay, no pictures. I just look, yes?"

The guard remained unmoved until his gaze dropped to the open guidebook and rested on the eighty Egyptian pounds protruding from the pages. There was two months' salary for each man there.

"One hour," Girling said firmly.

The guards looked first at each other, then down the street. The older one grabbed the money and gave a shrug of resignation. "Okay," he said.

Girling slipped off his shoes and entered the cool tranquillity of the mosque. He crossed the great *sahn,* the courtyard, and proceeded into the gardens on the other side. He found a bench among the trees and sat down. No one paid him any attention, for prayers had already begun. The sea of bodies moved as one, rising and falling with the exhortations of the prayer leader.

Girling began to gather his thoughts, to prepare himself for the encounter ahead. But in the stillness that followed, he became conscious only of the depth of his hatred. He told himself over and over that this was not the time or the place for his anger, that he had to forget this man's deeds. His first duty was to break Stansell out of captivity. The Guide offered a chance. But first he had to put Mona behind him.

When Girling looked up, the people had turned their faces to the pulpit. An air of expectancy filled the mosque. Across the courtyard, a slight figure was climbing the steps to the *miqra.* The Guide was older than Girling imagined; his face weatherbeaten, skin sallow from a life of asceticism. His hair was hidden by a turban; his cheeks and chin by a patchy, gray beard. He wore the long, flowing robes of all clerics.

The Guide's address rang out across the courtyard. Girling listened, trying to understand, but all he caught were snatches of meaning. The Guide was using classical Arabic, the language of literature, and vastly different from the colloquial patois he had taught himself. The Guide's address was inspirational; an appeal for patience, a reminder of rewards to come. His people listened thoughtfully, and every so often there were waves of assent.

When it was over, the crowd rose suddenly, much more quickly than Girling had expected. He leapt to his feet and rushed forward, but the Guide was already halfway from the *miqra* to a door in the far wall. He battled against the tide of people heading for the street, ignoring their cries of indignation. Girling burst through them just as the Guide was almost through the arch.

Girling shouted in English. "Hey, you!" The silence began with those closest to him. They stared accusingly as if he had uttered some deep profanity. Like concentric ripples in a pond, the silence emanated outward, until it reached the Guide and his entourage. When it touched him, the Guide hesitated, then turned.

"Do I know you, *'agnabi?*"

Girling tried to speak, but could not find the Arabic.

"Do you come as a friend?" the Guide asked. His voice rang clearly across the courtyard.

Girling's awkwardness had turned his curiosity to concern. He felt the crowd's hostility at his back.

"Who are you?" the Guide asked.

The words came suddenly. Girling spoke the local dialect of a Cairene. "I am a journalist, an English journalist. My name is Tom Girling. I have come a long way to see you, sheikh."

"A journalist? What could I possibly have to say to a journalist?" The Guide waved his hand in a gesture that indicated the high walls of his prison. He took another step toward the door.

"I did not come here to write down your words. I have come here with an appeal. An appeal for a life. For a man named Stansell, a writer, like me. Have you heard of this man?"

The Guide stopped.

"Do you know this man?" Girling repeated.

"Should I, *'agnabi?'*"

"He has been kidnapped by the Angels of Judgment, or people acting in their name. Here, in Cairo."

The Guide turned again. "What has this to do with me?"

"I think you can help."

"Why should I help you against the noble soldiers of Islam?"

"What nobility is there in the death of innocents, sheikh?" As he spoke, Girling heard Mona's cries echoing across the courtyard. "Stansell's only crime was that he did his job. He published a name, the name of the Angels of Judgment. Nothing more. Surely—" He stopped, searching for the merest sign of assent. "A word from you would spread through the mosques, the bazaars and the streets. They listen to you . . ."

The mosque was silent once more.

"And why do you assume I might have influence in this matter?" the Guide asked.

"Because I know who you are. I know they look up to you, sheikh."

There was a murmur from the crowd.

The Guide straightened his back and lifted his face to the sky. "Your friend's fate was determined by God. What has happened was written. I cannot change that." He reached for the door.

Girling shook his head. "That's bullshit," he said in English. Then in Arabic: "I was in Asyut. Three years ago. The riots, sheikh, I was there . . ."

The Guide stopped walking, but he did not turn.

Girling fought for space. The crowd had almost surrounded him. "I saw a young Egyptian woman stoned to death on a patch of dirt road. Like Stansell, she had done nothing. But that didn't stop the mob. They rained the rocks on her until her body was so badly broken even her husband could not recognize her. Could such a death be preordained?"

The Guide faced Girling once more. His eyes were bright, but there was a tremor in his voice. "More than likely she was unclean," he said. "An adulteress."

"Then I of all people should have known," Girling replied. "For this woman was my wife."

The Guide's shoulders rose as he drew breath. The crowd quivered in anticipation.

"Only God can save your friend, *'agnabi,'*" the Guide said. Then he stepped through the arch. The door slammed behind him, the noise echoing across the *sahn*.

Girling pounded the wood with his fists. On the other side, he could hear the Guide's steps retreating down the corridor. "You murdered her, sheikh, you killed her, you and Abu Tarek," he shouted. Before he could put his shoulder to the door, there was a howl of rage from the crowd. It surged forward. Girling felt himself being picked up like a swimmer in the grip of an immense, rolling wave. He tried to grab hold of something, the door handle, the balustrade of the *miqra,* but the people were too many. They dragged him to the top of the steps where he had entered the mosque. He knew this crowd. He had seen it at work before. Once outside the sanctuary of the mosque he was as good as dead.

He was tumbling down, images from the street spinning past his face as he fell. The crowd fell on him, blocking out the sun. They were kicking him, pulling his hair, ripping his clothes. He tried to shield his face with his hands, but his arms were nearly pulled from their sockets.

Then he heard a volley of shots and suddenly saw daylight again. He struggled to his feet, as his assailants scattered. He saw blood, his blood, dripping into an open drain. When he looked up, he found himself staring into the unsmiling face of Captain Lutfi al-Qadi of State Security.

■   ■   ■

THE GUIDE watched from the tiny latticed window of his second-floor room as the *'agnabi* Girling was led away, flanked by two plainclothes police officers, with a third, short and overweight, leading the way down the street.

The Guide found that his exchange with the *'agnabi* had vexed him deeply. It was partly the look in the young man's face, partly the reminder of times past, dredged up so publicly, that preyed on his mind.

Most of all, though, he caught in Girling's eyes a vision of troubled times to come. Not for himself; the Guide was beyond caring for his own physical well-being. He was old and ill; and his moment, the moment he had been waiting for all his adult life, was near. Death would not be an end, but a beginning.

Yet for his brothers, Girling spelled danger. The Guide knew nothing of the Sword or the Angels of Judgment, but their action in Lebanon had filled the True Believers with a new sense of purpose, a new vigor. The English journalist Stansell was not being held by the Muslim Brotherhood, of that he was certain; the Brothers did nothing without his blessing. Which meant that the Angels of Judgment, brother fundamentalists, were somewhere in his city. And with Girling on their tail, they needed protection. He must somehow pass on the warning.

He called over the *katib,* his scribe, and proceeded to dictate a letter. The Brotherhood had ways of seeing that it would be delivered. Then he summoned the boy. Though only thirteen, the boy had boasted once that he could find anyone or anything in Cairo. The Guide wanted Girling watched. It was time to put the boy to the test.

■   ■   ■

BOOKERMAN LEANED against the fuselage of his Sikorsky, smoking a cigarette. He watched the comings and goings of the Russians dispassionately. The Russian investigation team, a bunch of technicians from Qena, had been brought in on another Hind, accompanied by a fully armed detachment of Spetsnaz.

A Russian sergeant, in charge of the armed escort, informed Bookerman that the troops were there to ward off any inquisitive bedouin who strayed into the wadi. But Bookerman knew that was only part of the truth. He had little doubt their primary task was to discourage the Pathfinders from getting too close. Some things never changed. He had been at the Paris Air Show once when the Soviets' pride, the MiG-29, had crashed during the display. The Russians closed ranks and began blaming anyone or anything except their flawless fighter. He sniffed the same paranoia in the air in this hot and dusty wadi.

As the Sikorsky that Bookerman had requested as backup disgorged its complement of Pathfinders, he was able to relax. Bookerman didn't like to spend more time than he had to in the company of Russians, particularly when they outnumbered him.

As he pulled a last drag from his Marlboro and tossed the butt away, Bookerman became aware of a commotion around the twisted remains of the Hind's tail boom. He joined a group of three Pathfinders and set off toward it.

The boom had carved out an enormous trench in the center of the dried out riverbed. It was so deep that from where Bookerman had been standing beside his helicopter, it was possible to see only the mangled blades of the tail rotor. Now as he came closer Bookerman could see a group of technicians huddle around the boom like archaeologists gazing at a newly excavated dig.

The Pathfinder group was still thirty yards away when a young Spetsnaz soldier spun around, his Kalashnikov pointed right at them. The Russian screamed something, and Wallace, the leading American, stopped in his tracks. The two other Pathfinders made to unsling their weapons.

"*Stoi!*" the Russian shouted. There was a wild look in his eyes.

Wallace held his arms out, the palms of his hands face down. His escort let go of their weapons.

Wallace looked the Russian, a fair-haired corporal, squarely in the eye. "What the fuck is with you, boy?"

"Sabotage!" the soldier yelled, jabbing his weapon. "You killed them, Yankee."

Bookerman could tell from the expressions on the faces of the other Russians that the belief was shared.

A Russian officer, a major, sprinted across from another area of the crash site. He shouted at his corporal, but the soldier appeared not to hear. He kept his eyes fixed on Wallace, his gun aimed at the middle of the American's rib cage. Bookerman tensed. From the set of the Russian soldier's jaw and the look in his eyes, he was going to blow a hole through Wallace's chest. The major swung his nine-millimeter into a firing position. The corporal saw the movement and started to turn, bringing his assault rifle around with him, but the officer's pistol found its target first and jumped, the shots booming in the confines of the wadi. The bullets lifted the soldier off his feet and threw him into the pit gouged by the tail boom.

Bookerman was the first to unfreeze. He jumped into the pit and knelt beside the body. A shadow fell across him and Bookerman looked up into the face of the corporal's executioner. The officer was holstering his Makharov. His face was devoid of any expression.

"Perhaps it was the heat," the officer said.

Bookerman shook his head. "Don't give me that horseshit. He said something about sabotage."

The officer shrugged and turned away. Bookerman got to his feet, grabbed the Russian's shoulder and spun him around. "Tell me what he meant."

The Russian hesitated, then indicated that Bookerman should follow him to the center of the crash site. A small section of skin had been pulled back from the tail boom. Bookerman examined the guts of the machine. For the most part it was intact, with little sign of internal damage. His gaze skirted past the ribs, wires and incidental components of the helicopter's dynamic systems to rest at a point where the shaft linking the main transmission drive and the tail rotor had sheared in two. Orange hydraulic fluid dripped onto the gleaming metal.

"He thought this was sabotage," the officer said.

"And you?"

"No sabotage."

"Then what?"

"Structural failure, maybe."

"But this was a new helicopter," Bookerman said. They didn't come newer.

The officer clambered to the top of the trench and looked down. Bookerman had not moved.

"We go back to base now," the Russian said. "No doubt Colonel Shabanov will issue orders to recover the wreckage later."

Bookerman heard turboshaft engines spooling into life a little way down the wadi.

Bookerman climbed wearily to the top of the pit and paused before heading back to his Sikorsky. It was some moments before he realized Wallace was standing there beside him, waiting for orders.

"Are you all right, Major? You look like you were the one who nearly got blown away."

Bookerman didn't answer.

"It's time to get going, sir," the sergeant said, more firmly.

Bookerman nodded and started walking. "You're right, Wallace. The quicker the better."

"Sir?"

"Someone took a saw to that shaft and cut it almost in two. That Hind was flying on borrowed time. And the Russians think we did it."

■   ■   ■

AL-QADI CLICKED his fingers and the driver tore off down the road. A turn close by the train station confirmed they were heading for the *mukhabarat*'s interrogation center in Shubra.

The main drag gave way to the oppressive squalor of slums. Here, there were no children playing—no dogs even, roaming the gutters for scraps. The air was thick, every molecule charged. The Fiat splashed through open drains and the stench of the water rose to meet them. Al-Qadi removed a soiled handkerchief from his top pocket and wiped it under his nose.

The interrogation center seemed to have cast a pall over the surrounding area. It was a desolate place, a place you went to and never returned. As they pulled up before the red-and-white barrier and al-Qadi wound down his window, Girling realized there was something more. Shubra felt as if it had been sealed in a vacuum. There was no sound.

He was marched, a policeman on either side to support him, into the bowels of the building. Al-Qadi's plastic soles squeaked on the smooth flagstones as he led the way down the corridors of cells. From time to time the investigator would stop, slide back a hatch and peep inside. From one, Girling heard a sudden cry. Al-Qadi responded by gargling some phlegm in the back of his throat and spitting it to the floor.

At last, al-Qadi kicked in a door, letting it swing on its hinges as he groped in the darkness for the switch. Greasy yellow light pulsed from a bare bulb hanging in the center of the room. The current crackled as it fought against the buildup of damp in the ragged insulation of the wiring.

Al-Qadi gestured to a chair by a table, the only furniture in the cell. There was a strong odor of urine. Girling took three steps before his legs gave way and he fell. The concrete floor was cold and wet against his face.

The door crashed shut behind him and he looked up in time to see al-Qadi's face momentarily framed by the bars. Girling struggled to his feet and stuck his head as far as possible into the opening. He bellowed down the corridor, but all he heard was his own weak echo and the squeak of al-Qadi's soles disappearing into the distance. When he turned back to the room, the light had failed and the cell was quite dark.

Girling moved to a corner where the odor of excrement was less pungent. He tilted the chair, his back resting against the wall, and listened. At first he heard nothing. Slowly, however, sound bubbled up through the silence. He was able to identify the desolate cry he had heard before, the murmurings of a man deep in prayer ritual and a third voice, very weak, probably that of a woman.

It was several hours before Girling heard the approaching squeak of al-Qadi's shoes once more. He shook himself awake and waited for the door to be thrown open. But the sound wasn't anything to do with al-Qadi, nor was it coming from the corridor. The rats were inside his cell.

■   ■   ■

ULM STRODE purposefully down the center line of the hangar, glancing left and right at the squat shapes of the MH-53Js. His engineers swarmed over, under and inside them. The noise of engines spooling and the clatter of wrenches and power drills working against machines was the same sound he heard every time he walked into the maintenance shop at Kirtland. Yet there was also something missing. It was only when he was halfway down the hangar that he realized what it was. There was no conversation, no laughter as his men worked. He wasn't the only one who had been stung by the Russian's sabotage allegation. The order from the crew chiefs had been check and double-check the machines. Lightning was not going to strike twice.

It was not a good day to be leaving Qena, but he needed to make contact with the embassy in Cairo to collect the codes that would trigger the mission. He was due on the northbound express later that evening.

He found Jones in the back of one of the MH-53Js. The sergeant had just finished binding his head with bandage from the helicopter's first-aid box.

"How are you doing, Spades?"

"I've felt better, sir."

Ulm pulled down one of the folding troop seats and sat opposite his sergeant. "Tell me what happened."

Jones told him about their desperate search for water and the incident with the bedouin at the well.

"Bitov killed them?"

"I wouldn't be talking to you now if he hadn't." He paused. "If you ask me, we were never meant to find any wells. I'll bet that bastard doctored the maps."

"Who?"

"Shabanov. With respect, sir, the son of a bitch is capable of anything. Which reminds me. Who came in last on the E and E exercise?"

"Kerrigan and Tarantinov," Ulm said. "But they won't be doing it again."

"How come?"

"Our friend the colonel is too preoccupied with the crash of his Mi-24."

"What's the latest on the helicopter?" Jones asked.

"They're still bringing in the bits, but I think it's a fair assumption we won't be riding into Lebanon on Mils."

"Well, at least something's going our way," Jones said. "I never much liked the look of Russian hardware."

"Spades, there are two men dead because of that crash and the Russians think we had something to do with it."

"What do you think, sir?"

"I think Bookerman was mistaken, that it was most likely some kind of structural failure. Why would any of us want to sabotage one of their helicopters?"

"Maybe one of *them* tampered with it," Jones said.

"Come off it, Spades." Ulm put a hand on the sergeant's shoulder. "You look like you could use some rest."

Jones opened his mouth to speak again, but thought better of it.

Ulm looked at him thoughtfully. "What's on your mind, Spades?"

"It's probably nothing."

"Spit."

"He said something that's got me beat, that's all."

"Who's that?"

"Bitov. It was while we were on the cliff. He was telling me about some kind of mission impossible in Afghanistan that only he and Shabanov came back from. Thing was, the unit they were attached to wasn't Spetsnaz. Bitov called it Opnaz. I heard him loud and clear. When I tackled him on it he backtracked, saying I was going crazy. But

I know I heard him right.'' Jones stared Ulm in the face. ''You ever heard of Opnaz, sir?''

Ulm shook his head. ''That's impossible, Spades. Shabanov has been in Spetsnaz twenty years. And the Sovs went into Afghanistan in 1979. He had to have been in Spetsnaz then, same as he is now.''

''So where does Opnaz fit in?''

''Slip of the tongue?''

''I don't think so, sir.''

''Then maybe that bedouin hit you harder than you thought.''

Jones passed his hand over the newly applied bandage and managed a broad smile. ''You could be right there,'' he said.

■   ■   ■

DOYLE HAD just finished submitting his daily report to TERCOM when Ulm appeared at the door of the communications room. The intelligence officer followed him outside.

''Anything shaking out there?'' Ulm asked.

The IO shook his head. ''TERCOM's still in silent mode.''

''Shit, this is shaping up to be one big bitch of a day.''

''You're bound to pick up some news when you go to Cairo tonight.''

''I wouldn't count on it. The Angels of Judgment managed to give an entire task force the slip when they pulled that stunt at Beirut. Who's to say they've gotten any easier to find since?''

''It'll do you good to get off the base,'' Doyle said, then hesitated. ''You think there's anything in this sabotage shit?''

Ulm looked at him.

''I know what you've been telling the men, Elliot. But I want to know what you really think.''

Ulm kicked a toeful of sand across the edge of the concrete runway. ''I think we've got trouble, Charlie, that's what I think.'' He paused. ''Have you ever heard of something called Opnaz?''

Doyle shook his head. ''Nope. Should I?''

Ulm repeated the story that Jones had just told him.

''His brains are pretty badly shook up,'' Doyle said. ''That bedouin hit him hard.''

''He swears the guy said Opnaz, not Spetsnaz.''

''Okay, maybe he did. Is it that significant?''

"I want you to have it checked out. Raise Jacobson on SATCOM. I want answers. Bad luck has a habit of coming in threes. And Opnaz has got bad written all over it."

■   ■   ■

THE INVESTIGATOR leaned against the wall and nodded to the two others to take up positions by the door.

Girling rocked back and forth on the chair and clasped his sides for warmth.

"You are cold?" al-Qadi asked.

"Just tell me what I'm doing down here."

Al-Qadi examined a fingernail. "I have one or two questions for you, Mr. Girling. That is all. Once you have answered them, you will be free to go."

"Then ask them."

"Please, a little patience. We have been more than patient with you."

Girling opened his mouth to speak, but al-Qadi put a finger to his lips. "You are right to feel angry." His eyes darkened. "But then I, too, am angry. You make trouble in my country. You look into matters that do not concern you and you create only problems for us, for Egypt. You are a dangerous man, Mr. Tom Girling."

"Dangerous?"

"Don't be flattered, Mr. Girling. You are in very deep trouble. This should not be a matter for your private amusement."

"Why am I in trouble?"

"First of all, you have met with the Israeli, Lazan."

Girling shook his head disbelievingly. "I'm a journalist, Captain. I meet with many diplomats, even Israeli ones. There is no law, even here, against that."

Al-Qadi's voice rose. "Then tell me what you were doing with the internee of the al-Mu'ayyad Mosque."

"The internee?"

"Perhaps you know him as the Guide. The internee is not known for his knowledge of science and technology," the investigator said.

"You'd be surprised at his range of interests," Girling said.

"Be careful, Mr. Girling."

"There is something about the . . . internee that intrigues me," Girling said.

"And what is that?"

"If the Brotherhood does not exist, why is its spiritual leader locked up in a gilded cage by the *mukhabarat?*"

Al-Qadi tried unsuccessfully to mask his fury. "Listen to my truth, Mr. Girling. I do not like people who roam my streets, breaking my law. What did you hope to achieve by going to the sheikh?"

"Why not ask him?"

"He despises people like you."

Girling looked at him levelly. "And you, Captain."

A muscle twitched at the right side of the investigator's face. "Let me ask you again, Mr. Girling, what you were doing at the al-Mu'ayyad Mosque."

"I went to the sheikh with an appeal for Stansell's life."

The investigator's eyes blazed. "I told you to leave the matter of Stansell to us."

"Tell me what progress you have made since Stansell was first taken. Tell me what leads you have uncovered. You have done nothing that suggests Stansell's disappearance is in any way a priority for you, Captain. And you blame me for looking for him? For doing your job? You and I may have got off to a bad start, but we have the same aim, don't we? We both want Stansell. For God's sake, let's start acting like we're on the same side. I'm not interested in denigrating Egypt. I don't want to write an article about the Guide. Whatever he's doing in the al-Mu'ayyad Mosque is your business. I just want Stansell. He's the one—the only—reason I'm here."

Al-Qadi's features seemed to soften. "Then, Mr. Girling, perhaps we can do business together." He walked to the door. "Come," he said.

Together with the two bodyguards, they retraced their steps to the entrance. It was still light outside. A wall clock in the hallway stood at a little before six. Al-Qadi crossed the great courtyard, entering an outlying wing of the building via a wooden door. Once inside, Girling became aware of a pungent odor, a mixture of organic decay and chemicals.

Al-Qadi checked the number on a door at the end of yet another long corridor. He entered the room and flicked on the lights. Unlike the interrogation cell, the forensic laboratory was well-lit, although by Western standards, quite filthy. Archaic microscopes abutted bottles of strangely colored fluids scattered on a ledge that ran waist high around the room. In the center of the floor there was a large, solid-looking box. Next to it was a Formica work-surface the same height as the shelf, and there were various papers and instruments scattered on top. The smell he had first detected upon entering the building was stronger than ever.

Al-Qadi lifted the lid off the box, scattering the papers across the floor.

Al-Qadi beckoned. "You see, there really is no need for you to stay in Egypt any longer," he said.

The body, half-obscured by blocks of ice and semisubmerged in water, lay in a sarcophagus chiseled from the limestone quarries of the pharaohs.

Stansell had been shot twice. One bullet had nicked him on the side of the head; a second had hit him in the chest. There were cuts on the body which Girling recognized as pathologist's incisions.

Girling turned away. Parts of the torso were badly decomposed, and he felt the bile rise to the back of his throat. With a supreme effort he suppressed it. He didn't want to give al-Qadi the pleasure.

"When did you find him?" He heard his voice tremble. The question was a device, nothing more, to shield his pain from al-Qadi. Inside, all he could think of was his failure.

"Yesterday afternoon."

"Where?" Stansell had given him life. Kelso and he had taken it away. Kelso. Girling felt new anger and new pain. None of this needed to happen. Kelso and his lousy ambition. Tom Girling and his wretched stupidity.

"In the Nile. On a patch of beach, near Shari 'a al-Nil, across the river from the Meridien. Some fishermen caught the body in their nets and dragged him ashore. The body had been weighted down."

"Time of death?" Girling asked. His stomach churned. The smell was excruciating.

"The very day he was taken. It seems that from the beginning you have been wasting your time here, Mr. Girling."

Stansell stared at him from the fetid water. If there was one shred of solace for Girling, it was that Stansell's expression in death was of infinite wisdom. Had Stansell found the answers he'd been seeking?

"Has the discovery provided any new leads? What about our embassy—has anyone there been told?" Girling leaned against the shelf, staring down at the scattered tools of the pathologist's trade—scalpels, saws, microscopes, chemical fluids, powders. The questions had exhausted him.

"You are off the case now, Mr. Girling," al-Qadi said. "No more questions. You are being sent home, deported."

Girling felt himself sag. The anger, even the pain, had gone, leaving emptiness.

"As soon as the paperwork is complete," al-Qadi went on. "Forty-eight hours, at the most. Meanwhile, stray from the boundaries of this city, or make any further trouble, and I will be forced to detain you in less comfortable surroundings." He nodded in the direction of the courtyard.

The investigator looked at Girling contemptuously. "*Khalas,*" he said, clearing his throat and spitting into the icy water of the sarcophagus. "It is over."

CHAPTER 6

IT WAS A FIFTEEN-KILOMETER drive from Qena's main runway to the outside perimeter of the base complex. Doyle drove the jeep hard.

He waited until the checkpoint had dwindled to a dot in his mirror before he opened his mouth. He told Ulm he had filed a separate report to Washington about Opnaz, but true to form, TERCOM had returned an H3-grade reply, which translated as "monitor, but take no further action." His report of the Hind crash and the Russian accusation of sabotage had met with a similar response.

"Is that it?" Ulm asked.

"Not exactly," Doyle shouted over the whine of the jeep's engine. "I took the liberty of plugging into JWICS and seeing what I could find." JWICS was the Defense Intelligence Agency's Joint Worldwide Intelligence Communications System, a classified data network for U.S. operatives in the field; a very special encyclopedia for those cleared to use it.

"Well?"

Doyle gritted his teeth as they hit a particularly deep pothole. "Opnaz stands for Operativniy Naznacheniye," he said, the moment they cleared it.

"Don't tell me what it stands for. What is it?"

"The toughest antiterrorist squad at the Kremlin's disposal," Doyle said. "It was formed in the late seventies to deal with a potential terrorist threat at the 1980 Moscow Olympics. Opnaz is the Russian equivalent of Delta, or the SAS. Tough sons of bitches. Being only company strength in those days, it would have been led by a captain. We don't have the name of that officer—at least, he's not listed in JWICS—but given Shabanov's age and rank today, it's quite possible that he was the main man."

Ulm looked at his intelligence officer. "If they are this Opnaz, why hide the fact? They're the best, you say."

Doyle sucked his teeth. "They're good all right. They saw action right across the Soviet Union—Latvia, Georgia, Armenia and Uzbekistan, for example—before the breakup of the empire. But if Jones really heard Bitov right, I still don't get what the hell they were doing in Afghanistan."

"Uzbekistan, Afghanistan . . . what's the difference?"

Doyle took his eye off the road for a moment and turned to Ulm. "That's just it, Elliot. A whole lot. You see, Opnaz isn't even part of the Russian Army. It's the elite spearhead of the MVD, the Interior Ministry, the body tasked with keeping internal order. Uzbekistan, as a former Soviet republic, was very much its responsibility. Afghanistan wasn't.

"When the government needs something special done outside its borders—and this would have applied to the whole Afghan operation—it calls in army special forces, Spetsnaz. The MVD, even its special forces, Opnaz, is technically forbidden to operate outside Russia. It's a constitutional thing, like the rules governing the National Guard back home. And if that's what we're dealing with here—if we're teamed with Opnaz, not Spetsnaz, on this mission—someone ought to tell us what all the secrecy's about."

"Not to mention Opnaz being outside its own jurisdiction—twice. First Afghanistan and now here." It was several moments before Ulm said: "Jacobson must have known all this."

"Sure," Doyle said. "And if I were him, the first thing I would have wanted to know is what Shabanov, an MVD man, is doing taking orders from Aushev, a GRU army general."

"What the fuck's going on, Charlie?"

"I don't know, Elliot, but here's a thought for you to chew over while you're on the train to Cairo. I ain't never met this Jacobson, but if TERCOM is what I think it is, some kind of 'black ops' outfit, then none of them is going to be too upset if the Russians shaft us on this operation. For some people, man, the cold war will never be over."

"I want answers, Charlie."

"The embassy should be getting the big picture."

"Yeah, maybe."

Doyle pinched the top of his nose. He looked studious for a moment. "While you're there, ask them what's going on in Lebanon and Syria. The DIA's reporting movement out of Hizbollah, Fatah and the PFLP-GC."

"Movement?"

"Lots of radio traffic in the last couple of days. JWICS says it's encrypted, but it looks like these guys are planning something or going somewhere. And all at the same time."

"And in Lebanon, our next port of call."

"Have a nice day," Doyle said.

■   ■   ■

THE DOOR opened and for a while Girling stood there, just watching her. Sharifa was dressed in Levi jeans and a T-shirt. Her hair was uncombed and she had a faintly drowsy look about her.

He watched her expression alter as her eyes became accustomed to the shadows outside her apartment door. His clothes were ripped and scuffed, one eye was blackened and his face was a mass of cuts.

Her hands came up to her face. "My God, Tom, what happened to you?"

He took a step forward. "Sharifa, Stansell's dead." He gave her the briefest summary of the facts.

She looked at him uncomprehendingly. He could see her trying to establish a connection between his appearance and the news. Then, as the words registered fully, his condition ceased to be important and she let out a gasp of anguish. She stifled it by biting her lip, but her eyes brimmed with tears.

He took her in his arms and felt her body give.

"Poor Stansell," she said softly, her head on his shoulder.

She cried in silence, her chest rising and falling sharply as the grief flowed from her body. And then, when she was done, she pulled herself away from him and shut the door. She began to wipe away the tears, but Girling stopped her. He lifted her head and looked into her eyes. The kohl had run down her face in long, dark lines. She smiled sadly, almost apologetically.

He led her to the sofa and sat her down. Then he disappeared into the dining room and brought back brandy and two glasses. "I know what loving and losing means, Sharifa." He poured them both stiff measures and sat beside her. "Drink," he said, "it'll make you feel better."

"How long have you known about us?" she asked.

"Not very long."

She looked at him questioningly.

"When I was going through his things," Girling said. "There was a letter to you in his desk. He must have thought twice about sending it. I'm sorry. I didn't read more than I had to."

"We both knew in our hearts that it wouldn't work, but Stansell just refused to admit it." The tears started to come again. "After he was taken, I realized that this story, the Angels of Judgment . . . it was his way of trying to prove himself to me . . ."

"You mustn't blame yourself."

She gave him a look of infinite sadness. "Ah, Tom," she said, "but I must."

They sat in silence, Girling trying to blot out the image of the torn and bloated body in the sarcophagus. Suddenly he couldn't protect her from the truth any longer. He told her what had happened, from the meeting with the Guide to al-Qadi's brutal unveiling of Stansell's corpse. When he had finished, she had to wipe away his tears. Then, without warning, the concern in her eyes turned to anger.

"What on earth made you go to this sheikh? You were lucky not to have been killed."

Girling stared into his glass. "It seems stupid now, doesn't it? Stansell dead all along, before I even set foot in Egypt, and now I'm to be deported for trying to find him. What a bloody waste."

"Deported?"

"Al-Qadi didn't like me playing amateur detective. He's given me my marching orders."

"Then it's all over."

Girling shook his head. "Stansell's dead."

"So, he died for nothing?"

"No, Stansell died uncovering a story that's bigger than anyone ever imagined. The threads that bind the Brotherhood to the Angels of Judgment are just a tiny part of an enormous web. I realized that today. For the first time, I saw the size of the monster I've been running away from since Mona died."

She started to shake. He reached out and held her hand. "You'll be all right. When I leave, this will all be forgotten. Stansell, Mona—for everyone but us they'll just be names on a list."

Her fingers tightened around his. "I have nightmares about Mona, Tom. I see people watching me on the streets, al-Qadi and his men, I see the hatred in their eyes, everyone's eyes. I wonder when they will come for me with stones."

He held her gently, knowing there was nothing he could say. After a while she slipped into a troubled sleep. From time to time her body stiffened and she would cry out. Later he picked her up and carried her from the sofa to the bedroom. He placed her tenderly on the bed and pulled back to see her looking at him through half-closed eyes.

"Can we pretend?" she asked, her voice breaking. "Is that so wrong?"

He turned out the light and they undressed, the sound of their clothes and the rustle of the sheets seeming unnaturally loud in the darkness. He slipped in beside her and they held each other tightly, pressing the contours of their bodies against each other for comfort and warmth. Girling drifted into sleep as if he had been given an anesthetic. He could see demons still, but for the moment they were very far away.

They awoke in the night and clung to each other urgently, like swimmers trying to save themselves from drowning. Then she wrapped herself around him and he around her until shrill ululations of pleasure danced in her throat and he fell back, exhausted. Then they made love a second time, slowly, tenderly, their bodies hot from the first encounter. Their ecstasy rose together, hung there suspended, then fell in a simultaneous moment of release. And in that small window of time, Stansell, Mona, the Brotherhood and the Angels were a distant memory.

CHAPTER 7

SHARIFA AWOKE just before the dawn. She reached out for Girling, but he was not there. Slipping on her T-shirt, she found him hunched over her ancient typewriter at the dining room table, pounding away at the keys as if his life depended on it.

The first he knew she was there was when she touched him on the shoulder.

"What are you doing?"

"I'm writing Stansell's obituary."

She gave a puzzled look.

"I know. But believe me, it helps."

"Who's it for?" she asked.

"Reuters, the Associated Press . . . one of them will take it. News of his death will have the wires humming by midmorning."

"That sounds so cold."

"I'm sorry. It wasn't meant to."

"But you haven't even told Kelso yet."

Girling pulled the finished page from the roller and added it to the two others beside the machine.

"Kelso can read about it in the papers, or hear it on the radio, the same as everybody else. This way, the words will get to the right people."

She rubbed her eyes, wearily. "I don't understand."

"Read it."

It took her several minutes. It was less an obituary, more a news story. It pointed the finger squarely at the Angels of Judgment and their accomplices in Cairo, the Brotherhood. And finally, it revealed that the full story of the Angels of Judgment, the hijacking in Beirut and the reasons behind Stansell's death would be made public in the next issue of *Dispatches* in two days' time.

She put the sheets back on the table, puzzled. "You don't have a jot of evidence against the Angels of Judgment."

"Right, but they don't know that."

She stared at him.

"Don't you think they might just be a little bit curious about how I know so much?" Girling asked. "And, more to the point, who else knows what I know?"

"You're setting yourself up!"

"Something like that."

"No!"

"Sharifa, it's the only way."

"But what about last night? You said you were leaving. As soon as al-Qadi sorted out the paperwork."

"I changed my mind. Someone's got to get these bastards. It's as simple as that."

"Al-Qadi will put you straight back in that cell."

He reached out and held her hand. "Who's going to tell him?"

She recoiled like a sea anemone from a predator's touch.

"You were the only person who knew that I would be at the mosque. I'm not angry, Sharifa. You saved my life."

"I was scared I'd lose you, too."

"Tell me about al-Qadi. I want to help."

"Al-Qadi's evil, Tom. You've no idea of the things he can do."

Girling held her. "He's a playground bully," he said, and wondered whom he was trying to convince.

"If he touches me again," she said, "I'll kill him. I've been running away from him for too long."

"You used to inform on Stansell for him, didn't you?"

"How can you possibly know that?"

"When I was in the custody of the *mukhabarat* I realized that whatever hold al-Qadi has on you, it had to predate my arrival."

"Al-Qadi knew about me and Stansell; me sleeping with the alcoholic *'agnabi,* as he put it. He threatened to tell my father, if I didn't—" She stopped and looked up at him. "I'm sorry, Tom . . . I'll carry that for the rest of my life."

From the look in her eyes, he believed that she would.

"What are you going to do?" she asked.

Girling folded the sheaf of papers and tucked it into his jacket.

"First I take this to Reuters, then I'm going to the Khan. There's an old friend of mine there who might be able to get me access to the pathologist's report on Stansell."

"Is there anything I can do?" she asked.

"Yes, I believe there is."

He gave her the volume and page number of the piece missing from the *Dispatches* binder. Then he went to take a shower.

■   ■   ■

CYRUS McBAIN's face almost creased in two. He stood up from behind his desk and greeted his old friend warmly.

"Elliot Ulm. I might have fucking guessed."

"You mean, they didn't warn you?" Ulm said. "You always were slow, McBain."

"Your identity was 'need to know' right up until this minute, which is a piece of luck for you, Elliot. If I'd known, I wouldn't have shown up for work today. What kind of trouble have you gotten yourself into this time?"

Ulm threw his leather jacket over the back of a chair. He had made the overnight journey from Qena in good time, blending in amongst the tourists from Luxor and Aswan in his jeans, sweatshirt and beat-up jacket. "Shut up, Cy, and give me a drink. Where I've been the last three days, they don't even have Miller Lite on the menu."

"Colonel Beckwith always said Qena was a shit-hole. If you'd read up on Eagle Claw and Teheran before you signed on, Elliot, you might have elected to stay home."

"I didn't have a whole lot of choice."

McBain shrugged and moved to a small fridge beneath a shelf crammed with books about the Middle East, terrorism and military hardware. He threw the can of Budweiser across the room and Ulm caught it cleanly.

Ulm snapped the can open and poured half its contents down his throat before he came up for air. "So this is what it's like outside the firing line," he said, taking in the clean, businesslike appearance of McBain's office. "Judging by your beer gut I'd say they must be preparing you for a nice fat job in Washington."

"Repeat those words across a volleyball net sometime and I'll make you eat them, Elliot."

Ulm snorted and they both laughed. "It's good to see you again," Ulm said.

"You, too, Elliot. So, you finally managed to get away from that rest home in New Mexico."

"Yup. One fucking desert to another." Ulm waved his can around the room then lowered his voice. "I take it this place is clean."

"Swept every day."

"I need the big picture, Cy. Tell me what's been happening these past three days. Is there any news?"

McBain sat back at his desk and began rolling a pencil between his palms. "Not a squeak. It's like the Angels of Judgment and Franklin's negotiating team never existed. Don't they get newspapers out where you are?"

"We don't get jack," Ulm said.

"No *Early Bird?*" The *Early Bird* was the Pentagon's own cuttings service, a faxed digest of all the important news stories of the day.

"Minimum transmission, remember?" Ulm said. "That's why I'm here. Cyrus, there's a whole lot I don't like."

"I've known you a long time, Elliot. And the last time I saw you look this way was the day before the court-martial brought home its verdict. What's up? I guess it's got something to do with this guy Jacobson who keeps sending all this encrypted shit for you. I thought I'd seen some classification levels before, but . . ."

"There's not much I can tell you."

"What can I do, Elliot?"

"Tell me what's happening out there."

McBain shook his head. "Like I told you. Everybody's running around like headless chickens here. When it comes to the Angels of Judgment, nobody knows. Nobody.''

Ulm wondered what his old friend, dyed-in-the-wool Colonel Cyrus J. McBain, USAF, would say if he were to tell him that the Pathfinders were hooked up with Spetsnaz, or Opnaz, or whoever the fuck Shabanov and his men were.

"That's not exactly true," McBain said, correcting himself. "There's one guy around here who seems to know what's going on, but . . ."

"Who?"

McBain looked uncomfortable. "Well, he's not exactly cleared."

"Tell me about it."

"The guy's a journalist, Elliot. A British journalist from the magazine that broke the story, *Dispatches.*"

Ulm was immediately suspicious. "Shit, you don't think—"

"Relax. Girling's got too much on his mind to start digging into special operations activity here in Egypt. Besides, people's attentions are on the Lebanon task force. If there's going to be a rescue, that's where they think it's coming from. Read any of the papers."

"You said he had some things on his mind."

McBain put down his pencil. "A guy called Stansell, their Middle East correspondent, got himself snatched by the Angels of Judgment. Girling has been here the better part of a week trying to get him back. We just heard he didn't luck out. They fished Stansell out of the river a few days back with a couple of holes in him."

"So what good is Girling to me?"

"I never said he was good; in fact, he smells like trouble. But you asked who might be able to give you more on the Angels and Girling's the only guy I can think of who fits the bill. He's got the *mukhabarat,* the secret service, running around in a blue funk, he's stirred up a hornet's nest in the Islamic fundamentalist community, and he's even got the Israelis going. We intercepted a transmission from their embassy here to Tel Aviv the day before yesterday. And guess who's name was on it. The Israelis are convinced that Girling's going to lead them to the Angels of Judgment, and God knows, they've got just as much to be worried about as we have."

"So how do I get in touch? I haven't got much time, Cy."

McBain poured himself some coffee. "Something's really gotten under your skin, hasn't it?"

Ulm said nothing.

"Girling's already contacted our public affairs people here," McBain continued. "He wanted to meet with me, or someone who could give him updates on what's happening in Lebanon. So far, I've told the PA guys I'm out—permanently. I don't give intel briefs for people I don't know. I've even ducked a volleyball game with the guy. But there's no reason why we shouldn't have a change of heart. Someone from PA will sit in on the meeting, but there's no way they'll be able to guess who you are. Even if they do, they'll play dumb. You're just another suit from Washington, right? All you need is a name. Your mother's maiden name might not be a bad place to start. That's if you had a mother, Elliot."

Ulm sat back.

"Thanks, Cy. I owe you."

McBain said: "You can pay me back by forgetting I ever did this." He punched a four-digit extension number and held the phone to his ear.

"Get me Mike Schlitz," he said, as soon as he had a connection.

CHAPTER 8

GIRLING TURNED the BMW onto Shari 'a al-Ahram—the road that led almost from the center of Cairo to the pyramids of Giza—and settled down to a steady pace in the center lane. It was coming up to one o'clock. He was in good time for his lunch appointment at the Mena House Hotel, a luxury affair in the shadow of the Great Pyramid. The Mena House was just that little bit remote; he guessed that was why Schlitz and McBain had picked it.

It had been a busy morning and it was getting busier. First he had called on his old friend John Silverman at Reuters and dropped the story onto his desk. Silverman was shocked. He had known and liked Stansell. But Girling recognized a look in Silverman's face that said he also knew a good story when he saw one. With kidnapping and hijack in the air, the fact that a leading British journalist had been murdered by the world's latest public enemy made the story dynamite. And despite his previous visit from the *mukhabarat,* Silverman wasn't going to be deterred. With commendable restraint, Girling thought, Silverman had not pressed him for any of the details of *Dispatches'* forthcoming exclusive on the Angels of Judgment, which was just as well.

Next he had driven to the Khan, parked and retraced his steps to Kareem's coffeehouse on the Street of the Judges. This time, he had gained access to old Mansour without difficulty. Mansour had accepted Stansell's death with a sad, wise look in his face which said that he had known all along that Stansell would never again smoke and exchange banter at Kareem's. Girling had explained that it was important he get in touch with Uthman, the doctor from Duqqi, who worked part-time at *mukhabarat* HQ. He had given old Mansour Sharifa's number and told him to get Uthman to ring him, day or night.

It was when he had returned to the office, at about eleven o'clock, that he'd gotten the invitation from Schlitz.

Soon he caught his first glimpse of the pyramids' chipped, sand-blown peaks creeping above the houses lining the dead-straight road. Despite their overexposure—pyramid motifs emblazoned everything in Egypt from newspapers to gas stations—he never tired of seeing them. On the rare days, when neither the smoke nor the dust was too thick, you could see them with the help of a telephoto lens from any of the tall buildings downtown.

Mona and he had climbed to the top of the Great Cheops Pyramid on a day much like this. They had ignored the cautionary notices and made it to the summit a little before sundown. The view had been breathtaking. They had sat holding each other in the moonlight.

The sun glinted on the windshield of a Fiat three cars behind him. Girling spotted it in the mirror. They must have picked him up at the office. He adjusted his dark glasses.

He drove on for another kilometer without varying his speed, but instead of turning off at the hotel, he kept driving along the road that led up the escarpment of the pyramids. He parked in the shadow of the Great Pyramid and set out for the first row of meter-high stone blocks that marked the base. He heard the *mukhabarat* slow to a stop a little way behind. He began to climb.

Neither of the two *mukhabarat* field officers elected to follow him. While one of them watched his progress, the other reached for a newspaper. They knew Girling would be gone a long time. It was a forty-minute climb to the summit and probably a thirty-minute descent.

When he was about a hundred feet up, Girling began moving toward the corner of the pyramid, the safest route for the ascent. He paused to catch his breath and looked down. He could see the camels and horses for hire, their owners touting for customers, scores of milling tourists and a few white-clad police. In the blue Fiat, neither man had moved.

Girling stepped round the corner, out of the *mukhabarat*'s sight, and moved swiftly downward. There was a warm wind blowing in from the desert. He glanced toward the horizon and made out the crumbling remains of the Abusir pyramids eight kilometers to the south. A little farther off stood the distinctive shape of the stepped pyramid of Zozer at Saqqara nestling between the green valley strip and the desert.

It took him about five minutes to reach the ground. He dusted himself off and walked around to the back of the tomb before rejoining the road that led to the Mena House. He glimpsed the Fiat. The man reading the paper was smoking a cigarette. His companion looked as though he'd gone to sleep.

It took five more minutes to reach the hotel. Although the hotel was built at the turn of the century, successive owners had added new wings and outbuildings. Girling proceeded straight to the cocktail bar. He spotted Schlitz in the corner sharing a drink with two other men. One was dressed in a lightweight, tropical suit, the other in jeans, T-shirt, and a scuffed leather jacket.

Schlitz got to his feet. "Glad you could make it, Tom. We were just about to order another round. What'll it be?" Even in a jacket and tie Schlitz managed to look fat and disheveled.

The waitress appeared and Girling asked for a beer.

Schlitz made the introductions.

"Tom, this is Lieutenant Colonel Cyrus McBain, our defense attaché."

McBain shook his hand. He had sandy hair, thinning on top, and piercing blue eyes. A guy to depend on in a tight spot, Girling thought.

"And this is John Gudmundson of the DIA," Schlitz continued. "John just got in from Washington."

Girling matched the strength of Gudmundson's grip with difficulty. There was steel in the man's eyes, and a restless energy in his body that made it difficult for Girling to picture him behind a desk. He looked somehow out of place in the ornate surroundings of the hotel's cocktail bar.

"Seems like we picked a hell of a time to meet with you," Schlitz said, lighting up a Marlboro.

"I'm sorry?" Girling said, settling into his seat. For a moment he thought they were referring to the cuts and bruises he had received at the hands of the mob.

Schlitz said: "Come on, Tom. It's not a secret anymore. It came over the wires just before we left the embassy. And, by the way, before we go any further, I'd just like to say how sorry I am. Like I told you, Stansell was a good operator. A good guy, too. He'll be missed around here."

"Well, I guess I owe you an apology for that cock-and-bull line I gave you about him being sent back to England," Girling said. "The *mukhabarat* didn't want the news to leak while they were looking for him. I kind of had my hands tied."

"We've known for a few days now about Stansell's abduction," McBain said. "As you can imagine, the antennae are pretty sensitive at this time. There's a lot of things out there we're picking up."

"And a lot you're missing, too, perhaps?" Girling said.

McBain said nothing. He settled back in his armchair, relaxed, confident, every inch the diplomat. Gudmundson, on the other hand, seemed edgy.

"I've been reading your stuff," McBain said. "*Dispatches* seems to be way ahead of the game."

"At a price."

"Looks like it's taken something out of you, too." McBain nodded to Girling's cuts.

"In this business you get into the odd scrape," Girling said. He turned to Schlitz. "So, Mike, what's this little meeting all about? You never did explain on the phone."

"We wanted to talk with you. Exchange some views."

"So, let's talk."

Schlitz looked between his two colleagues, waiting for one of them to speak. But McBain and Gudmundson seemed content to let him handle the press.

"The thing of it is, Tom," Schlitz said, "we'd appreciate hearing what's going to go into your next Angels of Judgment story. Is there any chance we could see your copy early?"

Girling had expected the wire stories to flush out some interesting creatures from the woodwork, but not so soon. For an approach by U.S. intelligence, this seemed unusually ham-handed.

"That would kind of breach the rules," Girling replied.

"Rules go out the window at a time like this," McBain said.

"Then perhaps you could tell me what you guys at the DIA are working on right now, Mr. Gudmundson?"

Gudmundson shifted in his seat. "I'm afraid that's classified information."

"Quite," Girling said. He looked at the three of them in turn. He'd seen a hundred Gudmundsons in his years as a defense and technology journalist and none of them had been in intelligence. "So, who's calling the shots here, gentlemen?"

"We thought it would be useful to talk, that's all," Schlitz said. "For both of us."

Girling looked at Gudmundson again. Something about him definitely didn't fit.

"Have we ever met before?" he asked.

Gudmundson looked him in the eye. "No, sir."

"You sure?"

"I never forget a face," Gudmundson said.

"Me neither. That's what bothers me."

Girling sipped his beer. "What line of work do you do with the DIA?" he said.

"Government work," Schlitz interrupted.

"Sounds fascinating," Girling said.

Gudmundson leaned forward. "Girling, if there's anything you know that can help us, believe me, we ought to hear about it."

"Why don't you start by telling me what you know," Girling said.

"That's not the way we work."

"Well, that's how I work, Mr. Gudmundson. In my profession, we call it trading." The words tumbled out aggressively, because for Girling they had become a defense mechanism. He felt cornered. These people wanted information from him, yet ironically, he knew nothing. All that he knew about the Sword and the Angels of Judgment was already in print. He was overcome by a feeling of claustrophobia, a feeling compounded by the presence of Gudmundson, whom he had run into somewhere before, he just knew it. But because Girling couldn't make the face fit, Gudmundson's presence and that of his colleagues had become strangely threatening.

Schlitz began to stub his cigarette nervously. "Tom, I think I should say . . . er, just for the record, that this conversation is not really happening. I should have made the ground rules clear from the start. Clearly you appreciate the sensitivity of this meeting.''

"Maybe you should get to the point, Mike.''

"You said you wanted to meet with Colonel McBain the other day. Well, here he is.'' Schlitz was sweating.

"That was three days ago. A lot has happened to me since then. As you're clearly more than just a press officer, Schlitz, I could ask the same about you.''

"What do you mean?'' Schlitz said.

Girling ignored him. "Are you any closer to the hostages?'' he asked Gudmundson.

"I'm sorry, but we can't discuss that,'' Gudmundson said.

"I thought this was meant to be a frank exchange of views.''

"I'm sorry, Girling, there are certain things I can't go into. You must appreciate that. You, on the other hand, may have information that could be of immense value to us.''

"Are you telling me you don't know where the hostages are?'' Girling said.

"I didn't say that.''

"What exactly do you want from me, Gudmundson?''

"A little cooperation. That 's all.''

"It seems we're going round in circles,'' Girling said.

Schlitz grabbed Girling by the arm. "Unless you start cooperating, Girling, you won't get anywhere in this town. I'll see to that.''

Before McBain or Gudmundson could get Schlitz to back down, Girling got to his feet. "I don't need this,'' he said.

Across the room, a few people began to stare.

"It looks like I won't be joining you for lunch,'' Girling said. He turned and walked from the room.

■   ■   ■

FIVE MINUTES after Girling left, Ulm said good-bye, leaving McBain and Schlitz to argue about the rights and wrongs of their interviewing techniques. It was obvious that nothing short of physical violence would have induced Girling to divulge his secrets—if he had any in the first place, that was. The journalist's aggression, combined with that asshole Schlitz's heavy-handed questioning, saw to the meeting's somewhat swift conclusion.

Ulm was due on the six o'clock express to Qena, but hoped there might be an earlier train. He did not want to spend a moment longer in Cairo.

He stopped at the concierge's desk to ask for a timetable for southbound trains. Then he joined the small line of people waiting for taxis outside.

■   ■   ■

GIRLING WATCHED the man he knew as Gudmundson from a phone booth in the main lobby, shielded by the throng of tourists checking in and out at the front desk.

He was intrigued by Gudmundson. He watched impatiently as the queue grew shorter. Girling strained for a better look, willing a couple of tourists to get out of his line of sight. A taxi swung into view and Gudmundson raised his hand to flag the driver.

It was in that moment, that Gudmundson's body was three-quarters to him, that Girling tagged him. The American's entire bearing was military. This was a man used to giving orders, but not from behind a desk. And Girling suddenly realized he'd seen Gudmundson giving orders before.

He rushed outside as the taxi swept out of the forecourt. There were no others in sight. Taking a deep breath, he went back inside the hotel and asked the concierge what his American friend with the suntan and the leather jacket had asked her for a few moments earlier.

The girl smiled and pointed at a timetable for trains leaving Ramsis Station, Cairo, for the tourist centers of Middle and Upper Egypt: Minya, Asyut, Qena, Luxor and Aswan.

Girling thanked her and looked around for Schlitz and McBain. They hadn't emerged from the bar. The sound of crickets mingled with the buzz of traffic on Pyramids Road. He felt light-headed. He went back to the phone booth, lifted the handset and gave the hotel operator a London number.

In less than a minute, he was talking to Kieran Mallon.

"Girling, you rogue. Jesus, I can't believe I'm talking to you. Where are you, man? The world, not to mention Kelso, is going apeshit and you're nowhere to be found."

"Slow down, Kieran."

"Slow down, you say? Is it true about Stansell?"

"Yes, I'm afraid it is."

"Hell, I'm sorry, Tom. Kelso's been besieged with calls from Fleet Street ever since the story broke on the wire. They want to know everything. The facts behind the kidnapping, how he died and what we're going to file about the Angels of Judgment. I know Kelso wanted to capture a bit of attention, but I'm not sure this is exactly what he had in mind. He and Carey are both screaming for you. What do I tell them?"

"Tell them the story's on its way."

"Is it?"

"No. But keep that to yourself."

"Tom, why Reuters? What's going on?"

"I need your help, Kieran. Can you do something for me? It's very important."

"Name it."

It took Girling a little over two minutes to dictate his instructions. After he'd finished, he made Mallon read them back.

"What's this got to do with Stansell?" the Irishman asked.

"I'm not sure. When can you get back to me?"

"Hopefully within the hour."

"Good. I'll be waiting by the fax. And if you need to get hold of me by phone, I'm abandoning the office and my apartment for a while. I'll be here." He read out Sharifa's number.

"A woman?"

"It's not what you think."

"Tom?"

"Yes."

"You sound different."

"You should see how I look."

"No, you sound . . . well, better."

Girling felt himself smile. "I hope it lasts," he said.

He paid reception for the call and set out to retrieve his car.

■   ■   ■

I T   W A S   hotter than usual for late afternoon and nowhere more so than in al-Qadi's office, three floors above the basement cells at *mukha-*

barat headquarters. The air-conditioning unit had long since broken down. An electric fan mounted on his desk had suffered an undiagnosed mechanical failure three days before.

Al-Qadi mopped his brow and read the handwritten report from his deputy for the third time.

He took another sip of water and loosened his tie. When Girling had filed his report with Reuters he had declared war. The investigator wondered whether the Englishman had even begun to appreciate the power of his enemy.

Al-Qadi opened the top drawer of his desk, pulled out a tattered manila file and studied it one, final time. He lit one of the corners, made sure it had caught well, and tossed it into his metal wastepaper bin. As the flames took hold, the cardboard buckled and a blown-up passport picture of Stansell slipped from the dossier. Al-Qadi stared at it, mesmerized by the advance of the flames across the *'agnabi*'s face. Not until every scrap had been reduced to ash did he turn to the second drawer of his desk, open it and pull out his automatic.

He had resolved not to wait for the general's call.

■   ■   ■

IT WAS dark when Girling entered the office to find both telephones ringing and Sharifa nowhere in sight. Having checked the fax tray and found it empty, he took both phones off the hook. Then he locked the door, sat down on the floor beside the fax machine and waited in the gathering gloom.

Ten minutes later, the silence of the fifth floor was disturbed by the first bleep of the fax's built-in phone. He switched on the light as the teleprinter burst into life.

The picture formed before his eyes, pixel by pixel, line by line, until it grew into the face and body of a man. Mallon had enlarged the shot on the photocopier and still kept reasonable definition. When the transmission ended, he took the page over to his desk and placed it under a lamp.

Girling stared at the picture with some satisfaction. The thickset, balding guy in the fatigues standing with his hand raised before the Il-76 Candid at Machrihanish the day Girling thought he would die in the Tornado, was the man who called himself Gudmundson.

He lifted the phone and punched in the number the moment he

obtained a line. Ten seconds later, he was connected again to Mallon. This time, there was no small talk. Mallon's rapid breathing signaled his excitement.

"Who is that guy?"

"I don't know," Girling said. "That's what I want you to find out."

"Me?"

"It's all right, Kieran, I'm going to take you through it. Have you got the picture in front of you?"

"Yes."

"Okay. You're going to have to help me here, as some of the quality has been lost in the transmission." He brought the desk lamp lower. There was a name tag stitched onto the officer's combat fatigues, just above the left breast-pocket. With the frame enlarged it was possible to see that the person he had mistaken first for a technician was in fact a USAF officer—and a senior one too, judging by the insignia on his shoulders. He asked Mallon if he could read the name on the tag. One thing was for sure: the letters did not spell Gudmundson. Not that he had ever expected them to.

"What do you make of it?" Girling asked.

It was not easy—it was already grainy from the enlarging process—and to make matters worse, the man's arm was obscuring part of the word.

"Could be . . . Palmer," Mallon said. "It's a common enough name."

Girling found a magnifying glass on the desk and tilted it under the light. "Could be," he agreed. "But that doesn't look like an *A*, more like a *U*."

It took them a minute or so to agree that the three letters were *U-L-M*. Neither of them thought it sounded like much of a name.

"Whatever he's called, he's a colonel in the U.S. Air Force. See that eagle on his shoulder loop? I wonder why the hell he was meeting a Russian tactical transport aircraft on a remote Scottish air base eleven days ago?"

"And you met the same guy today? You think it has something to do with the hijacking?" Mallon asked.

Girling thought back to his flight in Rantz's Tornado.

"Could be. But why is Ulm interested in me, all of a sudden? Do the

Americans think I know where their hostages are? Do they think I'm going to blow the gaff?''

''That's not their style, Tom. If they thought you were going to compromise their mission, they'd have gagged you already. I reckon it's much simpler. They're still in the dark and they think you might be able to help.''

Girling's mind raced.

''Tom, are you still there?''

''Yeah.''

''What do you want me to do?''

''Who was on this Russian transport aircraft?''

''MoD lied. Said it was on a humanitarian mission, remember?''

''Okay, so we're going to have to try another route.'' He thought for a second and then dictated another set of instructions. After putting the phone down, he sat back in his chair and waited.

It took Mallon roughly half an hour to return with information.

''Machrihanish isn't any old base,'' he explained. ''A recent modernization program has turned it into Europe's principal storage site for U.S. nuclear weapons.''

Girling drummed his fingers on the desk.

The line was beginning to break up. Girling shouted to make himself heard. ''That's interesting, but it's not what I'm after.''

''How about this, then?'' Mallon said. ''There's a permanent detachment of SEALs there—you know, U.S. Navy special warfare troops.''

''Now you're getting warmer. Anything more on that tack?''

''Yes. Machrihanish has been extensively updated with U.S. cash since the early eighties. The underground nuclear storage sites account for some of it, but that's comparatively small—''

''Compared to?''

''Compared to what U.S. Special Operations Command has been doing there. Machrihanish is apparently the main staging post for American special forces coming to Europe. It's been built up since the Gulf war as a liaison point between the U.S. eastern seaboard and any hot spots that develop on this side of the Atlantic. The runway's been lengthened to take C-5s and C-141s and there's a new special operations command center on the base for controlling forces in the field. It's all hush-hush stuff. Even your contact started clamming up on me.''

Girling clenched his fist and held it in the air. ''Our man is special forces, which puts him in that USAF outfit . . . shit, what are they called? The Pathfinders, that's it. They dropped off the map a couple of years ago. Rumor had it they ran into some kind of trouble in Panama.''

''And you think they're in Egypt?''

''Yes. Ulm sure as hell hadn't just got off the plane from Washington.''

''Then everybody has been heading in the wrong direction,'' Mallon said. ''The conventional wisdom is that any rescue would be launched by Delta or the SEALs from a ship with the task force off the Lebanese coast.''

Girling nodded. ''Right.'' He only half-heard Mallon, because he was looking at the wall map behind Stansell's desk. He shone the lamp full on it.

''So where are they then, your Pathfinders?'' Mallon asked. Girling touched a spot in the desert just north of a wide bend in the Nile. ''Wadi Qena,'' he whispered.

''What? You're breaking up on me, Tom.''

''Nothing.'' Ulm had gone to the train station. He hadn't gone to the embassy, or the airport. He'd gone to the bloody train station. And he'd been southbound. There was only one possible place he could be heading. The same place Colonel Charlie Beckwith, the man who had led Eagle Claw had gone over ten years before. The place from which Delta Force had launched its abortive rescue attempt for the hostages in Teheran. With the U.S. Navy prowling in strength somewhere off Beirut, it was the perfect double-bluff.

He gathered his things. As he closed the door the phone began to ring, but Girling ignored it, locked up and headed for the elevator.

■   ■   ■

GIRLING KEPT his foot down as he left University Bridge and headed north along Shari'a al-Nil. A flash rainstorm had left the streets slippery and shiny under the bright city lights. He checked his mirror and saw a car pulling away from the junction behind him. The *mukhabarat* were back on his tail.

Half a mile ahead, he could see the lights of the Sheraton reflecting off the oil black water of the river. He glanced to his right at a barge sailing silently, almost invisibly, downstream toward Alexandria, its wake chopping the river's surface. The vessel would be laden with cotton, cane, or potatoes. As he slowed and the barge plowed on, Girling found himself staring at the Meridien Hotel on the opposite bank and realized that he was at the point where Stansell's body had been recovered from the river. He pulled the BMW into the side of the road, and a hundred yards away the driver of the Fiat followed suit. As he stepped onto the pavement, Girling gave the second car a glance, but the *mukhabarat* were staying put, invisible behind their lights. He stepped onto a low wall and stared down at the dross floating on the river's surface. The ripples from the barge's wake lapped against the small stretch of beach, depositing the water's jetsam in miniature tide lines on the fine silt. It was a lonely place to wind up dead. As he stared across the river Girling saw the lights of fishing boats bobbing up and down on the river, some of them quite close by. For all the myriad noises that made up the background hum of the big city, the sound of their oars dipping in the Nile was crisp and clear in the night.

Girling shivered, and he headed back toward the car. He did not want to keep Sharifa waiting any longer.

He gunned the engine and pushed on, past the Sheraton and the Cairo Tower, through the bright lights of the Gezira Club and into the gloomier tracts of al-Aguza, keeping a tributary of the river on his right. As he took the access road that led to the 26th of July Bridge, which would take him back to Zamalek and Sharifa's apartment, Girling lost sight of the *mukhabarat*. It was only when he glanced from the rearview to the right sideview mirror that he saw the Fiat, very close and slightly behind, sticking like glue to his blind spot. There was a sharp crack, as if his tires had kicked up a pebble. Everything seemed to happen so slowly that Girling found himself almost observing what followed. His eyes moved down to the speedometer. Accelerating up the ramp, he'd allowed the car to get up to eighty-seven kilometers per hour. The steering wheel suddenly went slack in his hands as the tire blew instantaneously. There was a demonic shriek as the bare metal rim scraped across the road. And then he lost control.

The BMW careened across the access road and smashed into the thin metal railings lining the turgid pedestrian walkway. Girling caught a fleeting glimpse of the brown, turbid waters of the river below him as the BMW upended and plunged over the side of the bridge. He was thrown against the door with such force he thought it would fly open, but it didn't; it held. Girling shut his eyes and prepared for the impact.

And then suddenly the lock gave and he was free, falling through space, images of his tumbling world imprinted at random on the back of his mind. He saw the bridge above him, the car spinning, the water and the trees . . .

He hit the ground twenty feet below the bridge, but the shock of the fall was absorbed by five feet of accumulated rubbish. He rolled down the bank and slid into a dense clump of papyrus. He lay there, half his face in the mud and detritus, panting for air, like a fish left high and dry by the tide. Then he began to pick up the sounds around him. He could hear the car sinking in the river, the water rushing in and the air bubbling out, the two meeting in a boiling confluence. He heard a car's doors open and close. Footsteps on the bridge. Shouts. Excitement. He rolled onto his back and saw his surroundings for the first time. Somehow the car had thrown him clear and under the bridge as it spun into the water. The concrete sections of the bridge's span filled his vision, obscured partially by the curtain of reeds and vegetation into which he had tumbled. He pulled himself onto his elbows, ignoring the stench from the nearby rubbish and the musty smell of the swamp. The BMW was all but submerged, with only its trunk and part of the roof showing above the water.

There were more voices on the bridge now. He thought of shouting for help, but something stopped him. He lay still, out of sight. He heard a twig snap on the bank above him and the light curse of a man struggling through undergrowth to get to the water's edge.

A last gasp from the car signaled its plunge to the riverbed. Moments later, Girling recognized a voice on the bridge. The investigator shouted down to the man by the water.

"Huwa maut," came the reply. He is dead.

"Tayib," al-Qadi said. Good.

Only then did Girling begin to edge toward the bridge's concrete pillar and the sanctuary of the dark road beyond.

■   ■   ■

"IF THEY dredge the river tomorrow they'll know I'm not dead. And this is the first place al-Qadi will come looking. You don't want to be here when that happens. The guy is out of control."

"Where will you go?" Sharifa asked.

Girling could see from her eyes that she was still in shock.

"I'm going south. If I get lucky, I should be back in thirty-six hours."

He looked at his watch. There wasn't a whole lot of time before the last train for Qena pulled out of Ramsis Station.

She sat on the edge of her bed, watching as he exchanged his clothes for a tropical suit of Stansell's. "You, meanwhile, are going to get some special protection."

"Who from?"

"The Israelis."

Girling wrote down Lazan's address in Ibn Zanki Street and passed it to her. "Get to him as soon as you can, either at this, his home address, or the embassy. Lazan knows most of the story already. You'll be safe with him."

"What's happening, Tom? What's going on?"

"I don't know. Maybe Al-Qadi's working for the Angels of Judgment, too. Or maybe he just decided to take the law into his own hands."

"This whole thing is getting out of hand," she whispered. "Stansell knew the Sword. He'd written about him. In 1979."

She produced the fax she had received from *Dispatches'* circulation department, the office that dealt with back issues.

Girling just stared at the sheet of paper. His mind tried to take in the words, but he never absorbed anything beyond the first paragraph. It was enough.

The report, datelined Kabul, bore Stansell's byline. Guerrillas had attacked a government convoy with rockets on the Salang Highway, leaving several trucks wrecked and a number of soldiers dead. No one group had claimed responsibility, but according to mujahideen sources, Stansell filed, the attack had been carried out by a nascent organization whose leader was said to be known at varying times as Ibn Husam or al-Saif, the Sword. The name of the tiny guerrilla organization he led was the same then as it was now.

"Jesus Christ." The Russians had known about the Angels of Judgment for years.

CHAPTER 9

THE TRAIN PULLED into Qena a little after dawn. Girling disembarked, feeling rested after the overnight journey from Cairo. The air was cool, but he could feel the temperature rising already. Qena was two degrees of latitude south of Cairo and it told.

He proceeded toward the town's trading quarter, a short but brisk walk from the station. The market was well under way by the time he entered the maze of stalls and twisting passageways. It was dominated by two commodities: camels and pottery. He rounded a stall piled high with kullas, the large porous water jugs fashioned from the local clay, and spotted the camel auction, his goal.

He walked cautiously amongst the bedouins and their beasts. The camels' front legs had been hobbled to prevent the camels wandering off. The smell of their excrement made his eyes water.

"*Ayiz hashish?*" a voice whispered.

Girling turned to see a middle-aged man whose bulk was conspicuous despite his flowing gray galabiya. He wore a tattered black baseball cap sporting the logo of an American petroleum company.

"*Hashish?*" the bedouin asked again, his eyes darting nervously around him.

Girling shook his head. "*La. Mish ayiz hashish.*" He reached into his pocket and produced a handful of notes and coins.

The bedouin's eyes shone. "*Ayiz gamal?*" He patted the behind of his nearest beast and guffawed.

Girling fought for the Arabic. He enunciated the words slowly, conscious that this man spoke a different dialect from his sketchy Cairene. "I need a man of resource and courage who can take me into the desert, to the place where the army keeps the *ta'iraat.*" The things that fly. It was ponderous, but it was the best he could do. No one had ever taught him the Arabic for helicopter.

For a moment, the bedouin's face creased. "The *ta'iraat* of Wadi Qena? Why?"

"That is my business, my friend."

"So be it," the bedouin said. "*Inter majnoon, ya sidiqi.*" You are mad, my friend. "Such a trip will cost you dearly."

"Money, I have," Girling said, pressing a wad of notes into the bedouin's hand. "Do you have the courage, my friend?"

The nomad snorted.

Girling handed over more money, the equivalent of 25 dollars. He explained there would be another wad if the bedouin could get him into the air base. They haggled for a while, but finally shook on a price of 130 Egyptian pounds, roughly 50 dollars.

The bedouin clapped Girling on the back. "My name is Abdullah," he said.

"And mine is Tom."

The bedouin laughed heartily. "*Al-majnoon* is better, I think, *ya* Tom."

Girling smiled. The Crazy One. "So be it," he said.

■　　　　■　　　　■

ULM SPOTTED Shabanov outside a bunker away from the main complex of buildings that Spetsnaz and the Pathfinders had turned into their operations center. The Russian was staring at a pile of junk dumped unceremoniously on the tarmac. There was little that was immediately recognizable of the Mi-24J.

As Ulm crossed the last stretch of sand-blown runway to where Shabanov was standing, a Hind lifted off behind the wreckage of its sibling. Looking like a malevolent insect, it clawed its way slowly into the dawn sky and picked up speed over the desert, the sound of its engines and rotors dwindling to a dull, asynchronous buzz. The pilot was heading for the crash site to carry out one last search for wreckage. Throughout the previous day, the Russians had been shuttling pieces back to Wadi Qena, the larger portions of the twisted remains carried in underslung nets. When the An-124s arrived to take them home, Shabanov wanted to make sure that all the pieces of this helicopter went too.

"Had they been with your unit long?" Ulm asked.

Shabanov half-turned toward the American. "I didn't know you were back, Elliot. How was Cairo?"

"A disappointment." He paused. "I'd always imagined it differently."

Shabanov flicked over a piece of main rotor with his foot. "Evgeny Pavlovich had been with us five years. He was an experienced pilot. And Gennady Georgevich, the gunner, even longer, from the beginning."

"They buzzed one of my helicopters."

"It was part of the training."

"Well, no one told me about it."

"There has to be an element of surprise in everything we do, Elliot."

Ulm didn't doubt it. "Do you believe all that talk about sabotage?"

"No Elliot. It's just the mood of the men. Tempers are strained. They want to get on with it."

"So do we. What's the word from Moscow?"

"Provided the dress rehearsal goes well tomorrow morning we go any time after that."

"The dummy camp, it's ready?"

"Yes. Have you ever seen a caravanserai, Elliot?"

"I can't say I have."

"It is a place of beauty, strangely enough. You will see pictures of it at the briefing tonight. We gather the men at twenty-two hundred hours."

Shabanov left Ulm to stare at the shattered carcass of the Hind.

■   ■   ■

AN HOUR after Girling and Abdullah left the alluvial plain behind, the lush richness of its crops and vegetation still shimmered across the desert like a mirage. They headed due north, the bedouin's camel maintaining a dead-straight course, without encouragement or correction. Girling's, on the other hand, seeming to sense the discomfort of its rider, kept wandering off track. Only through sharp tugs of the rough hemp reins would it maintain direction.

Girling's galabiya and headdress, purchased in the market, made him indistinguishable from the bedouin of the region. Abdullah had assured him that the meager defenses of the base would enable them to slip unnoticed onto the site. He raised his eyes to the horizon and announced that they would be at the outer perimeter in an hour.

The sun was directly over their heads, its heat pulsing down in waves. It seemed as if it had been hanging in the same position for all of the five hours they had been on the move. Girling glanced across to Abdullah, ten yards to his right, and wondered how the man could maintain an expression of complete disinterest when his brains were being fried through the flimsy cloth of his hat. Girling took his cue resolutely from the bedouin, stopping when he stopped, drinking when he drank. If he couldn't buy his respect, he knew he'd have to earn it. He needed Abdullah on his side, especially if things got rough.

Suddenly, Abdullah gave a whoop of satisfaction. Bobbing on the undulating waves of the heat haze, the perimeter fence of Wadi Qena air base stretched across the desert as far as the eye could see.

■   ■   ■

SHARIFA HAD finished bundling some things into an overnight bag and was taking a last look around her apartment when the phone rang. It had gone several times during the morning, but each time she had ignored it, suspecting it was Kelso or Carey wanting to know where the hell Girling was. The truth was she no longer knew what to tell them. She paused by the door, glancing from the scrap of paper with Lazan's address on it to the telephone, and back again.

A sudden thought that it might be Girling made her pick up the phone.

"Miss Fateem?"

She did not recognize the voice. It sounded hesitant, almost nervous. "Yes."

"Is Mr. Girling there, please?"

"No. Who is this?"

A long pause.

"I said—"

"My name is Uthman. Dr. Uthman. Mr. Girling and I have a mutual friend in Mansour, the old man at Kareem's coffeehouse. Mansour gave me this number. I am sorry, but I have only just received his message." Dr. Uthman spoke in English, his accent precise.

"Dr. Uthman," she stammered. "I'm so sorry. For a moment, I didn't–" She composed herself. "Tom Girling isn't here, doctor. Perhaps I can help."

"Well, I don't know. You see, it is a somewhat delicate matter."

Sharifa bit her lip. "You said 'delicate,' Dr. Uthman."

"There is the small matter of payment."

Sharifa thought fast. "Whatever Tom Girling promised, I'll see that you get it. I presume the transaction is to be made through Mansour."

"Precisely. Thank you, Miss Fateem."

"Please continue, doctor."

"Mr. Girling was interested in some files relating to the death of his friend, the British journalist Stansell."

"That's right. We both are."

"The fact is, Miss Fateem, there aren't any."

"I'm sorry, doctor?"

"The files, there aren't any. Oh, there were some. I know there were. You see, I wrote them. I carried out the autopsy."

"What happened to them?"

"I wouldn't like to say—"

"I don't suppose a certain Captain al-Qadi had anything to do with their disappearance," she said.

Uthman coughed. "Really. I wouldn't like to say."

"How was Stansell killed, doctor?"

"He was shot. Twice. Tom Girling knows this. I understand he was shown the body."

She mused aloud. "Then, why would . . . ? Was there anything particularly unusual about the case, doctor?"

"There were indications that he had been held in two different locations before he was killed and his body thrown in the river."

"Do you know their identity?"

"We know one of them. The City of the Dead. It has a particularly distinctive type of soil."

The mere thought of the necropolis chilled her.

"I still don't understand why anybody should want to lose that file, doctor—"

Sharifa stopped. She smelled it distinctly. There was something alien in her apartment, something that had no place there at all.

"Miss Fateem?"

"I'm sorry, doctor. I have to go."

She replaced the receiver with a dreadful sense of foreboding. The smoke was being carried to her by a light, warm draft from the sitting room. She thought about trying to escape out the back, but the only way was through the bathroom window. And from there, it was more than thirty feet to the ground.

She looked around for something, anything, with which to protect herself. All she could find was a small, ivory paper knife. She slipped it into the back pocket of her jeans and went into the next room.

The curtains were drawn to keep the apartment cool, so the room was dark but for a thin rectangle of light where the drapes met. All the same, Sharifa could see al-Qadi by the whites of his eyes and the soft glow of his cigarette. She reached for the switch and flicked on the lights. He was lolling in an armchair in the middle of the room. A button had popped on his shirt, exposing his belly. For a moment, the thought of him alone amongst her things made her feel more angry than frightened.

She managed to keep her voice even. "How did you get in?"

Al-Qadi made an exaggerated show of studying his surroundings. "These old apartments are not particularly secure. I thought I'd come and look you up, Sharifa, see how you are. I was in the neighborhood, feeling particularly good today and I thought—" He paused. "But enough of this. Uthman I can deal with anytime." He smiled.

Sharifa remained by the door. Oh God, what if he wanted to talk about Girling? What if he wanted to tell her Girling was dead? She was afraid beyond reason that her reactions would give Girling away.

Al-Qadi studied her slowly. He let the smoke from his Nefertiti curl from his mouth into his nostrils. Then he pried himself from the chair and moved toward her.

"Work and pleasure, pleasure and work. How many times has he had you, you bitch?"

"How dare you," she whispered. Suddenly, all she could think of was the missing file.

The gleam of triumph in his eyes turned cold.

"Remember who owns you, *ya* Sharifa. I feel somewhat let down by your recent efforts at keeping in touch. Why didn't you tell me about Girling's assignation by the Pyramids? Who was he meeting? Tell me."

"You don't own one hair of me. Not anymore. We're through."

Al-Qadi looked at the walls and the ceiling, his eyes making a great show of her comfortable surroundings.

"Your father's just a phone call away."

Fear and anger had turned her legs to water.

"What do you want from me?" she stammered.

"Since you're not letting on who he's been seeing, I thought we could have a little fun. Just you and me."

Her hand came up to her mouth. "Oh God, no . . ."

She turned to run, but al-Qadi was quicker. He grabbed a handful of her hair and began to march along the corridor to her bedroom. She yelped with the pain, but al-Qadi offered no respite. He threw open the door, paused to sniff the scented aroma of her boudoir, then threw her onto her bed.

She felt his weight on the bed. She turned to find him kneeling beside her, one hand reaching for his belt, the other undoing his zipper.

"They've all had you," al-Qadi said. "Now it's my turn."

Her slap caught al-Qadi full in the face. He fell backward, his hands behind him to cushion his fall. He fell against her wicker clothes basket and sent it flying.

For several seconds, he lay there, surrounded by her dirty laundry. Then he was on his feet, scattering items of her clothing around the room like confetti. With a roar of half triumph, half rage, al-Qadi produced Girling's soiled jacket from the basket, the one he had seen him wear the previous night.

He stood there, transfixed for a moment before rushing at her, his momentum driving her back onto the bed. In a second he was upon her, the full force of his weight piling down onto her stomach, expelling the wind from her lungs. She opened her mouth to scream, but all sound died in her throat.

"He's supposed to be dead, you bitch! His car plunged into the river off the 26th of July Bridge last night."

Al-Qadi pulled her shirt from the waistband of her Levi's. His small, pudgy fingers dispensed with undoing the buttons, ripping the garment open instead, one hand running over her breasts, the other plunging down toward her jeans.

She tried to draw breath, but she couldn't. She was suffocating.

Al-Qadi jabbered, calling her every obscenity she had ever heard. She could see the lust in his eyes as he pulled at her trousers. She felt she had been struck down by a snake, its poison paralyzing her muscles, but leaving her with a disturbing clarity of mind. She could do nothing without breath to her lungs.

The sweat of his palms allowed Al-Qadi to slip a hand under the waistband of her trousers. She felt the fingers inching their way lower, the blunt tips clawing at her underwear, past the elastic.

"So good, so good." His spittle splashed her face. Something had snapped inside him. "Girling won't get far." He licked her neck. "You whore! Did you think he would get away from me? That other *'agnabi* bastard bled like a pig when I shot him. Two bullets, that's all." He laughed and shoved his hand down deeper. "But with Girling, I'm going to make it five."

Suddenly, the air rushed into her throat, filling her lungs and banishing the paralysis. Al-Qadi had killed Stansell. Dear God. She lunged for the investigator's crotch, took both his testicles in her hand and squeezed with all her strength.

Al-Qadi's eyes bulged in their sockets, his mouth gaped, the fleshy lips curled back in agony. He rolled off her and her hand went to the back pocket of her jeans. She saw him going for the automatic inside his jacket. She grasped the paper knife and wrenched it from under her.

Despite the unyielding pain to his genitals, Al-Qadi pulled the gun from its holster. His face was gray. He brought the gun up to her head at the precise moment Sharifa plunged the ivory tip of the paper knife into his chest.

■   ■   ■

"I do not understand," Abdullah said. He was gazing into the middle distance, studying the outer defenses of the airfield.

"What?"

They were four hundred yards from the perimeter wire, two nomads riding at a lazy pace, rejoining their tribesman in the desert after a morning at Qena's market.

Abdullah spat on the sand, then gestured with a nod to the nearest of the watchtowers. They were spaced roughly half a kilometer apart.

"There are two men in the tower, see *'agnabi?* And one of them is watching us through long glasses."

Girling raised his head level with the horizon. He had wrapped the headcloth to hide his face but for a narrow slit across the eyes. He saw a glint from the watchtower. A pair of high-power binoculars reflecting the glare of the sun.

"Don't worry, there will be another tower, empty next time, *insh 'allah.*" Abdullah gestured ahead. "Do not show too much interest in them, *ya majnoon,* for if the soldiers become suspicious they will send trucks. And then it will be over for you."

"And for you also."

"Me they would never catch. But you . . . ?" He drew a finger across his throat and laughed.

Girling laughed, too. It helped to ease the tension.

Ten minutes later, they passed close to the next tower. It looked deserted. Suddenly, a head appeared above the parapet. The guard exchanged a series of greetings with Abdullah and Girling bit back his frustration.

"Most curious," Abdullah whispered. "Normally, it is deserted."

Prompted by Abdullah, the sentry explained that they were providing security for a military exercise on the base.

When they discovered that the third tower was also manned, Girling put a new plan to his guide. "We wait until nightfall and cross the perimeter under cover of darkness."

Abdullah shook his head. "Impossible, *ya majnoon.* There is a minefield on the other side."

"A what?"

"A minefield, *ya majnoon.*"

"You never mentioned the minefield."

Abdullah shrugged. "I did not think it important."

Girling threw his water bottle onto the sand. "Not important? How were we ever going to get to the *ta'iraat* with a minefield between the perimeter fence and the runway?" Girling swore under his breath. "I bet you knew about the bloody guards all along, too."

Abdullah dismounted at the same time as Girling. The two men confronted each other between the camels. "Are you calling me a liar, *'agnabi?*"

"I'm calling you a thief."

Abdullah reached into his galabiya and pulled a knife. Girling faced him, aware that they were in full view of the guard in his watchtower a few hundred yards away. He no longer cared. His anger was uncontrollable.

Abdullah's arm moved like a striking snake. But instead of lunging, the bedouin sheathed his knife.

Abdullah looked at Girling for a moment, then tipped his head back, his body racked with sobs of laughter. "I should have told you about the minefield. So keep your money." He thrust a bundle of screwed-up notes into Girling's hand.

The bedouin forced his camel to the ground and mounted it again. He looked down at Girling, who remained unmoved.

"There is nothing more for you here, *'agnabi.* Come. We go back to Qena." He gestured to the watchtower. "This is God's will. I knew about the minefield, yes, but I did not know about the guards."

Girling got back onto his camel and stared at the watchtower. "If I could just see what they're protecting," he said.

They turned the camels around and headed back toward Qena.

It was five minutes before Abdullah spoke. "Maybe they are protecting the *halikubtars.*"

At first Girling didn't register the bedouin's words.

"They say the *halikubtars* are very valuable," Abdullah added nonchalantly.

Girling stopped his camel. "*Halikubtars?*"

Abdullah nodded. "Yes." He made a whirling motion in the air with his finger. "But you are not interested in *halikubtars,* only *ta'iraat.* You said so in Qena."

"What is the difference?"

Abdullah held his hands out, arms level with his shoulders. He grinned self-consciously. "These are *ta'iraat.*"

This time, it was Girling who laughed.

"Do not insult me, *'agnabi.*"

"I'm not laughing at you, my friend, only my own stupidity."
Girling shook his head. *Halikubtars.* It was so simple. It had not
occurred to him that the word *"ta'iraat"* would not include the genus
halikubtar. Helicopter. He should have been more precise.

"Tell me about these *halikubtars.*"

Abdullah pointed to a spot on the horizon. "Every day they fly into
the mountains." His arm described an arc from the air base to the
jagged heights in the distance. "They say that one of them crashed."

"Recently?"

"Two days ago."

"Where?"

Abdullah pointed to two barely discernible peaks, their summits
arching slightly inward toward each other. "In the valley that lies
between the Horns of Shaytan."

"Take me there and you will receive the rest of your money."

"Never, *ya majnoon.* It is an evil place. They say *djinn,* evil spirits,
dwell there."

Girling studied the bedouin's face. There was fear there, certainly,
but . . .

"Would another fifty pounds lessen your fear?"

Abdullah smiled. "A hundred, maybe."

They agreed on seventy.

Abdullah nudged the nose of his beast. He looked to Girling, riding
beside him, and smiled. "Truly, you are mad, *'agnabi,*" he said.

CHAPTER 10

THE SUN WAS LOW in the sky when Girling and Abdullah rode up the dried riverbed that lay in the long shadows of the Horns of Shaytan.

The wadi had known death. It was not just the physical evidence—a camel's rotting carcass lay a dozen yards away—there was a malevolence there, too. Girling felt its imprint deep within the rocks. He almost found himself believing Abdullah's talk of genies and spirits.

They urged the camels on, following the course of the wadi deep into the mountain range.

After many miles and with the light diminishing, Abdullah reined up his camel and the beast sank to the ground.

"What are you doing?" Girling asked.

"We camp here for the night."

"No, my friend. We do not rest until we have found the *halikubtar*."

Abdullah raised his hands to the sky. "We have searched for hours with no sign of it. Perhaps those who gossiped in the market were mistaken."

"I don't think so," Girling said. But inside, he was beginning to have his doubts.

"And it is almost dark," Abdullah said.

"But not quite."

"I should never have told you about the *halikubtar, ya majnoon.*"

"Think of the money, Abdullah."

The bedouin groaned. "What good is money in this devilish place?"

They rode for another half hour, until the light was so poor Girling could see scarcely a few yards ahead. Then, without warning, Abdullah stopped.

Girling no longer had the stomach to argue. "*Khalas,*" he said.

In the gathering gloom, the bedouin scurried down the side of a sandy depression in the wadi bed and was lost from sight. A moment later, Girling heard a muffled shout.

"Come quickly, *ya majnoon.*"

Girling slid off his saddle and stumbled after the bedouin. He tripped over the edge of the hole, the sharp drop taking him by surprise. He tumbled down its side to land at Abdullah's feet.

Abdullah threw his arms out expansively, gesturing to the dimensions of the hole. "Is not this great trough the work of a *djinn, 'agnabi?*"

Girling said nothing.

"Tell me, *'agnabi.* How was it made?"

Girling looked around him. It seemed an unnatural hole in the otherwise flat riverbed. "A flash flood perhaps." Then his bare foot touched something hard but smooth beneath the surface of the sand. "This was made by man, not spirits."

He pulled a lighter from his robes and flicked the flint, the sparks like tracers in the darkness. The flame danced in the light, warm breeze that blew in from the far-off shores of the Red Sea.

The hole was big, probably thirty feet across. And deep.

He reached down and pulled the object from the sand and held it up to the light. Its geometry was almost perfect; a block of aluminum, two feet long and rectangular, with over thirty holes drilled into one face. He ran the light up and down the sides free of the perforations and saw the burnished identification plate, its Cyrillic lettering indecipherable. A group of letters and Arabic numerals was obviously a serial number. The machine for which the object was intended was a Mil Mi-24J.

The hole was big, because a helicopter had crashed there and then been removed. The flare dispenser he held in his hands, its thirty-two cartridges devised to seduce heat-seeking missiles away from their intended target, had been missed by the salvagers.

His thrill turned to disappointment. Girling had been positive he would find an American helicopter. But instead it was Russian. And the Egyptians had Russian-built helicopters coming out of their ears.

He let the flare rack fall to the ground and mounted the slope toward the place they left the camels.

Abdullah had been watching him expectantly. "There was a *halikubtar* here, *ya majnoon?*"

Girling turned to him. "Yes, my friend. You did well."

"Then why are you not pleased?"

"I was hoping we would find a different machine. But *ma'lesh.*" No matter. "My search is over."

When Abdullah came over the lip of the depression, he found Girling standing perfectly still, as if something had turned him to stone.

Girling swung round. There was a look of awe on his face. "My God," he whispered in English. "The Russians are here, too." He let out a whoop of glee that echoed off the valley walls. "The Russians and the Americans are here. They're working this thing together."

Everything came together in a whirl. The Ilyushin at Machrihanish, Stansell's visit to the Russian embassy the day he was taken, the fact that he had interviewed the Sword over a decade before in that distant corner of the once mighty Soviet empire, Afghanistan. And now this Mi-24J, a helicopter so new that it wasn't even listed in the reference books. "The Egyptians don't have any Mi-24s—they never did."

Abdullah rushed around to confront Girling, but the journalist was so absorbed he could not see him.

Girling laughed out loud. "This rescue mission's a joint operation. They're both going in together to get the Angels of Judgment. Because the Russians know who the Angels of Judgment are, they have all along. This is the New World Order at work." He did a little jig in the sand. "The Russians know where the Angels of Judgment are, but the Americans don't. That's why Ulm came looking for me. He wants to know for himself, because the Russians won't tell him."

Abdullah stared at him, horrified. "Are you possessed?"

Girling stopped dancing. "We found the right *halikubtar* after all," he said, reverting to Arabic. And not just the right helicopter. His mind was spinning so fast he didn't know how to stop it. One piece of metal, a flare dispenser, had unlocked an Aladdin's cave of information. Not least, it pinpointed Stansell's source for the story. It hadn't been the Israelis, the Americans or the Brits. Lazan had been right. It was the goddamned Russians who'd told Stansell about the Angels of Judgment.

He clapped a friendly hand on the bedouin's shoulder. "So let's eat."

They made a fire from wood washed down by flash floods from the mountains. Abdullah brewed tea, dark brown and sweet, in an old biscuit tin that he kept inside one of the saddlebags. Another saddlebag yielded their meal, a sack of *fool misra*—the small fava beans of Egypt—that Abdullah boiled and mashed into a paste, mixing in corn oil as he went. When he had finished, he motioned for Girling to scoop the glutinous mixture from the bowl with his fingers and gave him some bread to supplement the small meal.

The food was just enough for Girling to forget his hunger, and he lay down on the camel blanket. Above him the Milky Way shone with a magical clarity, the pinpoints of light dimmed only by the periodic contrast of shooting stars.

He felt a sudden burning wish for Mona to be there beside him. He would have loved more than anything to have shared this moment with her, to talk it through with her and listen to her soft words of wisdom. He wondered whether she would have seen things the way he saw them. He hoped so, for to him the evidence was indisputable. Stansell had learned of the Sword and the Angels of Judgment during the cocktail party at the Russian embassy, probably from a Russian diplomat who'd gotten plastered and spilled the beans by mistake. On the face of it, Stansell already had his scoop, but being the sort of journalist he was, he had to take it one step further. The names had triggered a hunt through past volumes of *Dispatches* until he struck gold and traced them back to Afghanistan. Knowing of the links that bound Muslim fundamentalist organizations from around the world, he'd gone to tap a source in the Brotherhood, perhaps the Guide himself, to push the story that extra bit along. Yet that determination to go further than he ever needed to go had cost Stansell his life.

Girling had never believed in anything like an afterlife, but under such a sky, on such a night, it was difficult not to feel that something existed out there for Mona and Stansell. He wondered whether her killer, Abu Tarek, was watching the sky that night. And whether the chance to make Abu Tarek pay would materialize.

Abdullah stoked the dying embers. As he did so, Girling saw him shiver.

"What is it, my friend?"

"I will get little sleep tonight."

"There is nothing to fear from this place."

"It is your soul that frightens me, *'agnabi.*"

Girling sat up.

"Something troubles you," Abdullah said. "Many times I have felt it while we were riding."

Girling felt compelled to answer.

"I lost my wife some years back," he said. "There is still pain."

"How did she die?"

Girling told the story of Asyut and the manner of Mona's death.

"I have heard of these people from the towns and cities who do wrongs in the name of our belief."

"I'm not sure I can forgive them, Abdullah."

"Then you will never truly live again, my friend."

"If Islam is vengeful, then perhaps so am I," Girling said.

"God says that evil should be rewarded with like evil," Abdullah said. "But the Koran also says that he who forgives and seeks reconcilement shall be rewarded by God." He paused. "It is for each man to choose his path. You should make peace with the world, *'agnabi.*"

Abdullah sighed and lay back on the sand to sleep.

The light wind that had brought with it the heat of the Red Sea by day had turned colder, and Girling pulled the blanket more tightly around his shoulders. Try as he might, sleep evaded him until the small hours before dawn.

■   ■   ■

THE SOUND cut into his dreams before Abdullah's rasping whisper roused him. He had not stirred before because he was convinced that the swishing noise of the blades only existed inside his head.

Girling's eyes snapped open. The sky had lightened in the east. He had been asleep for an hour, maybe two.

Abdullah shook him hard. His voice was tense. "That sound. What is it?"

The canyon reverberated as the blades carved through the air toward them.

It took Girling a moment to focus his mind, a moment longer to appreciate that he, Abdullah and the camels were out in the open, clear of cover.

Girling knew that wherever the machines were going, their course would take them right overhead.

He threw the blanket off his body and sprang to his feet, thinking blindly that it would be enough for him and Abdullah to run for the shelter of the rocks close by. But then he remembered the camels.

Could he risk leaving them out in the open, while he and Abdullah cowered behind the rocks? The camels were alert, their ears twitching to each blade beat that echoed off the rocks. It was if they sensed he might leave them behind.

"We must move the camels behind the boulders," Girling yelled.

He dragged the first camel to its feet. A moment later Abdullah was by his side.

They cajoled the creatures, their gangling legs resisting attempts to hurry them as the sound grew in Girling's head and the sand was whipped up by the rushing wind.

"It is Shaytan. He is coming for us," Abdullah said, gasping, eyes wide with fear.

"No, not Shaytan." But Girling was too breathless to explain.

They dragged the camels behind the nearest cluster of rocks just as the first helicopter swept around the bend in the wadi, the downwash from its rotors sending dust devils spiraling into the air.

The big machine roared past their position, its pilot holding a resolute course a few feet above the center of the wadi bed. Girling recognized it as a modified Jolly Green, the fabled MH-53J Pave Low III of USAF special forces. It was so close that he could see the concentration on the pilot's face; so close that the monotone star and bar was easily visible on the fuselage.

The MH-53J was followed by three more, each flying with the precision of the first.

Girling saw the special modifications—refueling probe and radar system in the nose, the miniguns protruding from the open cabin door—and knew that these helicopters were training for no ordinary mission.

When the last MH-53J had thundered past, he sprang out from behind the rock and watched as it skittered down the wadi like a giant dragonfly, eventually pulling up over the cliffs and disappearing from view.

He stood there, waiting for the din to recede, but the sound of their engines did not disappear into the desert as he thought they would. He could hear them roaring beyond the wall of the wadi.

Girling began to sprint for the cliffs just as the gunfire started.

Abdullah was behind him, rifle in hand. They reached the flat summit together and ran across the plateau, stopping only at the abyss that lay on the other side. What Girling saw took his breath away.

The helicopters were circling like vultures a few feet above the tops of the cliffs at the head of the wadi. Every second or so, a belch of flame leapt from the cabin doors, accompanied by a sound that ripped apart the last vestiges of the night.

The gunners were pouring fire into the ground at the base of the cliffs. The shooting was well disciplined, each burst aimed with pinpoint precision—Girling could tell as much by the isolated puffs of dust that jumped from the ground.

One of the helicopters broke away from the group and came into a hover a few feet above the cliffs at the end of the valley. Girling was dimly aware of shadows scurrying from the open cabin door.

Two more helicopters broke away, but Girling only tracked their passage on the periphery of his vision.

A complex at the base of the cliffs was beginning to take shape as his eyes grew accustomed to the light. It was as strange as any he had ever seen. Its rigid geometry looked incongruous against the desert setting, but the fact it was fifty kilometers from the nearest outpost of civilization made it absurd.

It was a perfect square, its sides some fifty yards long, its walls approximately fifteen feet high. In its midst was a great courtyard, covered, in part, by a flimsy roof. There were a number of smaller buildings, shacks, scattered around it, all whitewashed. Beyond the shacks a trench enclosed the cluster of buildings.

More details leapt into focus. In one of the corners he noticed a minaret set starkly against the rocky backdrop, a building within the building at its base.

Girling turned to Abdullah. "What is this place?"

"I do not understand," Abdullah replied. He had to shout over the gunfire. "It is a caravanserai."

Girling had never seen one close up.

"Did you know about this caravanserai here?"

"No, *ya majnoon.*" There was a mixture of puzzlement and anger on the bedouin's face. "A caravanserai is the desert's own miracle, a sacred place, where even rival tribes forget their differences."

It was only when Girling looked at one of the walls side-on that the pieces fell into place. "Look," he shouted. "Your caravanserai is made of wood."

Before Abdullah could ask him the purpose of such an edifice, the two Sikorskys that had broken away thirty seconds earlier swept in low and fast from the open end of the wadi. Their noses reared as the pilots bled off the excess speed. Then they began to settle on the expanse of dust between the caravanserai and the two shacks. Even before their wheels brushed the ground, men leapt from their ramps.

A group of eight soldiers rushed to one of the shacks amidst covering fire from the helos circling overhead. Accurate sniping fire came from the men who had been deposited earlier on the clifftops.

The soldiers were difficult to spot, dressed as they were in black, gas masks and hoods on their heads.

There was a flash like a firecracker detonation and the shack door blew off its hinges. Two men scurried inside. Another group dished out similar treatment to the second shack in a mirror-image operation. The second door blew open just as the first group of soldiers began hurrying back across open ground toward the helicopters. Each soldier supported mannequins, all dangling legs and deadweight. The second group reappeared and from somewhere a star shell rose into the sky, bursting in an incandescent shower of green phosphor.

The two Sikorskys lifted off from the ground and peeled away.

There was so much action that Girling did not know where to look. At the head of the wadi, the second pair of Sikorskys began to lower over the caravanserai, ropes spilling from their bodies like disemboweled entrails. In an instant men were abseiling to the ground.

It took, perhaps, less than two minutes for the soldiers to clear the rooms with gunfire and grenades. This time, they did not reappear with mannequins. As he watched, the caravanserai was torn apart.

Another star shell, red this time, burst in the sky. The Sikorskys reappeared and once more the ropes dangled from the cabins. Troops back aboard, the helicopters pulled away, clearing the cliffs just as a series of explosions blew the building apart.

Then the noise ceased, leaving only a ringing in Girling's ears.

■   ■   ■

SHABANOV JUMPED from the side door of his MH-53J onto the tarmac at Wadi Qena. The other three helicopters swept down from the sky one by one, each separating by a hundred yards as it lowered wheels to the ground.

Shabanov had exchanged his Russian combat fatigues for American ones. It had been decided that because they were using U.S. helicopters, they would standardize on U.S. military equipment, right down to the uniforms. Apart from anything else, it would lead to fewer identification problems when they took the Sword's caravanserai for real.

Shabanov waved to his pilot and took a last admiring look at the MH-53J. With mid-air refueling, it was big enough to ferry them all the way into and all the way out of the target area and yet Russian pilots who had flown it, his Russian pilots, said it performed like an agile combat helicopter. Remarkable. Would that their own technology was as good.

When he turned to the other Sikorskys, two of them were already trundling across the tarmac to their hangars, leaving Ulm's machine alone, facing his, the two birds looking like overweight gunslingers at a dawn showdown. He watched Ulm swing out of the copilot's seat, drop to the ground, catch sight of him and start walking over.

They met halfway.

"Well?" Ulm said.

Shabanov pulled off his helmet and ran a gloved hand through his bristle-length hair. "Tell Mr. Jacobson to alert the KC-130 tankers. We're ready to go as soon as General Aushev gives the all clear."

"When could that be?"

"Your guess is as good as mine, Elliot. When the weather's fine, when the hostages are all in the optimum position, when the Angels are asleep, when the gods smile . . .

"That could be weeks."

"Or tomorrow." Shabanov breathed deeply. He felt good. "You can tell Mr. Jacobson we're ready, Elliot. For the moment, that's all that matters."

CHAPTER 11

ONLY IN THE COOL, air-conditioned interior of the Misr Tours office at Ramsis Station did Girling notice the acrid odor of his body and clothes for the first time. His filth-ridden suit and sweat-stained skin had gone unremarked amongst his fellow travelers—mainly fellaheen, or peasant farmers—on the third-class coach on the train from Qena to Cairo. But here, surrounded by a busload of Italian tourists, their leader remonstrating angrily with a girl behind the desk who was disclaiming all knowledge of a block booking on that morning's express to Luxor, the smell of the camel saddle and the dust on his jacket almost choked him.

With the uproar at its height, Girling calmly reached across the desk, picked up the phone and dialed Sharifa's. He let the phone ring for almost two minutes, but there was no answer. He was relieved, because it meant she had done his bidding and gone to Lazan's.

Enduring hostile glances from a couple of elderly tourists at the back of the melee, Girling dialed a new number, Stansell's apartment, and waited for the answering machine to engage. He was reluctant to show up there personally in case he ran into one of al-Qadi's men. For the moment, being dead suited him just fine.

He activated the remote access code and listened to his messages. There were four from Kelso, his voice getting successively angrier. Interspersed amongst them were the calmer tones of Jack Carey, asking him to call with details of his forthcoming exclusive on the Angels of Judgment. Time was running short if he was going to make the edition. Girling smiled to himself. God, did he have a story for Carey now.

On the train, with eight hours to himself, Girling had resolved not to release details of what he had seen in the desert until after the rescue was complete. Not only did he want it to go ahead, uncompromised, but he felt consumed by the need for the Angels of Judgment to get what was coming to them. The fact that he had seen the rehearsal—and knew of the punishment the Americans and the Russians would unleash once the hostages were secured—gave him a glow of satisfaction. It was as if he would be going in with them. As if their revenge were his also.

His last message was from Lazan. The Israeli asked him to get around to see him as soon as possible, before he did anything else. At the embassy, day or night. He would be there, not home. There had, he said, been some interesting developments.

Girling wandered from the station into the chaos of Ramsis Square. Though it was filled with thousands of people heading off for work, he managed to find a taxi before long.

He reached the embassy after a protracted battle with the early-morning commuter traffic. The security was elaborate, the checks endless. Only after the armed guards, the video cameras, the remote entry-control systems and the air locks did he get to talk to Lazan on the lobby phone. The defense attaché told him to sit tight and wait for an escort who would take him to the second floor. A girl behind the desk handed him his pass, scarcely disguising her distaste for his appearance as she did so.

The escort was a taciturn man in his late twenties who looked almost Scandinavian. The atmosphere in the embassy was distinctly militaristic. But for the fact that everyone sported the relaxed dress-style of Israeli officialdom, Girling imagined he could have been in an IDF command bunker on the Golan Heights.

The elevator doors opened on the second floor and Girling was greeted by the quiet chatter of teleprinters and the businesslike rasp of Hebrew. He saw the sense of purpose in the comings and goings of the people in the corridor. The embassy seemed to be a microcosm of the Jewish state—a small patch of land under siege—and it showed in the determination of the people around him.

Lazan was at his desk, the phone jammed to his ear. He cupped his hand over the mouthpiece and told the Scandinavian to bring an extra chair and two cups of coffee.

The office was bare, functional. A picture on the wall of a younger, uniformed Lazan, free of facial scars, posing beside the burned-out hulk of a Syrian T-62, provided an ironic comment on the Islamic skyline beyond the window. The picture was an arrogant gesture, Girling thought, but he would have expecting nothing less.

The air-conditioning prickled Girling's skin. Outside, the sun rose a little higher above the minarets as Cairo began to cook.

The Scandinavian returned with a chair and coffees. Lazan nodded his thanks before the door was closed and the two of them were alone.

Lazan wound up his conversation and put the phone down. "Where have you been, Tom Girling?"

The rim of the coffee cup never reaching Girling's mouth. "I'm sorry?"

"I said—"

"I know what you said, Lazan. Didn't Sharifa tell you?"

"Sharifa? What are you talking about?"

"Oh my God. Al-Qadi . . ." Girling made a lunge for the door, but with surprising agility, Lazan beat him to it.

"Tell me what is going on, Girling."

"I have to get to Sharifa's. She was supposed to get in touch with you." Girling managed to blurt out the succession of events which had led to him ordering her to seek sanctuary with him. "I've got to get to her." He tried to twist from Lazan's grip, but the Israeli held him firm.

"No, wait." Lazan moved to his desk and punched in an extension number. He spoke quickly into the mouthpiece and hung up. "Take the elevator to the basement. Ariel Ram—the man who brought you to my office—will drive you to her place. I'll catch up with you there as soon as I can." He gestured to the cane by the door. "I'm afraid my leg would only hold you up on the way to the basement."

Girling opened the door, then hesitated. "Why did you call me here?"

"Think about this on your way. We're receiving intelligence from

Lebanon of something extraordinary. My people need answers,
Girling, and maybe you're the one to find them. It seems like every
important leader of the whole terrorist community in the Levant is on
the move. Al-Haqim of Black June, Sheikh Abu Jadid of Hizbollah,
Ahmed Jibril of the PFLP-GC, and others. They're mobilizing and we
don't know why. There are rumors of a *shura*—a council of war—
somewhere in Lebanon. Tel Aviv is screaming for information, but
everyone's drawing a blank.''

"Do you think it's got anything to do with the Angels of Judgment?'' Girling asked.

"I don't know. That's what I'm hoping you'll tell me.'' He slapped
him on the back. ''That elevator's waiting for you, Tom Girling. Go.''

■   ■   ■

GIRLING WAS out of the passenger seat and bounding up the steps of
the apartment block even before Ram had brought the car to a stop. He
dispensed with the elevator and took to the marble stairs, taking three
steps at a time in his impatience to reach the third floor.

Panting for breath, he stood outside her door and leaned on the bell.
He sensed someone close by, turned and saw Ram coming up the stairs.

Neither of them said a word. Ram raised his foot and gave the door
a sharp kick. It flew open and Girling was inside, calling her name and
getting nothing in reply. When he saw the overnight bag by the front
door, it only served to heighten his anxiety. He checked each room in
turn, moving down the corridor, Ram behind, the Israeli's outstretched
hand brandishing a small, compact automatic. Girling stood before the
bedroom, its door slightly ajar. It was the last room in the apartment.
He peeped through the crack and caught a glimpse of clothes strewn
around the end of the bed. He called out her name, but again there was
no reply. He took a deep breath and stepped inside. He had braced
himself for the worst, but nothing had prepared him for the sight that
confronted him.

Al-Qadi lay in the center of the bed, belly up, arms and legs
outstretched. His face had gone a shade that was something between a
pasty yellow and a watery gray, his lips a deeper hue of the same,
sickening color.

The tip of a blackened tongue poked from between his teeth. It was
just possible to see the hilt of the paper knife protruding from a hole

somewhere below the investigator's heart. There was blood all over the investigator's hands. In his last moments of life, it seemed al-Qadi had tried to pull the dagger from his chest, but the blade had stuck fast between two ribs. The blood had poured through the wound, running over his great stomach in rivulets, soaking the bedcover, the sheets and the pillows. Al-Qadi had bled like a stuck pig, unable to get up, unable to remove the paper knife, too shocked, too weak to shout for help. His eyes bulged, unblinking, sightless, like a fish lying gutted on the slab.

Behind him, Ram gagged. Girling fought to keep his mind clear. He, too, felt sickened, but the need to find Sharifa was uppermost in his mind. He saw al-Qadi's gun on the floor. As he reached for it, anxious to see if it had been fired, he heard a slight sound from the clothes closet in the far wall.

He found her hunched in the very corner, hidden behind suitcases and a pile of clothes. She stared at him, at first not comprehending who he was. He pulled her to him and she began to cry, softly at first, then less so as her mind regurgitated her last moments with the investigator.

Girling held her close until her sobs subsided. Then he took her face in his hands. "What happened?"

"I killed him, Tom." She stared at him, eyes wide. "I stood here, where you and I are standing now, and I watched him die, slowly, painfully. It must have taken him almost half an hour, just lying there, bleeding to death. And do you know something? I enjoyed every minute of it. I've dreamed of this moment for as long as I can remember. And now he's dead and I'm glad it was me who killed him."

"Sharifa, no."

She turned to him. "Why not? Is it so wrong to want for something like that? Isn't that what you have wished all along for Mona's killers?"

He found himself wanting, but unable to answer.

"He killed Stansell," she said.

"What?"

"He told me."

"But that makes no sense. Al-Qadi couldn't have been in league with the Angels of Judgment. If they're half as radical as the Brotherhood, then al-Qadi was the kind of person they would have despised." He shook his head. "No, there has to be some other explanation."

"He pulled Stansell's autopsy report, tried to bury it—"

"How do you know that?" Girling interrupted.

"Dr. Uthman told me, in so many words. He phoned yesterday, asking for you. I was just on my way out, to Lazan's. It was only when I was talking to Uthman that I realized al-Qadi was here, in the apartment, listening to every word."

"What happened then?"

"He dragged me into the bedroom where he found your jacket. It was then that he just . . ."

"Yes?"

"He just went berserk. He tried to rape me. If I hadn't had the paper knife he would have killed me."

Girling looked past her at the obscenity on the bed. "We've got to get rid of the body."

She couldn't bring herself to turn around. "Where?"

Girling found himself thinking fast. "There's only one place: the City of the Dead."

She was poised to remonstrate, but he put a finger to her lips. "This is one death the Brotherhood can take the rap for, whether the Guide likes it or not. The City of the Dead is very much the Brotherhood's own. If al-Qadi's body is ever found down there the Brotherhood will be the natural suspects."

"But how—?"

Ram appeared at the door. Sharifa gasped and grabbed Girling in alarm.

"It's all right," Girling said. "This is Ariel Ram. He's on Lazan's staff."

Girling looked at him. "I'm getting the body out of here. Al-Qadi's bound to have a car somewhere around here. I'll use that."

"How to get the body outside?" Ram asked.

"You're going to help me," Girling said. "We'll wrap it up in the blankets and shove it in the boot of the car. And then I'm going to drive his car to the City of the Dead and dump it there. The Brotherhood can have the lot." He turned to Sharifa. "You, meanwhile, are going to stay here with Ram until Lazan gets here. Then the three of you must go to the embassy and wait for me there."

"What happens then?" she asked.

"You and I are on the first plane out of here."

■   ■   ■

GIRLING TURNED the blue, unmarked Fiat off the airport road down a track whose tarred surface soon gave way to the bare sandstone soil, soil that characterized the land beneath the Muqattam Hills on the southeast side of the city.

He let the car coast, listening to its suspension protest as the wheels dipped in and out of potholes, or jarred against the protruding rocks. He had the windows down full. The sun was high in the sky and the heat was stifling. Girling thought he could smell al-Qadi's body decomposing, but it was nothing more than the regular odors of the city, odors that grew stronger the farther he ventured into the old, southeast side and the closer he got to the City of the Dead.

Behind him, the walls of the Citadel and the mosque at its pinnacle towered over the surrounding landscape. The great Mohammed Ali Mosque, at something over 150 years old, was a comparatively new addition to the skyline, but little else had changed in almost a thousand years. Girling's view was filled by the City of the Dead, a suburb of tombs, originally for the mighty, but over the centuries for anyone who could afford the money or the time to construct a mortuary for himself and his family. On his left were the egglike domes of the Circassian Mamelukes, a dynasty that had governed Egypt from the middle of the thirteenth century until the arrival of the Turks in 1517. Girling thought back to the morning of his arrival and his fleeting impressions of the necropolis as the sun had crept above the Muqattam Hills.

In the dawn light, the City of the Dead possessed a sinister kind of beauty, a thin curtain of mist softening its horrors, like muslin over a camera lens. It was here, at the turn of the millennium, that the Fatimid caliph al-Hakim liked to wander incognito, disguised as one of the simple peasants he had terrorized and ritually slaughtered during his reign. One evening he rode out in the direction of the Muqattam Hills and was never seen again, becoming a hero, his status embellished over the years, his return awaited by obscure Islamic sects across the Arab empire. It was here, too, that many of the stories of thieving and roguery were composed for *Arabian Nights*.

Under the harsh light of the noon sun, however, the City shimmered in its true colors. Interspersed amongst the mausoleums of the Mamelukes were small, bungalowlike tombs, some topped with fragile, crumbling domes and minarets, built in a pathetic emulation of the glorious sepulchers of the rich and the royal. It was to these tombs that the oppressed and the destitute of Cairo had flocked over the centuries. Too hungry and frightened to fear the dead, these people began to construct flimsy shanties, at first on any patch of land they could find, and then, as space ran out, on top of the graves themselves. As the shanties spread, so too did the City's reputation as a haven for murderers and thieves. Initially, the crime barons kept their distance, hugging the shadows for anonymity, and the traditions that had existed for so long in the City were allowed to continue. On certain days of the religious calendar, for instance, families would still come to the tombs of their forebears to leave food and drink for the departed. But as the criminal fraternity's grip on the City became firmer, so the visits of the simple law-abiding people became fewer and fewer. Staring across the City of the Dead's desolate expanse now, his car stopped, the engine idling, Girling understood why the meek at heart had stayed away.

Girling had halted the Fiat at the very boundary of the City. Behind him the air above the track still swirled with the dust thrown up by his tires. Ahead stretched a street whose buildings crumbled from the neglect of centuries. Every now and again, the desolate monotony of its facade was broken up by a whitewashed tomb here, a newly added shanty there. A dog crossed the street, stopped halfway to scratch its ear, then continued lazily on its way, lying down in a scant patch of shade on the other side of the road.

At first, Girling thought this part of the City was devoid of any human habitation. But as his eyes adjusted to the contrast of bright light and shade, he became aware of faces watching him from the gloomy recesses of windows, or the dark interiors of doorless rooms.

Girling climbed from the car. He did not want to stay in this place any longer than he had to. He knew that to the wary inhabitants of the City of the Dead, the very color of the car would reveal its identity. But as he stood under the sun, feeling as naked as a child, Girling realized that the disguise was paper thin and would not last long. As his watchers became accustomed to the sight of him, they would know that there was no way an *'agnabi* would be in the employ of the *mukhabarat.*

Girling moved quickly to the back of the car. He opened the trunk and stepped back as the smell of decomposition and the flies rushed to meet him. Al-Qadi's automatic, which Ram had replaced in the waistband of the investigator's trousers, had slipped from the folds of the blanket and now lay loose against the gas tank. Girling reached for it on impulse and stuffed it into the pocket of his suit jacket.

With one hand over his nose and mouth, Girling slammed the trunk shut. As he glanced up, he saw the first wave of people creep from their houses toward him. He could see the hunger in their eyes as they studied his car. Girling knew that, body in the back or not, within the next hour the Fiat would be stripped from the sideview mirrors to the chassis. After that, it would simply cease to exist, except in a thousand and one parts on the black market. Al-Qadi's body would be hungrily devoured by packs of scavenging dogs.

He began to advance back up the hill, one hand thrust into his jacket pocket where it held onto the reassuring grip of al-Qadi's pistol. A hundred yards from the car, Girling glanced back to see it surrounded by a crowd. He pressed on, anxious to regain the airport road, where he could find a taxi that would take him back to the Israeli embassy.

As he proceeded up the track, he saw a figure in the distance, moving down the hill toward him. It drew closer and he realized it was a boy, probably no more than thirteen years old, dressed in a traditional galabiya, which was dirty enough to indicate he possessed no other garment. The boy skipped down the hill seemingly without a care. He appeared to pay Girling no attention until he drew level. Then he stopped, just as Girling stopped, and studied him, head inclined over one shoulder to exaggerate the act of contemplation.

"*Agnabi*," he said. "I have a message for you."

Girling thought he misheard. He was convinced that this boy would ask him for money.

"A message? Who from?"

"From Sheikh Youssef, our Guide."

Girling felt his pulse quicken. "What does he say, *ya walad?*"

"If you come with me, I will show you the house of Abu Tarek. You want him, don't you?"

Girling fingered the butt of the automatic. "Why should the Guide do this?"

"He did not tell me."

Girling stared up the track. He could hear the traffic at the top of the road.

"Do you come, or not?" the boy asked impatiently.

Girling's every nerve ending tingled. To be so close to Mona's killer and not see where his house was . . .

"How far is it, *ya walad?*" he asked.

The boy pointed down the slopes of the wooded grove beside the road. "He lives just beyond these trees."

Girling looked from the trees to the road and back. He gripped the gun more firmly in his pocket.

"Well, *'agnabi?*"

"Come on."

The boy stopped him with a hand on his jacket. "First, you must pay." He held his hand out.

Girling actually allowed himself a smile. Somehow this simple act of enterprise made him feel better. He handed over a few piasters, notes which amounted to little more than a few cents, but were enough to sustain this artful boy for a week. They were bundled quickly into a pocket in the lining of his galabiya.

He followed the boy as he skipped nonchalantly between the trees. The sun broke through the branches and the boy used the shadows for a game, jumping from each of them, humming happily as he went.

And then they were out of the trees and moving through a cemetery. Girling slowed as he weaved between the headstones, but the boy waved him on. Finally they sat at the wall of the cemetery, the boy pointing at a collection of tombs across a clearing, the nearest of them about a hundred yards away. Girling crouched breathlessly, cradling al-Qadi's automatic in his lap.

The boy looked down at the gun. "Are you a policeman, *'agnabi?*"

"No."

"Then why do you have a gun?"

"It makes me feel safer. Which is the house of Abu Tarek?"

The boy pointed to the largest of the mausoleums, the one capped by a small, crumbling dome. "In there."

Girling studied it for a few moments, then turned to his small guide. But the boy was already weaving a path back through the graves. "How many people are inside?" Girling hissed after him.

The boy stopped. "He is alone," he said, before proceeding on his way.

Girling knew he should turn back. Before good sense could get too firm a hold, he darted across the clearing, gun in hand, and pressed his back against the nearest wall. He stopped still and listened. The place was perfectly quiet. He could hear nothing, not even so much as a dog's bark. He edged along the wall, stopped at a low gate and was over it, heading down a narrow passage, the tomb supposedly occupied by Abu Tarek straight ahead. He could see inside the mausoleum now. There was no door. Light streamed through a latticed window in the roof. There was a kind of raised platform in the center of the room, beneath the dome. It looked like the sarcophagus in which he had seen Stansell at police headquarters.

His heart in his mouth, Girling twisted through the doorway. There was no stopping him now. He felt that every minute he had been in Egypt had been in preparation for this moment. He stopped and listened again. His gun was ready, he had cocked it in the cemetery, and he held it out before him with both hands. The tomb was quiet. There was nobody there.

When he turned to the door, he caught only the merest glimpse of the figure just inside as it turned and slugged him in the face. At the moment Girling fell, he saw others. They were dressed in black, heads covered, moving into the room as nimbly as spirits. Girling rolled across the floor, coming to a halt against the sarcophagus. The figures advanced toward him. One of them held something in his hand.

Just before the cloth was clamped over his face, Girling asked the question to which his delirious mind thought it already knew the answer.

The mask moved. "We are the Angels of Judgment," it said.

CHAPTER 12

GIRLING AWOKE WITH A START. He sat up, trying to focus his eyes beyond the sunlight streaming through the window. The floor of the cell was of loosely raked earth, so cold he was shivering convulsively.

He tried to move toward the window, but his legs gave way. He lay there, the chilled earth against his cheek, and as the light started to fade he drifted back into unconsciousness.

As dusk fell he woke again. He groped for clues of his surroundings. The smell of the earth confused him. He was sure he remembered the rise and fall of a ship at sea, the smell of tar and salt spray.

Then he was running once more through the graveyard, al-Qadi's gun in his hand, trying to keep up with the sheikh's messenger.

Girling brought his hand up to his face and felt the bruise above his eye. He remembered rolling toward the sarcophagus, al-Qadi's gun skating across the floor.

Girling rose again and swayed. He felt pain and swelling in his upper arm. Whatever it was, it had been a powerful anesthetic. The hollowness in his stomach told him that he had been unconscious for a day, maybe two.

Before he made it to the window, a crude hole in the door crisscrossed by bars, a cool wind brushed his face, and brought with it the smell of cooking.

He grasped the bars and looked outside.

His prison lay now in the shadow of a high-sided rock face, at the end of a wadi. As his eyes adjusted to the light he made out a white, crenellated building shimmering in the distance like a mirage.

"A caravanserai . . . a sacred place," Abdullah had said, before the helicopters swept over Wadi Qena to destroy it.

Girling let go of the bars and teetered backward. He tried to regain balance, but fell against the far wall of the cell, cracking his head against the stones.

There was a scuffle outside the door and he looked up to see a man's face at the bars. Girling could not speak. He watched as a slice of unleavened bread was thrown to the floor. By the time he reached it, the face was gone and he was alone again.

■   ■   ■

THEY CAME for him several hours after nightfall.

Too faint from drugs and hunger to be afraid, Girling stumbled into the night. His hands were roped together in front of him; two soldiers held his arms and a third marched behind, holding a rifle to his back.

Girling felt as if he were caught in a strong current against which resistance was useless. He twisted in his escort's grip to take in his surroundings. The new moon did not cast much light, but as soon as they reached a small rise he was able to pick out the high walls of the caravanserai two hundred yards in front. Behind him was his prison, a shack with thick walls of caked mud and straw. A little way from it was a similar building, though slightly larger. He could make out the bars on the door and a roof reinforced with sheets of corrugated iron. It was then that he remembered the two small buildings, remote from the caravanserai itself, that had been picked out by the MH-53s in the valley near Qena. Was this where Franklin and his negotiating team were being held? To Girling, finally, it seemed he had arrived.

Dotted before the walls of the ancient caravanserai were a dozen campfires, each surrounded by five to ten men. It looked a little like a medieval battlefield.

In the glow of the fires, Girling could make out weapon emplacements. He saw antiaircraft guns mounted on station wagons and, amongst the portable weaponry, rocket-propelled grenades and shoulder-launched antiaircraft missiles by the dozen.

The night air was sharp against his face. He was maybe five or six thousand feet above sea level. Mountains—he was in the mountains.

They reached the caravanserai's double gates. The soldier in charge of his escort shouted a series of harsh commands in the night and the doors swung slowly open, hinges groaning under the strain.

Inside, women cooked over open stoves while the men sat talking and smoking. The air was thick with conversation and the smell of bean stew and spiced meats.

The caravanserai was lavishly detailed. It reminded Girling of the al-Mu'ayyad Mosque, where he had seen the Guide. A wooden balcony ran around the inside of the courtyard, supported by ornate, carved columns. The balcony was covered by a simple tiled roof, but the rest was open to the night. In the corner was a small mosque.

They reached a door set into the far wall and Girling was pushed inside with such force that he tripped and fell headlong.

He lifted his face off the smooth, paved floor. He was in a low-lit room and there was a crowd around him. The silence was palpable. As he climbed to his feet, Girling's gaze passed quickly across the sea of faces. Some were in traditional robes, others dressed in jeans and combat jackets. Several carried automatic rifles and pistols.

His guards grabbed him again and waded through the crowd, pushing it back with their rifles. He was forced onto a wooden chair.

Smoke hung in layers, from floor to ceiling. Facing him were three tables arranged in a semicircle. The crowd behind him was quieter now, but Girling could sense its every movement.

A door opened and two men entered. They sat down directly in front of him, on the opposite side of the middle table. One of them was Ahmed Jibril, the leader of the Popular Front for the Liberation of Palestine, General Command. He was older than his few published photographs gave him credit. His hair was gray, his stubble patchy. He wore a checkered Palestinian *gutra* around his neck.

The second man unbuckled his canvas combat belt and dropped it onto the table. Removing an old Colt .45 from its holster, he proceeded to clean it with a corner of his shirt. His dark hair, thinning at the temples, was swept back over his crown. His eyes were immensely dark and devoid of expression. Like Jibril, he wore military fatigues.

Jibril produced several pieces of paper from the top pocket of his tunic. He unfolded them slowly and placed them on the table. He put on a pair of reading glasses and studied the papers for a full two minutes without saying a word.

Girling could hear nothing except the sound of his own breathing. The entire room waited for Jibril to speak, but the other man held Girling's attention. As he watched the rhythmic movements of the second man's hands on the gun, a succession of images appeared before his eyes. The massacre at Beirut, bodies falling from the aircraft, explosions ripping it apart, flaming jet fuel incinerating the dead and the wounded. He saw al-Qadi spitting into Stansell's sarcophagus, felt the crowd close in on him outside the al-Mu'ayyad Mosque.

As he looked into this man's eyes he thought he saw the face of Abu Tarek, whose men had held him while the rocks rained down on Mona. He who had turned and laughed as he stood over her body on that dirt road in Asyut . . . Girling shook his head, clearing his mind of the flames and the stones, the dead and the wounded. He knew Tarek, the Guide's small-time thug, wasn't here. He had to tell himself that all these monsters were beginning to look alike.

Girling gripped the edge of his chair. His one solace was the knowledge he possessed. He knew the secret of Wadi Qena. Ulm and the Pathfinders were coming to kill this bastard and his friends. And he wanted to watch them do it.

Jibril looked up. "Tho-mas Gir-ling." He pronounced it badly, pronouncing the *th* as *th* rather than as *t* and softening the first *g*.

Girling turned slowly toward him.

"Who do you work for?" Jibril asked. Behind him a studious-looking man translated into Arabic for the audience.

"The British publication, *Dispatches.*"

Jibril clucked. "The whole truth . . ."

"I told you—"

"I heard first time," Jibril interrupted. It was a gravelly voice, heavily accented. "Perhaps I should be more clear." He waited for the translator to finish. "Who is paying you to write this material?" He waved the pieces of paper in his hand. "The Americans? the Israelis? Your own secret service?"

"I am a journalist," Girling said. "I don't work for any government."

"You expect us to believe that?" Jibril gestured around the room.

"It's the truth."

"One day you are writing about guns and airplanes from the safety of a desk in your own country. The next, you are here, sticking your nose into business that is not your concern."

"Murder is my concern."

"You do not answer the question."

Girling took a deep breath. "I was in Cairo a long time ago. Murder took me away, and murder brought me back."

The translator held his tongue.

"Then you have learned nothing," Jibril said. "Why did you write these lies about the Angels of Judgment?" He waved the paper again.

Girling looked back at the second man, who was no longer polishing his gun. "Because I wanted to see the face of the murderer," he said. "I wanted to see the Sword."

"Who are you working for?" Jibril repeated. The other man held up the Colt, examining it carefully under the light.

"You bastards aren't interested in the truth. It doesn't matter if you blow the leg off another kid, or waste one more pregnant woman. There's always the Cause, isn't there? The bloody cause justifies everything—"

The second man snapped a bullet into the chamber of the automatic. Girling looked straight into his eyes. Suddenly he didn't care about the hostages, the rescue, even about revenge. Past and future were the same. "You can't kill me again," he said, rising. "You bastards did that three years ago."

Jibril clicked his fingers and three bodyguards appeared from the shadows behind him.

The crowd took it as a signal and came for him from three sides of the room.

One of the bodyguards brought the butt of his Kalashnikov across Girling's face.

The pain temporarily drowned the cries of the crowd.

The first man to get to him had already drawn his pistol. At least six others held him down, pinioning him to the table.

Girling opened his eyes. He was staring straight into the snub barrel of an automatic. The man who held it was pleading with Jibril, shouting over and over. The crowd joined with him, a tuneless chant, an exhortation for him to pull the trigger and blow the *'agnabi* to hell.

Girling closed his eyes and the barrel was rammed against the bridge of his nose.

Then a voice rang out, silencing the crowd. It was deep and authoritative, but ice-cold, not angry. "Put your gun away, Adel."

"*Aiwa, ya Saif.*" Yes, Sword.

Girling tried to turn toward the voice, but it was impossible to see past the wall of men who surrounded him.

"Girling must live long enough to tell us what he knows. I will deal with him personally."

■   ■   ■

GIRLING LAY close to the door, his ears straining for sound. In the night, alone with his thoughts, a yearning to survive had returned. The thought that help was at hand sustained him.

On his way back to his cell he studied others, nearly identical: the same window bars, same thick wooden door with two armed guards either side. Was it large enough for an ambassador and a nine-strong team of negotiators?

He walked over to the door and looked outside. The moon had slipped behind the clouds. There was not a sound, not a single voice, not a laugh to be heard in the wadi. He clutched his sides for warmth. He could not see the other cell, but was tempted to call out. Then he felt the dried blood on his face from the Kalashnikov and remained silent.

When was Ulm coming?

Jibril and the Sword would put him through a further round of interrogation sometime after daybreak. They would want to know what he knew about them, but with boots and gun butts in his face, his groin and his kidneys, what else might he tell them?

He heard something.

An engine. A jet engine.

Girling pressed his head to the bars. It was very faint, very distant.

An airliner, crossing the night sky at altitude on its way to Europe, or the Gulf. Passengers inside, warm, relaxed, eating, sleeping . . .

Girling moved away from the bars to the corner farthest from the door and sat there waiting for the dawn.

■   ■   ■

GIRLING OPENED his eyes when it was not yet light. He lifted his head from the crook of his arm and heard a sound, very close. He stiffened, then got slowly to his feet. By the door he could see the outline of a man.

A match flared and he found himself staring into the eyes of a man he took at first to be a priest. He was dressed in a long robe and turban. His beard was white and full, the face strong.

The mullah watched him as he brought the flame to the wick. The lamp's flickering light illuminated a second man, rough-looking and armed, just beyond the door. The guard took a step toward Girling, but the mullah held him back. One word from the mullah, spoken lightly, but with authority, and the guard left them, closing the door behind him.

The mullah replaced the glass and hung the lamp on a hook by the door. To Girling's surprise, the eyes that held his were bright blue.

"Have you always been so angry, Mr. Girling?" The mullah lifted the hem of his robe and sat opposite him, eyes level.

"Who are you?" Girling asked.

"One who comes in peace." His English was accented, but smooth, unlike Jibril's.

"Does peace come from the barrel of a gun?"

The mullah raised his eyes. A muezzin had begun to call from the caravanserai.

Girling pointed to the door. "There are enough weapons out there to start another world war."

"The weapons belong to Jibril and Hizbollah, not the Angels of Judgment."

"What brings Jibril and Hizbollah here?"

"They have come to hear the Sword's message. They are here for the *shura*."

"The *shura* . . . ?" Lazan's last piece of intelligence came back to him.

"A meeting, a council. At the caravanserai. You know what a caravanserai is? It is a holy place—"

"Where even rival tribes forget their differences," Girling whispered.

"For one who knows our culture, it is strange that you should hate it so. What have the Angels of Judgment done to you?"

Girling felt a surge of anger. "What have you done—"

The mullah held up his hand. "I know about your wife. I know about your friend. I know about the hostages. But these things are not the work of the Angels of Judgment."

"The Brotherhood killed my wife—"

"Abu Tarek's men killed your wife. There is a difference."

Girling took a step toward him. "You know Abu Tarek?"

The mullah shook his head. "I know only that he worked for the Guide."

"Who answers to the Sword."

The mullah smiled sadly. "The Guide is an informant, nothing more. He sent a letter through the network. In it he warned the Sword of you—and told him about Abu Tarek." The mullah paused for a moment. "You should know, Mr. Girling, that Abu Tarek is dead. Two years ago, the man who ordered your wife's death met his own at the hands of God."

"How?" Girling whispered.

"Abu Tarek died a leper's death in the City of the Dead. The Guide wanted you to know this." Their eyes locked. "As I said, the Angels of Judgment are innocent."

His voice held such quiet conviction that Girling was still. News of Abu Tarek's death had brought him nearer the end of his long, arduous journey. Then he saw himself once more overlooking the valley outside Wadi Qena, Abdullah beside him. The helicopters were circling, pouring fire into the mock caravanserai. "Then why call this *shura*?"

"So that many can hear the message." He paused. "The Sword will tell the PFLP-GC, Fatah and Hizbollah that there is to be no *jihad*—no holy war."

"It's a bit late, isn't it? Wherever he goes, the Sword's message is pain."

"You know so little about him . . ."

"I know that he and his Angels of Judgment were murdering as long ago as the fighting in Afghanistan."

"What could such a tiny band, a score of men, do to the mighty Soviet Army? But *jihad,* holy war, is not a rational thing, is it, Mr. Girling?" He studied Girling's bruised face. "Has your own battle been worth it?"

"It would be if I could kill the Sword," Girling said.

The mullah suddenly got to his feet and walked over to the door. He uttered two words to the guard, but before Girling could register their meaning, he was back, alone, holding the guard's rifle. In one move, the mullah turned the gun around and held it out. "Take it," he said.

As if in a trance, Girling grasped the stock. The mullah took the barrel and held it against his heart.

The blue eyes regarded Girling with no fear. "Does peace come from the barrel of a gun?"

The question was asked softly, and Girling thought he detected a hint of a smile on the mullah's face. When he finally answered, Girling's tone, too, was soft.

"Why didn't you tell me who you are?"

"Your heart was too full of anger to see the truth." The Sword paused. "The things you wrote . . . Beirut Airport, murder in Cairo, hostages . . . none of it true."

"But they happened."

"Not on my orders."

"Then perhaps your Angels of Judgment are operating beyond your control."

"I may be an old man, Mr. Girling, but you should know that none of my men moves without a word from me first. You see, to them I am the Imam, the One Who Will Return. Even Jibril and Hizbollah, for all their guns and grenades, listen to me when I speak. And tomorrow I will tell them that my ways are the ways of peace."

"If it wasn't you . . . then who?"

"I was hoping you would tell me. Why do you think I brought you here? I need answers, too. I thought you knew . . ."

The muezzin's song rose. For a long time the two men watched each other in silence. Girling felt his tiredness leave him. The puzzle was almost complete. It had been since his journey to Qena. He just hadn't been watching it closely enough.

"You and the Angels of Judgment were in Afghanistan, a muja-hideen group. You saw action against the Russians . . ."

"A long time ago. Things were different . . ."

"In what way?"

"We were less sold on the ways of peace."

"Afghanistan, though. Why such a long way from home? I thought the struggle was here."

The Sword looked up. "In those days, the struggle was everywhere, Mr. Girling. But I wasn't far from home. You see, I am an Uzbek, born and raised in a village south of Samarkand."

Girling nodded slowly. "Samarkand, Uzbekistan?"

"Yes."

"The Soviet Union."

"The old Soviet Union." The Sword's eyes darkened. "For almost six decades the Communists tried to keep Islam out. They burned the mosques, rounded up the believers; they killed my people. The Muslims of Central Asia are by and large for peace, Mr. Girling, but one day, almost thirty years ago, I decided to stand up and fight. We were always a tiny group, my Angels of Judgment and I, but we fought back against the Soviets with a ferocity they could not believe. We kept moving: Uzbekistan, Kazakhstan, Tajikistan, and across the border even, into the mountains."

But like the Afghan mountains themselves, Girling was far, far away. "The Russians . . . there's no rescue . . . it's a trap."

"A trap?"

"Three days ago I watched a Russian-American task force destroy a valley identical to this one. I thought it was a dress rehearsal for a rescue. But if the hostages aren't here, those helicopters were on a mission to search and destroy."

The Sword bowed his head. "It's me they want, Mr. Girling. They've been hunting me down for over twenty years, but somehow we've always managed to stay one step ahead of them. When I came here I thought we'd be safe, safe to plot my return. It would have been quite a homecoming."

"How could I be so blind? It was the Russians all along. How many Muslims are there in the Soviet Union? Sixty million, more even? Sixty million Uzbeks, Khirghiz, Tajiks, Tatars, Kazakhs and Azer-baijanis all united by a common faith. Sixty million." Girling paused as the picture became complete. "You're their worst nightmare. You're the Imam. The One Who Will Return. They think you're going to take the holy war to the heart of Russia."

"But like you, Mr. Girling, they were wrong. My struggle was with the Communists, the Soviets. I called the *shura* to tell Jibril and his kind there will be no *jihad*. The Muslim revolution in Central Asia must be a peaceful one."

"I'm afraid it's too late. For you, for me, for the Americans . . ."

"The Americans?"

Girling thought back to his meeting with McBain and Ulm. They had been hoping he knew where the hostages were. They had been in the dark then, just like everyone else. Hostages. The Russians took the hostages. Stansell knew, because he'd tripped over the Angels of Judgment in Afghanistan. It had taken his booze-soaked mind most of the night to work it out, but he cracked it in the end; maybe only moments before the Russians had had him killed. Jesus, someone in Moscow had known which buttons to press all along. And to his eternal shame, Girling realized he had helped them do it.

He turned to Sword. "When the helicopters leave, this valley will be littered with the dead bodies of Arabs and Americans, unless we do something first."

■   ■   ■

As they stepped outside into the watery dawn there was an ear-splitting roar and a helicopter the size of a trawler rose up from behind the shack. Girling grabbed the Sword's hand and ran for an irrigation ditch in the lee of the cliffs.

Three more helicopters shot into the valley, one of them so low it had to climb sharply to avoid the roof of his cell.

A movement at the edge of his vision made him turn. A helicopter was heading straight for them, its guns firing.

Girling jumped into the ditch, pulling the Sword with him. The Pave Low's downwash clawed at their heels and bullets spattered around them. Sand stung his skin as the Sikorsky thundered overhead.

A nearby flak gun opened up, but the shots went wild. The Sikorskys twisted and weaved through the air, buzzing the defenders from all directions.

Girling looked for cover. There were some boulders, sixty yards away. He and the Sword began to run, but a Pave Low prowling in the valley spotted them and did a 180-degree turn.

Girling threw the Sword behind the rocks. The helicopter roared past, its momentum so great that it overshot. Girling saw the pilot wrestling with the controls as he fought to bring the helicopter back.

Thirty yards away was a path leading upward.

Girling heard the whoosh of an SA-16 launch. He turned to see the missile streaking across the valley toward the nearest Sikorsky, but the machine was too low for the heat-seeker to engage and the missile buried itself into the ground, exploding harmlessly.

Like a stuck bull, the helicopter wheeled.

Girling saw their chance. "Come on."

The Sword hesitated. "My people . . ."

"They need you alive, Sword." He pulled the old man after him.

They were almost at the top of the path when Girling snatched a glance into the valley. Jibril's missileman was in the open, defenseless, his empty launch tube discarded. Around him lay the broken bodies of his comrades. The MH-53J was hovering left and right, intercepting his every attempt to reach the safety of the caravanserai. Suddenly, the machine rotated, giving the ramp gunner unrestricted aim. There was a belch of flame and the Sikorsky moved on to some new hunting ground, its miniguns spitting remorselessly; Jibril's men and Hizbollah dying with every sweep of the muzzle.

The Sword's breathing became more labored. Girling pushed on to scout the ground up ahead. The cliff top was a plateau littered with outcrops and boulders—the first sign of a place to hide.

He turned to encourage the Sword, but the old man had collapsed facedown on the path. He was clutching his right side. When Girling rolled him over, he saw a face gouged with pain. Girling's hand moved down to the bullet wound. Blood seeped between his fingers as he lifted the Sword's arm from the sticky red stain spreading across his robe.

A helicopter passed close by, just below the level of the path. Girling had to bend lower to hear what the Sword was trying to tell him.

"You must go—"

A burst of machine-gun fire swallowed his words.

"—save yourself."

Girling slipped his hands under the Sword's body. He managed to carry him as far as a group of rocks just beyond the top of the path. He laid him down in the shade of an overhang.

"You are free now," the Sword said. "Start your life again. Leave me."

Girling shook his head.

"I will die with my Angels of Judgment."

"You're the only person who can tell the truth. Die and your people will declare a *jihad* against the Americans. There will be more hijackings, more Beiruts . . ."

Using the smoke and the dust for cover, Girling made his way back down to the outer walls of the caravanserai. One of the gates had a hole blown in it, just large enough for him to squeeze through. He stepped between the bodies and the guns littering the courtyard. He knew what he had to do; he just didn't know where to begin.

■　　　■　　　■

THEY CAME in low over the caravanserai, heading for the patch of scrub designated as the landing area, Shabanov's Pave Low in front, Ulm's just feet behind. Ulm's gaze swept the ground ahead, looking for the shack Shabanov had briefed them about; the shack where Franklin, Koltsov and their colleagues were being held.

Ulm could have been in a combat simulator back in Kirtland, watching images on a screen, his headphones filled with computer-generated sounds of weapons and war.

The bullet that snapped through the windshield and buried itself in the door above his head was a sudden reminder that this was no high-tech exercise.

Bookerman threw the helicopter around the narrow sky between the valley walls, responding to reports of incoming fire. Ulm gave few orders. Every man knew what to do. The scene was almost identical to the dummy camp outside Wadi Qena.

Everywhere people were running for cover. He could see old men and women cowering under the eaves of the caravanserai. A gunner was slumped over the breeches of a flak gun on a truck in the middle of the courtyard. Others poured small-arms fire at the Pave Low from the balcony, their bullets cracking and whining off the thick armor plate behind him. The right-side and rear minigunners let rip a synchronized volley of shots, catching three of the terrorists out in the open. One of the bodies split open like a bag of overripe fruit, the remains spattering the white walls behind. With pinpoint precision, Ulm's gunners raked their fire along the balcony, carefully avoiding the innocents in the courtyard below. The bullets picked their way into the upper rooms, whole patches of wall crumbling to dust under the onslaught. Through a dark doorway Ulm could see the first flickerings of a fire ignited by tracer. And then they were out over the open ground that stretched between the caravanserai and the two small buildings they were looking for.

The Pave Low jinked and weaved as Bookerman responded to the calls of his gunners. Ulm's search for the shacks was momentarily diverted by the sight of terrorist bodies, dozens of them, lying where they had fallen, some mutilated beyond recognition by the miniguns of the two mixed-crew helicopters that had preceded theirs into the valley. A glance over his shoulder told him that they were safe, too; both were now landing on the plateau above the caravanserai, ready to cut off any terrorists trying to escape up the pathway that led to the top of the cliffs.

A shout from Bookerman drew his attention to two reinforced shacks a hundred yards beyond the nose of the Sikorsky. Shabanov's helicopter was throwing up clouds of dust already as it recovered to the ground. The next minute they were down, Ulm throwing off his straps and heading for the ramp. Someone chucked him his Heckler and Koch and a moment later he was out of the helicopter, feet pounding the earth. The swirling downwash from the rotors screened him from enemy fire. Ulm made it across the open ground just as the two-man explosives team from Shabanov's helicopter was putting the finishing touches to the plastic around the hinges of the shack door. He pressed against the wall and waited for the synchronized detonation.

When it blew, Shabanov was first through the smoking doorway, followed by Bitov and Jones. Ulm took a deep breath and rolled in behind them.

A pall of smoke hung in the room. It was impossible to see more than a few feet. He could make out the three soldiers in front of him, but beyond that only shades of dark and light. Ulm's every nerve ending tingled. A stray shot from any of them would mean the difference between success and failure, life and death for hostage and captor. He waited for the first bullet, the first scream.

A gust blew in through the door, parting the smoke. The cell was empty. Ambassador Franklin and Minister Koltsov were gone.

Ulm pulled the balaclava off his face. He sucked in the musty air, trying to suppress the stirrings of a feeling that before meeting Shabanov he had not had since Panama.

"They must have been moved to the caravanserai," the Russian said. His voice bore no trace of surprise.

Ulm stared at him. "Do you realize what our chances are?"

"We have to try, Elliot."

Ulm pulled a walkie-talkie from his uniform and barked orders for the helicopters to take as many men as they could gather quickly and get away, get airborne, while he thought. Seconds later, both machines lifted into the sky, their guns audible even above the din of the rotors.

An explosion outside rocked the foundations of the shack. Through the doorway, Ulm saw a crater burst close to the spot vacated a moment before by the helicopters. Someone had managed to rig up a mortar.

He braced himself for the next round when a ripple of fire from one of the Pave Lows split the sky above his head. The mortar fell silent.

The miniguns would give them covering fire as they ran toward the perimeter of the Sword's hideaway.

"All right," Ulm said, turning to Shabanov. "We'll split into pairs and search the caravanserai room by room." He went outside and did a head count. Apart from Jones, only three Pathfinders were left; the others had all made it back to the helicopters. The Russians, on the other hand, had remained on the ground in strength: at least fifteen now rallied to Shabanov for the charge to the walls of the caravanserai.

■   ■   ■

ULM AND Jones reached the first door leading off the caravanserai courtyard.

They flanked the entranceway. Ulm had pulled his balaclava down around his neck. Jones, still wearing his, lifted his eyes and nodded.

Ulm kicked down the door and threw the flash-bang into the room. The second it hit the floor and detonated, Jones was moving, Ulm right behind him. Inside, light streamed through a window close to the ceiling. It was a storeroom; bags of grain and rice stacked to the roof.

The next room was exactly the same; dark and cool, like a church.

The thick stone walls drowned the noise of battle, allowing the two men to stop and listen. Inside there was no sound, no movement.

They turned and moved outside, stealing beneath the eaves of the balcony towards the third silo. Jones stopped before they even reached the door. Without saying a word, he signaled Ulm. It was ajar, swinging gently on its hinges. Jones threw the stun grenade and Ulm careered inside. He rolled, coming to his feet in a crouch on the far side of the room.

Another larder. One of the rice bags had split, scattering grains across the floor. In the echoing silence, it was like walking across broken glass.

Ulm looked at Jones, covering him from the door. He heard a high-pitched note, an ultrasonic alarm inside his head. There was someone else in the room, someone besides Jones. He could feel something, a presence . . .

He began to turn when the gun barrel hit him in the base of the spine. Ulm froze.

Jones took a step into the room. He squinted against the light. ''Sir?''

Girling came up from behind the sacks of grain. He moved the pistol up Ulm's spine and held it between his shoulder blades. ''Drop your weapon, Sergeant.''

Jones looked at Ulm.

''Do it now!'' Girling shouted. ''You, too, Colonel.''

Ulm flinched, ''Girling!''

''Drop your gun, Colonel.''

There was a clatter as Ulm let his MP5 fall to the floor.

Seconds passed, then Jones did the same.

''Don't say anything, Colonel. Don't say a fucking word. Just listen and listen good.''

Girling stepped out from behind his cover. He kept Ulm's body between himself and Jones. ''You've been set up. There are no hostages. No Franklin. There's only one reason the Russians are here. The Sword's an Uzbek, a Muslim from Central Asia, the former Soviet Union. The Russians need him dead, and they need you to take the fall.''

Ulm gritted his teeth. ''What the hell are you doing here, Girling?''

Girling's voice rose to a shout. "Don't you ever learn, Ulm? The Sword wants out, but the Russians don't know that."

"This is bullshit," Jones said. "There are terrorists with surface-to-air missiles out there."

"They're Palestinians, Hizbollah," Girling said. "The Sword got them here to say the deal's off. They listen to him. He's some kind of religious leader, something like an ayatollah."

"There are Russians among the hostages, too, Girling."

"Colonel, they've gone to a lot of trouble to make this ruse work. And any minute now they're going to turn on your men."

Jones took a step forward. "Who is this crank?"

Girling swung the pistol. "Far enough, Sergeant." He kept the barrel locked on Jones's head. "Let's just say your colonel and I ran into each other in Cairo."

"Well, you're full of shit." Jones turned to Ulm. "Shabanov and Bitov could have killed us anytime back there in the shack, boss."

"They need you while there are still terrorists out there," Girling said. "When they're safe from Jibril and Hizbollah, that's when the Pathfinders start dying."

Jones was about to speak but Ulm silenced him. "You'd better talk fast, Girling."

"The Sword's been shot, Colonel, and there's a good chance he'll bleed to death unless . . ." He hesitated. "If he dies, Washington takes the fall for this whole operation. Those are American helicopters up there."

"With Russian soldiers on board!"

"Are they wearing red stars on their uniforms?"

Ulm faltered. Opnaz were the goddamned crack troops of the Russian Interior Ministry. It began to hit him. Uzbekistan . . . Jesus.

Ulm tried to turn, but Girling told him to keep his eyes front. "Girling, this can't be happening . . ." Then he thought of TER-COM's discreet offices, the blacked-out windows and Joel Jacobson. TERCOM had him taped from the beginning. If he brought back the hostages, they shared his glory. If it was a trap, it was back to the cold war, TERCOM's old stamping ground. Jacobson and General Aushev had been playing the same tune all along, only neither of them knew it. He suddenly felt tired. "There won't be any further need for the gun."

Girling stood firm.

"For God's sake, man, if you're right, I've got to warn the men."

"Okay," Girling said. "Then let's go."

They ran across the courtyard, Ulm trying to raise Bookerman and the other pilots on the walkie-talkie. He couldn't see anything for the smoke and dust drifting across the valley.

Once through the gates, Ulm ran ahead of Girling, while Jones brought up the rear. Girling was thankful for the escort. The pistol in his hand felt unwieldy. All around him Arabs were either dead or dying. He looked briefly for Jibril amongst them, but saw no sign of him or the group of men that had terrorized him the night before.

They reached an abandoned pickup truck and ducked down by the driver's door. Sharp cracks from the cliffs signaled the presence of snipers. Ulm continued to work the radio, but his voice was met by a wall of static. Girling edged round the side of the truck, hand raised against the smoke. He wanted to pick out the path again. He had to get back to the Sword.

It was then that he saw the Pave Lows through the smoke. "There," he called, pointing them out against the bright early dawn.

Ulm and Jones turned to see the two helicopters begin their descent over the caravanserai.

"They're going for those snipers," Jones said, thoughts of Shabanov momentarily forgotten.

Girling's eye was drawn to the spinning barrel of a minigun in the first helicopter, then the puff of dust from the rocks as the gunner found his target, an Arab marksman at the base of the cliffs. He thought the flash of light away to the right of the caravanserai was the strike of more bullets on another sniper position, but then he saw the accompanying threadlike trail of smoke as first one missile, then two, pulled away from the ground and into the sky.

Both helicopters exploded simultaneously as the two shoulder-launched heat-seekers found their mark. The first crashed close to the caravanserai, carving a great trench across the valley. The second seemed to take its time, the lift in its spinning blades holding it aloft as the conflagration tore through the hold and into the deck. It sank to the ground like a stricken airship, finally tearing itself into a thousand pieces as the main rotor bit into rock and sand a hundred yards away.

Ulm took a step forward, but Jones held him back. "No, Colonel. It's too late."

An explosion shook the wreck of the first Pave Low, sending more smoke and flames billowing into the sky. Girling felt the heat searing his exposed skin.

"Christ, Spades! Charlie, Bookerman, the men—"

Jones wrestled against the strength of his superior. "There's nothing you can do, boss. There's just two helos left now and they're up there." He forced Ulm's gaze to the top of the cliffs. "The mixed-crew birds," Jones added with grim emphasis.

Jones turned and almost walked straight into Bitov. Ulm was mesmerized still by the burning wreckage. Girling saw the confrontation between the two sergeants, but from the broad smile on Bitov's face he thought the big son of a bitch was American.

Jones hesitated. "Bitov . . ."

The Russian raised his arm and shot the American once, straight through the forehead.

Girling tried to move, but he couldn't. He couldn't tear himself away from the sight of Jones, still falling, his brains spilling through the jagged hole in the back of his balaclava. It was only when the body hit the ground that the spell was shattered. And by then, Bitov had shifted his aim.

Girling stared straight into the barrel of the pistol. Behind him, he heard Ulm's shout of rage, but it was a faint echo amongst the screams and gunfire.

Bitov squeezed the trigger. Once, twice . . . Strange, Girling thought, that there should be no sound.

The gun had jammed.

Ulm brought up his MP5, pulled Girling out of the way and fired.

Bitov was already diving for the truck. He rolled, but the bullet caught him in the back, close to the spine. His body kept rolling, out of Ulm's line of fire. And then it lay perfectly still.

Ulm was ready to go back into the caravanserai to find the three Pathfinders who had accompanied him on his last charge, when he and Girling all but tripped over the bodies on the way to the path that led up the cliff. Ulm examined each for life signs, but the three neat head shots and the frozen look of surprise on their faces told Girling the effort was a sorry waste of time.

Girling reminded Ulm of the imperative to get to the Sword and, on the merest basis that the remaining helicopters were still under

Pathfinder control, fly him out of the valley to salvation. An occasional volley of shots emanating from the caravanserai told him that the Russians were polishing off the last traces of Arab resistance. Soon they would intensify their search for the man they had traveled a continent to find. Denying them the opportunity was the last duty Ulm had left, Girling remonstrated. It was also the best possible revenge.

The Sword was weak but conscious when they reached him. While Ulm did what he could, staunching the flow of blood with a field dressing and killing the pain with morphine, Girling disappeared over the other side of the rocks to reconnoiter the land ahead.

He returned two minutes later, breathless from the exertion in the rarified atmosphere. "I've found the helicopters," he said. "You'd better come and take a look."

Keeping behind cover, they worked their way toward a cluster of boulders that afforded an unencumbered view across the plateau at the head of the valley.

The sun was coming up behind the two Pave Lows, casting long shadows across the rocks. The helicopters were a little over three hundred meters apart, separated from each other by another cluster of large boulders. Their main blades drooped, motionless. It was as if the machines had been drained of energy.

For a second, Girling thought the helicopters had been left unprotected, but then he saw movement on the ramp of the nearest machine. As his eyes became more used to the light, he could make out the figure behind the minigun. He was training it left and right, back and forth, with the restlessness of an insect.

"Yours?" Girling asked.

Ulm shielded his eyes against the glare. It took him a few seconds to come up with a prognosis. "I don't think so," he said simply.

Girling felt himself sag. With the Sword's deadweight to carry, they would not get more than a few yards across the open stretch of land before being cut down by a hail of 7.62-millimeter bullets.

"What are we going to do?"

"We've got to fly one of those birds out of here." Ulm seemed gripped by some new determination. "No time to waste. There's a U.S. task force a dozen miles or so off the Lebanese coast. We'll make for there."

Ulm slapped in a new magazine and snapped back the bolt of his

MP5. "Those two helicopters can't see each other. Now if we go for the nearest one . . ."

He leaned against the rocks, unslung his weapon and reached into a thigh pocket. He screwed the silencer onto the barrel of the MP5, never taking his eyes off the nearest of the two helicopters. Then he attached the laser sighting system.

"I could take out that guy from here, but I don't know how many others are inside. This way, I might stay alive long enough to find out and fly us out of here both." He looked at Girling. "When I signal, bring the old man over to the back of the helicopter. Meanwhile, keep watching that trail. Still got your weapon?"

Girling held up the pistol.

Ulm disappeared behind the rocks. Girling tried to follow his progress amongst the shadows, but lost him. The American was working his way around to the other side of the helicopter so as to approach it with the sun at his back.

■   ■   ■

ULM STEPPED out into the open and began walking towards the nearest MH-53J when the helicopter was no more than thirty meters away. He could see the minigunner's forearms; the rest of his body was hidden behind the wall of the Sikorsky's cargo hold. If there were other gunners inside, he hoped they were looking the other way. For all the concentrated firepower in the helicopter before him, it was the second machine, away to his left, that worried him most. If any of its crew caught wind of what was happening, they could destroy their only means of escape with a few well-aimed bursts of automatic fire.

Just before the second helicopter slipped from view, Ulm raised his arm and waved in case any of its crewmembers were watching him. He hoped he would pass for a Russian. He brought the Heckler and Koch up routinely, flicked the catch to semiautomatic and switched on the laser sighting system. The red spot beam danced over the rocks by his feet.

He reached the sponson midway between nose and tail and stopped. Beneath the helicopter he saw the bodies of its American crew. All three of them had been shot in the base of the neck. He did not let it divert him. The cockpit appeared to be empty, as did the left-hand minigun station just aft of the forward bulkhead.

Ulm stole along the fuselage, pausing for one last check of his MP5 before reaching the ramp. He pulled his mask down and stepped round the wall of the cargo hold.

He had perhaps a second to assess the situation. There were two gunners inside. The one on the ramp, the other well forward, manning the right-hand defensive position by the flight deck bulkhead. Both were training their weapons in the direction of the cliff where Girling and the Sword were hidden. Ulm smiled and nodded to put the far gunner at his ease then put the barrel of his MP5 against the ribs of the Russian on the ramp, pulled him in toward the gun and shot him twice through the heart. The body jumped and pitched forward, the folds of the jacket catching on the silencer of the American's gun.

The second Russian lunged for his MP5 as Ulm struggled to pull the ramp gunner's deadweight off him. Hearing the machine pistol being cocked in the confines of the aircraft gave him a new burst of energy and he hurled the body off the ramp. Suddenly free of the obstruction, the red laser sight spot danced on the bulkhead. The gunner saw it, too, and raised his weapon. Ulm knew that a bullet through a fuel line or a critical piece of avionics would dash any hope they had of getting away.

His hands wet with sweat, he waited till the spot beam held on the Russian's forehead before firing. The gunner's body slammed back against the opening for the minigun, catching on the pintle mounting. It hung, twitching, half-in, half-out of the helicopter.

Ulm ran outside the hold and snatched a glance toward the rocks that obscured the second Pave Low. There was no sign of any movement. Then he waved Girling over.

There was a flurry of movement as Girling eased the Sword's body over his shoulder in a fireman's carry. Then the journalist made his way across the clearing. When they reached the ramp, Ulm helped Girling ease the Sword into the back of the hold. He pointed to some parachute packs hanging on the wall and told Girling to use them to make the old man as comfortable as possible for the flight.

"You know how to work a minigun?" Ulm asked.

"I think so."

"Chances are you're going to have to." Ulm slipped out of the back of the helicopter and jogged up the right side of the fuselage, stopping only to pull the dead gunner from his window.

Ulm turned the handle on the door to the flight deck and tugged it open to find himself staring into the barrel of a gun. He twisted instinctively, like a fish on the end of a line, in a bid to get away. He curved off the footrest into space at the precise moment the Russian pilot fired his pistol. The slug caught Ulm in the upper chest, spinning him in the air. He landed face down in the dirt, fully conscious. He could see the wheels of the Sikorsky a little way off, but could not raise his head any higher. He heard a single crack of gunfire in the valley below. He heard, too, the cabin door swing as the Russian prepared to finish him.

■   ■   ■

GIRLING HAD made the Sword's body secure, when he heard the shot from the flight deck. Drawing his pistol, he ran through the hold toward the bulkhead. He wrenched the connecting door open just as the Russian was stepping out. Girling had no time to think. Still only halfway through the access hatch, he fired off two rounds. The first went high, but it made the Russian turn. The second bullet took him in the face.

Girling wriggled through the hatch and was out of the commander's door. He rolled Ulm over, convinced that he was already dead. The American's blood was trickling down the gentle gradient that led to the cliff drop-off.

As Girling moved him, Ulm coughed violently. Girling pulled the mask off his face and Ulm spat a mixture of dirt, blood and saliva into the dust. He tried to speak, but Girling couldn't make out the words. From the look on his face, though, he took it as some sort of apology.

"Don't talk," Girling said.

Ulm's half-choked laugh made Girling realize that talking was all they had left, because the Russians had them now. Their helplessness stirred anger in him and his anger gave him strength. He pulled Ulm onto his feet, ignoring his groans. Half-carrying, half-dragging the American, Girling moved around the front of the helicopter and opened the copilot's door.

It took him a full two minutes to get Ulm strapped in, during which time he had lost and regained consciousness. Girling took off his own jacket and pressed it between Ulm's wound and his inertia-reel harness.

"Forget it, Girling, we're fucked."

Girling stared at the bank of switches and dials in front of him. "Not if I can help it. Not while there's still a chance."

"A chance for you maybe if you run for the hills. But the old man and me are all out of luck."

Girling snatched a glance over his shoulder toward the trail that led up from the cliff.

"I'm going to fly us out of here," he said.

"You never said you were a helo pilot."

"I've flown simulators."

"Simulators?" The blood made his throat rattle. "This isn't a penny-fucking-arcade game."

"Tell me what I have to do."

Ulm twisted painfully in his seat until he saw Girling's face and knew he wasn't kidding.

■   ■   ■

BITOV WAS alive, but only just, when Shabanov found him. The finger stumps of the sergeant's mutilated hand beckoned and the colonel got down on his knees to put his ear to the *starshina*'s lips. He listened patiently, then got slowly to his feet.

They stared at each other for several seconds, Bitov's eyes showing they comprehended.

"It is time, my friend," Shabanov said, raising his MP5.

He shot Bitov twice. Once through the chest and once in the head, just to be sure. Bitov, who had fought with him since the very formation of Opnaz, was now one more dead American in the Sword's valley.

Shabanov turned to the platoon leader, a corporal. He noticed the man had acquired an RPG-7 rocket launcher and an SA-16 SAM system from the field of battle and was carrying them over his shoulders.

"The signal, *yefreytor*. Fire it."

The soldier pointed his flare pistol in the air and pulled the trigger. The green signal flare shot into the sky.

"The Sword, Ulm and one other are on the cliff," Shabanov announced to his men. "Kill them and we can all go home."

■   ■   ■

GIRLING FOUND the battery switch and flicked it to ON. "Now what?"

There was a hum of electrical power as the lights came up on the instrument panel. Girling found two headsets. He put one on Ulm and plugged the lead into the comms panel between them. Then he donned his own.

Girling turned to the American and waited.

"There are two levers above you on the overhead," Ulm said.

Girling raised his eyes. The roof was a maze of switches, dials and levers.

"Right in the center."

"Got them." Girling grasped them with his left hand.

"Push them forward to ground idle. You should feel a slight click as they hit the detent."

Girling brought the twin levers slowly forward until he felt it.

Ulm pointed. "Flick the left-hand ignition switch on."

Girling's finger hovered momentarily over the switch.

"For Christ's sake, Girling, you wanted action! Throw the switch."

Girling pushed it forward.

"Now the starter."

There was a whirring sound from the roof as the left engine began to turn over.

"Watch the RPM gauge."

Back to the instrument panel. "Where is it?"

"A little ways down and to the left of your finger."

Girling found it.

"Wait till that dial reads twelve percent, then turn the fuel switch on. See it? It's a toggle switch to the right of the others."

The engine whine intensified. Lights all over the instrument panel were flashing.

For a second, Girling was dazzled. "Jesus."

"Don't worry about the lights. I'll take care of them." Ulm flinched as a wave of pain washed through him.

Girling's gaze weaved a path through the lights back to the RPM gauge. "Eight . . . ten percent," he called. His thumb felt the fuel toggle. "Twelve percent."

"Give her fuel now and repeat the whole process again for the right-hand engine."

Under Ulm's orders, Girling threw switches and punched buttons. As he called the shots, Ulm inched his right hand down to the comms console and flicked through the frequencies, but the set was dead. Shabanov must have given orders for his men to pull all the circuit breakers in case the Pathfinders realized what was happening and began trying to warn each other.

"Engine temperature's coming up," Ulm said wearily. His head fell as drowsiness began to replace pain.

Girling roused him with a shake of the arm. Ulm winced as the pain returned.

"Colonel, you've got to stay with me." It was then that Girling saw the green flare through the window above his head. Someone was signaling them.

The American forced his eyes to focus on the instruments. "Okay, we have ground idle. Bring your left hand up to the overhead and prepare to release the rotor brake."

Girling waited for Ulm's command, then pushed the lever forward. There was a groan from the bowels of the helicopter. Girling watched one of the six main blades inch impossibly slowly past the cockpit window.

"Advance the throttles to flight idle."

Girling pushed the levers toward the next notch.

"Slowly, Girling, slowly."

The blades turned faster, making the cabin rock. Girling kept advancing the levers until they clicked into the second notch.

Ulm watched the revs, calling them out all the way. Within a minute, the rocking stopped. There was a resonant hum from the engine joined by the whoosh of the blades as they rotated above the cabin at 100 percent RPM.

"On the center console, between the seats, there's a parking brake. Release it."

Girling groped with his left hand. "Brake off."

"From now on, don't think about what you're doing, or you'll bury us in that valley down there." He paused. "Here goes. Push the cyclic forward a fraction and keep your foot down on the right pedal. We need to be pointing away from those rocks."

Girling inched the control column away from him, and the helicopter trundled along the ground for no more than a few feet before coming to an abrupt halt.

"Shit," Ulm said.

Girling could feel the helicopter's wheels straining against the obstruction.

"Pull up on the collective."

Girling reached for the lever beside the seat with his left hand and lifted it toward him. It came up far too quickly. The helicopter tipped forward on its nose wheel, tail rising in the air. Girling froze as the horizon whipped away past the top of the windshield and it seemed the Sikorsky would flip over onto its back.

Ulm fell forward on the collective and the helicopter crashed back to the ground.

It took Girling vital seconds to heave the American off the pitch lever and back into his seat.

Ulm gritted his teeth. "Let's try that again, only this time, go easy on the power."

Girling pulled the collective toward him again and the helicopter lurched forward. He kept the cyclic column pushed fractionally away from the seat and the right rudder pedal all the way down until the nose of the MH-53J heaved around and away from the rocky outcrop. He held the position with a touch of brakes.

Dust and stones flew around the cockpit. It would have been impossible to make out the posse of soldiers advancing up the cliff path but for the flash of sunlight on an assault rifle. Girling saw it out of the corner of his eye just as there was a crack from the Perspex in front of him. A bullet slammed into the bulkhead behind his head.

"No time for a dress rehearsal," Ulm said. "Pull on the collective until she lifts off."

Girling eased up the lever. He felt the helicopter getting light on its wheels.

"Higher," Ulm said. "Pull it higher. And bring back the cyclic. Just a fraction."

The Pave Low rose and teetered uncertainly six feet above the ground. Girling heard another bullet glance off some armor plate somewhere below him.

"Pull the cyclic into your fucking armpit, Girling, or we die. Here, now."

Girling heaved the lever up, but the helicopter rose only another few feet and stayed there, floating from side to side like a leaf in the wind. Girling fought to hold the Sikorsky steady, but it seemed that every corrective touch on the cyclic made the helicopter veer more wildly.

Ulm checked the temperature and torque gauges. "No wonder. We're at fifty-eight hundred feet. Power margins are way too low." He shouted over the vibration. "Only one thing for it, Girling. Fly it over the edge of the cliff. Let her drop and pick up airspeed. Then haul back and pray."

Girling felt the blood drain from his face.

"Do it now, before they shoot us down," Ulm yelled.

Girling pressed the cyclic forward and the helicopter advanced at little more than walking pace toward the edge of the cliff. For a brief few seconds, the Perspex windshield was filled with a view of the wadi below. It was like being poised at the highest point of a roller coaster, in that instant before the carriage plunges to the bottom of the track. He could see the cell where he had been held, bodies littered across the open ground, wrecked gun emplacements, and finally, through the Perspex by his feet, the blazing roof and courtyard of the caravanserai.

"Now!" Ulm shouted. "Push the stick right forward."

Girling advanced the cyclic as far as it would go and forty-five thousand pounds of helicopter tipped on its nose and plunged over the side of the cliff. Girling fell against his straps and the ground filled the windshield.

The Pave Low dropped like a stone.

"Don't freeze up on me, you bastard!" Ulm roared. "Pull back on the stick!"

Girling pulled for their lives.

Inside the cockpit, everything happened so slowly. Ulm jockeying the power levers, his own efforts on the cyclic, the altimeter winding down.

Outside, the ground zoomed toward them. Had it not been for his harness he would have fallen straight through the Perspex and onto the roof of the caravanserai. Fighting gravity, Girling raised his foot and pushed against the instrument coaming, while pulling on the cyclic with his hands.

The Sikorsky's nose moved fractionally, then some more. With agonizing slowness, it began to come out of the dive.

Before he knew it, the helicopter was scudding a few feet over the battlefield. Too late, he heard Ulm's warning and the shacks leaped out of the smoke. Girling pulled and felt a sickening crash as the tail boom clipped the roof.

■   ■   ■

THE SIGHT of the Sikorsky advancing precariously toward the edge of the cliff, teetering there and then diving almost vertically for the caravanserai made Shabanov and the rest of his men freeze. Initially, the Russian thought the helicopter had taken a hit in the tail rotor. Then, when it tipped onto its nose he had a clear view into the flight deck and saw Ulm's body, slumped and bloody in the left-hand seat.

The civilian Bitov told him about was at the controls.

There was a roar from the Pave Low as the rotors bit through the thin air and the helicopter disappeared beneath the level of the cliff top. Shabanov rushed forward and watched as it arced toward the ground and disappeared behind a pall of smoke billowing up from the caravanserai. He waited for the explosion, but it never came. The vortex wake of the Sikorsky's rotors parted the smoke in time for Shabanov to see it heading straight for one of the two shacks farther down the wadi. The helicopter's tail boom grazed the roof of the building, but the machine kept going. With a sickening feeling that it was too late to make any difference, Shabanov yelled at his missile-man.

The sharp tone of the SA-16's infrared seeker head locking onto the hot exhausts of the Sikorsky was audible even over the din of exploding ammunition in the valley below. The operator steadied the missile launch tube on his shoulder and adjusted his aim.

"Fire it!" Shabanov roared.

There was a deafening crack as the missile left the tube and shot into the valley.

■   ■   ■

A SCREECH filled the cockpit and a whole section of the instrument panel lit up as the inbound SA-16 tripped the automatic alarm system rigged to the missile approach warner on the helicopter's boom.

"Holy Jesus," Ulm said.

Girling, still wrestling to steady the Pave Low after the glancing blow to the roof, thought they were about to crash.

"We've got a launch." Ulm saw the white dot winking on the approach warner panel. "It's probably an SA-16, a heat-homer, and it's coming in fast on our six."

"What do I do?" Girling shouted.

"Pray."

"Can't we fire flares?"

"The countermeasures aren't armed," Ulm said. In the rush to get airborne, he'd forgotten to prime them. And it was certainly too late now.

The screech warbled with each course deviation of the missile. Its seeker head was struggling to maintain a lock on the Sikorsky's engine exhausts through the smoke of the battlefield. But still it came at them.

Girling's whole body braced for the SAM's imminent detonation. When an explosion blossomed in the window in front of them, he was convinced they had been hit.

Instead, the screech from the approach warner intensified. The missile was still there.

The billowing flame ahead was a truck's fuel tank blowing up, the flames rising like a geyser fifty feet into the air.

Even before the colonel yelled the command, Girling banked the helicopter straight for the fountain of fire.

The dot converged with the helicopter at the center of the panel. Ulm looked up just as the cockpit windows were engulfed.

For a moment neither man could breathe as the fire sucked the oxygen from the air around them. The sky and the ground disappeared as the helicopter was lost in the conflagration.

Girling heard the explosion behind him. When he opened his eyes, the Pave Low was streaking through clear sunshine between the cliffs.

The screech stopped.

Girling snatched a glance over his shoulder. Through the open ramp he could see a crater where the burning truck had been. The heat-seeking SA-16 had homed straight in on it, the force of its exploding warhead snuffing out the flames.

With the tips of the blades and the belly of the helicopter no more than a split second's flight time from the rocks, there was no time for self-congratulation. Girling flew on, knowing that he was just as capable of killing them as any SAM.

■   ■   ■

SHABANOV WAS pounding up the cliff path again, his men behind, when the air above him reverberated with a new sound. The second Sikorsky rose up behind the outcrop that had shielded it from view, pirouetted before them and dropped down onto the clear patch of scrub where the first machine had been stationed. Shabanov made it onto the ramp before the Pave Low had even settled onto the ground. Rushing forward to the cabin, he turned to check that all his men were on board, then opened the door in the bulkhead and shouted to the pilot to head the other helicopter off before it reached the coast and the enemy ships that lay somewhere beyond.

■   ■   ■

THE WADI walls rushed at Girling faster than reason. His instinct was to lift the Sikorsky out of the valley, but a voice at the back of his head reminded him about triple-A and SAMs. The Russians might be way behind him, but Girling knew that if he flew high, away from the ground, there was still enough hardware in southern Lebanon to knock him out of the sky.

Girling gripped the cyclic so hard his fingers bled. For the moment, his entire world consisted of the control column and the narrow tunnel of airspace through which he coaxed the MH-53J. When the valley became too narrow, he eased the helicopter a little higher, but still he hugged the contours of the earth. Like a robot, he pulled back when the land rose and pushed down when it fell. By the time he first considered the matter of navigation, he had been in the air for almost five minutes. And in all that time, he realized, he'd been heading God knows where.

Keeping his eyes fixed on the terrain ahead, he yelled at Ulm to give him a bearing for the coast.

From out of the early-morning mist a shadow metamorphosed into a minaret and Girling slammed the cyclic to port. There was a flash of white masonry and the obstruction whistled past a few feet beyond the end of the rotor tips. Girling steadied the helicopter and flew on toward the indistinct horizon. His arms had turned to jelly.

Some ingrained instinct had kept him flying away from the sun, heading him west, toward the coast. But he had no idea of his position. Somewhere in the maze of instrumentation ahead of him there was an indicator that fed constantly updated coordinates of his position via satellite, but he did not know where it was, much less how to plot a course from here to safety.

He snatched a glance to his left. Ulm had slumped against the cabin door. Girling reached out and pulled the American toward him.

Ulm groaned.

"Don't black out on me, Colonel."

The American opened his eyes. There seemed to be very little comprehension behind them.

"You've got to guide me to the ships," Girling said, his voice desperate.

Girling thought Ulm was going to pass out on him again. Instead, the American leaned forward, primed the countermeasures and turned on the radar warning receiver—the RWR. "This thing starts yelling at you . . . get lower. Start punching chaff."

"How?"

"There's a switch on the cyclic. Controls both the chaff and the flares."

Girling pried his fingers off the control column. He found the rocker switch with its worn writing just beneath his thumb. Forward for chaff, the tinsellike substance for spoofing radar-guided SAMS; back for flares, used against heat-seeking missiles.

Both of the decoys were contained in a panel, half the length of a man, in either side of the rear fuselage. There were some forty flares and twenty chaff bundles in each dispenser. All Girling had to do was select which decoy he needed, toggle the switch and fire them out the side of the helo.

"If we're really in the shit, hold the switch down and you ripple fire all the decoys at once. But we're talking last resort, okay?"

A picture formed in Girling's mind's eye of the flares firing straight out the side of the helo, then falling back as the aircraft moved on. The image momentarily distracted him from the concern that was now uppermost in his thoughts: locating the task force.

"The fleet, Ulm. How do I find the fleet?"

"Hit coast and turn north. Keep the beach on your right. Five miles north of Sidon . . . only large coastal town around here . . . turn east. You'll reach fleet in . . .''

Ulm passed out.

■   ■   ■

SHABANOV SAT on the jump seat behind his pilot and copilot, eyes straining for a glimpse of their quarry. While the pilot pulled up for a snap visual sweep of the skies around them, his copilot monitored the RWR, looking and listening for any trace of a search radar, or worse still, a missile fire-control system.

Shabanov barked orders for every man to scan the skies for the fleeing MH-53J. They all knew that finding and destroying the Sikorsky was their only chance of returning home. General Aushev had left no provision in his scheme for failure.

The pilot turned and shook his head. There was nothing else in the sky.

Shabanov thought fast. Ulm had a choice. Either fly south to Israel and risk negotiating one of the best air defense systems in the world, or stick to plan, fly east and find the U.S. Sixth Fleet.

"Make for the coast," Shabanov said.

"He may already be there, Comrade Colonel," the pilot said. "The coast is less than fifteen minutes away."

"Are you telling me you can't outfly a civilian?"

The pilot responded by locking the helicopter onto the most direct course for the coast. He adjusted the power to full boost and pushed the Sikorsky down, away from the SAMs and triple-A. The scrub terrain whipped past the belly of the helicopter at 320 kilometers per hour.

A near miss with a rock outcrop prompted the copilot to switch the terrain-following radar from STANDBY to SEARCH. He also turned on the FLIR, flicking it alternately from infrared to low-light TV in an effort to determine which mode best cut through the early-morning mist.

The pilot switched the range scale on the radar picture and saw the hills give way to a short stretch of coastal plain. Beyond that, the sea disappeared off the edge of the screen.

They were less than five minutes' flight time from the coast when the copilot gave a warning shout and pointed to the FLIR screen. Shabanov craned over his shoulder. The copilot had the monitor in infrared mode. In the center was the unmistakable outline of a helicopter, its engines showing up as shimmering black heat spots. The copilot brought up the magnification and the shape grew into the other MH-53J.

"He's coming in on an almost perpendicular course," the copilot said. "From the northeast."

"Cut him off," Shabanov said.

"Then what, Comrade Colonel?"

"We pull alongside and shoot him out of the sky."

The smell of the sea was strong on the warm wind blowing through the open window in the cockpit.

"Two minutes to intercept," the copilot called.

■   ■   ■

GIRLING COULD see waves breaking on a beach a few miles beyond the nose of the Sikorsky. He pushed the helicopter lower, preparing to adjust his course onto a heading parallel with the coastline. Suddenly, the cockpit filled with a sharp audible warning and the RWR panel in front of him lit up like Broadway. He held his breath, convinced that, at any moment, the helicopter would be hit by a SAM, or rocked by the blast of radar-guided triple-A. In the midst of his fear, he remembered what Ulm had said about countermeasures. He hit the button beneath his thumb and knew that somewhere behind the helicopter little bundles of radar-spoofing chaff would be billowing into the slipstream.

The audible warning kept on coming, cutting through his concentration like a migraine. He spotted a switch on the RWR panel labeled AUDIO and turned it off. The noise stopped immediately, but he could see the threat still winking at him on the panel—a flashing box with the alphanumeric "E-2C" beside it. It took him a few seconds to realize that the helicopter was being swept by a Hawkeye airborne early-warning aircraft from the Sixth Fleet. Girling knew that Ulm's mission was so secret that the Sikorsky's IFF transponders would have been switched off for the duration of the flight. He hoped somebody on the Hawkeye had been briefed to look out for them.

Unaware the radio was dead, he was preparing to raise the Hawkeye on VHF when he spotted a second box winking on the flat panel display. He peered at the screen, anxious to identify the threat on his left. Unlike the Hawkeye, there was no recognition code beside the box. All Girling could tell was that something was painting his RWR with radar signals and it was closing fast.

He adjusted course until the E-2C was dead ahead, though impossible to tell how far. He began to pray that the crew was vectoring a couple of navy fighters toward him. For Girling knew now why the radar emitter on his nine o'clock bore no identification. It was a MH-53J, just like his. The Russians were right on his tail.

The sound, shrill and piercing, exploded in the cockpit. Wide-eyed, Girling swept the instrument panel, hoping it was only the ground-proximity warner, but he was too high and, in any case, this was a sound he knew already.

He spotted the warning light. It was pulsing MISSILE ALERT, over and over. The clock face of the missile-approach warner indicated it was heading for his left-hand rear quadrant.

Girling banged the stick hard to the right and pushed the helicopter down. He was so close to the waves that salt spray showered the Perspex. A snaking trail of gunfire lashed the water in front. There was no missile. The RWR had picked up the storm of bullets from the Russians' miniguns.

A last look at the threat warner told him there were no F-14 fighters to rescue him. He was on his own.

■   ■   ■

THE RUSSIAN-crewed helicopter had had only one chance for a shot before the other Sikorsky banked away beyond the deflection of its guns.

Shabanov roared his disgust with his crew, then ordered the pilot to slip into Girling's wake.

Using the low-light television on supermagnification, Shabanov was able to gain a perfect close-up view of the helicopter.

The ramp was down, but no one was manning the minigun station. He could see right through the hold and into the flight deck. Ulm's body slumped listlessly, his hanging head silhouetted in the frame of the doorway. The pilot he could not see, but that did not matter. Shabanov already knew that the man was inexperienced. It was a miracle he had kept the Pave Low in the air this long.

The wind rushed through the open, unmanned windows in the helicopter's hold; loose straps and canvas seats flapped like streamers in the wind. Clearly discernible on the floor was the trussed form of the Sword, his head supported by parachute packs. He was either unconscious or dead. Shabanov wanted to remove the element of doubt.

The Sikorsky was utterly defenseless. It remained for them to maneuver alongside and blast it out of the sky with a prolonged broadside from the miniguns.

The copilot turned to him and announced that they were being painted by a U.S. E-2C Hawkeye. Judging from the strength of the signal he estimated it to be about fifty miles ahead.

Shabanov was unconcerned by the American radar plane. He told the pilot to pull all available power from the engines, haul parallel with the other helicopter and hold a close course while he and the ramp gunner poured thousands of rounds into the flight deck and hold.

The colonel moved back and briefed the ramp gunner before assuming position in the window immediately aft of the flight deck.

He stuck his head out the window and watched as the other Sikorsky drew closer. He checked the minigun, rotating its six barrels slowly just to make sure there was no malfunction.

Everything was in perfect working order.

■　　　■　　　■

GIRLING THREW a glance over his shoulder and saw the Russian-crewed Pave Low creeping up on his tail, as predatory as a deep-water shark. It was so close that its nose filled the frame of the ramp opening, so close he could see not just the flight crew, but the darkened forms of soldiers on the cargo deck below. Fifty feet below, the sea boiled under the vortex of the machine's six-bladed main rotor.

He had pushed the Sikorsky as low as he dared. He had used up all the available sky. Due to his inexperience, the second helicopter was outrunning him and there was nothing he could do about it.

He knew that Shabanov was preparing to maneuver alongside to bring his guns to bear. He could try twisting and turning, but it would only delay the agony. If he maneuvered, he would lose his bearing on the E-2C; and the Hawkeye was his one guiding light.

Girling faced front and scanned the horizon for a ship, a U.S. Navy frigate acting as picket for the fleet, but the early-morning mist allowed only a few miles' visibility. There was not so much as a fishing boat in sight.

Girling turned to Ulm. He shouted once, but the colonel's head continued to hang on his chest. Girling felt a rush of loneliness. He wanted to hear another voice before he died. He wanted Ulm to talk. Girling felt a mad compulsion to laugh. He wanted Ulm to make him laugh. There was no need now for fighting talk, no time anymore for his advice . . .

Advice. Ulm's advice.

Dear God.

He looked over his shoulder, but the second Pave Low had gone. He glanced to the left and saw its shadow on the sea. Two shadows almost parallel. His aircraft and Shabanov's. Together. Side by side.

He lifted his eyes and there it was. The second helicopter level pegging with his own. He could see the Russian pilot toggling the throttle levers, squeezing that last bit of power from the engines. He could see the concentration and the sweat on his face. The helicopter inched forward and there was Shabanov in the forward gunner's window, his minigun leveled right at the cockpit, right at him. There was a moment in which their eyes met.

Girling pushed the throttles to the gates and his helicopter edged forward twenty feet. His thumb found the toggle switch on the cyclic. There was no time to look. Forward or back? Chaff or flares?

Back. That was what Ulm had said. Girling pulled the switch toward him and held it there.

Barely a few feet separated the blades of the two helicopters when fifty flares, each possessing the peak intensity of a mini-sun, ripple-fired out of the flare rack and punched into Shabanov's Sikorsky. They exploded through the Perspex windshield of the flight deck and into the open windows of the cargo hold. Once inside, they burned holes through flesh and bone, through metal deck plates, through control rods and fuel lines.

Shabanov took the full force of the salvo. The flares that hit him were so hot his clothes ignited instantaneously. His flaming body fell onto the ammunition box.

Girling pulled up into the sky just before the other Sikorsky exploded like a giant catherine wheel. The force of the blast lifted his helicopter another two hundred feet and for several seconds he thought he had lost it. Behind him, the dawn was momentarily eclipsed by a billowing fireball.

He kept climbing until he reached two thousand feet and throttled back. He felt the onset of the reaction then. His hands began to shake uncontrollably and the instrumentation swam before his eyes. Had it not been for Ulm's voice, weak but calm beside him, he might have panicked.

"Are we going to make it, Girling?"

"We might just, Colonel." He paused. "As long as you stick around long enough to teach me how to land this thing."

There was a glint in the sky as something caught the sun up ahead. Before Girling had time to tense, two F-14 Tomcats appeared out of the mist. They roared past so close that the sound of their engines reverberated over the noise and vibration of the Sikorsky's rotor.

Ulm reached for the flare pistol in the door compartment and fired their recognition signal out of the window. The F-14s reappeared, wings swept fully forward, engines throttled right back, hanging on the edge of the stall to maintain speed with the Sikorsky. The pilot of the one off their right side rocked his wings and pointed a little way south of their present heading. Girling responded by putting the Sikorsky into a gradual turn toward the fleet.

CHAPTER 13

GIRLING WAS AWARE of the constant throb of the deck plates as he made his way from the communications room to the infirmary. The USS *Groves* was steaming full tilt through the Ionian Sea to the Strait of Messina en route for Naples.

The U.S. Navy had let him make two calls. The first was to his parents, a second to *Dispatches*. Atmospheric distortion on the lines had not made conversation easy; he just wanted to let them know he was on his way back.

The USS *Groves* had been designed to spearhead assault landings from the sea; the infirmary was big enough to pick up the pieces. Girling made his way between the beds. One or two of them were occupied. A marine with a broken arm, another with some indeterminate illness, a third with a scalded leg. It was a far cry from the mayhem of the caravanserai.

From the equipment surrounding Ulm's bed, it looked like the air force colonel had just come through a heart-lung operation. There were wires attached to his chest, bandages lacing his torso, two drips in his arm and a tube up his nose.

As soon as the nurse saw Girling, she headed him off. Girling looked over her shoulder and noticed Ulm giving her the once-over.

Girling asked for—and was granted—five minutes, but no more. Colonel Ulm, she said, was still a very sick man.

He sat down beside the bed. Ulm's eyes were on him and alert.

"They say you're going to make a complete recovery, Colonel."

"Physically, yes." Ulm's voice cracked.

For a moment, Girling's face registered concern.

"Some shrink captain said he ought to take a look inside my head after the way you landed that thing."

Girling smiled. "I took you for an arrogant arsehole first time we met, Colonel."

"Us 'arseholes' have got to stick together, Girling." Ulm laughed, then winced as the pain shot through his body. When he had controlled the coughing bout that followed, he brought a hand up from the bed. "It's Elliot."

Girling smiled as they shook.

"Was it true—all that shit about only ever having flown simulators?"

"Yes and no." Girling paused. "I've flown helicopters, but nothing the size of a Pave Low. When it comes to heavy lift, then I'm afraid simulator experience is it. A background in technical journalism has its advantages."

"The sooner you're back flying a desk, the better," Ulm said.

"I'm in no hurry."

"Well, here's one thing you can keep out of the notebook. The hostages, Franklin and the rest of them, were freed at ten hundred hours this morning. They're all safe. Shaken, but safe."

"I'm glad. What happened?"

"Aushev had had them detained in some top-secret military complex in the Crimea. Koltsov too. A GRU listening post, way up in the mountains, close to the Black Sea. He'd got them out of the Med by submarine, our guys think. Incidentally, the navy has detected a suspicious-looking Russian trawler off Crete. Seems likely that's where Shabanov would have headed if things had gone his way."

"Why didn't Aushev just kill the hostages?"

Ulm shrugged, then wished he hadn't. "Who knows? The hostages were just bait, devices to entice us to hit the Angels of Judgment.

Aushev needed the Sword dead, but it was vital it shouldn't be seen by the Muslim world as a Russian operation.''

Girling nodded. Vital, yes. For many years the Sword had been planning a revolutionary-style return to his people in the former Soviet republics, a return that would have made Ayatollah Khomeini's Iranian revolution seem like a Sunday-school outing. When Aushev found out about it, he spent the rest of his professional life hunting down the Sword. By the time he'd tracked the Angels of Judgment to Lebanon, Aushev had had plenty of time to formulate a plan that would rid Russia of the militant Muslim threat in the south and still leave Moscow's hands clean: join with the Americans and get them to take the blame for the Sword's death. For without the Sword, there could be no revolution, because no other religious leader had the power or the charisma to unite the different Islamic groups of Central Asia.

"He might just have got away with it, too," Girling said, thinking aloud. "Washington could have bleated about Russian complicity all it liked. Face it: when did the Islamic world ever trust the U.S. government, the Great Satan?''

"The whole affair would have dealt a mortal blow to U.S.-Russian relations, which would have suited Aushev just fine.'' Ulm massaged part of his shoulder beneath the bandages. "Like Shabanov, the man was a committed Communist. A return to the cold war through this plan of his may also have been part of the agenda. The Russian government swears he was out on his own, that this was a maverick operation. Let's hope they're telling the truth. God knows there are enough Russians who think like Aushev did.''

"Did? What happened to him?''

"The word from Moscow is that he hanged himself in his cell this morning,'' Ulm said. And the word from Washington was that Jacobson and the other TERCOM members had been rounded up, too; but he kept that to himself.

"So what's the official version to all this?'' Girling asked.

Ulm raised an eyebrow. "A joint Russian-American initiative brought about the rescue of the hostages. It'll all be in the White House press release soon enough, I should think. The world needs to believe we're all moving forward together.''

Ulm was silent for a moment, and when he spoke again there was no irony in his voice. "They're talking about giving me a medal, Tom. The Pathfinders deserve a lot more than that."

"I'm sorry, Elliot."

"Yeah, me too." Ulm swore that he would rebuild the Pathfinders. It was the only testament he could think of to the twenty-three men who had died in the Sword's valley. It was little consolation that they had helped wipe out a small terrorist army before Opnaz turned on them. Somehow, though, Ulm had the feeling they hadn't heard the last of Ahmed Jibril and Hizbollah.

"And the Sword?" Girling asked.

"The Sword will make public the declaration he was to have made at the *shura*. He is for peace, not armed struggle."

"But he and the Angels of Judgment take the rap for the whole thing."

"He gets what he wants. Islam will be allowed to thrive in Central Asia. Even within Russia itself. The Russian president gave his word."

Girling's face darkened. "His word?"

Ulm said: "If anyone fucks about, Tom, then everything I just said goes on the record. Until then, I'm prepared to give them a chance. Are you?"

"It'd make a damned good story." He paused. "But what the hell, we've all got to start somewhere . . ."

The nurse reappeared at the far end of the ward and began walking toward them.

"Do you think they'd let me see him?" Girling asked.

"You'll have to hurry. They're shipping him out."

"Where to?"

"A hospital in Tunis. His presence aboard the *Groves* could be somewhat embarrassing when we dock in Naples."

"Then I'd better go."

Girling held his hand out. "If you ever need a pilot . . ."

"Fly low, fly slow, Tom."

Girling smiled. "I will."

He made his way back up through the bowels of the ship to the hangar on deck two, his mind churning over the facts. Aushev's flair for strategy had made him a grand master of the old school, one who'd kept an eye on every detail, right down to the smallest piece on the board. The general had been in Egypt until President Sadat's expulsion of all Soviet advisers in 1972. It seemed likely, therefore, that al-Qadi, Stansell's murderer, had been doing the general's bidding, off and on, ever since.

From the hangar, it was just a ride on an aircraft hoist to the open air. A sharp sea breeze whipped across the deck of the minicarrier. It seemed as if every spare inch of deck space was packed with hardware: AV-8B jump jets, CH-46 medium-lift helos, several MH-53E mine-sweeping choppers and last but not least, their Pave Low, sitting it out alone, above the fantail.

At the other end of the ship, toward the bow, Girling could see an MH-53E warming up, the sunlight catching on its rotors as they started to turn. He quickened his step, heading for the cordon of armed marines between the helicopter and the island, the conning tower from which the captain commanded his ship.

Twenty feet from the helo, a marine lieutenant flagged him down. There was a special security restriction around the flight. Definitely no civilians allowed.

Girling turned just as the party of orderlies brought the Sword on deck. He was lying on a stretcher, but his head moved from side to side, his eyes sharp as they took in the details of the walk from the island to the helicopter.

Girling stopped and watched him go. The orderlies lifted the stretcher onto the ramp and it was then that their eyes met. The Sword raised his arm and the procession stopped. He said something to one of the orderlies, who looked briefly in Girling's direction before walking over to the cordon and talking to the marine. The lieutenant listened, shrugged, then waved Girling over.

Before Girling knew it, he was under the swirling downdraft of the helicopter's rotors. The stretcher was on the ramp, the orderlies standing slightly back. Girling knelt and the Sword reached out and touched his arm.

"So you get to go home after all," Girling said.

"Yes. There is much to do." His watery eyes twinkled. "And you, Tom Girling?"

Girling wrapped his fingers around the gnarled hand. "Me too."

As Girling walked back to the island, he heard the helicopter lift off and turn south.

He did not look back.

EPILOGUE

KELSO CLEARED HIS desk top of papers and personal effects with a fervor that belied his appearance. Since the news an hour earlier that Girling was safely on his way home, all he'd been able to think about was getting away.

Not that he'd be long gone. After a few weeks at his holiday retreat in Marbella he'd be back. Thanks to the injection of cash from the board, there was enough money to take care of anyone who was thinking of indulging in a little loose talk about his conduct over the Angels of Judgment story. There would be generous pay raises all round. And that would be the end of the matter.

With the Stansell affair soon forgotten, Kelso believed he could get back to the serious business of editing the world's best—and make no mistake, it would be—weekly current-affairs magazine.

He'd reckoned without Kieran Mallon, his star reporter, Girling's protégé.

The phone was on the third ring when Kelso picked it up with a cluck of irritation.

"Mr. Kelso?"

"Yes." He couldn't place the voice.

"The name's Gee, Jack Gee. I'm a reporter with *The Sun.*"

Kelso drew breath to swear, but the tabloid journalist on the other end of the line cut him short. "I should warn you, Mr. Kelso, that you are on the record . . ."